MW00789816

MAKE BELIEVE

A NOVEL OF HOLLYWOOD

PRAISE FOR PREVIOUS BOOKS

ROBERTO TO THE DARK TOWER CAME

"Epperson immerses readers in a dense jungle seething with treacherous flora and fauna and murderous men, punctuating terror with startling moments of beauty."
—PUBLISHERS WEEKLY

"Heart-stopping . . . page-turning." —ANDREA KEMPF, LIBRARY JOURNAL

"It's like Raymond Chandler and Joseph Conrad teamed up to write a thriller."
—PHILIP MARTIN, ARKANSAS DEMOCRAT-GAZETTE

"Mr. Epperson, a veteran screenwriter as well as a novelist, keeps readers guessing until the very last." —TOM NOLAN, WALL STREET JOURNAL

THE KIND ONE

"A beautifully written take on the dark Hollywood of the 30's—a perfect noir novel." —ROBERT CRAIS

"With his boyhood pal Billy Bob Thornton, Epperson cowrote one of the great crime films of recent vintage, 'One False Move.' His screenwriter's sense is evident on almost every page."
—EDDIE MULLER, SAN FRANCISCO CHRONICLE

"Tom Epperson recalls Horace McCoy, Raoul Whitfield, and of course, Nathanael West. The spirits of the classics haunt this book." —CAROLYN SEE

SAILOR

"Exquisitely written, expertly plotted." —BOOKLIST, starred review

"This book is as au courant as any crime-fiction novel or neo-noir flick, but its themes (courage, morality, loyalty, grace under pressure) are as old as Hemingway or Lao-Tzu." —TOM NOLAN, WALL STREET JOURNAL

"Simply a great thriller—full of action but about people, fast and yet thoughtful."
—LEE CHILD

Also by Tom Epperson

The Kind One
Sailor
Roberto to the Dark Tower Came

MAKE BELIEVE

A NOVEL OF HOLLYWOOD

TOM EPPERSON

ALAYA PRESS

Los Angeles

MAKE BELIEVE. Copyright © 2022 by Tom Epperson.

All rights reserved. No part of this publication may be used, reproduced, distributed, or transmit-ted in any form or by any means without prior written permission from the publisher, except in the case of brief quotations embodied in critical reviews and certain other noncommercial uses permitted by copyright law.

ISBN-13: 979-8-9851958-1-1 (Cloth)
ISBN-13: 979-8-9851958-0-4 (Paperback)
ISBN-13 979-8-9851958-2-8 (eBook)

This is a work of fiction. Names, characters, businesses, places, events and incidents are either the products of the author's imagination or used in a fictitious manner. Any resemblance to actual persons, living or dead, or actual events is purely coincidental.

Book cover and interior book design by Tricia Reeks

Printed in the United States of America
Alaya Press
Los Angeles, California

*To all the mad people who have come to Los Angeles
in pursuit of their crazy dreams.*

"But I don't want to go about among mad people," Alice remarked.

"Oh, you can't help that," said the Cat: "we're all mad here. I'm mad. You're mad."

"How do you know I'm mad?" said Alice.

"You must be," said the Cat, "or you wouldn't have come here."

—*Alice's Adventures in Wonderland*

LAURA

1

There's an old joke in Hollywood. Did you hear about the Polish actress? She fucked the writer. Well, I am a Hollywood writer, and I actually did have an affair with an actress from Poland. Not that she was dumb, as the joke suggests. She spoke five languages. She always had her adorably snub, freckle-dusted nose stuck in a book. Her favorite writer was Nabokov. She told me he was an even greater stylist in Russian than in English, but she thought Edmond Wilson had scored a few points in his attack on Nabokov's translation of *Eugene Onegin*.

My wife reacted poorly when she found out about her; in fact, she jumped out a window. Not to her death, since we were on the first floor, but as the quickest means of escaping my odious, two-timing presence. She ran across a flagstoned patio and then a crisp expanse of just-mowed grass, shedding her clothes all the way. It was her habit to take her clothes off at moments of crisis. She was down to bra and panties by the time she reached the tall adobe wall at the back of our property and threw herself into the trumpet vines.

Cesar, our gardener, was holding a pair of pruning shears, transfixed by the sight of the beautiful and nearly naked lady of the house clawing her way athletically up the tangle of green vines with their big red flowers. "Get her, Cesar!" I shouted, and he dropped the shears and took off towards her.

Thoughts of career are never far away in Hollywood, and I had such a thought now: on the other side of the wall lived Magnus Storndrop, the movie director. We hadn't lived in the house long, and I hadn't met Storndrop yet, and I certainly didn't want to meet him *this* way, fetching my shrieking lunatic wife out of his back yard, especially since I had written a romantic comedy that was perfect for his sappy sensibility. For one so dissolute, Laura had remained in amazingly good shape, and within seconds had got her elbows up on top of the wall. She was just about to clamber over and land perhaps right in Storndrop's scandalized lap when Cesar reached her. He wrapped his arms around her, his baseball cap falling off, his neatly trimmed moustache pressed against her pantied buttocks. Cesar was about five foot five, while Laura was five ten in her bare feet and had big bones and broad shoulders, so he had his hands full with her. She wiggled and kicked and yelled, "Let go of me, you greasy little beaner!" but Cesar held on doggedly until I got there.

"Laura, calm down!" I said as I grabbed her and she screamed, "Don't touch me, don't touch me!" and then one of her flailing heels smashed Cesar right in the mouth. Finally the three of us tumbled down together on the grass, and lay panting in the quiet of the soft Beverly Hills April afternoon. Now all the fight seemed to go out of Laura. She sobbed into the lawn: "Oh, I can't believe it! Dustin! How could you do it?" As if she never had. With the goateed Argentinian Marxist film critic Alfredo Disorbo, or with Harry Pegg, a grip on her last flop, or with Toby Holland, her costar in the same clunker, a skinny crackhead barely out of his teens who played Laura's *son* in the film (Toby made the mistake of getting in a fight with Pegg over Laura; Pegg, a tough Australian probably descended from vicious convicts, put Toby in the hospital, and production had to be shut down for two weeks to allow his allegedly handsome features to get back to normal), or with Brad, her supposedly gay Pilates instructor, or—but you get the picture. If I had reacted to all her gross couplings with goateed old goats and hairy grips the way she had to my brief, freckled, sunlit romance, I'd never have had the time to do anything at all except streak around the streets of Los Angeles in my underwear. Cesar spat blood into a rag he pulled out of his pocket, then he patted his split lip with it.

"You okay, Cesar?" I said. "You want me to take you to the hospital?"

Cesar smiled sadly and shook his head. "Oh no. It's nothing. Is the *señora* all right?"

"*No*," Laura said emphatically into the lawn. "The *señora* is *not* all right. The *señora* wants to *die*."

I gave Cesar a little nod to indicate I had the situation under control now. He stood up and, continuing to dab at his mouth, walked back to his shears.

"Laura's sorry about the name she called you," I said. "She didn't mean it."

He gave a dismissive wave. "It's okay, Dustin. Don't worry about it."

Cesar was a sweet guy who'd been with us for years. He lived with a wife and a passel of kids in one of those mysterious neighborhoods to the south where white people never ventured.

"Did you hear what I said? I want to *die*."

"No you don't. I know you. What you really want is a drink. To replace the one you threw at my head. Come on."

I helped her to her feet. Her cheeks were covered with tears and clear snot was dripping out her nose and she was scratched up from the vines and speckled with grass cuttings. If what remained of her public could only see her now. I took her arm and guided her back toward the house as if she were a frail old lady. We passed her Dolce & Gabbana pants and Jimmy Choo shoes and Pierre Balmain blouse. "What's her *name*?" she moaned. "Tell me her *name*!"

"Her name doesn't matter. It's over between us. I'll never see her again."

I was telling the truth for a change. The bitter irony was,

Helena—I'll tell *you* her name—had broken it off with me that very day, so this whole preposterous scene had been unnecessary.

I'd met her for lunch at a restaurant way, way up the Pacific Coast Highway, out past Pepperdine, nearly to Point Dume. It seemed a reasonably safe place for a tryst. The restaurant was on a bluff above the ocean. We sat outside, under an umbrella. I had the halibut, she the seared scallops. We split a bottle of 2000 Domaine de Chevalier Blanc, which cost 250 bucks but it was worth it, what with the immeasurable ocean and the unending sky and the three pelicans skimming in formation just over the waves and, of course, Helena herself. At twenty-eight, she was a little less than two-thirds my age. I'd met her six weeks ago, at a screening of a movie directed by Richard Downward, a not too talented but amiable Brit who'd thrown me a bit of work over the years. It was a big-budget action picture that was due to be released in the summer. About thirty of us were gathered in a small screening room in the Thalberg Building on the Sony lot in Culver City.

An hour or so into it, I was happy to realize my bladder was full and I had an excuse to leave for a few minutes. I was walking toward the door when a bony arm shot out from an aisle seat and grabbed my wrist.

It was Dick Downward. He had a long, narrow head, with a wispy, graying fringe of hair, and there was something skull-like and terrible about his face as he gazed up at me in the changeful cinematic light. "Where are you going?" he gasped.

I could hardly hear him over the boom and bam of high explosives as the terrorist training base was destroyed.

"Just to the men's room."

"Are you coming back?"

"Of course I'm coming back. Dick—I love the movie."

"Dear boy, do you?"

"I think it's the best thing you've ever done."

Downward smiled, which made his face look like a Greek comedy mask. I patted his hand, then detached it from my wrist and exited.

I found the men's room and peed, but didn't go straight back to the screening room. I wandered down the hallway. The Thalberg Building was deserted at this time of night. Or maybe not, according to a friend of mine who used to be an executive here. One night she'd been working late and had looked up and been startled to see a man standing on the other side of the desk. He was wearing a dark, old-fashioned-looking suit, and was short, pale, and very handsome. He was smiling musingly at her, and then he had just faded away. My friend was positive it had been the ghost of the boy wonder Irving Thalberg himself, who'd had a bad heart since he was a baby and had died of pneumonia at the age of only thirty-seven. Maybe the shade of Louis B. Mayer, his megalomaniacal little boss, was roaming the corridors too, looking for the ghost of some wretched writer to berate.

In the lobby, an obese black security guard sat behind a counter, eating yogurt with a plastic spoon and talking on his cellphone. He chuckled and said in a rich Barry White baritone: "Baby, you know that ain't true. Huh huh huh. Now you know *that* ain't true." He didn't even give me a glance as I ambled by; I could have been an Arab terrorist like the ones in Downward's movie who'd had plastic surgery and their skin bleached so they could look like white people and now I was about to carry out my plot to blow up the Thalberg Building for all that he knew.

I went outside. A girl was there, smoking a cigarette. She was wearing tight jeans tucked into black lace-up boots and a furry jacket. She had big pouty lips and honey-colored hair. I was a little taken aback, she was so beautiful.

"Hi," I said.

She looked at me and nodded. Took another quick puff. She seemed nervous, or maybe angry.

Then I recognized her. She played the hero's love interest, who might or might not be a surgically disguised terrorist.

"You're in the movie."

She gave a mirthless laugh. "Is that an accusation?"

"Well, no, I—"

"It's ghastly, isn't it?"

I shrugged.

"My nude scene is coming up. I can't bear to watch it. It's so humiliating."

"What's your name?"

"Helena."

"I'm Dustin."

"Why are *you* here?"

"I'm a friend of Dick's."

"Dick," she sighed. "A nice man, but—do you think he knows his movie is no good?"

"No. They never do."

"Yes. How sad."

"Maybe sometimes it's better not to know the truth."

Helena shook her head as she twisted out her cigarette in the dirty sand of an ash receptacle. "No. The truth is always better."

"You seem to have a little bit of an accent."

"Oh shit, is it that obvious? And I've been trying to expunge it."

"You have nearly expunged it. I've got an ear for accents or I'd never have noticed it. What is it? Russian?"

"Polish."

"Were you an actress in Poland?"

"A student. I was visiting Paris with my boyfriend, and one night a funny-looking man with a big nose came up to me on the street. He asked me if I was an actress, and I said no, and he asked if I wished to be an actress, and I said no, and he said, '*Mademoiselle*, you may bray no, no, no until the sun comes up, but you are going to be the star of my next movie!' The man with the big nose was Philippe de la Touche, the director, and I *was* the star of his next movie. The silly, frightened, laughably inept star, but the movie became a big hit. That was six years ago. Now I am here, in America. Still silly. Still frightened. Still inept."

In the minute or two I'd been standing here, I'd fallen three-quarters or maybe even four-fifths in love with Helena.

"I think you're very ept."

"'Ept'? That's not a word, is it?"

"It is now. It's a nice night. Want to take a walk?"

She looked at me. She thought about it.

"Or else we could go back to the movie," I said. "Maybe arrive right in the middle of your nude scene. I know *I'd* certainly find that highly unpleasant."

She smiled a little, for the first time.

"We can't be gone for long," she said.

We strolled off across the lot. We went under a hundred-foot-tall steel sculpture of *The Wizard of Oz* rainbow. It was February and chilly, and our breath steamed out of our mouths. "It's cold tonight," I observed.

"You think this is cold?" she scoffed. "Poland is cold," and then: "Are you an actor?"

I find this subject awkward and uncomfortable, but it is necessary that it be dealt with so here it goes. I am what many people consider to be a handsome man. I'm a wide-shouldered, narrow-hipped mesomorph, athletic enough to have played baseball professionally. My dark hair is so thick it's hard to pull a comb through it. I have blue eyes set in deep sockets under a beetling brow that gives me a slightly (and misleadingly, I hope) brutish look. Anyway. It's not surprising Helena thought I was an actor. It happens to me a lot.

"No," I said. "A writer."

"A writer?" I nodded. I sensed an uptick of interest. "Do you write movies?"

"Yeah. And I've done some TV too."

I expected her to ask, as people always do, if I'd written anything they might have seen, but she lit another cigarette instead.

"This used to be the old MGM lot," I said.

"Yes. Of course."

"All the great old stars used to walk exactly where we're walking now. Gable, Lombard, Judy Garland, Spencer Tracy—and now Helena."

She rolled her eyes. "Please, Dustin. Cut the crap."

It's always cute when foreigners use American slang, especially when they're cute foreigners.

"You Europeans are all going to smoke yourselves to death."

"Why not? There are far too many people on the planet already."

We passed between the Cohn and the Kelly Buildings, then walked up a fake, small-town main street, past a bowling alley, a bank, a police station, an ice cream parlor.

"We are make-believe people," said Helena, "walking through a make-believe town."

"I don't know about you, but I'm real enough."

"Are you sure? Maybe you're just part of a dream I am dreaming."

"Well, you know, Nabokov said 'reality' is a word that should always have quotation marks around it."

Bingo! You should have seen the smile she smiled at me! The next day, we met for lunch at a restaurant in West Hollywood; after lunch we wound up at her apartment, which wasn't far away. There I discovered she had freckles across her shoulders and breasts as well as her nose and cheeks. She had a dab of a scar on her right buttock; when she was a kid, her brother had got a toy bow-and-arrow set for his birthday, and he had thought it would be hilarious to take the rubber suction cup off the tip of one of the arrows and sharpen it with a knife and then shoot his sister in the ass with it. Despite its smog and traffic and crime and fires and earthquakes, there yet remains a shimmering magical something about Los Angeles. I think it has at least a little to do with the fact that the golden girls and boys of movies and TV actually live and work here. You might go to your local supermarket and see one of them taking a box of Wheaties off the shelf just like a regular person. You might strike up a conversation: "You like Wheaties too, huh?" Who knows where that could lead? Maybe an invitation to come to the party tonight up at the Hollywood Hills mansion. Friendship might follow. Even romance. It's possible. Anything's possible. You might in a few hours be covering his or her body with kisses, might be being caressed in your most intimate places by her or him. Just like in ancient Greece, where the gods and goddesses would sometimes tire of one another and descend from Mount Olympus to dally with mere mortals. Last night I'd been admiring a lovely luminous two-dimensional image, not realizing its real-life counterpart was sitting in the dark just ten or fifteen feet from me. Now today I was in her bedroom, flat on my back on her bed, with her astride me, blissfully moaning, her breasts dangling above me like the freckled fruits of Paradise.

It was easy to fool my wife. In Hollywood, life is a tedious round of mostly meaningless meetings, so I would just tell Laura, if she happened to be sober enough to be paying any attention, that I was up for a rewrite job at Warners and was off to Burbank to give them my "take," and then would jump in my silver Maserati Quattroporte and head like a heat-seeking missile for Helena. In March I got a gift. Laura was still a star of sorts in Japan, and she flew there for a week to shoot a series of perfume commercials for a sum of money that would make you weep and shake your fist helplessly at the sky at the cosmic injustice of it all were I to disclose it to you. I had a few unhurried, halcyon days with my new girlfriend. We drove out to Palm Springs, and walked around in the desert, and communed with Joshua trees and cacti, then that night at our hotel, out on our private patio, drinking wine under the stars in the indolent thermal swirl of the Jacuzzi, she explained to me Nietzsche's theory of the Eternal Recurrence. Not only will each moment of our lives happen again, but it will happen a million, a billion, a trillion times. Since any real heaven and hell would have to be eternal, we can create in a very literal way hell or heaven at every moment of our lives. What's done once is done forever. I am not a deep person, but I thought I got her drift. I set down my glass of wine, reached for her, and said, "Then let's fuck."

"You're smart for an American," she murmured, and then kissed me.

Unfortunately our idyll was cut short when I got word from Japan that Laura had collapsed on the set due to "exhaustion" (probably too much saki) and was coming home two days early. Then a week later we were drinking Domaine de Chevalier Blanc at the restaurant in Malibu.

While we were waiting for our dessert and coffee, she went to the ladies' room. She was wearing her usual tight jeans and a fringed buckskin jacket and a waiter nearly had a tray knocked out of his hand by a guy walking back to his table who was looking over his shoulder at her, she had the kind of beauty that caused disruptions wherever she went as though she were a wild animal that had escaped from the circus or wandered out of the forest, and she's mine, I thought, eat your heart out, she belongs to Dustin Prewitt. But those were the last happy seconds I was to have with Helena.

When she came back, she gave me a long look, then didn't look at me at all. She was a dessert lover, but after just a bite or two she abandoned her chocolate crème brûlée, lit a cigarette, and gazed out moodily at the ocean. A gentle breeze blew over us. I asked her if anything was the matter.

She looked at me and said: "It is McFate."

"What?"

"Aubrey McFate? In *Lolita*. One of Dolores's classmates."

"What are you talking about?"

"While I was peeing. I heard two women come in. They were talking, and then one woman started to cry. She said she had just learned her husband was having an affair. She sounded like her heart was broken."

"Okay. So?"

"I don't feel good about this, Dustin. About your being married. I don't think we should see each other anymore."

"You can't smoke here!" I looked around. At the next table a young guy was sitting with a much older woman. He was wearing a black Armani jacket and Armani sunglasses, and had sharp but handsome features. The woman was plump, bedecked with jewelry, and overly made up. A gigolo, probably, and his wealthy client. The gigolo was waving his hand in front of his face. "It's blowing right on us."

"Fuck off," I said, and turned back to Helena. "Look, I've told you about Laura. She's an alcoholic. She's a horrible person. She's had a thousand affairs."

"I'm sorry you're in a bad marriage. Perhaps you should think of leaving it."

"Is that it? You want me to leave Laura and marry you?"

She looked repulsed, as though we'd seen something nasty lying on the ground and I'd suggested she take a bite of it. "*No*. I don't want to be married. Not ever."

"This doesn't make any sense, Helena. You want to end it with me just because you were sitting on the toilet and you happened to overhear a conversation between two strangers."

"That was just the . . . what is the word . . . catalyst. It has bothered me from the beginning. I don't like sneaking around and not being able to call you whenever I want to and so forth. It makes me feel like a bad girl and I am not a bad girl. I don't want to hurt other people."

"What do you think you're doing to *me*?" I said, just a decibel or two below a shout. "Helena, I love you!"

"I doubt it. But if you do, you'll get over it. *I* always do."

The waiter came by and dropped off the check. Helena reached for it, but I took it away from her.

"Oh Dustin, don't be macho. I do this and spoil our lovely lunch, then I should pay."

I shrugged, and took out my wallet. I couldn't believe the sudden nightmare turn my life had taken. This is just Hollywood to a T, I thought. Everyone's immoral here except when you want them to be.

"I don't suppose it would do any good to argue with you," I said.

She shook her head. Good-bye, freckles. Good-bye, honey-colored hair. She reached across the table and put her hand on mine. Good-bye, the touch, the taste, the sound, the smell of her.

"I don't regret taking that walk with you, Dustin, or any of the rest of it. I like you very much. Do you believe me?"

I nodded. I felt numb. I felt like I was a giant hand puppet and somebody's finger was doing the nodding for me.

And then she got up and she was gone. Her chair across from me empty just like that. Life's favorite magic trick. Making stuff disappear. I just sat there for a while after I paid the check. The water and sky had lost their charm. I hoped this moment wouldn't eternally recur. To hell with pelicans! Finally I sighed, and rose.

The gigolo guy was smirking at me.

"She dumped you, huh, dude?"

I gazed into the dark Armani depths of his sunglasses, then reached down and tipped his water glass over into his lap. "Jesus fucking Christ!" he gasped. He started to stand up, and I thought I was about to get in my first fight since 2003, when I'd scuffled with some idiot in a Porsche who'd bumped into my Jag in front of the Viper Room, but the plump woman leaned across the table and clutched his arm.

"No, darling, don't! He's crazy! Don't you see?"

She sounded scared to death. I suddenly felt bad about the whole thing, and walked away quickly.

I drove fast back down the PCH. I imagined coming upon Helena's car broken down on the roadside, Helena standing by it helplessly. I pulled over and, before you knew it, I was pressing her quivering

buckskinned beauty against me as she proclaimed her love for me
in five languages, then we hopped in my Maserati. But instead of
continuing towards Los Angeles, we put that crazy town behind us
forever as I made a swift decisive U-turn and headed the other way,
up the windy coast, past Pepperdine and Point Dume and towards
unknown points beyond . . . In the make-believe world of Hollywood
movies, that's always how it happens: an apparent sad ending, and
then the "real" happy one.

My wife ordinarily spent her afternoons drinking vodka and
leafing listlessly through magazines filled with glossy pictures of
women that looked a lot like her, and that's how I found her when
I got home.

"How was lunch?" she said, not even bothering to look up; the
cover of her magazine posed the burning question: "Is Short Hair
Coming Back?"

"Oh, fine."

"And how's Brian?"

Supposedly I'd been having lunch with Brian Nasry, my manager.

"You know." I was too disheartened to come up with the lively
details that would give some verisimilitude to my cover story. "Brian's Brian."

"Does he still want to go to Syria?"

Brian's father came from Syria and Brian was very distressed
by the bloody civil war taking place there. He'd begun talking of
traveling to Syria and shooting a documentary about it, which was
laughable if you knew Brian, an archetypically Hollywood fellow
for whom hardship and peril consisted of his phone going dead
when he was stuck in traffic or his assistant messing up a restaurant
reservation.

"Yeah," I smiled, and shook my head. "The crazy guy. He'll never
do it in a million years."

"You went to the Grill?"

"Yeah."

"That's funny," she said casually, still turning pages. "I thought you went to Geoffrey's."

After a stunned pause, I managed to produce halting, speech-like noises suggesting that yes indeed I *had* had lunch at the Grill.

She looked up at me, her face suddenly twisted and ugly.

"Liar! You were *seen* at Geoffrey's! You and your little blonde bitch!"

I chuckled, closed my eyes, held my hands up, and nodded. "Okay. Okay. You got me. You're going to feel *so* bad when you hear this. That girl was a party planner. One of the best in L.A. Your birthday's next month, you know, and we were planning a surprise party, something really elaborate, hundreds of guests, acrobats from the Cirque du Soleil—"

I thought it a damn good lie for the spur of the moment, but when she threw her tumbler of vodka at me it was clear she wasn't buying it. I ducked a little and it sailed over my shoulder and smashed against the wall. Then she jumped up from the couch and ran toward the big French windows which were open to the balmy spring day and went through them like a high hurdler and this is where you came in.

We had a dog named Topper, a golden-brown Irish terrier. He had cost us $2000, which seems like a lot to spend just to get a dog that hates your guts. I would be barked at like a burglar whenever I entered the house. He would chew up my new Italian loafers, piss on any of my clothes I was unwise enough to leave lying around. Laura, on the other hand, he loved, and was very protective of. On the rare occasions when I was physically affectionate with her, he would stand nearby and glare at me as he growled and trembled. Once when we were having sex and Laura was in the middle of a rather loud and protracted climax, he leapt up on the bed and sank his teeth into my calf and sent me to the emergency room. He liked to hang out on the balcony off the master bedroom on the second floor, and maybe he'd been up there watching Cesar and me as we struggled with Laura. At any rate, as soon as I walked in the house with her, Topper came charging at full speed around a corner, skidding as he changed direction, his claws scrabbling for traction on the hardwood floor, and then he came at me.

He grabbed hold of my pants leg and pulled and shook it as he growled louder than you would think such a small dog possibly could.

"Topper, stop it! Laura, make him stop!"

"Why should I?"

"Come on, Laura! Please!"

"No, Topper! Leave Daddy alone! Now!"

Topper reluctantly relinquished my leg. I helped Laura back to the couch. She curled up in a corner of it and I draped an afghan over her and she sniffled and wiped her face with it and said, "Get me that drink, you bastard."

"Grey Goose?"

"Sipsmith."

She was very picky about her vodka, frequently switching brands according to what she'd heard the latest favorite was amongst the Hollywood young and hip. I walked over to our well-stocked bar, put some ice in a glass, then filled it to the brim with Smirnoff, knowing she'd never know the difference.

When I went back to the couch, Topper was under the afghan with her, only his head showing as he licked her face. He eyed my arm as I handed her her drink as though it was taking all his willpower to restrain himself from chomping down on it.

"If you'd hit me in the forehead with that glass," I said, "you might have killed me."

"You deserve to die, you pig."

"Who told you? How'd you find out?"

"I'm not telling."

"Here's the truth, Laura. The god-honest truth. Yes, I've been having an affair. A meaningless affair with a silly little bimbo. I was unfaithful to you because I know you've been unfaithful to me *and don't bother to deny it*. It only started a few weeks ago and now it's over. I broke it off with her today because I realized in spite of Alfredo and Harry and Toby and Brad and God knows who else, I still love you and want to make our marriage work. I'll give you a second chance if you'll give me a second chance. What do you say?"

I could see in her bleary eyes that she was listening to me and I was likely to get away with it. Though I couldn't remember having seen her raise the glass to her lips, I noticed now it was half empty, as if she were taking the booze into her body through some sort of mysterious osmotic process.

2

I was born and raised ten miles from West Point, on the Hudson River, in Newburgh, New York. My father managed the Sears store, my mother was a junior high history teacher. My parents weren't rich but they were ambitious for me, and when I was fourteen they sent me off to a prestigious prep school in Pottstown, Pennsylvania. At the Hill School I studied Greek and Latin and was a star pitcher for the baseball team, then I went to the frozen wilds of New Hampshire and became a star pitcher for Dartmouth. Upon graduation, I signed with the Boston Red Sox organization, and found myself back in New York, playing for the Elmira Pioneers in the New York-Penn League. My second year I played in the Florida State League for Winter Haven. At the end of the season I got the word that I wasn't going to be asked back to spring training, and my baseball career was effectively over.

I felt I'd been pitching pretty well and I was shocked, but I really shouldn't have been. My fastball was in the high eighties, maybe ninety on a good day, excellent for the Ivy League but so-so for the majors. I had good control, but with that kind of speed it needed to be better. Plus, I was a college guy. They were more patient with guys who'd signed straight out of high school, figuring they'd be maturing more, than with college guys who were already probably close to their peak.

Not knowing where else to go, I went back to my parents' house in Newburgh. I had planned to play in the Big Leagues until my late thirties, whereupon, rich, famous, and revered, I would tip my cap to the cheering crowd with a tear in my eye and slowly walk back to the dugout one last time, then spend the rest of my life playing golf in sunny southern climes. Now here I was in the bedroom of my boyhood, surrounded by baseball paraphernalia—trophies, scrapbooks, autographed balls, my first glove, Yankee pennants, a framed photograph of an eleven-year-old me grinning up at the Yankees' first baseman Don Mattingly—which seemed to mock me and all my dead and foolish dreams.

I'd gotten a B.A. in English from Dartmouth, and I finally decided, for want of anything better to do, to go back to school and get my master's. I applied to several different programs, but since it was already too late to make the fall semester I had at least several months to kill. So I started work on a novel.

It was about baseball—about my love of it, and my grief at the loss of it. It focused on the summer I'd just spent in Winter Haven. Some of it I made up, but it was mostly true. I became obsessed. I seldom left my room except for meals. My parents feared I was having some sort of breakdown, which I think I was, except somehow I was getting it all down on paper. The autumn scene outside my bedroom window became a winter scene and yet I hardly noticed for I had found a haven from winter and snow and cold and early dark and failure in that illimitable space inside my own cranium where white baseballs flew to the plate at eighty-eight miles per hour under the buggy lights and beer was drunk and girls were chased and on the day after Christmas, when I wrote the final pages about how David Cole, the cocky pitcher from Dartmouth, was saved from disaster by the self-sacrificial action of Lumpy Ogonowski, the uneducated catcher and steel-mill-worker's son from Pittsburgh, I was weeping, weeping, even though that scene was a hundred percent make-believe.

I never did make it to grad school. I sent *Strike Four*, as I called it, to Hanover, New Hampshire, to one of my English professors who was also a novelist. He sent it on to his agent in New York, who called me not long after to tell me a publisher was offering a hundred-thousand-dollar advance for the book (as at the climax of a sentimental movie, I ran through the ecstatic snow of Newburgh, shouting my news to the icicled houses and the frozen trees!).

The reviews could hardly have been better had I written them myself ("The best baseball book in many a year." "Lumpy Ogonowski's final speech would put a lump in the throat of a stone statue"), and it was thrilling to see *Strike Four* climb onto the lower rungs of the *New York Times* Bestseller List for a week or two.

And then Hollywood came a-callin'. Wined me and dined me and had its way with me and even remembered my name the next morning. Not only did I sell the movie rights for a pile of dough but I got hired to write the screenplay. I remember the plane floating over snow-topped mountains then drifting down towards Los Angeles, and my face filled a window in the first-class cabin as I gazed upon the giant white letters of the Hollywood Sign marching across the Hollywood Hills, and I had just turned twenty-five and my head was buzzing with scotch and I knew it was unlikely I would ever die and it might as well have been DUSTIN PREWITT spelled out in those giant white letters. The producers professed themselves pleased with what I wrote then promptly, in that communal, more-the-merrier way that Hollywood fashions scripts, brought in other writers to rewrite me. When the movie came out, I was sent a thick stack of reviews, of which I read about half, then triggered the smoke alarm in my apartment by setting fire to the rest. "It swings for the fences but pops the ball up," was one of the more respectful comments. "Too bad movies can't be rained out like baseball games," was more cruelly typical. The reviewers were right all right, it was a big fat ugly gobbling turkey, and the pretty-boy actor they cast as me threw like a girl. The only notable thing about *Strike Four* the movie was the performance of Matt Price as Lumpy Ogonowski. This was Price's breakout role, the one that propelled him toward his present all-devouring world-historical superstardom.

But the failure of the movie didn't seem to matter, I was a hot young writer repped by one of the top agencies and I made deals all over town. I bought a house in Bel-Air. I roared around the city in a red Jaguar. I rubbed suntan lotion on lithe starlets on the white beaches of Cancun, dazzled poorly paid D-girls by flying them to Saint Kitts. I went through a wild, feverish cocaine phase, then returned to my senses and went back to drinking half a quart of whiskey a night. I got married, to a person who will not be allowed the satisfaction of seeing her name or a single detail either positive or negative about herself in these pages. The marriage ended after three years, then I resumed my blissful bachelor's life for three more years, and then I met Laura Keene.

Her career had just reached its apogee and was about to head downward, although of course one never knows such a thing at the time. *Jill and Jack*, a romantic comedy she'd starred in with George Clooney, had made north of a hundred mil and gotten her a Golden Globe nomination. Universal, which made the movie, rewarded her with an on-the-lot production deal. To me, giving someone like Laura her very own company to run was sort of like the mad emperor in ancient Rome appointing his horse to the senate, but that's the protean nature of power in Hollywood, horse to senator or senator to horse in the twinkling of an eye. My agent got me a meeting with Laura to discuss her "dream" project. I seem to remember it was about the first woman to swim the English Channel. Or maybe it was the first woman to fly solo across the Atlantic. Or it could have been the first woman to teach hummingbirds to fly upside-down. All I'm sure is I knew it was something the studio would never greenlight in a million years, and yet screenwriters can make very healthy (or unhealthy) livings writing such projects.

I launched into my pitch: "I see this as a movie not about hummingbirds flying upside-down but about a shy, retiring woman discovering her own strength and beauty. I think we open on a shot of her favorite hummingbird Harold crashing into a tree and knocking himself out." My actual words don't matter now and didn't matter then because, if not for the irritating presence of her partner, a fey young man named Alan who was making notes on his laptop and occasionally giggling at one of my witticisms or perhaps just at the absurdity of the drivel I was spouting, Laura and I probably would have been coupling animalistically on the couch I was sitting on within five minutes of my walking through the door. We could hardly keep a grin off our faces we were so gaga over each other. As I've mentioned, she was quite a big girl. She'd been a star swimmer as a teenager, and still looked fit enough to dive in a pool and win another trophy. I'm a big fan of female legs, and Laura must have had the best set of Hollywood gams since Betty Grable. She was wearing a skirt with a slit in it, and her legs were crossed, and the top leg was rocking a little, and she was taut of calf and firm of thigh and noble of knee, and her big shoe was dangling from her big foot and seemed about to fall off, and she saw me looking at it as I soldiered on about the hummingbirds, and she gave me a throaty, knowing laugh, and I laughed too, and even Alan, eyes still glued to the laptop, joined in with a convivial giggle.

I didn't write the hummingbird script nor any other for Laura's short-lived company because we both decided it would be better not to mix business with our rapturous pleasure. I became, in short order, her boyfriend, fiancé, and husband. The marriage took place in Woodbury, Connecticut, and this brings us to something very important about Laura. In her heyday, she was often the recipient of seven-figure checks, but that was like bringing coals to Newcastle since Laura was a member of one of the wealthiest families in America. Her grandfather, William Keene, had founded a very successful engineering firm in Newark, New Jersey, which he had passed down to his son, and Laura's father, William Junior. Junior was a college drop-out of whom nothing much was expected, but it turned out he had a genius for making money, diversifying into real estate and gold mines and oil wells and cattle ranches and earning the nickname Billionaire Bill. I was told that our wedding (hundreds of repugnant Republicans arriving by private jet, entertainment by Elton John, paparazzi swooping about in helicopters) cost Bill millions.

You're probably thinking I married Laura for the money. And I don't blame you for being cynical about me or anything else in this corrupt and decadent and fallen and wicked and doomed world of ours and yet I must fervently yelp not guilty! In the beginning, I loved Laura. After all, she was a gorgeous woman, and we had a great deal in common. Our love of sports for instance. You should have seen her whack a ball 250 yards down the middle of a fairway, and she would beat my brains out in tennis, though I couldn't share her passion for horses, gigantic, nervous, snorting beasts that didn't want me up on their backs any more than I wanted to be there. But as her career waned and her drinking increased and her affairs proliferated like rotting toadstools, it's true that the financial aspect of our relationship grew in importance. Regrettably, I've never been very good with money, and though I made a lot as a screenwriter I spent even more, then a couple of years ago my career began to grow unaccountably cold. It was unexpected and horrible. It was like being cut by the Red Sox all over again. I began wondering if I had unwittingly offended some powerful Hollywood figure and been put on some secret blacklist. I wasn't making any money at all except for occasional meager residual checks. If it hadn't been for my marriage to Laura, I don't know what would have become of me.

Billionaire Bill, a chain-smoking, whiskey-drinking old bastard whom I was actually very fond of despite his obvious utter disdain for me, had died four years ago of bladder cancer at the age of seventy-eight. He was survived by his wife Peggy, a woman whose most interesting characteristic was an alarming sneeze that sounded exactly like a scream, and their three children: Laura; Katherine, called "Kitty" by everyone; and William III, known as

"Buzzy" because of some obscure childhood prank involving bees. I'm sure no one wished Mrs. Keene anything other than the longest life possible, but the reality was she was extremely frail, beset by many ailments, and often talked poignantly of her longing to join her husband in heaven. Upon her death the Keene money, thought to be in the ballpark of twelve billion dollars, would pass equally to the three children.

So maybe I was staying with a woman that I didn't love anymore; but ye who would blithely walk away from four billion bucks may cast the first stone.

3

About a week after my imaginary lunch with Brian Nasry, I had a real lunch with him. It too was at the Grill on the Alley. It was a renowned Hollywood spot packed with producers and studio execs and agents and managers—a perfect place, I often thought, for an embittered, end-of-his-rope screenwriter to come strolling in wearing a suicide vest.

Brian was a cute little guy, with a boyish flop of hair over his forehead. He had the dark complexion of his Syrian father and the green eyes of his American mother. He looked on with disapproval as Don, our white-jacketed waiter, brought me a vodka tonic.

"Nobody drinks at lunch anymore," said Brian.

I smiled and lifted my glass. "To the Last of the Mohicans!"

"It's no joke, man. It's fucking competitive out there. You need every edge you can get."

"So why aren't I working? Have I been blackballed? Is that the fucking deal?"

"No, dude, you haven't been blackballed. The business has changed. The studios go to the same ten writers for everything. And if they can't get them, then they get some snot-nosed little punk just out of film school that'll work for peanuts. And guys like you in the middle are getting creamed. There is no middle class in Hollywood anymore. You're either a star or a peasant. It's becoming like a third-world country."

"Well, I shouldn't be in the middle. I should be one of the ten assholes that get all the action."

"Agreed. But we have to deal with reality. Anyway, all the studios are making these days is that superhero shit. Cable and streaming is where it's at. Netflix, Amazon, they're voracious monsters, they're gonna take over the world. They'd be perfect for you."

"Yeah?"

"Yeah. It's not like the movies. It's a writer's medium. The writer is king."

"I'm not opposed to being a king."

"Good. So how's Laura?"

"Drinking like a fish. Freaked out about turning forty."

"My god. Laura's forty?"

"In three weeks."

"Jesus." Brian shook his head, and took a somber sip of his iced tea; it was as though I'd said: Laura has been diagnosed with cancer.

"She's mad at me. I'm in the doghouse big time."

"How come?"

"She caught me screwing some Polish chick."

"What Polish chick?"

"Helena Dabrowski. She's in Dick Downward's new movie."

"Oh, she's hot."

"Yeah, she's really beautiful."

"No, I mean hot in a business sense. Everybody says she's gonna be a big star."

"You're kidding me. I mean, I thought she wasn't bad, but you know, the movie's terrible."

"That's not what I hear. The buzz on it's unbelievable. What are you doing fucking around on Laura for, anyway? She loves you, dude."

"She's got a weird way of showing it sometimes."

"Everybody's weird. We're all weird. We're all nuts."

Don brought us our food: meatloaf for me, the grilled vegetable plate for Brian.

"Can I get you gentlemen anything else?"

"You know what?" said Brian. "I'll have what he's having."

He was pointing at my vodka tonic.

"You got it."

I looked at Brian, mystified. He wouldn't meet my eye. He poked at his food with his fork.

"Brian . . . what's up?"

"You're not gonna like this."

I shrugged. "Okay."

"I can't be your manager anymore."

"Shit. Brian. You're dropping me?"

"It's not like that. I'm not gonna be a manager anymore. At least not for a while."

"What are you gonna do?"

Now he looked up at me. His eyes had a strange intensity in them. His lips had the hint of a smile.

"I'm going to Syria."

I relaxed. "Oh."

"No. Really. It's just gonna be me and this guy named Grayson Neihardt, he's this great documentary filmmaker, he's won awards. We're leaving next Tuesday. Everything's ready to go. We fly into Turkey, and from there we cross into Syria. My cousin Mahmoud will meet us at the border."

I stared at him. "You're serious."

"Don't try and talk me out of this. I gotta do this. Syria's like a second home to me. I'd spend whole summers there when I was a kid. I have lots of friends and family there. The world needs to know how horrible this war is."

"I know how horrible it is, that's why you shouldn't go."

But Brian went on, as if he hadn't heard me. "It's all I can think about. I even dream about it. I dream about explosions. And fire, and blood. And black smoke drifting across a red sun. The dreams are fucking weird. It's like I've already been there. It's like I'm dreaming about things I've already done."

"Maybe your subconscious is trying to tell you something, Brian. Like if you go to Syria you're gonna get your nuts shot off. Or you're gonna get kidnapped. And your head cut off! Journalists are dying like flies there!"

"This all has to do with Trump, in some weird kind of way. The fact we have an evil idiot as our president. It's like there's been some kind of cloud covering the earth ever since he was elected. And it makes me want to do something with my life. Something decent. Just one decent thing."

Don returned with the vodka tonic. "Thanks, Don," said Brian, and then to me, softly: "Wish me luck, Dustin."

I shook my head, and laughed a little. "You're my hero, man. And a fucking lunatic."

We clicked glasses. Brian dug into his grilled vegetables. "You're gonna be fine, you'll see. Ben'll take care of you. He's still one of the best agents in town."

"You think I should get another manager?"

"What for? Save yourself the ten percent. Hey, what do you do all day anyway? I mean, besides chase Polish chicks."

"Read. Fart around on the Internet. Work out. Play golf some-times. Why?"

"Why don't you come up with a concept for a TV show? Write a treatment? And then have Ben set up some meetings for you?"

I nodded. "I could do that."

"Or you could write a novel."

"A novel?"

"Yeah. I loved your first one."

I considered the green lime wedge floating in my sparkling drink. "Nah. That's what got me into this mess."

4

We had a wonderful house. It was a white stucco Mediterranean built in the twenties, with forest-green wood trim and a terra-cotta tile roof. At six thousand square feet, it was a modest cottage by Beverly Hills standards, but it was just right for us. You walked in the front door and found yourself in a circular foyer, with a majestic staircase with a wrought-iron bannister leading up to the second floor, where there were three bedrooms and a game room and a workout room. On the first floor were a den and a living room and my office and her office and a dining room and a big kitchen and a butler's pantry and a maid's room. There was no butler in the pantry or maid in the maid's room. Nor were there any shenanigans with the butler in the maid's bed with the maid, or the maid in the butler's pantry on her knees in front of the butler. We had no live-in help. We both valued our privacy. The *Sturm und Drang* of our relationship was witnessed mostly only by Topper.

We had lived previously for several years in Mandeville Canyon. It was green and rustic and peaceful out there, with lots of amusing critters. A family of chipmunks lived by the swimming pool; they would tumble and play and tire themselves out then curl up together in the shade and nap and seemed less like flesh-and-blood animals than living cartoon characters. One night we heard a noise then found a masked intruder in our kitchen, a raccoon that had come in through the doggie door and was eating Topper's food. But come

October and the scorch and howl of the Santa Ana winds, we were always nervous that fire would sweep through the canyon and destroy us, and then one day Laura saw a deer that had tried to jump over a neighbor's spiky fence and impaled itself; it was still alive, and was struggling, and Laura became so hysterical I had to rush her to her doctor for sedation, and soon we had bought the house in Beverly Hills on Bedford Drive.

It had its charms but needed work. Laura tended to be dithering and lazy, but she remodeled that house the way Hitler invaded Poland, zestfully hiring and firing contractors and torturing interior decorators and bringing seasoned landscape artists to the verge of tears. It had been a long time since I had seen her so happy. She furnished the place with down-filled dreamily comfortable pieces in dark chocolates and ruby reds. Renovated the kitchen with brutally efficient-looking stainless-steel Viking and Wolf appliances. Hung a huge hundreds-of-years-old French tapestry in the living room, showing unicorns and dragons, knights and fair ladies. Laura knew a lot more about art than did her philistine husband, and we had a valuable collection of mostly modern stuff, paintings by Warhol and Hockney and Pollack and de Kooning, and sculptures of scrawny-looking women by Robert Graham, the late sculptor to the stars. Also a bust by Graham of the Lady of the House herself.

Beverly Hills had a biannual art show, Affaire at the Gardens. It was held within walking distance of our house, on four blocks on the north side of Santa Monica Boulevard in Beverly Gardens Park. One Sunday in May, Laura and Topper and I took a stroll down to the Affaire. Artists were selling their paintings, watercolors, sculptures, photographs, jewelry, and ceramics in hundreds of white tents. Thousands of people were milling about. A large percentage of them had dogs, and Topper seemed compelled to sniff, lick, bark at, bite, or attempt to mount every one of them. One dog in particular seemed to incite Topper's fury, a medium-sized dog without any hair. It looked like a burn victim. Its wrinkled skin was exactly the same shade of brown as its sad, liquescent eyes. It cringed and shivered as Topper strained at the end of the leash held by Laura and bared his teeth and snarled at it.

"Control your dog, lady!" snapped the dog's owner.

"*My* dog's not the problem!" Laura claimed ridiculously.

"Like hell he's not!"

"Just chill out, pal," I said.

"Chill out yourself, asshole!"

He was a lean guy in a tight T-shirt, with a stubble of beard and a shiny shaved head. I felt the blood rush to my face, and stepped towards him.

"What kind of idiot would breed a dog without any hair?" I ranted. "What's next? A dog without legs? A dog without eyes?"

I wasn't being exactly fair since presumably *he* didn't breed the dog. Maybe he had rescued it from dire circumstances and they were just out for a nice Sunday walk only to be set upon by a vicious terrier and a bellowing, red-faced fellow.

"Come on, Daniel," he said. "Let's get out of here."

Poor Daniel cast a puzzled, woebegone look over his shoulder as his huffy master led him away through the crowd. Laura slipped her arm through mine as she beamed at me. She always loved it when I got angry, as long as it wasn't directed at her.

I have limited endurance for such things as shopping and sightseeing and wandering around museums or art shows, and within fifteen minutes I could have been staggering across a desert in a desperate search for water for all the fun I was having. Sometimes I'm afflicted with an aching right hip, a result of wear-and-tear from my pitching days. Today it felt fine, but I began to subtly limp anyway. Laura found something she liked—a three-and-a-half-foot-tall bronze of a heavily muscled, mythological-looking warrior, armed with a short sword. It had a purple and green and gold patina, strange growths coming out of its head, and was naked except for a codpiece studded with knobs. She told me it "reminds me of you," and bought it for $9000, then as we headed across Canon toward the next tent-covered block, I began to limp more heavily. Finally Laura noticed.

"Oh Dustin. Is it your hip?"

"Huh? Oh. Yeah, it's a little sore."

"Do you want to rest for a while?"

"No, are you kidding me? This is great. Looking at all these statues and things."

But I couldn't help but wince as I stepped back up on the sidewalk, and Laura insisted we find some place to sit down.

The park was pleasant, with lots of tall cypress and ficus trees. Under the spreading limbs of one of the trees a place called the Wine Garden was selling food and wine. Tables were covered with purple and white tablecloths. A swarthy man in a black suit was passionately playing the violin. We bought two plastic glasses of Chardonnay and a turkey and brie sandwich, then sat down at one of the tables.

It was a gray, cool day, with gusts of wind sweeping through the leaves above. Rain was in the forecast, a rarity for May. I sipped my wine, and ate my half of the sandwich. Laura downed her glass quickly, got up and got another, and fed most of her sandwich to Topper.

We had both been making an effort since the big blowup over Helena, and had been getting along reasonably well. And it was agreeable now to be with her under the windy tree. We held hands, and listened to the violinist give a sprightly rendition of "If I Were a Rich Man." When he finished, Laura lifted her hands over her head and clapped and cried, "Bravo, Pablo! Bravo!"

Pablo—I don't know if Laura somehow knew that was his name or just thought he looked like a Pablo—smiled and bowed to Laura. Now she was recognized by some fans, and graciously deigned to pose for a selfie or two. (This could have gone the other way. Once in a hotel lobby she was approached by a grandmotherly lady, who told Laura she was her favorite actress and politely asked for her autograph. Laura, deep in her cups, called her an old cunt and told her to get away from her and continued screaming at the unfortunate woman as she fled back across the lobby in tears.)

A sudden rush of wind blew our empty plastic wine glasses off the table. Pablo began to play the Carpenters tune "Close to You." "Oh, I love this!" said Laura, then she began to sing directly to me in a swoony, wide-eyed way, *"Just like me, they long to be close to you!"*

Now she jumped up and grabbed my hand.

"Let's dance."

I hadn't danced since our wedding. I dance only under duress. And I wasn't in the mood now to make a public spectacle of myself by dancing under a tree with my madcap wife in front of a lot of strangers. I smiled, and made some negative murmuring noises. She pulled on my hand and being a powerful girl nearly lifted me off my chair.

"Oh, come on, Dustin, dance with me!"

"Dance with her, Dustin!" said a fat guy in a baseball cap at a nearby table, then other spectators chimed in, enjoying a little hobnobbing with a Hollywood celebrity (*You eat Wheaties too, huh?*). Now I noticed half a dozen different people snapping pictures or shooting video of us with their phones.

"My hip," I remembered. "It hurts too much."

"I'll bet you'd dance if *she* asked you."

"Who?"

She threw down my hand and grabbed Topper's leash.

"Laura, don't be silly. Sit down!"

She yanked the leash and Topper trotted after her as she stormed off.

Pablo was still sawing away at his violin, eliciting the dulcet sounds of the Carpenters song. The people who'd been egging us on were staring at me silently now, thrilled no doubt at having played a small role in a real-life Hollywood drama. I didn't want to follow Laura's intended script and go chasing after her, but of course within seconds I was doing exactly that.

"Laura, where are you going?" I said as I caught up with her and Topper.

"Home!" she said without looking at me or slowing down.

"Look, don't be this way. We were having such a good time. Let's go back. Let's keep it going."

She glanced over at me.

"Your hip seems all right now," she observed.

I gave up. Stopped walking. Watched her striding up Canon on those magnificent legs of hers.

I went back to the Wine Garden and sat down with another glass of wine. Pablo played "Hello, Dolly." Soon it began to rain. The cypress tree offered some temporary protection, so I stayed where I was. I felt bad for all the artists in their white tents. They had worked hard on their stuff and here was their chance to get it seen, but now they had to watch their customers scatter, watch them scurry away like bedraggled rats through the unlikely rain.

A vast sadness descended on me, and I forgot where I was. I was brought back to myself by raindrops trickling down through the leaves and dripping on me. All the other Wine Garden customers were gone, Pablo was gone. I was quite alone under the tree.

5

The BHPD car eased by, the cop inside taking a good look at the weirdo walking through the rain. Two crows hopped like hobgoblins across my path, then rose into the air and flapped away. Palm fronds had been torn loose by the wind and lay broken and fluttering on the gleaming street.

I found Laura in the den, standing behind the bar. She had a new favorite vodka, Roberto Cavalli, named after an Italian designer, and she was splashing some over the ice in a glass.

"So that's your solution to everything," I said. "Get drunk."

"What's your solution? Fuck a bimbo?"

"I thought you were gonna try and get over that. Like I'm trying to get over all the shit you've pulled."

"You know what? We both fuck around for exactly the same reason."

"Yeah? What's that?"

"You fuck other women because you don't love me. And I fuck other guys because you don't love me."

She didn't act mad as she said this, mad I could deal with. Sad was more difficult. I made the expected pro forma protestation of love. She took a long drink of Roberto Cavalli as she listened, but when I finished she just shook her head.

"Oh, just shut up about it, Dustin. It's Sunday, and I hate Sundays.

And it's raining, and I hate rain. And I'm turning forty in four days, and I hate that. And I hate that you don't love me."

There wasn't much to say after that. Following Laura's lead I made myself a drink, then retired to my office and finished up reading the Sunday *L.A. Times*. When I went back in the den for a refill, Laura wasn't there. Then I saw that the door that led out onto the patio was open.

I went outside. It was late in the day. The rain had stopped, but it was still cloudy and blustery. Laura's clothes were lying on a lounge chair, and she was swimming laps in the pool. I sipped my single-malt scotch and watched her. Her naked body was so graceful and beautiful as it cut through the water. She had always reminded me of Esther Williams, another teen swimming champ and movie star. I remember thinking that the water was Laura's natural element, that it was a shame she ever had to leave it.

I went back to my office. Turned on the TV and watched an NBA play-off game. Got hungry, and went in the kitchen. As I microwaved a beef-and-beans burrito, I heard a floorboard creak overhead, and knew that Laura was now upstairs.

The game finished, and I channel-surfed. Finally I settled down with the Western Channel. Gary Cooper was playing an Army officer unjustly accused of cowardice in *They Came to Cordura*. "If there's any piece of truth in your insect soul," Coop snarled, "I want it!" Next thing I knew, "I want you to 'elp us," a woman was saying in a Mexican accent, and I opened my eyes to Raquel Welch and Jim Brown in *100 Rifles*. I looked at the clock. It was nearly eleven. I'd been asleep for a couple of hours.

I made sure everything was locked and turned on the burglar alarm and turned off all the lights and climbed up the stairs.

Our bedroom door was closed. I tried the doorknob. Locked. I could see a strip of light under the door. I knocked.

"Laura? Laura?"

Topper began to bark. All at once, I felt worried. I continued knocking and calling and Topper continued barking, and then I heard Laura: "Topper! Shut up!"

"Laura? Are you okay?"

"I'm fine. Just go away, Dustin."

"Open the door."

Silence. I gave the doorknob a last futile jiggle, then went down the hallway to one of the guest bedrooms. I had been a guest there before. I fell asleep quickly, and dreamt I was lost in a hellish jungle in the rain. Daniel, the hairless dog, was my companion. We wandered miserably and tediously for what seemed like hours. I was thirsty and scooped up water in my hands and drank and drank but my thirst was unslaked and then I woke up. The rain had started again. My hangover was kicking in, and my head hurt and I was very thirsty. I went in the bathroom and peed and drank water straight from the tap. Then I went back in the bedroom and looked out the window.

There were lights on around the pool, and it glowed blue beneath me. Its surface was ripped and lashed by the wind and rain. I felt a crushing sense of desolation, like I had arrived after a long journey at the place I had been seeking, only to find this empty pool in the stormy dark.

Later in the night I was awakened by Topper howling hideously like the Hound of the Baskervilles, and I remember thinking I should get up and see what's wrong, and then I opened my eyes again and the room was filled with sunlight.

It was about 8:30. I pulled on some clothes and headed downstairs. The door to our bedroom was still closed.

I made coffee, then went outside and got the *Times.* The morning was bright and sparkly. An earthworm squirmed over the wet cobblestones of the driveway. On an obscure impulse I picked it up and put it on the grass.

I sat in the kitchen at the marble-topped island and drank my coffee and looked over the sports section. The Yankees had won.

The Dodgers had lost. Then the bell to the front gate rang. I walked to the intercom, mildly puzzled as to who could be here so early. I pressed the button and said, "Who's there?"

"Los Angeles Police Department," came the unsettling reply. "Detective Dempster. Can we come in?"

"What's this about?"

"Laura Keene."

My god, I thought, as I hit the button that opened the gate. Has Laura committed some kind of crime?

An unmarked Chevrolet was pulling up as I came out the door. Two middle-aged men in suits got out. They both had small, well-trimmed moustaches. They could have been brothers in their bland nondescriptness.

"John Dempster," said the one on the left, as we shook hands. "And this is Detective Gunston."

"Dustin Prewitt. Mind if I see some ID?"

They didn't mind at all and showed me shiny badges.

"You're Mrs. Keene's husband?" asked Gunston.

"Yes. What's going on?"

"Do you know where your wife is?" asked Dempster.

"Of course I know. She's upstairs. She's still asleep."

Dempster and Gunston exchanged a look.

"You've seen her this morning?" said Dempster.

"Well, no. Not yet."

"When's the last time you saw her?" said Gunston.

"Last night. Before I went to bed."

"You have separate bedrooms?" said Gunston.

"Not usually, no, but—"

"Do me a favor, Mr. Keene," said Dempster. "Just check and make sure your wife is actually in the house."

Feeling a sudden sense of foreboding, I nodded. I started to go back in, then paused.

"What kind of detectives are you?"

"Homicide," said Dempster.

I went upstairs. Our bedroom door wasn't locked anymore. As it swung open, I saw Topper lying on the foot of the bed. Now his head popped up and he looked at me.

The room smelled bad; Topper had peed and shat on the floor. Laura wasn't in the bed, nor was she on the balcony. As Topper followed my every move, growling softly, I walked toward the bathroom. "Laura?" I called, but she wasn't in there either.

I checked the rest of the rooms on the second floor and then, moving faster and faster as my heart beat harder and harder, did the same thing downstairs, then went out in the back yard. Finally I went in the garage. My Maserati was there, but the space next to it, where Laura's Mercedes usually was, was empty. Jesus Christ, has she killed somebody? I thought. Is she on the lam? But who would she want to kill but me?

I went back out front. The homicide detectives were standing in the driveway talking, but they fell silent as they saw me approach.

"She's not here," I said. "And her car's gone."

Gunston was holding a small spiral notebook; now he opened it up. "White Mercedes? License number CAO 655?"

"Yes. You guys gotta tell me what's happening."

Looking at his notebook, Gunston cleared his throat.

"At 5:26 a.m., 911 received a call from a man who'd been walking his dog at Dockweiler Beach. That's the beach by LAX. He'd found a woman's clothes—shirt, pants, shoes, underwear—not far from the water. He'd also found a purse. Contents in the purse showed it belonged to Laura Keene. A patrol unit was dispatched to the scene. They searched the area but failed to find Mrs. Keene. But they did find her car, parked nearby on Vista del Mar. That's the road that runs by the beach."

"You okay, Mr. Keene?" said Detective Dempster. "You want a glass of water or something?"

I shook my head.

"We found this in your wife's purse," said Gunston. He handed me a transparent plastic sleeve inside of which was a business card for a dermatologist in Santa Monica. Scribbled on the back of the card in ink, in Laura's handwriting, was this message:

Dear Dustin—
   I killed myself because you wouldn't dance with me.
                      Laura

6

L.A. is briefly beautiful after a storm blows through. The smog was gone. Hills and buildings were etched sharply against the crystal sky, and cool winds gusted through the tops of the rattling palms. When the ocean came in sight, it was as blue and brilliant as I had ever seen it.

Word about what had happened had got out somehow, and Vista del Mar was lined with satellite trucks and camera crews. As the detectives and I walked away from their Chevy, a couple dozen media folks suddenly began to stampede our way. Boom mikes waved above them like pitchforks above a mob of enraged peasants. Uniformed cops kept them at bay as Dempster and Gunston hustled me down to the beach.

The ocean and the sky were swarming with boats and helicopters looking for Laura. Cops and lifeguards wandered near the hissing foam at the water's edge, looking at what the waves brought in. TV choppers buzzed over our heads. The detectives and I trudged across the sand, and got it in our shoes. A police lieutenant told us there had been no sign of Laura.

We heard a roaring, and looked south, towards Manhattan Beach. Beyond a low rise covered with scruffy vegetation lay the airport. Now we watched as a huge jetliner shot skyward. It was a Hawaiian Airlines plane, with a pretty girl with a flower in her hair painted on its tail.

"Any chance your wife faked this?" said Gunston. "You think it could just be a publicity stunt?"

I considered the possibility, then shook my head.

"That's just not Laura. Not that she doesn't have her faults, but she's not really the scheming or the cunning type."

The ringtone on my phone was "La Bamba," and now the incongruously cheerful tune began to issue from the pocket of my windbreaker. I took the phone out and said, "Hello?"

"Dustin, it's Kitty! What the hell's going on? What happened to Laura?"

"Kitty—I was going to call you."

"CNN's saying she's missing and she might be dead! She might be drowned!"

"It's true. I'm at the beach now with the police. We're looking for her."

"My god, Dustin. I think I see you. Are you wearing a light-blue jacket?"

I looked up. A chopper from Channel 7 was hovering almost directly above us.

"Yeah. That's me."

"Who are those two guys with you?"

"Detectives."

"I hope Mother's not watching this! Oh, everything's so messed up, I'm in a hotel room, in the Bahamas—"

"Look, just call Buzzy. Tell him to go to your mother's house."

"Dustin, what happened? Was she swimming? What was she doing swimming in the ocean?"

"I'm not sure what happened. Hold on."

There was some kind of commotion down by the water. People were running past us.

"What's going on?" I said.

"They must've found something," said Gunston, and then we heard somebody yell, "They found her! They found her!"

"Jesus Christ," I said.

"Dustin! Dustin, what's happening?" Kitty cried hysterically.

"I'll have to call you back." I put the phone in my pocket and began to run in the direction everybody else was running. I felt somebody grab my arm, it was Dempster.

"You sure you wanna see this?" he said, and I gasped yes and kept running. It is hard to run through sand, and Dempster, Gunston, and I advanced with a dreamlike slowness. Dempster's tie had blown over his shoulder and was flapping in the wind. I felt as if my nose and mouth had been taped over and I couldn't breathe. Divers in black wetsuits and lifeguards and cops were clustered around something on the hard-packed, gleaming, wave-washed sand. I stumbled and felt dizzy and pain stabbed through my chest and I thought I might be having a heart attack, and Gunston was holding me up, and then I saw the thing on the sand.

It was a very large, quite alive, and extremely active snake. It had doubtless been washed out to sea by the storm. Somebody said it was a rattlesnake, but somebody else pointed out it didn't have any rattles, then a third somebody suggested it could have lost its rattles as it was swept down a storm drain. There was a debate about whether to dispatch the creature on the spot or rescue it. Finally the rescue faction won out, and a call was made to the Humane Society.

~

After several hours on the beach and no Laura, the detectives took me back home. Outside the front gate, two Hispanic guys were standing by their pickup truck. They had come to deliver the sculpture that Laura had bought at the art show. The multicolored mystic warrior with the things coming out of its head and the codpiece with knobs on it was standing in the back of the truck, and was being filmed avidly by several camera crews. This struck me for some reason as a gross invasion of privacy, an outrageous ultimate straw.

"Bastards!" I said, fumbling at the door handle.

"Just hold on there, Dustin," said Gunston, but I threw the door open and jumped out.

"Get the fuck away from here!" I screamed. "It's none of your business!"

The cameras swung in unison in the direction of the grief-deranged husband, and the many-legged media beast scurried towards me. The detectives hastily exited their car and pulled me away.

"Come on, Dustin," said Dempster. "Don't give them what they want."

I opened the gate and yelled to the Hispanic guys, "Okay, let's go!" Looking a little wide-eyed, they got back in their truck, and in a few moments they, the detectives, and I were safe on the private side of the gate. But then I heard a loud clattering, and looked up. A chopper from Channel 4 drifted along under the blur of its rotary blades. Where's a Stinger missile when you need one?

The sculpture weighed a ton, and the guys rolled it inside on a rattling metal cart. As they crossed the foyer, Topper ran up and lunged at the leg of the smaller and younger of the two. He looked terrified, and kicked at Topper and shouted in Spanish.

"No, Topper!" I said. "Stop it! Bad dog!"

Now Topper turned around and took off.

"Sorry about that," I said. "It's my wife's dog. He's upset." I wasn't sure they understood, so I used some of the Spanish I'd picked up when I had a girlfriend from Colombia. "The *perro* of my *esposa*! He's *muy enojado*!"

They nodded uneasily. I had no idea where Laura had planned to put the thing, so I just had them leave it in the middle of the living room. I tipped them lavishly and they left, looking glad to get out of there.

Dempster pointed at the statue's codpiece.

"Looks like somebody stole your jockstrap, Steve."

"Doesn't matter," said Gunston. "I got a drawerful of 'em."

Like most cops, they joked around a lot. I went in a bathroom to take a long-suppressed piss. I noticed my penis was trembling a little, then saw it was my hand that was trembling. Now my irrepressible windbreaker pocket erupted in "La Bamba."

It was my lawyer, Larry Hochheiser. He was calling from his car. He said he'd been out on the golf course all day and somebody had just texted him the news about Laura. He wanted to know the latest.

"They still can't find her and can't find her body."

"Un-fucking-believable. Where are you?"

"Home."

"Are you by yourself?"

"No. Two cops are with me."

"Cops! What kind of cops?"

"Homicide cops."

"Jesus Christ! You're not talking to them, are you?"

"Sure. Why not?"

"Dustin. *Don't ever talk to cops without your lawyer present.*"

"I don't know why you're so upset. Laura killed herself, she wasn't murdered. They don't think I did it."

"How do you know what they think?"

"Larry, they're nice guys. They've been great to me today."

"I'll be there in twenty minutes. Don't say another word to those bastards. And remember: the prisons are full of innocent men!"

I put my phone back in my pocket and tried to remember everything I had told them. It turned out to be quite a lot. They knew about Laura's drinking and infidelities, and that I hadn't been any Boy Scout either. They had had me go over the last twenty-four hours in exhaustive detail. They understood the allusion in Laura's note. Of course the note, in Laura's own handwriting, proved that it was a suicide. Unless I had imitated Laura's handwriting and forged the note or had forced her to write it. Is that what they thought? All day, whenever they had been out of earshot, I would see them talking to each other and occasionally glancing my way. What kind of monstrous web were they trying to weave around me? And what kind of chance would a guy like me, with my blue eyes and thick hair, stand in prison? Sure, I was big and strong, but I wouldn't be able to fight them off forever.

My face in the mirror looked pale and pasty. I bent over the sink and splashed water on it, then returned to the living room.

The detectives were gone, but now Topper was in there. He was standing next to the statue with a hind leg lifted, and was giving the warrior a good hosing.

"Goddamn it, Topper!" I said and ran towards him. He dashed past me and out of the room. A big puddle of urine gleamed on the floor. Well, I would deal with that later. Where were the cops? What were they up to?

As I walked around the house looking for them, my chest started to hurt again. I heard voices in the kitchen. The detectives were standing by the sink, with glasses of water in their hands. They turned their calm, pleasant faces toward me.

"Hope you don't mind us helping ourselves," said Dempster.

"No. Of course not. I was gonna make some coffee. You guys want some?"

"Cops and coffee go together," said Gunston.

"I thought it was cops and donuts."

"Them too," said Dempster.

"Afraid I don't have any donuts," I said, and then I began to stagger backward. I was probably already unconscious by the time the back of my head bounced off the Italian tiles of the floor.

7

I was with Laura. We were on a hillside overlooking the ocean
in some tropical land. A cool, delicious breeze was blowing as
we walked hand in hand among palm trees and many-colored
flowers that seemed to glow with their own light. Laura had a red
flower in her hair. "Dustin?" she said. "Dustin?"

Then I opened my eyes. Two strangers with moustaches were
looming above me and peering down at me. "Dustin? You're gonna
be okay," said one of them, and the other said, "Just take it easy,
Dustin. An ambulance is on the way." One took his coat off and
folded it and put it under my head, and the other draped his coat
over me, tucking it carefully under my chin; I thought they were the
nicest, tenderest strangers I had ever met, and then I remembered
that they were detectives, and that my wife was dead. Had drowned
herself in the sea because I wouldn't dance with her.

Soon several paramedics, as well-built and handsome as if they
were actors playing paramedics on TV, came trooping into the
kitchen. They were gurneying me out the front door when Larry
Hochheiser arrived. He was a short, curly-headed fat guy, wearing
golfing togs in sherbety orange and green colors. He looked at me,
aghast.

"Jesus, Dustin. What have they done to you?"

"They haven't done anything to me," I whispered. "I'm having
a heart attack."

As they rolled me over to the ambulance, I stared straight up at the sky. It was athrob with helicopters. But the sight didn't vex me. Didn't in fact seem to have anything to do with me. The helicopters could have been dust motes floating through a beam of light, or shadows rippling at the bottom of my swimming pool. Or maybe it was me that was the mote of dust, the rippling shadow.

Then we were speeding through the stunned, shady streets of Beverly Hills, with the siren keeping up an apocalyptic wailing. Could this actually be it? I thought. Was I hurrying to keep my appointment in Samarra? I'm a resolute materialist, but that hasn't stopped me from being superstitious. My favorite writer is Scott Fitzgerald, and I'd noticed some parallels in our lives: we'd both gone to Ivy League schools, both had great success in our early twenties with our first novels, then both moved to Hollywood to write scripts. Fitzgerald had died of a heart attack maybe a mile away from our house on Bedford on a Saturday afternoon in Sheilah Graham's apartment at the age of forty-four, and ever since I'd turned forty-four last November I'd been nervous a similar fate awaited me.

I imagined Helena hearing about my passing. She would probably remember her last sight of me, sitting with a sick, befuddled look on my face under the umbrella at Geoffrey's, just before she had turned her back and gone tripping away in her buckskin jacket and her little black boots. I imagined her becoming distraught at the news, throwing herself down on her bed and weeping, and I became so moved by this image that I felt a tickling at my temple and realized a tear had trickled out of my eye. The paramedic attending to me saw the tear too, and gave my arm a reassuring pat.

At Cedars-Sinai Medical Center, the doctors gave me a lot of tests, then pronounced my heart as fit as a fiddle. It was, they thought, stress, understandable under the circumstances, that had caused me to pass out. They wanted to keep me till tomorrow just in case, but I said no. Larry drove me home, then stayed with me that night. He fell asleep in his golf clothes on the couch in the den in front of the TV. Sleeping beside him was Topper, Larry being one of the few people he seemed to like. But sleep didn't seem in the cards for me.

I made a drink, and went outside. Went over to the pool, and sat down in one of the lounge chairs. I wondered where Laura was right at this moment. Full fathom five thy *esposa* lies. Many emotions were swirling around inside me—horror, confusion, fear, dismay, regret, but mainly guilt, guilt, not only over the role I had played in her death, but at the pleasure I was feeling as it dawned on me that I was free.

PETE

8

The media had been obsessed with the malignant moron Donald Trump to the exclusion of every other story for a very long time, but on that Monday it changed, at least for a few days. The country that had nearly forgotten Laura Keene now couldn't get enough of her. It held its collective breath as it waited for her tragic remains to wash up on the beach. But the ocean seemed to want to keep Laura for itself. Those are pearls that were her eyes.

Despite the fears of my lawyer Larry, Detectives Dempster and Gunston never seemed to seriously consider me or anyone else as a murder suspect. They had picked up Laura's trail in Playa del Rey, a funky little beach town just north of Dockweiler Beach. A liquor-store owner there told them he'd closed up at two a.m. on Sunday and was counting the receipts, when a woman started banging on the door demanding to be let in. He shook his head and pointed at the CLOSED sign, but the obviously intoxicated woman kept on banging and yelled she'd give him a hundred bucks for a bottle of vodka. Finally she gave up and wobbled away. The owner thought there was something familiar about her. He went to the door and watched her get in her car, and at that point realized it was Laura Keene. He watched the white Mercedes pull out of the parking lot and turn west on Culver, toward Vista del Mar. Soon after, my detective friends suspected, Laura had shed her clothes and gone in the water.

They thought it was probably an impulsive act, the suicide note in her purse scribbled in the last mad moments.

As you might imagine, I wanted to keep the contents of that note private, but the media got hold of it within twenty-four hours, and it created, as they say, a sensation. Several of the people who had witnessed our argument at the art show came forward and talked about it on *Anderson Cooper 360* and *Good Morning America* and other shows; the fat guy in the baseball cap was especially ubiquitous. The cellphone footage of Laura and me shot by the fat guy and others was all over TV and the Internet. All the cable news shows had panels of pundits heatedly debating whether or not I had been a villain for not having danced with her. I was offered the chance to come on these shows and tell my side of the story, but I maintained a dignified silence.

Laura as Poor Little Rich Girl was a favorite theme of the coverage. How could an heir to one of America's most fabulous fortunes, a woman blessed with beauty and athletic ability and fame and a Golden Globes nomination and a hunky screenwriter hubby, discard her own life like a used Kleenex? It didn't go unnoticed that she killed herself four days before the big Four-O. "Did Hollywood kill Laura Keene?" was the solemn question on many a lip, as experts expounded on ageism in show business and wasn't it a shame that gorgeous forty-year-old females in Hollywood were considered to be sway-backed, shuffling nags good for nothing but the glue factory.

But with no new news to feed it, the story inevitably began to die. On Wednesday the search for Laura was called off. The police issued a report on Thursday declaring her "presumed dead, as a result of suicide." On Friday there was breaking news that Laura had turned up alive and well at an L.A. television station, where she claimed that she had indeed tried to drown herself but had been saved by a pod of dolphins who had carried her to Catalina, where she had been recuperating the last few days in a hotel room in Avalon. Nearly immediately, though, this news was broken into by the news that the woman was an imposter named Brenda Caskey, who was represented by a celebrity-look-alike agency, and for years had been parlaying her striking resemblance to Laura into a lucrative living. (Her motives were unclear. Had she just been trying to capitalize on the moment to get a little free publicity? Or had her identification with Laura been so complete as to cause her to become unhinged on hearing of her death and imagine she really was Laura Keene, miraculously saved by dolphins and ready for her close-up?) By the weekend, it was all over. The caravan had moved on. The country had forgotten that it had ever remembered Laura.

~

But I must back up a bit. There are some more things you need to know about that week.

Laura's siblings, Kitty and Buzzy, flew in on Tuesday; their elderly mother wasn't up to making the trip. I offered them the hospitality of our house, of course, but I wasn't unhappy when they said they preferred a hotel.

Buzzy resembled his father in one respect—nothing much had been expected of him—but the similarities ended there. Buzzy was content to be a parasite on the family fortune. He never had a job. He loved fast cars. He got speeding tickets by the bushel basket. He had several spectacular accidents, but always crawled out of the smoking wreckage laughing and unscathed.

Buzzy had never married, but he loved women. He had one beautiful girlfriend after another. Whenever he broke up with one, he would soften the blow by buying her a business of her choice. One girl got a nightclub in Miami. Another a bed and breakfast in Vermont. A third a ski lodge in Utah. He stayed friends with all his exes, and involved them in each other's lives. For instance, when Valentina, a former Miss Venezuela and the future owner of a hot-air-balloon operation in Arizona, wanted to launch her American singing career, she did so at Glam, Nina's nightclub in Miami. And when poor Nancy Jo found out she needed a kidney transplant, it was intrepid little Darrin who flew in the middle of winter, from a snowstorm in Vermont to a snowstorm in Salt Lake City, to give her one. Every year or so Buzzy would gather up all his girlfriends past and present, along with their current boyfriends and husbands, and take them to some wonderful place—to Stonehenge at the summer solstice to see the sun rise, or to the volcanic black-sand beaches of Tahiti Iti, to open sumptuous gifts on Christmas morning.

Despite his utter worthlessness, I found Buzzy impossible not to like. He was forty-seven, but seemed more like a precocious ten-year-old. He was cheerfully enthusiastic about nearly everything. He was tall and soft, with a potbelly. He had ruddy apple cheeks, and wore wire-framed glasses that were always slipping down his nose and that he was always pushing back up with a forefinger in a nerdish way.

Kitty was more of a chip off the old Billionaire Bill. She had a degree from Harvard Business School and a top job in New York with the Guggenheim Museum. She had been divorced twice, and tended to be acerbic and unhappy. She was two years older than Laura. She looked quite a bit like her—just as pretty, I always thought, though in a quieter, less Amazonian way. We had flirted with each other from the moment we met. Once it had gone a little beyond that.

Laura and I were spending Thanksgiving with the Keenes at their house in Nantucket. Bill sent me outside to get some more logs for the fireplace. Kitty offered to help.

A cold front was moving through, and the temperature was plunging. Ordinarily Kitty wasn't much of a drinker, but she was pretty sloshed that night—probably because she'd just separated from her second husband and so was even unhappier than usual. I, less surprisingly, was pretty sloshed too. It was dark out where the woodpile was. I picked up a stick of wood, then tossed it back down, and then more or less simultaneously we threw our arms around each other and our lips collided. I slipped my hand under her bulky sweater and shoved her bra up and grabbed a warm, tingling handful of tit and then, in heart-stopping proximity, we heard the sneeze that sounded like a scream of my mother-in-law, Peggy. We looked over and saw Peggy standing not more than twenty feet away. She had an obnoxious little dog, a Pekinese pug named Leo, and she had taken him outside to do his business; he had chronic digestive problems because of the junk Peggy was always feeding him. Fortunately for us, her eyesight was failing, and she didn't seem to have seen us. We gathered up our wood and walked past them. Peggy peered at us benignly and said it certainly was a cold night, and Kitty and I agreed wholeheartedly, but I think Leo smelled a rat. He glared and yelped at us as he crapped in the snow. This incident hadn't been discussed since by Kitty and me, though at times she would give me a certain look that I knew meant she was remembering Nantucket.

Late Thursday afternoon Kitty and Buzzy and I were having a drink in the bar of the Four Seasons, where they were staying. Our spirits were low. The police had just announced that Laura was presumed dead. Also, it was her birthday.

Buzzy raised his gin rickey and said, "Let's drink to sis."

Kitty and I bumped glasses with him. "To Laura," I said, and Kitty said, "Yeah, happy freaking birthday."

Buzzy was smiling, but at the same time he lifted up his glasses and dabbed at his eyes with a bar napkin. "When we were children, Laura loved birthdays more than any of us. She couldn't wait to grow up. But I loved being a child. I was horrified by puberty. Hair in my armpits. Pimples. Erections."

"Erections aren't all bad," I said.

"But I know what he means," said Kitty. "I was happier then too."

"What about you, Dustin?" said Buzzy. "Did you like being a kid?"

"Loved it. I was an only child, and my parents treated me like a little prince. I was popular at school, and good in sports. I had it made."

Buzzy beamed at me and repeated, "Had it made!"

A large, striking black woman walked by, accompanied by three young black men. They sat down at a table across the room.

"She looks very familiar," said Buzzy.

"That's Queen Latifah," I said.

"Oh yes. The singer!"

"And actress."

"And actress! She's very beautiful."

Kitty was munching morosely on some mixed nuts. "I wonder why they can't find a body."

"Maybe it was eaten," Buzzy suggested. "By sharks!"

"What a pleasant thought," said Kitty.

"Or whales!" said Buzzy.

"Buzzy," said Kitty, "whales don't eat people."

"But what about Jonah?"

"Jonah was *swallowed* by a whale but not digested. Plus, there was no Jonah. It's just a fairy tale."

"I suppose we should have some kind of funeral," I said.

"But how can you have a funeral without a body?" Buzzy asked.

"Well, a memorial service then."

"No," said Kitty firmly. "It's too soon. I'm not convinced she's really dead. Maybe she just got confused and wandered away. Maybe she was kidnapped."

Buzzy pushed his glasses back up his nose. "Funerals are sad anyway. Who wants to go to a funeral?"

He left for the men's room. Kitty and I had not really been alone together since they had come out. Now, somewhat warily, we looked each other over.

"I've quit smoking," she said.

"I noticed. Congratulations."

"But I'm dying for one now."

"Don't do it. Just take it a day at a time."

"So why wouldn't you?"

"Why wouldn't I what?"

"Dance with her."

"You know I hate to dance."

"Sometimes you have to do things you don't want to do."

"So you blame me for what happened?"

"No, Dustin," she said softly. "I don't. I know you loved her, in your own way."

I nodded. Robert Duvall went by, in jeans and cowboy boots. He must have been well into his eighties, but he was still walking his cocky, bowlegged walk.

"But I guess the timing stinks for you. I mean, assuming she's actually dead."

"What are you talking about?"

"If she had waited till Mother was gone, you would have been wealthy beyond your wildest dreams. But now you'll never get any of the family money."

"That's extremely cynical, Kitty."

"Don't tell me it's never crossed your mind, and I won't call you a liar."

I shrugged, and swallowed some scotch. "So now there'll be more for you and Buzzy. I'm sure you'll both spend it wisely. Maybe set up a foundation to fight global warming."

"Of course, Laura had a lot of her own money. What was she worth? Thirty million? Forty?"

"I really have no idea."

I really didn't. Our finances mingled only in a joint checking account. She kept everything else in her own name, and didn't seem to want me to know anything about it.

"Did she leave a will?"

"Yes."

"And?"

"And everything goes to me. You know, Kitty, I find all this talk about money really gross."

"Oh, has vulgar Kitty offended Dustin's delicate sensibilities?" she said, reaching across the table and putting her hand on mine. "I'm sorry."

Her hand lingered. Her fingertips explored the hills and valleys of my knuckles. She was giving me that *Remember Nantucket?* look.

"You look tired," she said.

"I am."

"I know this must have been a terrible ordeal for you."

I nodded.

"I was planning on going back tomorrow, but I could stay on for a few days. I know you must have a million things to deal with, but I also know how unpractical you are, but I am very practical. I'd be happy to stay and help out."

Ye gods, I thought, what is she proposing? It was true it was a brave new Lauraless world I was now living in, and lots of things were going to be different, but the thought of bedding my comely sister-in-law while my drowned wife was still floating around somewhere in the watery vastness of the Pacific was too much even for me.

"Thanks, Kitty. I just think I need some time by myself."

She gave my hand an understanding squeeze, and nodded; and then, "Good grief," she said. "What's that idiot doing now?"

Buzzy was standing at the Queen Latifah table. He was talking and gesturing animatedly, while Latifah and her friends stared up at him in total silence.

"Dustin, let's go. I can't stand to watch this."

"Are you kidding? This is great."

"It's like watching a car wreck. What in hell could he be saying?"

Suddenly the Latifah table exploded into laughter. Buzzy received a warm round of high fives and complicated soul handshakes, then headed back to our table, grinning happily.

"Delightful people," he said as he sat down.

"So what was that all about?" I asked.

"I told Miss Latifah I didn't wish to intrude, but I was one of her biggest fans and I simply wanted to pay my respects. And then I told them all a joke that Vinnie, the young man who cleans my swimming pool, told me last week. Would you like to hear it?"

Assuming that *you* wouldn't, let's move on to something that happened Tuesday night.

I was in the den, watching TV, when my cellphone rang. I'd been getting lots of calls, and was leaving most of them to voicemail; but when I saw the number of the caller, I couldn't answer fast enough.

"Helena?"

"How are you?"

"Oh, okay—you know—"

"I'm so sorry, Dustin. It's fucking horrible. I saw you on the news, in front of your house, when you were running at all the cameras and cursing at them. The look on your face . . . I just found myself bursting into tears. And then the ambulance taking you to the hospital, and they were saying you may be having a heart attack!"

"I'm fine. They said it was just stress."

"Have they found her yet?"

"No. No sign of her."

I could hear a faint whooshing noise that I knew was her expelling a chestful of cigarette smoke. "My god. I feel so guilty."

She'd really feel guilty if she knew that Laura had found out about us. But no need to tell her that.

"It's not your fault, Helena. No reason to feel bad."

"You cannot always help how you feel."

I couldn't help how I was feeling right now. I thought about the freckled, fragrant reality of her on the other end of the line, I could all but feel her body heat coming through the phone, I felt nearly dizzy with the desire for her, my brilliant Polish princess who—did you notice?—*had* cried for me.

"How are things with you?" I asked. "I hear you've become a hot commodity."

"Yes, it's crazy. I am running from meeting to meeting all over town. Everyone is whispering the most beautiful bullshit into my ear. All on the basis of a weak performance in a poor film. The existentialists are right. Life is absurd. It is enough to make me wish to shave my head and become a Buddhist. To wander about the world and beg for food."

"Could I give you some advice?"

"Of course."

"Relax. Enjoy the ride. Make a big pile of fuck-you money. Then you can do whatever you want."

"Yes, you're probably right. I always tie myself up into these silly knots."

I heard the brisk clicking of claws on hardwood, then Topper entered the room. He didn't even glance at me as he trotted out the other door, intent on some secret mission of destruction.

"I've missed you," I said.

Silence on her end, except for the sound of cigarette smoke.

"Have you missed me?"

"I've moved on with my life, Dustin. You should do the same."

"Are you seeing someone else?"

"It doesn't matter."

"Why don't you come over? I mean, just to talk. Nothing else."

"We're talking now."

"Or I could come over there."

"Dustin? Could I offer *you* advice?"

"Sure."

"You have just lost your wife. Maybe it wasn't a good marriage, but it *was* a marriage, for many years. Now your life will be very different. You should think about what you want your life to be. You thought you were having a heart attack. Listen to your heart. Maybe it's trying to tell you something. Will you do that, Dustin? Will you think, and listen?"

"Okay."

"Good-bye, Dustin."

"Good-bye."

And now, reluctantly, I have to address the sad topic of Topper.

You'll probably think me despicable when you learn I gave away my dead wife's dog, but I think you would have done the same thing in my (peed-on, chewed-up) shoes. Without Laura's mitigating influence, existence with Topper became intolerable. It reached the point I actually had a nightmare about him. I dreamed I was sleeping, then dreamed I woke up to find Topper on top of me, snarling viciously and trying to rip out my throat like a werewolf. Then I woke up for real with a strangled cry—and there, eerily, was Topper next to the bed. He was sitting on his haunches in the darkness staring up at me; then he stood up and turned and slowly clicked his way out of the room.

I could present you with a long list of crimes and misdemeanors committed by Topper in the days following that awful Monday—but one example should do. I took him out for a walk one morning, like the dutiful pet guardian I was trying to be. And the walk started out just fine. Topper seemed in high spirits as he sniffed and pissed and shat and barked at birds, his auburn coat shining in the sunlight. And then I saw ahead of us a jogger rounding a corner and coming our way.

The jogger was wearing short red shorts and a yellow ABBA T-shirt. He was broad and burly, maybe five ten or eleven and 245. His hair was about the same color as Topper's, and fell off his head in long, humid tendrils. He had little pale-blue eyes and a voluminous red beard. Breathing heavily and drenched with sweat, he stopped and put his hands on his knees, then took a long drink from a water bottle then squirted it on his head. Now I realized this was Magnus Storndrop, the movie director who lived in the house behind us. My first thought was of the script I wanted to give him.

"Good morning!" I said, just a friendly neighbor walking his dog.

I could see amidst his beard a very small mouth that was so red it looked as if he had lipstick on; now it smiled at me.

"Good morning, yeah!" he said heartily, and with an accent. "But maybe not so good for me, eh?"

"What do you mean?"

"I am running and I say, 'You old fat piece of shit, Magnus! You have run not even two kilometers and already you are gasping like fish out of the water!'"

Topper walked over to him, his tail stump wagging. Storndrop looked down at him and laughed. "Well, hello, little poochie! And what is your name?"

"Topper," I said, watching nervously. "Be careful. He's a little high-strung."

Topper lifted up one of his floppy ears, and with his shiny black nose and alert dark eyes looked as adorable as a dog in a Norman Rockwell painting.

"All dogs love me," said Storndrop categorically. He leaned down and offered his hand to Topper. Topper sniffed it with polite interest, as Storndrop looked up at me.

"He is Irish terrier, yeah?"

"Yeah," I said, and so afraid I was that Topper would bite Storndrop that it was as though it happened twice: once in front of my mind's eye, and then in front of my horrified actual eyes an instant later. Storndrop screamed and tried to get his hand away while I pulled on Topper's leash and yelled, "TOPPER, NO, NO, STOP IT, STOP IT!"

Storndrop was grimacing and clutching his hand as I got Topper away from him. I saw as in a bad dream red blood spilling onto the street.

"Shit! We need to get you to a hospital!"

Storndrop managed a weak, wincing chuckle. "Oh no, no, no, no, no. It's nothing, yeah."

"What do you mean nothing? He bit you, you're bleeding!"

"You're calling this a bite? This is no bite! I'll show you fucking bites!"

He turned around and pulled up his T-shirt. His back was a welter of pink and purple scars. I was shocked into silence. He looked over his shoulder at me and grinned and nodded.

"Yeah? Yeah?"

"Jesus."

He let the shirt drop then hooked his thumbs in the waistband of his shorts. He bent over and pulled them down and presented to me his broad white butt. A big ragged chunk of flesh was missing from the right cheek.

An SUV rolled by. The heads of a woman and two young boys in baseball uniforms swiveled in our direction.

"What happened?" I said.

Storndrop pulled his shorts back up. He began to squirt water over his bleeding hand.

"I was making movie about wildlife in Siberia. A documentary, you see. I get too close to cub of Siberian brown bear, and she attack me from behind, yeah."

"How did you survive?"

"I say to myself, 'Magnus, you are big and fat, but you need to become very small.' So I put my hands on my head and curl up in little ball. After a while she gets tired of chewing me and she goes away, her and her baby, yeah. She didn't want to eat me, she wanted just to teach me lesson. And she teaches me a goddamn lesson, fuck yeah! No more movies about real life! Only movies with actors in them! And actresses! With big beautiful breasts! Ha ha ha ha ha ha!"

Magnus the madman stood there laughing and bleeding as Topper and I stared at him.

"Anyway," I said. "Sorry about my dog."

"It's okay. I like Irish terriers. They're brave little buggers, yeah."

Then he gave us a wave and jogged off, leaving a trail of blood drops down Bedford Drive. I turned sternly to Topper.

"We were lucky today. It could have gone the other way. He could have called the police. They could have sent Animal Control to pick you up. Animal Control deals harshly with dogs that bite people. Do you know what the word 'euthanize' means?"

He seemed to, and started to bark. On Sunday, Larry Hochheiser came over to watch baseball with me. He brought with him bags of food from a barbecue joint on La Cienega. We sat in front of my fifty-inch screen and in an orgiastic frenzy ate beef sandwiches and pork ribs and grilled sausages and barbecue beans and potato salad and biscuits and honey butter and 7 Up Cake and drank beer after beer. Topper sat at Larry's feet, and gazed up at him with an intensity that suggested this was some kind of mind-over-matter experiment and he was trying to levitate Larry off the couch. Every now and then Larry slipped him a choice morsel.

"You sure have a way with animals," I said admiringly.

"Yeah?"

"Topper just loves you."

Larry scratched Topper behind the ear.

"Yep. Animals and women. I got this magnetism."

"He really misses Laura."

Larry's barbecue-sauce-slathered face grew somber, and the pace of his chewing slowed down a little.

"We all do, man. She was a great lady."

"You know, he was really Laura's dog, not mine. I never really wanted a dog, and I guess he senses that. He's been driving me crazy ever since Laura—you know. I think I'm gonna have to find a new home for him."

Larry leaned forward and his jaws froze in mid-chew as he watched a close play at the plate.

"*No!*" he hollered hoarsely. "Bullshit! He was out! He was out!"

"Larry?"

"Huh?"

"I'm going to give Topper away."

"Give him away? What for?"

"I just told you. We don't get along. I was wondering if you could take him."

"Aw, no. Not me."

"Why not?"

"I had a dog when I was a kid. Wally. When he died, it broke my fucking heart. I cried like a baby. I don't wanna go through *that* again."

"But Topper's not gonna die. He's young and healthy."

"Wally was young. He was just a puppy. He got some kind of disease. Distemper, I think it was."

"Topper's been vaccinated for distemper. He's in the clear."

"But you said he's really difficult. That he bites people and pees all over everything and tears stuff up."

"I think maybe I was being overly dramatic. All dogs are difficult sometimes, just like people. But I don't think you'll have any problems with him. I mean, you guys are beautiful together. When I watch you playing and romping around with Topper, it nearly brings tears to my eyes."

"When have we ever 'romped'? Usually I just sit here and feed him stuff."

"Oh, you guys have romped. Definitely. You've just forgotten."

Finally I got him talked into it. After the game we loaded up his Cadillac Escalade with all of Topper's food and dishes and toys and carriers and furniture and so forth. Larry lured him in with a doggie treat and then I shut the door on him. Larry started up the engine, then headed down the driveway. Topper jumped up and began scratching frantically at the window glass and barking at me. I didn't know if he was just showing his usual hostility toward me, or if he understood that he was being taken away from a home he loved and he was outraged. Maybe he was still waiting for Laura to come back. How could she find him if he wasn't there? But as I watched them go out the front gate, I knew it was the best thing for both of them. Larry had a big heart and would take good care of Topper. And Topper would provide companionship for Larry, whose wife had left him for another man about a year ago. The wife had gotten the house, and Larry was living now in a rental house in Brentwood. It had a big back yard. Topper would love it there. Larry would have to take him for walks, and thus get some much-needed exercise and maybe lose some weight. Maybe he would meet a girl who was walking *her* dog and they would hit it off. And Larry and the girl and the girl's dog and Topper would all make a happy life together.

9

On Thursday morning I drove down to Dockweiler Beach. Pulled off the side of the road and just sat there for a while. It was cloudy, damp, and cool; May gray had just turned into June gloom. To the south, smoke plumed from the red and white smokestack of the sewage-treatment plant. To the north, the mountains of Malibu disappeared into the morning mist. To the west, weary-looking waves staggered out of the dirty-green ocean and collapsed against the beach. The black shapes of shore birds were silhouetted against the white foam.

There weren't many people out. A few bikers and skaters gliding along the bike path. Stretched out in bathing suits on beach towels, an out-of-shape man and woman, tourists probably, sunbathing under the hidden sun. An old man jogging along the edge of the beach in a chugging, determined way. It seemed strange to think that Laura had been on this very beach only eleven days ago. She was so utterly gone now, as were millions of other people who must have been here over the years, and the bikers and the skaters, the two sunbathers, the elderly jogger, and the somber man in the Maserati watching them all on this particular Thursday morning in the early part of the twenty-first century—they too would soon be utterly gone. According to the scientists, the beach itself would probably be gone before too much longer, drowned by global warming, and suddenly the whole scene seemed phantasmal to me, as if it might at any moment flicker out like a candle in a draft.

My car shook in the wakes of other cars speeding past on Vista del Mar. I wondered what Laura's last moments had been like. There would have been no moon or stars that night above her, only stormy, wind-whipped clouds. Had she allowed herself to be overwhelmed quickly by the wild black water? Or had she fought it as long as she could? She was a strong, competitive swimmer. Maybe she had wanted to see how far she could get before flesh and spirit failed. Or at some point maybe she had changed her mind, had turned back toward the beach, had struggled for her life as she had shouted out my name—

My phone rang. Or rather, *la bamba'd*.

It was Chelsea, the assistant of my agent, Ben Benjamin.

"I got kind of a strange phone call. This guy called up and said he was trying to get in touch with you. He said he was an old friend of yours. I don't know if he was some kind of nut or what."

"What was his name?"

"It was kind of a weird name," but just as she said it to me a jetliner taking off from LAX came thundering over my head.

"I'm sorry, Chelsea, could you say that again?"

"Lumpy. Lumpy Ogonowski."

Since Lumpy Ogonowski was a character in a work of fiction I had created, it was a bit odd to hear that. Maybe something like Fitzgerald hearing a gentleman named Gatsby had left a message for him, or a certain Russian-American writer being told there was a Monsieur Humbert at the door (not that I'm suggesting I'm good enough to shine the shoes of those guys).

"Lumpy" had left a number for me to call. The area code, 412, was not one I recognized. I thanked Chelsea, started up the car, and went towards Manhattan Beach. I passed the shit factory, reached Rosecrans, and made a left. As I drove away from the ghostly sea, I pondered Lumpy.

He'd had a real-life prototype. Pete Holacek had been a team-mate of mine in Winter Haven. A minimally talented catcher, like Lumpy. A Pittsburgh native, like Lumpy. And like Lumpy, a loveable, high-spirited, not-terribly-bright fuck-up. The last time I'd talked to Pete was after *Strike Four* had been published. He wasn't exactly a literary guy, but he'd heard about the book somehow. He said he'd called to tell me it was the best book he'd ever read and how thrilled he was to recognize himself in Lumpy (which in itself was very "Lumpy" of him, since most people would have been insulted to be used as the model for somebody like Lumpy). A couple of years later, Pete left a message on my answering machine after the movie came out. He was beside himself with joy that a handsome guy like Matt Price was playing "him." I never got around to calling him back; that was during my flying-high days in Hollywood, when I didn't get around to calling back a lot of people. Now, eighteen years later, as I turned north on Sepulveda and headed back to Beverly Hills, I was debating whether or not to return this call.

Assuming "Lumpy" actually was Pete and not some deranged fan or stalker, the question was: Did I really want to talk to Pete? He was a guy I'd known for a few months long ago. We'd been buddies of a sort. I remember one particular night very fondly, speeding along the highway in Pete's old crummy Chrysler, drinking beer and throwing the empty cans out the window, "Ghost Riders in the Sky" blasting out of the radio and us singing along with it. We'd shared an apartment for a while, until his slovenliness, drunkenness, and womanizing (not that I have anything against womanizing, but Pete's standards had been so low there was never any telling what kind of snaggletoothed creature from the Florida swamps he might bring home) had driven me elsewhere. Now he probably wanted something from me. Probably had his own secret, selfish agenda like everyone else on the planet. Maybe he wanted to borrow money, which would be embarrassing for both of us. There was no doubt meeting him had been a lucky thing for me, but that didn't mean I owed him anything. Does a still-life painter owe something to the banana he paints? Yes, the best and easiest thing would be simply not to call.

But I couldn't help myself. I was curious. At a red light, I tapped the number in.

"Hello," said a voice.

"Is this Pete?"

"Yeah."

"This is Dustin."

"Duustiin!"

"How you doing, man?"

"Aw, I'm great, buddy. How the hell are *you* doing?"

"I'm okay."

"Hey, I heard about your wife. Laura Keene. I'm really sorry."

"Thanks."

"I just wanted to give you a jingle, and let you know I was thinking about you."

"I appreciate that."

I heard a laugh.

"So you figured out who Lumpy was, huh?"

"Yeah. It's been a long time, Pete."

"Too damn long. But I've been watching your life from afar. You've really done something with yourself."

"I'm not so sure about that but—thanks."

"Hey, I saw that TV movie you wrote that had Tom Selleck in it. Where he played a police chief?"

"Oh yeah."

"I thought it was pretty good. But I guessed the ending."

"You did?"

"Saw it coming a mile away."

"Oh, darn."

"Did you meet Tom Selleck?"

"Sure."

"What was he like?"

"Tall. Friendly. Drove a Hummer."

"*Magnum, P.I.*, man! He's a legend."

"Hey, Pete? Just curious. How'd you get my agent's name and number?"

"Just called up your union. It was no problemo. Sounded like a cute little girl that answered the phone."

"Chelsea? Yeah, she's very cute."

"You ever nail her?"

"Course not. Come on. She's young enough to be my daughter."

"So?"

"And I'm a married man. Or was."

"Shit. Right. Yeah. I'm sorry."

"That's okay. You still in Pittsburgh?"

"No. I mean yes, but not right at this moment."

"Where are you?"

"Oh, I'm rolling down," and then his voice began to disintegrate. "I-70 about. St. Lou."

"Pete? Pete? You're breaking up!"

"Can you hear me? Prewitt?! Prewitt!"

"I can hear you now. Can you hear me?"

"Loud and clear, buddy."

"Did you say something about St. Louis?"

"Yeah, I'm about fifty miles from there."

"You're traveling to St. Louis?"

"Naw, as a matter of fact, I'm heading your way."

"My way?"

"Yeah, I should be there in two or three days, I guess."

"In L.A.?"

"Yeah."

I continued up Sepulveda, trying to process this information. Lumpy in L.A.!

"Prewitt? You still there?"

"I'm here. What are you coming to L.A. for?"

"I just felt like taking a little road trip. Never been to the west coast before. Now, don't you worry, buddy, I'm not expecting you to put me up or anything. But maybe you could recommend a good motel or hotel I could stay at. Nothing too expensive though."

"Let me think about it."

"It'd be great to get together with you. Maybe suck down some suds."

"Okay. Why don't you give me a call when you get into town?"

"Will do. See you soon, buddy!"

10

Chelsea called me again the next morning.

"I heard from your friend again. Lumpy, Pete, whatever his name is."

"What did he want?"

"He wants you to call him. He says your mobile number's blocked so he didn't get it yesterday. Who is this guy anyway?"

"Just an old friend."

"We talked for quite a while."

"I hope he wasn't too obnoxious."

"No, he was fine. He was funny. He seemed nice."

"Yeah, I guess he's nice enough."

"Is he cute?"

"I guess he used to look okay. But I haven't seen him in twenty years. Now he's an old guy. Like me."

"Oh. Too bad."

"Chelsea—you're supposed to say, 'Oh, you're not so old, Dustin.'"

"Oh, you're not so old, Dustin."

The die still hadn't been cast. I could still just not call Pete back and thus never have to talk with or see him again. But after living with the idea for twenty-four hours, I was actually beginning to sort of look forward to seeing Pete. Sucking down some suds. Finding out why he was really coming out here.

He was on I-44 midway between Tulsa and Oklahoma City when I caught up with him. I asked him how he was doing.

"I'm sleepy as hell," he yawned. "The plumbing in the motel kept making these noises like a jackhammer. And I had these fucking dreams, man. One dream, I was in bed with this beautiful girl, you remember Heather Locklear?"

"Of course."

"Well, she looked just like Heather Locklear, and then I went to sleep, and when I woke up she was a skeleton!"

"Shit."

"I think that room was haunted. I think somebody must've been murdered in there."

"Chelsea told me you called. I'm sorry I forgot to give you my number."

"That's okay. You had any more thoughts about accommodations? Like I said, I don't want anything fancy. Just as long as it ain't haunted," and he laughed.

"You know, I've got plenty of room," I said, regretting the words even as they came tumbling out of my mouth. "Why don't you just stay with me?"

"You mean it?"

"Sure I mean it," I had no choice but to say.

"You're a fucking prince, man!"

Pete made sure this time that before the call ended he got my number. Over the next three days, I received periodic calls and texts charting his progress across the country. He was passing through the Texas panhandle. Spending the night in Tucumcari, New Mexico. Looking at Albuquerque in his rearview mirror. He called me up excitedly when he reached Winslow, Arizona, and started howling out the Eagles' "Take It Easy": *Well I'm standin' on a corner in Winslow, Arizona!*

His steady, relentless approach began to take on an awesome, portentous aspect, as if it were a hurricane that was headed my way,

MAKE BELIEVE · 75

or a comet that was on a path to strike the earth. Early Sunday afternoon I received word he'd crossed the Colorado River and entered California. He still had to traverse the furnace-like wasteland of the Mojave Desert, but he must have been speeding down the freeway like a rocket because in practically no time at all he was calling to say he had reached the outskirts of L.A. I gave him the address of my house, then poured myself a drink and waited.

A little after five the gate bell rang. I buzzed the gate open, then went out the front door.

A red Dodge Durango was coming down the driveway. Pete stuck his hand out the window and waved. I was surprised to see he wasn't alone. A girl with long straight brown hair was sitting in the passenger seat. As Pete pulled up in front of me, the girl looked me over in a nakedly appraising way. Then Pete jumped out and headed toward me.

"Prewitt!"

"Pete!"

He was wearing a red polo shirt, baggy navy-blue shorts, a Pittsburgh Steelers cap, sunglasses, and flip-flops. He knocked aside my proffered hand and enveloped me in a vertebrae-crackling hug. He used to have gorilla-like strength and obviously still had it.

"Hey, buddy," he said, "you're looking great! You ain't changed a bit!"

"No, man, you're the one that's looking great!"

I wasn't lying. Pete was the kind of guy I could imagine letting himself go and putting on fifty pounds after his playing days were over, but he looked lean and fit. The major change I noticed was a thick dark moustache.

I heard a car door opening. The girl was getting out.

"I'd like you to meet a friend of mine," said Pete. "Jodi, uh—Anderson."

"Overton," said the girl. "Don't you even know my fuckin' name yet?"

"Hi, Jodi," I said, holding my hand out. "I'm Dustin Prewitt."

She offered me a limp hand and a wan smile.

"Hey."

On her forearm was a tattoo of a heart, with SLUGGO on a golden banner that was wrapped around it.

"Who's Sluggo?"

"Just a guy I used to know. Wasn't worth two dead flies."

"Hell of a house," said Pete.

"Thanks. Let's go inside. You guys must be tired."

"I'm not tired," said Jodi, her long *i*'s flat and southern. "I don't ever get tired. Do I, Pete?"

"That's right, baby."

Jodi looked to be in her early twenties. She had a slender, sexy body, hazel eyes set abnormally far apart, a wide slash of a mouth. Her small breasts had prominent nipples that poked into her tight T-shirt. The shirt bore a message: "It's only funny 'til someone gets hurt. Then it's hilarious." The shirt ended just below her belly button. Her faded and ripped jeans were so low-slung one wondered why no pubic hair was visible. As soon as we walked through the front door, she veered off towards the living room.

"What the fuck's that?" she said.

She was referring to my multicolored mystic warrior, still in the place the delivery guys had left it two weeks ago.

"Oh, just a statue."

"What are them things comin' out of its head?"

"I couldn't really tell you."

"It's art, Jodi," said Pete; he was standing in front of the statue with his hands on his hips, gazing intently at it. "You're not supposed to understand every last damn thing about it. I love it."

"My bladder's fixin' to pop," said Jodi. "Where's your bathroom?"

I gave her directions. Pete and I watched her go. The crack of her butt crept up out of her jeans. A portion of a big, elaborate tattoo on her back could be seen below her shirt. She was pretty in a skanky kind of way.

"She nearly fucked me to death last night," said Pete.

"You didn't tell me you were bringing somebody with you."

"I didn't know until yesterday. I met her at a truck stop in Santa Rosa, New Mexico. She looked pretty hungry, so I bought her a plate of huevos rancheros. She said she needed a ride, so—" He gave me an uncertain look. "I hope it's okay, man."

"Well, I don't know. What do you know about her? She could be some kind of criminal."

He laughed a little. "Oh, I don't think she's dangerous. I mean, look at her, come on. She's just this skinny girl."

"The women in the Manson gang were skinny girls too. And they were crazed killers."

"Shit. You're right. You never know, huh?"

"It's just that I lead a very private life here. I have to be careful about who I let in."

"Yeah, yeah, I get it. Look. When she comes out of the bathroom I'll just tell her she has to leave."

"Does she know anyone out here?"

"Naw, I don't think so. I think she's pretty much on her own. From what she's told me, she's had a real run of bad luck lately."

Pete looked at me hopefully.

"Ah, forget it," I said. "I'm probably just being paranoid."

He looked relieved. "Don't worry, I'll keep an eye on her. Make sure she doesn't steal the silverware."

"So she turned you every which way but loose, huh?"

"She had me begging for mercy, buddy! Begging for mercy!"

It seemed as if a long time passed before she finally reappeared. I took them in the den and went behind the bar and made drinks. A Jack and Coke for him. A seven and seven for her. Scotch rocks for me.

"To your trip," I said.

"No, buddy. To old friends."

"And new ones," said Jodi, and we all bumped glasses and drank. I showed them around.

"This ain't the biggest house I ever been in," Jodi said.

"What house have you been in that's bigger?" asked Pete.

"Graceland. It was way bigger."

They both seemed very interested in the artwork. The Jackson Pollack wasn't a hit—

"Just a bunch of paint splatters," said Pete.

"A monkey coulda done it," agreed Jodi.

But the Hockney painting of a swimming pool was a different matter.

"Now I like this'un," said Jodi. "This'un's real pretty."

"Looks like you could just dive right in it," said Pete. "Cool off on a hot summer day."

"How much you pay for this?" asked Jodi.

"Oh, I don't remember exactly."

I did remember exactly, but I didn't particularly want her to know. I took them upstairs and showed them their bedroom. Jodi took her shoes off and jumped up and down on the bed. I had a foosball table in the game room. Pete and I had played a lot of foosball together at Winter Haven, and he insisted we play a game now. Jodi watched for about thirty seconds, then got bored and wandered over to the pool table and crawled on top of it and curled up and fell instantly asleep, like a cat. I defeated Pete in a close game, but he insisted we make it two out of three. I beat him again. We woke up Jodi and went back downstairs, where we ordered and ate two supreme pizzas. Then we went in the den and I made more drinks and started playing music. I was all set for a nice session of remember-when-ing about Winter Haven, but Pete started breathing noisily and I saw that now *he* had fallen asleep.

"You're a lively pair," I said.

He was sprawled on the couch with his head lolled back and his mouth open. Jodi was sitting with her legs across his lap. She said, "Let's put somethin' in his mouth. A dead bug or somethin'."

"Afraid I don't have any dead bugs handy. So where are you from, Jodi?"

"Arkansas. Little town called Augusta. Everybody called it Disgusta." She gave me a long, level look with her strange, far-apart eyes. "Pete told me he was comin' to visit this rich buddy that lived in Beverly Hills. I didn't really believe him but I guess I should have."

She took a pack of cigarettes out of her purse.

"You can't smoke in here, Jodi. You're welcome to smoke outside if you like."

"And you're welcome to kiss my ass," she said, returning the cigarettes to her purse. "Were you really married to Laura Keene?"

"Yes."

"Sorry she died."

"Thanks."

"You know any other movie stars?"

"A few."

"What are they like? Movie stars."

"Most of them? Smart. Charming. Self-centered."

Pete groaned then stirred a little, smacking his lips. I said, "Pete's quite a guy, huh?"

Jodi looked at Pete. He began to snore.

"Got any weed?" she said.

"No."

"You think I'm pretty?"

"Um . . . sure."

"I look in the mirror sometimes, and I can't make up my mind about it."

"I think you're very pretty."

"You wanna see my titties?"

"What?"

"You wanna see my titties?"

"Out of respect to Pete, I'm gonna have to say no."

She showed them to me anyway, giggling as she jerked her shirt up. Pete started moving around again, and she pulled down her shirt as he opened his eyes.

"Shit. Sorry," he said, giving us a groggy, good-natured smile. "Guess I'm still on Pittsburgh time."

We all went to bed pretty early. I couldn't handle being in mine and Laura's room anymore, so I'd moved into my favorite guest bedroom. I couldn't fall asleep though. I kept getting yanked back from the brink of sleep by the idea that Jodi was coming into the room, was creeping toward my bed with the intention of either fucking me to death or plunging a steak knife she'd got from the kitchen into my chest. I would stare anxiously into the darkness with my heart racing until I gradually realized I was alone, then I would roll over and close my eyes again until the next visit of the phantom Jodi.

Finally I gave up on sleep. I swung my legs out of bed and just sat there for a while thinking. I found myself missing Topper. Topper would be barking his ass off if he caught somebody up to no good sneaking around the house. Hell, he'd do a lot more than bark, the vicious little bastard.

I got up and pulled on my pants. Went down the hallway to Pete and Jodi's bedroom. Stood at the closed door and listened. It would have been reassuring to hear wild lovemaking sounds, but Pete could have been in there with Heather Locklear's skeleton, so silent it was.

11

I was awakened the next morning by shouts and laughter coming in my window. I walked over to it and looked out.

Pete and Jodi were in the swimming pool, ducking and splashing each other in a frolicsome way. Now Jodi climbed out, completely naked. As she ran around the pool to the diving board, I got a good look at the tattoo on her back: some kind of hairy, writhing monster with claws.

She walked out on the diving board. Her nipples were dark against her pale skin, but the expected patch of dark at her crotch wasn't there. Now she happened to look up and see me. She pointed at me as she shouted at Pete: "Hey, lookie there! Prewitt's up there spyin' on us!"

Pete looked around and waved. "Hey, buddy! Come on down and join us!"

Jodi bounced on the board and then knifed gracefully into the water. I put on some clothes and went downstairs. Made myself a mug of strong coffee and joined them.

They were sitting at an umbrella'd table, drinking long-necked Buds. Jodi had a towel draped carelessly over her. Her hair hung down in long wet tresses. I was relieved to see that Pete was wearing a bathing suit. It was far too early in the morning to face the sight of his bare genitals.

"You sleep okay?" I asked.

"Like a dead man," said Pete. "Man, it's beautiful out here. Like the Garden of Eden. Isn't it, baby?"

"Uh-huh," Jodi said, taking a swig of beer and looking at me.

"What are you guys gonna do today?"

"I wanna go to Disneyland," said Jodi.

"I won't take you to Disneyland, but I'll be glad to drive you around town if you'd like. Show you the sights."

"Hey, that'd be great," said Pete. "But you sure you got the time? I mean, if you got work you need to do—"

"Nope. No work."

Jodi stood up, tossed the towel in my face, ran and leapt and let out a whoop and cannonballed into the water.

"You see her snatch?" said Pete.

I nodded. "Fuzzy Wuzzy was a bear. Fuzzy Wuzzy had no hair. Fuzzy Wuzzy wasn't very fuzzy, was he?"

Pete laughed. Then it became quiet under the umbrella. A huge crimson dragonfly flew past, hovered, then zipped away. I looked at Pete, still wondering why he was here.

"So Pete, you got married, right? I forgot her name."

"Carolyn. Yeah, we were married for nineteen years. We just split up about six months ago. But we're still friends and everything. We just drifted apart. You know how it is."

"Kids?"

"Boy and a girl. They're both in high school now, if you can believe that. The boy's a linebacker. He likes to hit people. The girl's real pretty. Good student too."

"What do you do for a living? Didn't you used to be in construction?"

"Well, I had an electrical-supply business for quite a few years, but I just sold it. Made a shitload of money."

"Why'd you sell it?"

"I just got bored with it, I guess."

Pete took a sip of his beer, and sighed. Seeming sad all at once. Then he said, "I guess we better get a move-on, huh?" He yelled out toward the swimming pool: "Fuzzy! Hey, Fuzzy! Get your skinny ass outa there and put some clothes on! We're going!"

Jodi swam over to the metal ladder and climbed out, water sluicing brightly off her body. "What are you callin' me 'Fuzzy' for?"

Pete looked at me and we both laughed. She walked over and took the towel from me and started drying off.

"Y'all are talkin' about me behind my back. Makin' up dirty names for me."

Since the accusation was completely true, we had no answer.

We walked and gawked on Rodeo Drive. Did the hand- and footprint thing at the Chinese Theater on Hollywood Boulevard. Took Sunset toward the beach through West Hollywood, Beverly Hills, Bel-Air, and Brentwood. The road got twisty and hilly. "Go faster, Prewitt!" urged Jodi from the back seat of my silver Quattroporte; she was wearing purple-tinted sunglasses, skin-tight lime-green pants, and a light-blue T-shirt that said INMATE on it.

"I'm going fast enough," I said.

"What's the point of havin' a car like this if you're just gonna poke along in it?"

"Settle down," said Pete.

A moment later I smelled smoke. I looked in the rearview mirror and saw her puffing on a cigarette.

"Sorry, Jodi. You can't smoke in here."

"Can't do this, can't do that. I hate that word. 'Can't.'" Except she said "cain't." And she didn't get rid of the cigarette.

Pete turned around and glared at her. "Lose the cigarette. *Now.*"

"Don't talk to me like you're my fuckin' daddy," she said, but she lowered the window and threw the cigarette out.

We drove all the way out to where Sunset ended at the Pacific

Coast Highway. There was a restaurant there, Gladstones, and that's where we had lunch. It was a big place thronged with tourists. We walked in past a long tank filled with doomed seafood. The lobsters were all huddled together and seemed to be awaiting their fate passively, while three gigantic crabs were rearing up on their bony legs and pugnaciously waving their claws around as if daring somebody to order them.

We got a table that had a nice view of the ocean. Pete and I got beers and Jodi a Long Island iced tea.

"I think Pete's a damn liar," said Jodi.

"Why's that?" I said.

"He said you wrote a book and put him in it and then it was a movie and Matt Price played him."

"Every bit of that's true."

"See?" Pete said. "Told you."

Jodi made a startlingly unpleasant face at him.

"Lumpy was his name in the book," I said. "Lumpy Ogonowski."

"Lumpy," snorted Jodi. "Now that's a dumb name."

"Well, maybe it's dumb," said Pete. "But Lumpy turned out to be the fucking hero. Isn't that right, Prewitt?"

"That's right," I said.

"How come?" said Jodi. "What'd he do?"

"Well, at the end of the book," I said, "Lumpy's in his car with David. David's the character that's based on me. They've both realized by now that they're not gonna make it in baseball, and they're gonna have to move on to something else. David's a guy that's had all the advantages. Great parents, an Ivy League education, and he plans on going to law school and becoming a lawyer and maybe entering politics someday. But Lumpy came up the hard way. His parents were both drunks. His dad couldn't keep a job."

"So they were in the fucking car," said Jodi, obviously not big on backstory. "Then what happened?"

"One of the taillights was out on the old jalopy Lumpy was

driving, and the cops pulled them over. Everything probably would've been okay, except David smarted off at the cops and pissed them off."

"You really were a smartass," said Pete. "You still like that?"

"Of course not. Anyway, David had a drug problem. He'd just bought quite a bit of cocaine, and he had it stashed under the seat. The cops searched the car and found it, and asked who it belonged to. And Lumpy said it was his. David couldn't believe what he was hearing, he tried to tell the cops that the coke belonged to *him*, but they believed Lumpy and arrested him."

I noticed Pete was hanging on every word, like a kid listening to an oft-told but still-fascinating bedtime story.

"So David bails Lumpy out of jail, and they go to a coffee shop. David asks Lumpy why he did it. Lumpy says he figured that getting convicted of drug possession would ruin David's life, since he wanted to be a lawyer and a politician and all, but serving a stretch in prison wouldn't make much difference in Lumpy's life. He'd be going back home to the same kind of dead-end job he would've had anyway. He says David's the best friend he's ever had and doing this makes him feel happier than he's ever felt. He says everybody deserves a second chance in life. Everybody deserves one more swing at the ball. An extra strike."

"*Strike Four*," said Pete. "That's what the book's called."

Jodi looked perplexed. "So that's *it*? Lumpy goes to fuckin' prison?"

"Well, yeah. And at the end of the book you're left pondering the question of whether Lumpy will ever get a second chance in life. A strike four."

Jodi gave Pete a pitying sneer. "I can't believe you went to the joint for Prewitt."

"I've never been in the joint."

"See," I said, "that part of it didn't really happen. Pete and I were driving around once and the cops stopped us, and I had a doobie on me so I was really nervous—"

"But they let us go when they found out we were baseball players."

"Sounds to me like all the borin' shit's true," said Jodi, "and all the excitin' shit's made up."

"But that's how writers work," I said. "Some little thing happens, and it's like a seed planted in your imagination. And then it grows and—" A loud slurping noise interrupted my explication of the creative process. Jodie was sucking up through a straw the last of her Long Island iced tea. Our food came: a fish sandwich for me and seafood platters for them. We ordered another round of drinks. Pete and Jodi had been presented with humongous amounts of fried fish and shrimp and scallops and calamari and french fries, but Jodi seemed determined to drink her lunch. L.I. iced teas are notoriously potent mixtures of different kinds of liquor, and Jodi was swiftly getting blitzed.

I felt something touch my ankle. Either a small animal was loose under the table, or Jodi was playing footsie with me. She was giving me a straight purple gaze through her sunglasses. I pointedly moved my foot away, but the small animal or Jodi's foot pursued it. Then Pete got up to go to the can, and left me alone with her.

"Stop it," I said.

"Stop what?"

"The foot thing."

"I know you like me. I seen you lookin' at my pussy out by the swimmin' pool. You couldn't keep your eyes off it."

"Look, Jodi. As a healthy heterosexual male, I enjoy looking at attractive females. But that doesn't mean I necessarily want to, uh—"

"Fuck me? Course you do. Can't fool a girl about that. In fact, I'll bet you're poppin' a boner right now."

Suddenly I felt her foot on my crotch. I grabbed her foot and pushed it away. "Goddamn it! Stop it!"

Jodi sucked up some more of her drink and giggled.

"If you don't start behaving," I said, "I'm gonna tell Pete."

"Guess what, Prewitt."

"What?"

"I got an endless supply of pussy. More'n enough for you and Lumpy both."

I stared across the table at her. "I've never been around a girl that talked like you."

She giggled again, then pushed away her seafood platter, put her arms on the table and her head on her arms, and passed out.

Pete came back. We both looked at her. "You know, we could just leave her here," he said.

"Yeah. We could."

"It's tempting."

"Damn tempting."

But we wound up having the waitress put her seafood in a doggie bag (actually a gold foil package in the shape of a whale), and then we grabbed her under the arms and hauled her out of there. She moaned and whimpered and cursed as she stumbled along between us. All at once her eyes widened and her cheeks ballooned out.

"I'm fixin' to puke!"

We let her go, and she ran toward the ladies' room. When she came back out, she was white-faced and trembling. "It's all your fault, Prewitt," she mumbled. "Everything's your fault."

We got her into the back seat of my car. She lay down and passed out again. We headed down the coast toward wacky Venice Beach, the next stop on the tour. After a while, I noticed movement in the rearview mirror, and saw that Jodi was rising up, like some unkillable monster in a horror movie. Her purple sunglasses stood out against the ghastly pallor of her face. She didn't utter a sound. It became increasingly creepy, seeing her there, and I was greatly relieved when the mirror emptied as she subsided slowly from my sight.

12

Jodi was out on the patio talking on her phone when I went downstairs the next morning.

"Who's she talking to?" I said.

Pete was sitting at the island in the middle of the kitchen eating a bowl of cornflakes and reading the *L.A. Times*. He glanced out the window. "Dunno." Then he returned to the paper, and smiled. "Man, he's really kicking ass."

"Who?"

"Trump."

"Jesus, Pete. You voted for Trump?"

"Course I did. Who the hell else was I gonna vote for," and then he snorted, "*Hillary?*"

"Trump's an asshole, and a dangerous dingbat. He's going to kill us all. Don't you see that?"

"He's gonna drain that swamp, buddy. Build that wall."

I shook my head and sighed. "Jesus, Pete."

I limped over to the coffeemaker and poured myself a mug. I'd woken up with a severely sore hip. I also felt exhausted, as if I'd spent the whole night wrestling crocodiles in a muddy river. I was sleeping lousy practically every night now.

Jodi came in.

"Who were you talking to, babe?" said Pete.

"My mama. Back in Disgusta." She watched me walking to the

shiny Viking refrigerator to get milk for my coffee. "How come you're limpin'?"

"I've had a bum hip for years. It acts up every now and then."

Pete looked sympathetic. "That's still bothering you, huh?"

"Yeah. Orthopedist says I'll probably need a hip replacement eventually."

"Shit." And then he laughed. "You remember that night you were limping around, man, you could hardly *walk*, and Rack came out to pull you?"

"And I just told him no."

"Son of a bitch just refused to leave the fucking mound," Pete said to Jodi. "Rack couldn't believe it."

"You know how he'd spit all over you when he yelled? Boy, I was just getting *sprayed*. And he chewed tobacco, which made it worse."

"Yeah, that was some nasty shit that'd come out of his mouth."

"Poor old Rack. Something about me just drove him crazy."

Jodi grabbed a big red apple out of the fruit bowl. "Who's Rack?"

"Rack McCormick," I said. "He was our manager in Winter Haven."

"I'll give you this, Prewitt," said Pete. "You weren't much of a pitcher, but you were a hell of a competitor."

"Gee, thanks. You weren't much of a catcher either."

"Bullshit. I carried your ass. You owed your whole short, pathetic career to me."

"Oh yeah, you were great all right. Like that night you called twenty-three straight fastballs."

"What's wrong with that?"

"A catcher's supposed to mix things up. Keep the batter off balance. Not call the same pitch *every time*."

"But that was the only pitch you had."

"Not true. I had a very decent curve."

"A curve in your dick, maybe," said Pete, and we both laughed. Jodi had been observing our bantering without a trace of amusement.

Now she said through a mouthful of apple: "Let's get a move-on for fuckin' Disneyland."

~

After they left, like a strict parent checking up on a difficult teenager, I took a peek into their bedroom. It looked as though it had been burglarized. Clothes and shoes and brightly colored underwear were strewn everywhere. It was really remarkable they could make such a mess in only two days. And I caught a definite whiff of cigarette smoke.

At eleven, I had a meeting with my agent, Ben Benjamin. It was true that I was a soon-to-be-wealthy widower. I'd met last week with mine and Laura's accountant, from whom I received the not-unwelcome news that Laura's assets were even bigger than I had thought, around forty-five million. After a court declared Laura legally dead, it would all be mine. If I chose, I could easily lead the Buzzy-like life of an idle playboy. I hadn't given up, though, on the hope of making a mark in the world. I was determined to get my screenwriting career up and running again, and that's why I was on my way to see Ben.

The agency he was with, one of Hollywood's biggest, was just a few minutes from my house. I'd gone only a block or two when I became aware of an unpleasant smell. I pulled over and took a look around. Discovered Jodi's gold foil whale from Gladstones sitting on the floor in the back seat. The foil had been peeled back, exposing several pounds of putrefying seafood. Jody must have awakened and pawed it open and fed from it sometime during the course of yesterday.

I drove down into the underground parking garage of my agency, and turned my car over to Carlos, one of the valets. I carried the ruptured whale to a trash receptacle and dropped it in. I was walking toward the elevator when I heard a sharp "Sir? *Sir!*" behind me.

I looked around. A security guard was standing by the trash receptacle with a suspicious look on his face. "What did you put in here?"

"Uh—a seafood platter."

"A seafood platter," he repeated, with an east-European accent. "And why did you put it in *here*?"

"Well, it's a day old. I have guests from out of town and—"

"You can't leave it here, sir. It will smell up the whole garage."

"Well, what am I supposed to do with it?"

He lifted his eyebrows, and smiled a little. "I believe that falls under the category of . . . *your* problem."

I walked slowly back to the trash receptacle. The security guard was a skinny guy with a big Adam's apple. His pseudo police uniform hung loosely on him, and he had a big, ugly gun on his hip. He watched me with a smirk as I reached in the trash and withdrew the whale.

"Guess I'll put it back in my car," I said.

He pretended to be pleased. "*Good* idea, sir."

As I started to walk away, I said under my breath: "Fucking police state."

"I'm sorry? I couldn't quite hear that."

And then I lost it. "I said ever since 9-11 we've been living in a *fucking* police state! Everywhere you go there's little guys like you, yelling at you to stay behind the lines, open this, close that, step forward, step back, take off your shoes, pull out your dick, bend over and get *fucked* in the ass!"

His Adam's apple bobbed as he gulped indignantly. "I advise you to calm down, sir!"

"You know what you'd be if this was 1930? You'd be one of Hitler's Brown Shirts!"

"As someone who's Jewish, I deeply resent that!"

"Oh, come on! *You're* Jewish? Jews are powerful in this town! They run Hollywood! They're not crummy little rent-a-cops! What's the fucking matter with you if you're Jewish?"

I was vaguely aware of a pair of men in suits eying me curiously as they walked past us toward the elevator. A beautiful long-legged girl in a skimpy green dress scurried by, looking frightened. Carlos and two other parking valets gathered around to watch.

"If you don't get control of yourself, I'll have to take you into custody!"

"Take me into—? For what? For *this*?" I said, thrusting the doggie bag at him. "What do you think this is, a fucking chemical weapon? You think I'm a *terrorist*? You think I'm going to *poison* everybody in the parking garage with some day-old seafood?"

He took a step back, putting his hand on the butt of his gun. "Stay back! I mean it!"

I stared at him in disbelief. "Oh, great. You're gonna fucking *shoot* me?"

"Hey, nobody's gonna be shootin' nobody," said Carlos, and he put his hand on my back and gently guided me away. "Come on, man. Your car's over here."

Carlos had been a valet here for years. He was a nice guy, and I always tipped him well. As we walked back to my car, I looked over my shoulder. The security guard was still standing with his hand on his gun, glaring at me, panting irately with his mouth open, his face as red as mine probably was.

"Did you see that asshole?" I said.

"We call him *el Rey del Aparcamiento*," said Carlos. "The King of the Parking Garage."

13

I cooled my heels for a while in the lobby, then Chelsea came to conduct me into the inner sancta of the agency. She was a petite and energetic blonde from Chicago with a short shiny helmet of hair.

"How's Lumpy?" she said as we rode up in the elevator.

"Okay. He went to Disneyland today with his degenerate girlfriend."

"Why is she degenerate?"

"Oh, you know—she has tattoos and stuff."

"Lots of girls have tattoos these days. It's no big deal. *I* have one."

The elevator doors opened, and we stepped out.

"I won't ask you where it is—but I'll bet it's a tasteful tattoo."

"Nope. Gross and disgusting."

"Maybe *you're* degenerate."

"Maybe I am."

Chelsea went charging down the corridor on her short but shapely legs, and I had to hurry to keep up. She had an aura of success about her; one could easily imagine her running this joint in twenty years. Ahead of us I saw the beautiful girl in the green dress. She was standing in a doorway talking to a cocky-looking guy wearing red suspenders who was about a foot shorter than she. As Chelsea and I went past, she regarded me with alarm. Chelsea, who noticed everything, noticed.

"Do you know her?"

"Nope."

Ben Benjamin was seventy—unbelievably old for an agent. To translate it into sports terms, it was as if Dan Marino were still quarterbacking the Dolphins, or Barry Bonds were still swatting the ball in the stands for the Giants. His silver hair was perfectly coiffed. He sported a permanent tan. His suits were all custom-made in London. His fingernails were polished, gleaming works of art. But don't get the wrong idea; there wasn't an effete atom in Ben Benjamin's body. He grew up poor in a rough neighborhood in Brooklyn. Rumor had it that he got in with the wrong crowd in his youth, that perhaps even he was an out-and-out gangster and spent some time in prison. It was also rumored that the source of the rumors was Ben himself, who had calculated that possessing a make-believe mobbed-up past would help him operate more efficiently in Hollywood. But don't get another wrong idea. Ben wasn't some profanity-spewing tough guy. He was as gentlemanly a fellow as you could ever hope to meet.

He got up from his desk and grasped my hand firmly and put his other hand on my shoulder and looked searchingly into my eyes. "Dustin," he said in his gravelly voice. "The truth. How are you doing?"

"I'm okay, Ben."

I sat down on a comfortable couch, Ben in an armchair. He was wearing a tan suit, with a lavender shirt and a lavender-patterned tie. A lavender handkerchief was arranged just so in his breast pocket. Even his cologne smelled vaguely lavenderish. He shook his head and sighed. "My god. What a thing to happen. And they still haven't found her . . . remains?"

"No."

"I admire your strength, Dustin. You seem to be holding up well."

"Thanks. How's Miriam?" His wife.

"Like the Rock of Gibraltar. I don't know what I'd do without her."

"Give her my best," I said.

"I'll do that."

"Anyway. Like I told you on the phone. I want to get my career back. And I'm willing to do whatever it takes to make that happen."

"I'm happy to hear that. Very happy."

Ben had a long, aquiline nose with a bump in it. Rumor had it his nose had been broken by a guard in a riot when he was a prisoner on Ryker's Island. Now he started to rub the bump, as he always did when pensive.

"Once I saw a headline in a newspaper: 'Forty-Seven-Year-Old Fruitcake Discovered Near Milwaukee.' And it's always stuck with me that that must have been the most boring story ever written. I have to read many screenplays, and whenever I open one, I usually have that same feeling—this is going to be very boring—and I'm seldom disappointed. But I never feel that way about your scripts, Dustin. There's always some kind of sparkle about them that makes them interesting. That's the reason I've continued to represent you all these years, through thick and, as now, through thin."

"I appreciate that."

"Now if you're serious about all this—"

"And I am."

"Then you've got to promise me some things. One, you need to be more disciplined—you can't be turning in scripts weeks, or even months, late—and two, you've got to start getting along with people better. If you want to be your own boss, open up a hot dog stand—but in this town, you're gonna be working *for* somebody, and you can't be yelling at people and calling them idiots just because they don't agree with you about every little thing."

"I couldn't agree with you more, Ben. And maybe you're not aware of it, but I've mellowed a lot in the last couple of years. I have a much more Zen way of looking at life."

He listened, and nodded solemnly. How many lies over the decades must have drifted into his ancient ears. If he peered back into his Hollywood past, what mountains of mendacity, and seas of deceit, and dark, trackless forests of obfuscation must he observe.

"All right, Dustin. Here's what I suggest. We make a new beginning. Fortunately this town has a high turnover rate. Many of the people you've antagonized aren't even in the business anymore. We'll send out samples of your work to the new people. And I'll set up a series of meet-and-greets for you. And you'll shine your shoes, and put a fresh carnation in your buttonhole, and then charm the crapola out of them. How does that sound?"

"Sounds great. I had lunch with Brian, just before he left for Syria. He suggested I come up with a TV series and sell it to Netflix or Amazon or one of the cable networks. He said he thought it would be a great fit for me."

"I concur. I would be very supportive of that. I could put you in the room with the right people."

I nodded. This was going well. Yes, I would get a carnation. Hollywood would meet the new Dustin. The Zen Dustin.

"Have you heard from Brian?" I said.

"Not a word. I've e-mailed him, texted him, left messages on his cellphone . . . but no reply."

"Same here."

"I'm worried about him, Dustin. Syria is a hellhole. The Brian Nasry I know is not equipped to handle it."

"You know what I think? I think he's not anywhere *near* Syria."

"Where do you think he is, then?"

"Probably in some little hotel somewhere. Shacked up with a beautiful girl he met at the airport. He probably chickened out at the last minute and now he's too embarrassed to come back."

Ben rubbed the bump on his nose, and smiled sadly, as if we were reminiscing about someone who had died long ago.

"It would be nice if you were right."

~

Pete and Jodi got back around four, wearing matching sky-blue

Disneyland caps and carrying bagfuls of Disneyland merchandise. Jodi seemed exhilarated, Pete dazed and exhausted. They were both eager to start drinking.

"I've never seen so many kids, buddy. Thousands and thousands of them. When I shut my eyes, I still see them coming at me. Swarms of them. No end to them."

"I know what you mean," I said, and I handed him a Jack and Coke. "They're voracious. They want to ride more rides, eat more crap, buy more junk. They're like vast schools of piranha."

"You mean them fish that eat up people?" said Jodi. "You're sayin' that's what little kids are like? You're sick, Prewitt. You and your buddy both. Y'all are sick old perverts."

Pete shrugged and said, "I gotta piss." Then I was left alone with Jodi, and her far-apart, mocking eyes, and her nipples poking into her flimsy halter top; I would have thought Disneyland would have had some kind of policy against nipples like that.

"Got somethin' for you," she said, and pulled a Donald Duck mug out of her bag. "It's a Donald Duck mug," she explained. "For your coffee. I noticed you drink a lot of coffee."

"Gee, thanks, Jodi. That was very nice of you."

"You really like it?"

"Uh-huh. Tomorrow morning I'll drink my coffee out of it."

She seemed pleased. She took a pull from her bottle of Bohemia.

"Got a question for you, Prewitt."

"Okay."

"Mickey Mouse asked me for a date. Well, it wasn't really Mickey Mouse. It was just a guy in a costume. He said I looked just like Miley Cyrus. He said he knew lots of people in the entertainment business and he could probably get me an agent if I went out with him."

"So what's the question?"

"You think he's full of shit, or you think he really could get me an agent?"

"Full of shit. Sorry."

"Yeah, that's kinda what I figured. Guys'll say just about anything to get in your panties, huh?"

"I've heard there are guys like that."

The phone rang. It was Ben's office calling. Great, I thought. Maybe he's already working on those meetings.

"Dustin," said Chelsea, "I have Ben for you."

"Okay."

But she stayed on the phone. "What in the world happened?"

"What do you mean?"

"Everybody's going crazy here."

"Chelsea, I don't know what you're—"

"Here's Ben."

"Dustin! Tell me what happened."

"What are you talking about?"

"In the parking garage. Did you really get in a fight with a security guard?"

"Well, not a physical fight, but—"

"They say he stopped you when you tried to leave a bag of rotting fish in a trash can, and then when you found out he was Jewish, you went on an anti-Semitic tirade, ranting and raving at the top of your lungs about how the Jews run Hollywood and you're going to take them out with chemical weapons and—"

"Hey! Stop! Wait! That's a totally twisted version of what happened! And who's 'they' anyway?"

"Besides the security guard himself, there were three witnesses, all with the agency. Michael Blumenthal and Adam Brog, two very well-respected talent agents, and Maggie Peek."

"The girl in the green dress?"

"I don't know what kind of dress she was wearing. Don't you know who she is?"

"No."

"She's the latest winner of *The Voice*. She's a singer, with acting aspirations. Every agency in town wanted her, and we just signed her. And now her agent, Scott Kelly, says that she's terrified to come back here . . . that she's afraid she might encounter *you* again."

"Ben, I'm stunned. This is really . . . laughable."

"I'm not laughing, Dustin. This is a serious matter. I'm under heavy pressure to . . . discontinue our relationship."

"Jesus."

"But I said I had to get your side of the story first."

"Well, first of all, that security guard was an asshole. He provoked me. And second of all, yes, I did say something about how powerful the Jews are in Hollywood. But I was just stating the obvious. Ben, you know me. I'm no bigot. Some of my best friends are Jews."

"Do you realize how that sounds?"

"I can't help how it sounds! It's true! What am I supposed to say, some of my worst enemies are Jews?!"

"Dustin, please, quit yelling. I thought you said you'd mellowed."

"I have mellowed. I have."

I realized I was breathing hard, my heart was thumping, and my face felt hot. Pete had come back, and was looking at me with concern. Jodi was sitting at the bar, eating from a dish of macadamia nuts and watching me like I was a brand-new television in a broken-down house trailer.

"Take a few deep breaths," said Ben.

"Okay."

"So what was the bag of rotten fish all about?"

"It was just a doggie bag of seafood. I'd left it in my car by mistake."

"And you didn't think of it as a chemical weapon aimed against the agency or against the Jews."

"No. Of course not."

Silence. I knew Ben was rubbing the bump on his nose. Finally . . .

"You don't want to make the Jews in this town mad, Dustin. They're like elephants. They never forget. And I, as a Jew, can say that. That said . . . I think I can fix this."

I expelled a sigh. "Great."

"I've already reminded everyone of the terrible tragedy you've just suffered, and the enormous pressure you've been under. I think you need to write a letter of apology to the security guard, his name's Yuri Eisenberg, he's an immigrant from Russia, they're tough, those Russian Jews, you don't want to get on their bad side."

"Yeah, I thought he was going to shoot me."

"Also letters to Blumenthal, Brog, and Maggie Peek."

"What should I say, exactly?"

"You're the writer, Dustin. You'll know what to say. But the key is Maggie Peek. If she jumps ship to CAA or WME because of you, then . . . God help you."

"Okay. Well . . . sorry about all this, Ben. And thanks."

"This too will pass," said Ben.

I hung up the phone, and began to make myself a drink.

"Everything okay, buddy?" said Pete.

"Oh, yeah. Just a little misunderstanding."

"You don't look so hot. Your face is real pale."

I felt an odd sensation on my chest, as if the skin across it were being stretched tighter and tighter. I poured eighteen-year-old Glenlivet over glittering chunks of ice.

"And look!" cried Jodi. "His hands are shakin'!"

14

That night, I dreamt of Topper. He was lost in a hedge maze, and I was trying to find him. Sometimes I could hear his bark faint in the distance, at other times close at hand, and I would rush down an avenue of the strange green maze thinking he would be around the next turn, only to discover a dead end and hear his barks coming from an entirely different direction. Then suddenly it dawned on me: *I* was the one who was lost, and Topper was trying to find *me*.

I woke up in a panic, soaked in sweat, and for just a moment it was as if I could hear Topper's dream barks echoing down the night then fading away.

I looked at the glowing digital dial of the clock; it was not quite three. I thought about Fitzgerald's observation that in a real dark night of the soul it's always three in the morning and I wondered if this was what a dark night of the soul felt like.

I was unaware I had fallen back asleep till I found myself waking up again. It was a strange kind of awaking, my brain was active but my body felt paralyzed, as if I were a spider that had been stung by a wasp and was now being carried away to be fed alive to its young. Then I realized what had awakened me; somebody had come into the room, and was now slipping quietly into my bed. And I was glad. Sure, she had tattoos, and she was crazy, and mean, and the girlfriend of my friend, and her private parts were probably teeming with pathogens, but still I had been wanting this, precisely this. I was naked. I always slept naked. I was lying on my side facing the window. And now I felt warm breath on the back of my neck, and a hand on my hip, and then the hand slid on over. "Oh, yeah," I murmured, then I heard a deep voice close by my ear: "Feels good, buddy?"

I jumped up with a guttural yell, flailing my arms about . . . but I was fighting only the bedclothes. I was alone in the room. I turned the TV on, determined to sleep no more.

$\sim$

Matter-of-fact morning was filling up the bedroom with sunlight and birdsong when I woke up. *Terminator 2: Judgement Day* was on the TV. "Listen to me carefully," said the cyborg played by former Governor Schwarzenegger.

It was 10:37, which meant I was alone in the house. Pete had a friend from high school who was now living in San Diego, and Pete and Jodi had planned to leave early and drive down and go with him to the Wild Animal Park. They were supposed to come back sometime tonight, assuming they weren't arrested for public drunkenness or Pete wasn't arrested for assault after discovering Jodi giving his friend a blow job or the mountain gorilla didn't leap over the moat and throw Jodi over his shoulder and scamper away with her.

I went in the bathroom and took two aspirin, then headed downstairs. I kept running across their spoor. An empty Dr. Pepper can perched like a target on the railing of the landing. A pair of purple flip-flops at the foot of the stairs. Sugar spilt on the kitchen counter. Some cornflakes, soggy and sad, in a bowl in the sink.

I brewed some coffee. Took a sip. Savored being alone. Walked toward the front door to get the paper.

Something made me glance into the living room as I went by, and then I stopped dead in my tracks. Above the back of the sofa, I could see the limp brown hair of Jodi.

I walked around the sofa and looked down at her. She was wearing short green shorts, and her long skinny legs were propped up on the edge of the coffee table. She was barefoot, and had black polish on her toenails that made them look as if they had been beaten by a hammer and were about to fall off. Her thumbs were busy tapping out a message on her phone. She barely glanced up at me.

"Hey, Prewitt. You slept late."

"I thought you guys had already left."

"Lumpy left. I didn't go."

"Why not?"

"Bellyache," and now she gave me a longer look. "Liar."

"Huh?"

"You're not usin' my mug."

"Oh." I looked at the La Brea Tar Pits mastodon mug I was holding; I'd bought it about ten years ago when my parents were out for a visit. "Sorry. I forgot. I'll use it for my next cup."

"Who gives a shit?" she said, and then returned to her phone.

"So what are you doing?"

"Writin' to my friends. About bein' in Beverly Hills and all. You probably think somebody like me don't have any friends, but I got lots of 'em. All over the country. I wasn't popular in high school, but I'm real popular now."

"Well, that's good." My eyes traveled over her, up her lissome legs to her flat, allegedly aching belly, and her firm little boobs, and her wide, sullen split of a mouth, and, as it began to sink in that I would be alone with her all day, I felt a kind of premonitory tingling in my loins. "How's your stomachache?"

"Better."

"Good."

I started to walk out, then: "Hey, Prewitt?"

"Yeah?"

"*Work*'s spelled w-o-r-n-k?"

"W-o-r-k. No *n*."

"No *n*? Sounds like there's an *n* in it."

"Nope."

Three crows flapped over and cawed down at me out of their glossy blackness as I went outside to get the paper. I took it into my office. It had the same headline as always, "World Still Careening Towards Destruction." I spent about half an hour with it, then, unable to shake the dream about Topper, I called Larry Hochheiser. He told me Topper was doing just fine.

"No peeing or biting problems?"

"Some inappropriate peeing the first few days, but since then . . . nada. He loves Brentwood, man. And we've been doing some serious man-dog bonding."

"Yeah?"

"Yeah, we've been romping around like crazy all over the place together."

"That's great. You know, I think I'm gonna come over and see him."

"I don't think that's a good idea."

"Why not?"

"I think it's too soon. Give him some time to adjust. Seeing you might confuse him."

"Yeah, maybe you're right."

Larry didn't ask me anything about rotten fish or Maggie Peek, which was good, since it seemed to mean that the story hadn't as yet metastasized across Hollywood. It was time to pucker up and kiss some hiney. I turned to my computer.

"Dear Yuri: Sorry about the misunderstanding over the seafood. Instead of putting it in the trash, I should have shoved it up your officious ass, you skinny Bolshevik bastard! Go back to Russia! From Beverly Hills, with love, Dustin."

I had fun in this vein for a while, but I kept catching my mind drifting back to Jodi. Though on a certain level I found her loathsome, that just added in some sick way to her allure. But what about Pete? Yes, he was a pain in the ass, but he was still my friend. And maybe

I hadn't always been the most moral guy in the world, but I'd made it a rule never to go after the women of my friends. I didn't intend to seek Jodi out, but if she were to come walking through the door and sit down in my lap, put her arms around my neck and look at me with her weird, witchy eyes, I wasn't sure I could control myself. I started thinking that maybe the best thing to do was just leave. Call Larry back and see if he wanted to play some golf. But the thought of leaving Jodi alone in the house made me queazy too.

I needed more coffee. I walked toward the kitchen. A wisp of smoke was floating out the door. I smelled tobacco. I got pissed off. "Jodi," I yelled as I entered, "I've told you you can't smoke in here!"

But then I saw that I had been unjust. The cigarette wasn't Jodi's.

15

A guy was standing with his back to me, poking around in the stainless-steel refrigerator.

"Who the hell are you?" I said.

He looked over his shoulder at me, and smiled. "Hey, there. Where you hiding your mustard?"

"What are you doing here?"

His bushy eyebrows lifted in an interrogative way. "Mustard?"

He was wearing a dirty-looking black baseball cap that said "I collect antique radios." He had a foot-long brown beard streaked with gray. Lengths of colored thread were tied around the beard at regular intervals, narrowing it in a wavy fashion as it descended.

"To your right," I said, "in the door. Bottom shelf."

He found it. He shut the fridge and read the label as he walked over to the island. "'Hamilton House. Stone ground mustard. Gourmet.'" He smiled at me again. "Fancy mustard. For a fancy man."

He set the mustard down by a loaf of whole wheat bread and a package of sliced turkey. Smoke ribboned up from his cigarette, which was resting on the edge of a saucer. He picked it up and took a drag and looked me over.

"I guess you're Prewitt."

"How'd you get in here?"

"Jodi let me in."

"You're a friend of hers?"

"Oh yeah. We're real friendly."

He started making himself a sandwich. He seemed to be a little older than me. He was wearing a black Hawaiian shirt with golden pineapples on it and khaki cargo pants. He wasn't a physically imposing guy. Under six feet. Thin nearly to the point of frailty.

"Where is Jodi?"

He shrugged. "She's around here someplace." He spread mustard on a slice of bread with a steak knife.

"Look," I said. "You're gonna have to leave."

"But I just got here."

"I'm sorry."

He cut his sandwich diagonally in half, and began to eat. He waggled his eyebrows at me. "Hamilton House. Mmm."

"Okay," I said, turning around, walking away, "I'm calling the police."

"Prewitt?"

I looked around. The bearded man reached under his Hawaiian shirt, pulled a gun out of the waistband of his pants. He laid it down on the marble top of the island. Now he sat down in a chair, and kept eating.

"Come on back here," he said amiably. I hesitated. "Come on now."

I walked over to the island.

"Sit down."

I sat down across from him. I looked at the gun. I've put many a firearm in many a script, but I don't know a thing about them. All I can tell you is it was some kind of big revolver, capable of blowing big holes in my body. "What do you want?" I said.

"We can start with that watch."

I slipped my Franck Muller watch off my wrist and handed it over to him. He put it on, turned it this way and that, smiling, admiring it. Tattoos covered his arms: An ax-wielding Viking who looked a lot like Magnus Storndrop. BLUT UND EHRE. A death's-head with ZYCLON B under it. A heart and a golden banner with JODI on it.

"Is your name Sluggo?"

He looked pleasantly surprised. "Now how'd you know that?"

I pointed to his Jodi tattoo. "Jodi's got a tattoo just like that, except it says 'Sluggo.'"

"Well, you're just a real smart fella to figure that out. So now you know my name."

Sluggo returned to his sandwich. I looked again at the gun. It lay within easy reach. It wasn't so much that I minded being robbed as that I was afraid I was about to be murdered, because I had looked into Sluggo's eyes and seen an icy vacuum there. All I had to do was make a sudden lunge like they do in the movies, and . . .

I looked up at Sluggo. He was regarding me with amused contempt.

"There's no need for any trouble," I said. "I'll give you whatever you want."

"Damn right you will."

I heard footsteps on the tiled floor behind me. Jodi was coming in. She had raided Laura's closet. She was wearing a red jersey dress and matching spike-heeled shoes, and multiple strands of pearls around her neck, and dangling diamond earrings. The dress and the shoes were far too big for her, so that she looked like a kid playing dress-up in her mother's clothes. I saw as she came tottering across the kitchen toward us that she was carrying Laura's jewelry box.

"How do I look?"

"I'll show you how you look," said Sluggo. "Come here."

He put his arm around her waist and tried to kiss her, but she averted her face. "No! You got mustard on your mouth!"

"But it's Hamilton House, honey," he said as he persisted.

"Yuk! Quit it!"

He laughed, and let her go. He gave me a wink. "She'll scratch. She's a wildcat."

She picked up his cigarette and sucked in some smoke, then blew it out at me. "So what do you think of Prewitt?"

"I don't care what anyone says," said Sluggo. "I think he's a great guy." He opened the jewelry box, and began to look through it. Jodi picked up the gun and pointed it experimentally at me.

"He don't like Jews either."

Sluggo held a ruby ring up to the light.

"Is that right?"

"I heard him talkin' on the phone about it yesterday. He got in trouble 'cause he cussed out a Jew."

"How much is this worth, Prewitt?"

"I don't really know. My wife got it a long time ago."

Jodi had one eye closed as she sighted down the barrel at me. "I shot a possum once. I didn't kill it though. It's hard to kill a possum."

"Hey, quit playing around," Sluggo said and grabbed the gun but she didn't want to give it up.

"Leave me alone, you butthole!"

As they struggled over the gun, the barrel veered about wildly. I was scared it was about to go off accidentally. I stood up and began to back away, dodging this way and that as the gun pointed that way and this.

"Where the fuck you think you're going?" Sluggo roared at me, spit flying out of his barbaric beard, and now he wrenched the gun away from Jodi and aimed it at me. "Get back over here! Sit down! I didn't say you could move!"

"Okay," I said as I complied. "Just calm down."

With a casual movement, as if he were shooing away a fly, Sluggo backhanded the barrel of the revolver into my right temple. It was like a flare exploded in the starless night sky of my brain, and I clutched at the island and tried not to fall off my chair. Blood spattered the marble and my clothes and the floor.

"You probably think I've invaded your world," said Sluggo, observing me dispassionately. "But the truth is, I've invited you into *my* world. I carry my world around with me. Wherever I go is my world. Sluggo's world. You understand?"

I nodded.

"You're a citizen of Sluggo's world now, and you do have certain rights. You have the rights of a lab rat. A puppet. A Barbie doll."

Sluggo took a bite of his turkey sandwich. Jodi was pawing through the jewelry box and putting one of Laura's rings on every one of her fingers. I was holding my temple, trying to stanch the blood, feeling woozy and sick, and afraid beyond what I had known was possible.

"Where is it?" said Sluggo.

"What?"

"The safe. Where you keep all your jewelry. The good stuff. Not this costume junk."

"I don't have a safe. This is the good stuff. It's worth a lot of money."

"You expect me to believe you keep valuable jewelry just laying around in a jewelry box?"

"Well, my wife did, yeah. This all belongs to her."

"What about all your cash? Where do you keep that?"

"I got maybe a hundred bucks in my wallet. That's it."

"Where's your wallet?"

"In my office. Top drawer of my desk."

"What about your priceless coin collection?"

"I don't collect coins."

"Stamp collection?"

"Not stamps either. I promise you, there isn't any safe. I'm not stupid. I'm not gonna die to protect my coin collection. Everything's insured anyway. Take whatever you want. I really don't care."

Sluggo wiped his mouth with a paper towel, and looked at me. I realized that my fate depended on the unfathomable workings of the deranged brain that sat on the other side of those lightless eyes. As casually as you or I might decide to go to the movies or to have chicken for dinner instead of fish, he could decide to . . . well, to do absolutely anything at all.

Jodi held up and admired the rings on her flashing fingers.

"I don't wanna sell all this shit. I wanna keep some of it."

Sluggo shrugged. "Sure. Whatever you want. It's only costume jewelry anyway."

He got up and walked around the island and motioned toward the floor with his gun.

"Get down there."

I was shaking all over as I lay down on my stomach. I said, "Please don't kill me."

"Shut up. Put your hands behind your back."

I did so. He took a coil of thin, bright-blue rope out of one of the capacious pockets of his cargo pants. It looked like the kind of rope you use for water skiing. We would get a lot of spiders in our garden, particularly in the late summer and early fall, and I found it fascinating how most of the time they were the most torpid creatures imaginable, hanging motionless in their webs for hour after hour as if asleep or dead, but when an insect blundered into their web they transformed themselves with shocking suddenness into dynamos of demonic energy, arachnid acrobats twirling their hapless prey with their spindly legs as they encased it in silk and Sluggo and I were like that. In the twinkling of an eye, it seemed, he had tied my hands together then tied my feet together then had tied together behind my back my hands and feet. "Hog-tied" is I believe the term. And then he and Jodi walked out of the kitchen and left me there.

I could hear them moving about the house and talking. Once I heard a big crash, followed by hoarse cursing and girlish laughter. And then it was quiet for a while and I wondered if they had left and it was time for me to start yelling for help, then I heard clomping headed my way and Jodi came back. Blood was still oozing out of my temple and I squinted up at her, half blinded by the blood.

"You're a mess, Prewitt."

"Yeah, I know."

She squatted down beside me on her haunches, resplendent in

her red dress. She was puffing on a cigarette. "Sluggo and me just did it. In *your* bed."

"Yeah?"

"Got a question for ya."

"Okay."

"You got any idea how I could get on one of them reality shows? Like the one where cute guys and girls go on an island and go around naked and get in arguments and fuck one another and all that? I think I'd be good at that."

"I don't know anything about reality shows, Jodi. Sorry."

"Shit."

"But I could look into it for you. Just untie me. Let me go."

The cigarette hung out of her wide, bullfroggish mouth. She hugged her knees, and looked at me.

"You shoulda fucked me when you had the chance. Everything woulda been different. I coulda moved in with you. Took care of you. Since your wife's dead, you need somebody for that. I can cook and clean real good. My mama taught me how. Maybe we coulda got married. And then maybe you coulda got me on a reality show. But it's all too late now."

Sluggo returned, wearing my beloved leather bomber jacket.

"Guess we better giddy-up on outa here, baby."

"Okay," Jodi said, standing up. She dropped her cigarette on the floor, crushed it out under her Italian shoe. "What about Prewitt?"

They both looked at me. Pondered me in silence for several unnerving seconds. That age-old philosophical conundrum. The problem of Prewitt.

"Don't kill me," I said. "I promise I won't tell the cops about you."

Sluggo laughed. "And you love me. And the check's in the mail."

He reached in one of his pockets and took out his phone and took a selfie and then a picture of me then pulled out a roll of duct tape. He bent over me and in his efficient, spidery way wrapped tape around and around my head, covering up my mouth. It was awful having my mouth taped shut. Even though I could breathe perfectly well through my nose, I felt like I was suffocating and I began to hyperventilate. Sluggo tore off the end of the tape and returned the roll to his pocket. He and Jodi gazed down upon me. She had put her purple sunglasses on.

Sluggo smiled slyly. "Watch this."

His tattooed hand came down toward me and pinched my nostrils closed with his thumb and forefinger. I thrashed my head about and he lost his grip, but then he stabilized my head with his other hand and pinched my nose again. I struggled, but he was extremely strong for a scrawny guy; I heard him giggling as I felt like my chest was about to burst, and black spots began to form in front of my eyes. The spots were like crows swarming across the sky at dusk, seeking trees to roost in, a refuge from the night. More and more crows until there wasn't even a sky anymore, just a chaotic, cawing, crowlike darkness.

16

My eyes opened. A silvery monolith gleamed above me, some sort of holy object fraught with meaning, but then gradually it turned into the Viking refrigerator. I was relieved I wasn't dead. Relieved Jodi and Sluggo seemed to have gone away.

My head was lying in a pool of sticky blood. My groin felt warm and wet. I realized I had pissed myself.

Cesar, the gardener, had come on Monday, and Rufina, our Salvadorean maid, who came twice a week, wasn't due again until Friday. Day after tomorrow. Which meant it was unlikely anyone would come to the house till Pete wandered back from San Diego. Tonight, supposedly, but who knew with Pete?

It did not seem possible that I could last until tonight. Marinating in my own body fluids. Trussed up like some pig or chicken in a third-world market waiting to be bought and slaughtered. Dangling like an earthworm in God's beak.

~

It was quiet in the kitchen, except for the occasional mechanical humming when the motor of the refrigerator kicked in. And then the phone rang four times; I heard a faint murmuring from my office as someone left a message, but I couldn't make out the voice.

I found myself thinking about Laura, lying in her oozy bed on the sea bottom. I knew now a little of how it must have been with her in her final moments. It was no fun to suffocate.

Poor woman. I should have treated her better. I should have danced with her. Probably I wouldn't have found myself in the present predicament if I had only danced with her.

~

Sunlight crept across the kitchen floor, as the day moved along in its pokey way. I heard a leaf blower blasting on the other side of the back wall in Magnus Storndrop's yard. All around me life was going on as usual, and it was clear that my presence on this planet or lack of same didn't make a damn bit of difference.

Arms, legs, neck, shoulders . . . everything was beginning to hurt like hell. It was hard to breathe, with my chest pressed against the floor, and then I became aware of my heartbeat. It was beating like crazy, and then I felt a sharp, savage pain on the left side of my chest. This time it wasn't a false alarm. I was sure this really was a heart attack. I was about to die on the floor of the kitchen in my man-sion in Beverly Hills, after being tied up and robbed by white-trash sociopaths. It would make a good chapter someday in a *Hollywood Babylon* kind of book, recounting the dark and ridiculous fates of various unlucky showbiz types, and then I kind of lost it, rocking from side to side and making hooting monkey-like noises through the duct tape as I frenziedly tried to pull my hands and feet free. This resulted only in a still-faster heartbeat and intenser pain. So I decided to try the opposite tack. I wouldn't move at all. I would put as little stress as possible on my heart. I would think calm thoughts. Peaceful thoughts. A gentle waterfall in a beautiful forest. Clouds drifting across a soft blue sky.

And then I saw it. Something brown. Crouching in a far corner of the kitchen. It began to crawl across the floor toward me.

It was Daniel, the hairless dog from the art show. He was approaching in a cringing way, his tail wagging submissively. He didn't seem to mean any harm, yet he filled me with dread. "What do you want?" I said, and then as he got closer I cried, "Go away!"

He stopped about a foot from my face. At the edge of the puddle of blood. Then he began to lap it up, his long pink tongue rapidly turning red. I understood now. He was thirsty, terribly thirsty, and I felt bad for him but still I was afraid. "Don't," I said, "please," and he rolled his soft brown eyes in an apologetic way but continued to lick-lick-lick. "Please don't," I croaked, my mouth so dry I could hardly get out the words, and I realized that I was thirsty too, as thirsty as I had ever been, then the burnt-up-looking dog was gone. And I passed out for a second time.

~

"Hey, buddy!" somebody was calling. "Where you at?"

When Pete walked into the kitchen, I thought at first I was hallucinating again. But maybe he thought *I* was the hallucination, the way he gaped at me.

"Holy shit, man! What the fuck?"

I made some urgent *mmff-mmff*ing noises. Finally it occurred to him to take the tape off my mouth.

"Dustin, what happened?"

"Just cut me loose, okay?"

He grabbed the mustardy steak knife and cut the bright-blue rope. It turned out it was he who had called earlier and left the message. He'd been at his friend's house in San Diego only a little while when he'd gotten a feeling something was wrong back in Beverly Hills. When he couldn't get hold of either me or Jodi, he decided to skip the Wild Animal Park, and hopped in his Durango and sped back here.

Pete gave me a glass of water then called 911, and cops and paramedics arrived quickly. Pete told the police what he knew about Jodi and I gave them a description of Sluggo as the paramedics trundled me out of the house. I saw the mystic warrior lying on its back in the anteroom, sword sticking in the air. Sluggo and Jodi evidently had tried to make off with it and the crash I'd heard must have been when they'd dropped it and abandoned it. They'd looted some other things more successfully: all of the paintings, including the Hockney, the Pollack, the de Kooning, and the Warhol, that I'd pointed out to Pete and Jodi as being particularly valuable; several Lalique vases and bowls; Laura's menagerie of Steuben animals and her collection of Fabergé eggs; and various silver platters and golden goblets and jade dragons and vases from the Ming dynasty. Along with, of course, Laura's jewels, worth, Sluggo would be pleased to discover, many hundreds of thousands of dollars. They had left for me two signs of their passing: Sluggo, like Topper before him, had taken a piss on the mystic warrior, and one of them, probably Jodi, had gotten into Laura's set of acrylic paints and had written in a rainbow of colors on the floor-to-ceiling mirror in the workout room PRUINT IS A FAGOT. She'd also drawn a gigantic happy face.

Being rushed in a howling ambulance to Cedars-Sinai and thinking I was dying was becoming nearly routine. A memory popped into my head about my parents. One summer day when I was six, an older boy had dared me to throw a rock at a large, thriving yellow jacket nest. I'd done so, and scored a direct hit, and been promptly attacked by dozens of justifiably outraged yellow jackets. All I was wearing was a red bathing suit, and I was stung all over. I remembered my father's grim, tight-lipped face as he had driven fast through traffic to the emergency room, honking his horn, with me sitting in my mother's lap, wrapped in her tender arms, whimpering pitifully as I tried not to cry. And I wished now it was my parents taking me to the emergency room instead of these cheerful strangers.

At the hospital, they stitched up my head and EKG'd me and so forth and determined I wasn't having a heart attack, but this time I didn't argue when they insisted I spend the night. It wasn't a nice night. In the slivers of sleep between long stretches of wakefulness, I dreamt of tempests and being drowned at sea. The next morning, Pete drove me home.

He started to cry in the car. He was distraught about what Jodi had done, pointing out accurately that none of this would have happened if he hadn't come to visit me. His life, he said, had bottomed out. His electrical-supply business had gone belly-up and his wife had left him for some guy she met at work and his kids thought he was a loser. Coming to California had been an act of desperation on his part, and he had fucked it all up like he always fucked up everything, and if I wanted him to he would stay and help clean up the mess he had caused but then he would get out of my hair and go back to Pittsburgh.

But I didn't really want him to go.

Truth was, I was afraid to be alone. Afraid of bad dreams. Of memories of Laura. Of Sluggo and Jodi coming back.

I told him he could stay as long as he wished.

PENNY

17

"Pirates lost again," said Pete.

"Yeah, I saw."

We were in the kitchen, sitting at the island, reading the paper and eating bowls of cereal in a semi-dressed state like an old married couple. Pete picked up his cup of coffee and took a drink.

"Guess I oughta start looking for a job or something," he said.

"Why?"

"Well, I can't just keep mooching off of you."

"You're not mooching. Don't worry about it."

"I just feel kind of funny sitting here in the lap of luxury doing nothing. Not that I don't like it. But I've always had a job."

"Hey, you want a job? I'll give you one. You can be my assistant."

"What would that involve?"

"A little bit of everything. You can drive me around. Run errands. Even be my bodyguard."

Pete's eyes lit up.

"Your bodyguard?"

"A thousand a week okay?"

"Jesus. You sure you can afford it?"

"Oh yeah. I'm gonna be richer than hell soon."

Pete's moustache lifted like hairy wings as he grinned. We reached across the island and shook hands on it.

"I'd take a bullet for you anyway, buddy. You wouldn't have to pay me."

It had been about two weeks since I had been beaten, robbed, and tortured. Thank god Pete had been around. Several nights I had screamed myself awake and then Pete had been there within seconds, and had stayed with me to keep the boogyman away. And we would talk for hours, about baseball mostly, because baseball seemed a realm of exuberance and innocence and endless youth, as far away from Sluggo's world as I could get.

Chain of Lakes Park was surrounded by orange groves. Seventy-five or so fans would be sitting in the bleachers every night, and one of them, a one-armed Vietnam vet with long, tangled hair held in check with a red headband, would yell hoarsely and repeatedly, "Hit it in the trees, redsuckers!"

The whole town of Winter Haven smelled like orange juice. After a night of carousing, Pete and I would wake up around ten or eleven then plod in shorts and flip-flops down the fragrant street to a coffee shop where we would be revivified by coffee and orange juice and eggs and bacon and biscuits and the strange southern substance called grits. I always carried around a book with me, and after breakfast I would settle down with a fresh cup of coffee and *A Farewell to Arms* or *This Side of Paradise*, while Pete played the pinball machine. He would shake and pound and curse at the machine so violently that finally the manager of the coffee shop, Betty, a dumpy middle-aged redhead, would holler at him to cool it because he was scaring away her customers (I'm convinced Pete bedded Betty at some point in the summer, though he never would admit to it).

Florida was hot, especially for a Yankee kid like me. You'd work up a sweat just brushing your teeth in the morning. And it was wet too. Frequently thunderstorms would come boiling up out of the night and interrupt games. I remember sitting in the flooding dugout and seeing whitecaps in the outfield.

Nobody at Dartmouth chewed tobacco but at Winter Haven

everybody did. I held out for a long time, but eventually Pete talked me into it. I took a little nibble of his Redman, then he egged me on and I bit off a big chunk. I took a few chews, thinking it wasn't so bad, but all of a sudden the taste really hit me. I spat it out but it was too late. I began retching and puking, and my grossed-out teammates like some kind of crazed lynch mob grabbed me and threw me out of the dugout into the full view of the fans where I continued throwing up. I could hear the one-armed veteran screaming out obscene encouragement to me, and I looked up and saw Pete standing on the dugout steps, pointing at me and laughing so hard I thought he was about to break a rib. But within a few days I had avenged myself, chemically burning Pete's balls by putting Atomic Balm in his jockstrap.

"'Member the night Brainiac went maniac?" Pete asked me after one of my nightmares; it was 2:30 in the morning and we had moved into the game room to play foosball.

He used to call me Brainiac because of all the books and my Ivy League background. On the night in question, with two out and a man on third, the batter bounced my fastball to the shortstop, who threw him out from deep in the hole. Except the whey-faced slob of a first-base umpire called him safe, and the runner scored from third. I went berserk. "That run's on you, that run's on you!" I bellowed at the ump. He gave me a dismissive wave and turned his back on me. I threw my resin bag in his general direction and when he saw it sail past him, he whirled around and threw me out of the game. Whereupon I took off my glove and flung it down and went charging across the infield towards him. I probably would have ended up with a suspension or worse if Pete hadn't tackled me and dragged me off the field, to face the toxic spray of the wrath of Rack.

"I saved your butt that night, buddy," said Pete.

I faked him out of his socks then rattled the foosball home.

"Hey," I said, "remember when Turtle hit into the triple play?"

I called Pete Turtle because of his nearly comical slowness.

Nobody out. Runners at first and second. Turtle at the plate. He bunts. Badly. The pitcher pounces on the ball and throws to third for the force-out. The third baseman sees Pete chugging down the first-base line and thinks he has an easy double play, but he throws the ball over the first baseman's head. The runner on first comes all the way around but gets gunned down at the plate by the right fielder. Then the catcher fires the ball to second, where the second baseman tags out a sliding Pete to complete the triple play.

"Bullshit," said Pete. "I was out at third."

"No way. It was second. I remember it vividly."

"You'd have to be some kind of fucking retard or something to get thrown out at second in a situation like that."

"Yeah, well, okay."

"Goddamn it, Prewitt! It was third! Third!"

No clock. That's the magic of baseball. A game theoretically can go on forever. Even a single at-bat can, the hitter fouling off the three and two pitch till the end of time. But there's a problem with the players. The game is immortal but the players perish. At least until Schwarzeneggerian cyborgs take over the game.

~

After breakfast I went for my morning walk, a habit with a history of exactly three days. I was hoping to bump into my neighbor, jogger/ director Magnus Storndrop, so I could get friendly enough with him to pass along *The Ladies' Man*. It was my one and only spec script, written not long after I'd hit Hollywood. Ben Benjamin thought it was commercial as hell, and hoped to manufacture a bidding war over it. I was sure I was about to become a millionaire, but for whatever reason, or more likely, considering the general brain-deadness of Hollywood, for no reason at all, it didn't sell.

I'd been revising *The Ladies' Man* for the last few days (seemed like a good way to keep my mind off blue ski rope and such things). Structurally I thought it held up pretty well, but the setting seemed quaint and dated. So much had changed in twenty years. Not only was it now a world of Instagram and Facebook and YouTube and Twitter and Uber and Google, but the culture had driven off a cliff and was falling through a phantasmagoric nightmare of hatred, paranoia, environmental collapse, and Donald Trump, and though my screenplay was a comedy, I wanted to give it a little bit of an end-of-the-road, love-in-the-ruins feel.

The fourth day was the charm, Storndrop-wise. I saw him up ahead jogging west in yellow shorts and a black tank top across the intersection of Bedford and Elevado. I broke into a jog too. My hip hurt but I ignored it. I was like a Siberian wolf loping across the tundra on the trail of my oblivious prey. It had been unusually hot and humid for June, and I quickly began to sweat. It didn't take me long to catch up. Storndrop heard me behind him and looked over his shoulder, suspiciously at first, but then he seemed to recognize me and smiled out of his big red beard.

"Good morning!" I called out.

"Hey! Yeah! Good morning! But it's hot, yeah? Very fucking hot!" He slowed to a walk, gasping for breath, and I fell in beside him.

"Global warming," I said.

"Yeah?"

"No doubt about it."

"I guess we are all fucked, yeah?"

"I guess we are."

This seemed to please Storndrop, and he laughed. Sweat was dripping out of his beard. He squirted his water bottle into his mouth, then offered it to me.

"No thanks."

"And where is your little dog?"

"I gave him away."

"Oh, the brave little poochie, you give him away?"

"For his own good. See, he wasn't really my dog. He was my wife's dog."

"And your wife? It's okay for her you give away her dog?"

"Well—she's dead. She died about a month ago."

Storndrop looked shocked.

"Oh my Jesus! I'm so sorry." He shook his shaggy, long-haired, bearded head. "Fucking life, huh?"

"Yeah."

"The Russians have old saying: '*Zhizn eto zhizn.*' Life is life."

"'Life is life.' That's very true."

"Your wife, she was sick?"

"No. She committed suicide."

"Oh my Jesus!"

"It was quite a surprise, I have to say. I didn't see it coming."

"And you loved her very much?"

I nodded. Suddenly Storndrop grabbed me and pulled me against the hot, sweating bulk of himself, tickling my neck with his whiskers, heartily slapping my back.

"In one way you are lucky man," he said as we resumed walking. "You love your wife, but me? I hate my wife like crazy. She is a bitch."

"I'm sorry to hear that," I said, then I stuck my hand out. "By the way, my name is Dustin Prewitt."

"Magnus Storndrop, yeah," he said, subjecting my hand to a painful squeeze.

"The director?"

"Yeah, you know me, huh?"

"Sure. I'm a big fan."

"Yeah?"

"I think *Café au Lait* is the best romantic comedy of the last ten years."

"No shit?"

"No shit. It was very funny of course, but also sexy and provocative, and it made you think. And Will Smith and Kate Winslet were better than I've ever seen them."

"They were fantastic, yeah," then he gave me a wink. "But they have a good director."

"No, not good. *Great.*"

Storndrop was speechless with delight. He beamed at me, his blue eyes sparkling, his humid beard glittering, and then he began to laugh hugely, hugging his stomach like Santa Claus.

"You know," I said, "I live in the house right behind you. On Bedford."

The laughter stopped. He gave me a quizzical look.

"Hold on just one goddamn moment. Your wife is Laura Keene?"

"Yes."

"Laura Keene! My god!" and then he patted my shoulder. "To have such beautiful woman and then to lose her is shitty luck, yeah."

I sighed. "*Zhizn eto zhizn!*"

"I tell you something. For twenty years, I have had a crush in her."

"Really?"

"In Sweden I dream only of her on cold winter nights that never have no sunrise. So beautiful. Like a goddess! When I find out she move in the house behind, I am so excited, only in America, and I say, 'Magnus, go say hello to your new neighbor. Welcome her to neighborhood, yeah. Bring her a cake, and a bottle of vodka!' But I never did."

"Too bad. She would have liked that. Especially the vodka."

"You are in the business? An actor also, maybe?"

"No, I'm a writer. Actually, speaking of romantic comedies, I've just written one. It's about a womanizer brought low by true love."

He looked intrigued. "A womanizer. Like me. And like you too maybe, huh? Maybe the script it is autographical, yeah?"

I grinned sheepishly. "Well, maybe a little."

He laughed, and gave me a playful push.

"I can read it?"

"Of course. I'm still polishing it up a little, but it should be ready in a week or two."

"Maybe you and me we make a movie together, Dustin, yeah?

And we make a dedication: 'To Laura Keene. Beloved wife. Beautiful neighbor.' What do you say about that?"

"I think that would be just wonderful, Magnus."

18

Next morning I was sitting at my computer, chuckling over some changes I'd made in the script, when Ben Benjamin called.

"Dustin, what in the world did you write to Maggie Peek?"

"Oh shit. You mean I'm in trouble again?"

"No, to the contrary. I just got off the phone with Scott Kelly. He said that Maggie was over the moon about your letter. It made her laugh, it made her cry. She wants to meet you!"

"You're kidding."

"Every screenwriter in town would like to take this meeting, Dustin. All the studios want to be in business with her. She's being offered everything by everybody."

"But she's just some singer that won a talent contest, right? She's never even acted before?"

"Dustin—what I don't want to hear from you is doubt, or cynicism. Maggie Peek could be your ticket back out of the wilderness."

"I understand, Ben. And I promise I won't mess this up."

Chelsea called me back a little later, and arrangements were made for Maggie and me to meet for lunch the following Tuesday. I was glad it was a lunch meeting; that meant I could have a drink or two, loosen up a little. When Tuesday came, Pete wanted to drive me and be my bodyguard, but I explained that my whole Hollywood career might depend on this meeting and having him hanging around wearing sunglasses and pretending to be Kevin Costner might make me uptight.

"Don't sweat it, man, I'll be in the background. You won't even know I'm there. I'll see you, but you won't see me."

"Thanks. But I don't think so."

"Okay. But anything happens just call me on your cell. I'll be there in a flash."

Then Pete and I each slammed two shots of Laura's Roberto Cavalli vodka, so I had a pleasant buzz as I drove west across Los Angeles to lunch. Maybe it was just the vodka, but I was feeling better than at any time since Laura had taken her one-way swim at Dockweiler Beach; it was as if some turning point were at hand, as if I and my Maserati were emerging from a bank of cold gray fog into unending sunlight.

The restaurant was on Wilshire Boulevard, near the eastern edge of Santa Monica, across the street from a park. I turned my car over to a valet, then went inside. Jazzy music was playing. I walked up to a young hostess who, when I gave her my name, seemed to recognize and be pleased by it. She led me through the deserted dining room and onto a crowded patio. Several tall trees were scattered about. Talk and laughter arose from the diners sitting in wrought-iron chairs at poured-concrete tables. I followed the graceful, swaying hips of the hostess to a table at one end of the patio, under a pine tree.

I settled down in my seat, tugged at my soft Italian clothes, looked at my watch. I was a few minutes early.

Apple, my waitress, appeared—a skinny blonde with a short upper lip and big, friendly front teeth. She left menus and fetched me a glass of Amarone. I sipped it, and looked around.

Ten women, in their forties and fifties and in stylish, expensive clothes, were sitting nearby at a long table. They seemed more Beverly Hills than Santa Monica. It was the birthday of one of them, I figured out after listening in for a while. They were drinking a lot, wine mostly. I doubt if any of them had jobs. They probably spent their time at home planning their next eye job or Botox treatment, while their rich husbands were at work trying to fuck each other over. One of them saw me watching them. She cocked one nearly plucked-to-death eyebrow at me, gave me an inquisitive smile. I smiled back, raised my gallant glass to hers, and she raised hers to mine. She was wearing a silk, mint-green pantsuit. Had short blonde hair, a pert little nose, burnt-orange lip gloss.

I can't explain what happened next. The air in the patio seemed to brighten, as the woman in the mint-green pantsuit became a being of transcendent beauty. She was regarding me with sly amusement, as if she had sensed my misplaced condescension and had deigned to let me see her now as she really was. And then I saw that all the sun-dappled diners at the table had been likewise transfigured. The bored Beverly Hills socialites were gone, replaced with wild and passionate goddesses partying away an eternal afternoon on Mount Olympus.

Apple came up with a basket of bread and broke the spell.

"Where'd you get the name 'Apple'? Were your parents hippies?"

Apple giggled. "Whatever's the opposite of 'hippie' is what my parents are. I was named after my great-grandmother. Her maiden name was Abigail Apple. How's the wine?"

Her voice was like a child's, very soft and high-pitched.

"It's great," I said, and then I saw Maggie Peek. She and the hostess were heading my way across the patio, leaving behind a rippling wake of turning heads and fascinated looks. Her long legs, in red tights with a pattern of squiggly golden swirls, descended from a denim miniskirt. She had on a sleeveless top with wide red and brown horizontal stripes and high-heeled brown suede boots. An enormous red velvet Chanel bag with chain handles hung from one shoulder. As I rose to greet her, I noticed she was nearly as tall as me.

"Hi, Dustin," she said, giving me a nice smile and a mannishly firm handshake. "Sorry I'm late. The traffic was murder."

"That's okay. I haven't been here long."

As we sat down, I caught a whiff of potent perfume. Apple had been standing by in an alert posture, hands clasped behind her back, reminding me of a ball girl at a tennis tournament. Now she said, in effect dashing across the court to retrieve a ball: "Can I get you something to drink, Miss Peek?"

Maggie looked at my wine. "Oh, we're drinking? Good. How about a glass of cabernet?"

She had a little trouble finding a place for her Chanel bag, finally putting it down between her chair and the trunk of the pine tree.

"That's a big purse," I observed.

"Yeah, big bags are back."

"Is that right?"

"Oh yeah. They'd gotten so tiny it was ridiculous."

I nodded, then cleared my throat.

"Listen. I just want to apologize again for my behavior that day."

"You don't have to. You said it all in your letter." She began to laugh. "I mean, it was hilarious. 'The King of the Parking Garage'! And Lumpy's crazy girlfriend leaving her seafood in your car!"

"Yeah, it was one of those days, all right."

"And of course I had no idea about your wife. I was a big fan of hers, by the way. When I was growing up, she was one of my role models."

Laura a role model . . . it was enough to make your head spin.

"I just loved that movie she was in with Hugh Jackman," Maggie continued. "Where she was this big important lawyer and he was the carpenter that was building her a new deck?"

"*Jill and Jack.*"

"I was surprised she didn't become a big star after that."

"So was she."

"Is that why she did it? Because she was disappointed with her career?"

"Oh, I don't know."

I fingered my wineglass; Maggie looked abashed.

"Shit. That was dumb of me. I just met you, and I'm asking a question like that. Will you forgive me?"

"Well—maybe you should write me a letter."

She gave a loud laugh. Apple came back with the cabernet. She began enthusiastically reciting the specials but I didn't catch much of it. I was preoccupied with what was on the other side of the table. Creamy skin. The softly firm swelling of breasts. A curly mass of raven hair. Pink lips so plump they seemed about to split their skins like overripe fruit.

"Would you like a few minutes to think about it?" asked Apple.

"I'm ready if Dustin is," said Maggie.

"Sure, I'm ready."

Maggie ordered the grilled shrimp Greek salad and I the New York steak sandwich. Apple collected our menus and left. "Cheers," I said.

"Cheers."

We bumped glasses, then looked at each other as we sipped our wine.

"You been here before?" I asked.

"Mm-hm. I like it. I like the trees. I'm really into nature."

"Where'd you grow up?"

"Santa Barbara. We had a ranch up in the hills, not a working ranch, my father's a neurosurgeon, but we had a lot of horses. My horse's name was Warrior. You know how some girls get crushes on their horses before they discover boys? Well, I had a crush on Warrior. Warrior and I went all over those hills."

"What ever happened to him?"

"He's still alive. Still at the ranch. I try to visit him every few weeks. He's too old to ride, but I bring him sugar, and he eats it out of my hand."

"Lucky Warrior."

"Do you like horses?"

"Not really. I'm kind of scared of them."

She seemed amused.

"Why? What do you think they're going to do to you?"

"Bite me. Or buck me off their backs and kill me."

She took some bread from the basket and began to spread butter on it.

"You know, Dustin—I'm surprised that a big, rugged guy like you would be afraid of anything."

"Well, when you're truly macho, like me, you're not afraid to admit that you're afraid."

Maggie laughed, and bit into her bread and butter.

We both became aware of a teenage girl diffidently approaching the table. When she saw us looking at her, she froze, eyelids fluttering in alarm, as if she'd been holding not a small notebook and a ballpoint pen in her hands but a length of rope with which she'd been intending to throttle Maggie.

"It's okay, sweetie," Maggie said.

She came to the table. She was a tall, gawky Asian gal.

"What's your name?" said Maggie.

"Kiki?" she said, as though hazarding a guess.

"So Kiki, do you want me to sign that?"

Kiki smiled, reluctantly revealing a mouthful of pink rubber bands and gleaming metal.

"If you don't mind."

"K-i-k-i?" said Maggie as she took the notebook and pen.

"Yes."

Kiki watched Maggie writing, and then "Maggie?" she ventured. "You were my favorite from the very beginning. I knew you were going to win."

"Well, thank you. But you know the funny thing, Kiki? I knew I was going to win too!"

"Really?"

"Ever since I was a little girl, the first thing I do when I wake up in the morning is repeat a hundred times: 'I'm Maggie Peek, and

I get what I want!' And when I go to bed, same thing, a hundred times: 'I'm Maggie Peek, and I get what I want!'"

"And it works?"

"Like magic. It's all about being determined, Kiki. And never giving up."

Kiki nodded eagerly, lapping up every drop. Maggie handed pen and notebook back to her.

"What's your last name?"

"Denawa?"

"*You* try it. Say: 'I'm Kiki Denawa, and I get what I want!'"

"Right now?"

"Right now."

"I'm Kiki Denawa, and I get what I want!"

Maggie laughed and applauded.

"Wonderful, Kiki!"

Kiki began to smile widely, forgetting to be self-conscious about the hardware in her mouth.

"Thank you, Maggie."

"No problem, Kiki."

Kiki leaned in and took the obligatory selfie with Maggie then went back to her table, where her family had been waiting and watching. She showed what Maggie had written to Mom and Dad, who were thrilled, but her brother wouldn't even glance at it. He was tall and thin like his sister, and wore wire-framed glasses that made him look like a handsome egghead. With his arms folded across his chest, he cast a contemptuous look at Maggie and me, as if he saw completely through us.

~

"So how does it feel?" I said. "Being the girl everybody's talking about."

"Fucking fantastic," Maggie said. She forked a shrimp in her mouth and chewed it up vigorously. "You haven't told me what you think."

"About what?"

"Me. My singing. You know."

"I'm sure you're an amazing talent. But the truth is, I'm not familiar with your work."

She seemed taken aback.

"You didn't see me on *The Voice*?"

"I've never seen one second of *The Voice*."

"You don't watch TV?"

"I don't watch that kind of TV."

"What do you watch?"

"Sports. Movies. Documentaries on the Nazis. Cable shows like *Homeland* and *Better Call Saul*. *Downton Abby* was my favorite. I still haven't gotten over Mathew's death. Poor Lady Mary."

"You're a snob, Dustin. How's your sandwich?"

"Good. How's your salad?"

"Delicious. Want a bite?"

"Sure."

She stabbed another shrimp then leaned over the table, and I took it straight in my mouth right off her fork. You can see we were starting to get pretty cozy. I caught another heady whiff of her.

"I like your perfume. What's it called?"

"Le Baiser Du Dragon. The Kiss of the Dragon."

"Hm. Suits you."

"What do you mean? I remind you of a dragon?"

"In a good way. I understand you're interested in acting."

"Yes, that's the next mountain I intend to climb. You're an old pro. You have any advice for me?"

"Well, I think it was Spencer Tracy who said about acting, know your lines, and don't bump into the furniture."

"Who's Spencer Tracy?"

I was unsurprised she didn't know, but before I could enlighten her, the waitress for the table of Beverly Hills women brought out a birthday cake. The women started singing "Happy Birthday" to the birthday girl, a bony redhead, and as happens in restaurants, people at other tables joined in. Including Maggie. But her voice separated itself from all the others, soared gorgeously above them. The song concluded and applause followed as the redhead made a wish and blew her candles out, but the applause wasn't for her but instead was for Maggie, who graciously smiled and waved to her fans.

Now she gave me a challenging look. "Well?"

"Some voice."

I took a bite of my steak sandwich.

"You're a hard guy to impress."

"Not really."

"Don't BS me, Dustin. You've been around the block. You've seen 'em come. You've seen 'em go. You probably think you've seen a thousand girls like me. You're wrong, though. Maggie Peek is one of a kind. The real deal."

"I'm sure you are. But do me a favor. Quit talking about me like I'm a million years old."

"Oh, don't be so defensive. I like the mature look. This is such a phony town, but you're obviously the real you. Authenticity. That's what I value more than everything. Right now all I want is to be the best twenty-five-year-old singer I can be. And if someday I'm a seventy-five-year-old bag lady, then I want to be the best damn bag lady on the block!"

"Very admirable."

"Dustin? Would you do something for me?"

"Sure. If I can."

"Would you write me a great role in a great script? I promise when I win the Oscar I won't forget to thank you!"

"I appreciate that. Is there a particular kind of movie you want to do?"

"Well, I'm being offered a lot of things, but they're all crap. The hero's sexy girlfriend, that kind of thing. Squeaking and moaning with pleasure whenever he takes time off from saving the world to do her the favor of fucking her. I told my team of agents, if I'm gonna do a movie like that, then *I* save the world, *I* fuck the guy, I make *him* moan and squeak. *Wonder Woman*, for example. I would have been perfect for that. So I need to be proactive. Create my own reality. I didn't win *The Voice* by sitting at home waiting for the phone to ring or somebody to knock on my door. It wasn't given to me, I took it, I grabbed that motherfucker and made it mine!"

"You came, you saw, you conquered. As Spencer Tracey said."

"Exactly."

"How about we do this. We take a few days, you think about what kind of movie you want to do, I'll come up with some ideas of my own, then we get back together and kick things around. Come up with something that'll win you that Oscar."

"Perfect," she smiled. She picked up a shrimp by the tail and bit it in two with her bright-white teeth. "You know, Dustin, I'll be honest with you. All my agents tried to talk me out of this lunch. They said all the hippest, hottest writers in town want to work with you so what do you want to meet with *him* for. But I had a feeling about you. In fact, I had a *dream* about you."

"Really?"

"Yeah. I haven't been able to get you out of my mind. Ever since I saw you in the parking garage. You were scary, but you were also . . . fascinating."

I felt a twitchy sensation in my groin.

"What happened?" I said. "In the dream?"

"I was camping out up in the mountains. It was night. Warrior was tied up to a tree, and I was sitting by a campfire. Then I heard some noise out in the darkness, and you came walking into the firelight.

"You were wearing blue jeans, cowboy boots, and a blue work shirt with the sleeves rolled up. You're a big guy anyway, but in the dream you were *huge*, about six and a half feet tall. I didn't know your name, but I knew who you were. You were the new hired hand at the ranch. You'd never said a word to me, but I knew you'd had your eye on me.

"My heart started beating fast. I wanted to escape. I looked around at Warrior, but he was gone. I looked back at you. Your eyes were burning like blue fire. Your hands were hanging at your side, and slowly clenching and unclenching. I knew if I ran you'd catch me before I got twenty feet. I knew you had me right where you wanted me."

She drank some wine, her eyes looking at me over the rim of the glass.

"Jesus," I said. "Then what happened?"

"I woke up."

"Aw, shucks, ma'am. Things was just gettin' interestin'."

She expelled a snort of a laugh. A busboy cleared away our dishes. Apple handed us dessert menus.

"I don't usually have dessert," I said, "but listen to this: 'Warm chocolate hazelnut ice cream float.'"

"Sounds revolting," said Maggie, handing her menu back to Apple. "I'll have an expresso."

"But it's got this ring to it," I insisted. "'Warm chocolate hazelnut ice cream float.' Kind of like: 'Shave and a haircut, six bits.'"

"Wanna try it?" asked Apple.

"Is it any good?"

"I don't really know, it's brand-new on the menu. But you can be my guinea pig."

"Let's go for it."

Maggie waited till Apple was out of earshot, then did something with her lips in imitation of Apple's rabbity mouth, and said, in dead-on mimicry of her little-girl's voice: "You can be my guinea pig."

I excused myself, walked through the still-almost-empty dining room, and entered the men's room.

It was the darkest men's room I'd ever been in. The only illumination was provided by three directional lights set in the ceiling above the toilet, the urinal, and the sink. The jazzy music from the dining room was playing in here too.

I went to the urinal, and unzipped. My member was mildly tumescent. I stood there in the cone of light, looking at my glittering stream, mulling over Maggie. It was unsettling to learn that some grotesque, Harlequin Romance version of myself had invaded Maggie's dreams.

I zipped up, then traversed the darkness between the urinal and the sink. I gazed at myself in the mirror, turning my head this way and that. The mature look. I was obviously the real me. What had she meant by that? That I obviously hadn't had plastic surgery even though I needed it? I didn't think I looked so bad. There were some lines around my eyes, but they fell, I felt, well short of being "crow's feet." My jaw line was holding up. But then I looked at the hair at my temples. Ever so slightly, but undeniably, it was going gray. I'd never noticed it before. It must have happened during the tumultuous course of the last few weeks. My god, I thought, can that really be? Can you really grow significantly older in just a few weeks?

Shaking my head and sighing, I turned the water on in the sink. As I washed my hands, I thought about how I ought to handle Maggie. Things with her were clearly moving in a carnal direction, but maybe I should put the brakes on, at least till I nailed down some kind of deal to write some silly screenplay for her. Keep my distance, yes. Just stare at her with my burning eyes, just clench and unclench my hands.

To my right there was a brief brightness, as the door opened and closed. I looked over, and saw emerging from the gloom the miniskirted form of Maggie. I turned to her, my hands still wet, and her arms slid over my shoulders then around my neck and we kissed. My hands moved across her back, and then one found a buttock and the other a breast. Her hand began to rub my crotch, which responded in a situationally appropriate fashion.

She pulled back a little; she was smiling.

"I took care of the check," she said, her voice somewhere between a growl and a whisper. "Let's get out of here."

"But what about my warm chocolate hazelnut ice cream float?"

"Fuck it."

19

Maggie was driving a black Bentley—sleek and beautiful and new, like her. I was right behind her in my Maserati. We were headed west on Wilshire, toward her condo, which was on Tenth Street.

The wide boulevard was lined with palm trees and trendy stores. The streets arithmetically ticked by: Twenty-fourth, Twenty-third, Twenty-second. We passed a lightbulb store, a Whole Foods Market, a red-brick church, a Mercedes dealership. I could see the back of her black hair through her rear window. In mere minutes, I would run my stiff, splayed fingers through that hair, I would strip the red tights off those glorious legs. The car seemed to be moving along as smoothly as if I were in a boat being carried by the current down a dreamy river. I would plunge into the unknown abyss of another person, of the girl I scared in the parking garage, of Maggie Peek of Santa Barbara in mere minutes. Sixteenth, Fifteenth, Fourteenth, but then geometry interrupted arithmetic. Where Thirteenth should have been was a street called Euclid. Superstitious city fathers trying to ward off bad luck, one assumed. And then the countdown resumed. Twelfth, Eleventh . . .

The right-turn signal on the Bentley began to blink, and the car moved into the right lane. I turned my own turn signal on, and followed. Maggie lifted her hand and waved to me, and I waved to her. Now she turned right on Tenth Street, as my Maserati and I went straight on through the intersection, continuing down the palmy prospect towards the sea.

I crossed Lincoln Boulevard, went past a park where people were playing tennis. A guy on a motorcycle had been behind me for a couple of blocks, and now, as I stopped at a red light on Third Street, he swung around and pulled up beside me. "Your turn signal's on, asshole!" he informed me helpfully, then roared away as the light changed.

I clicked the signal off. Ahead of me Wilshire terminated at Ocean Avenue. I moved into the left lane. I was stopped by another red light. Directly ahead of me, across Ocean, was a white statue of Saint Monica. It was about twenty feet tall, showing a woman dressed like a nun with her hands piously crossed upon her bosom. I stared at the statue as I waited at the light. It was shining in the sun. It seemed to have some meaning for me. Should I turn my back on the world and enter a monastery?

A horn honked behind me, and I saw the light was green. I turned onto Ocean. A car conveniently vacated a parking space right in front of me, and I slid in and took it.

I put some quarters in the meter. Took a walk through Palisades Park.

It was a long strip of grass and trees that ran along the bluff overlooking the PCH and the Pacific. I headed north along a paved walkway. I went by a homeless guy lying facedown on the grass beside a messy pile of belongings; he was covered with a blanket, only his feet and ankles showing. Good way to hide a body. In plain sight, in a public park.

All the energy and optimism I had been feeling had utterly drained out of me. I felt like some gray, phantomlike figure creeping along beneath the trees. I passed behind the blank white back of Saint Monica. I saw more homeless people, and then even more. Suddenly they seemed to be everywhere, sitting on benches or sleeping in the grass or ambling aimlessly along. They were very similar to one another, all male, lean, shabby, and unshaven, they were like a tribe of weary wayfarers who had come to the end of the road.

I walked over to the concrete railing at the edge of the bluff, leaned on it and looked out at the peaceful blue ocean. A cool breeze, welcome on a hot day, hit me in the face. A boat was pulling a yellow parasail. The beach was heavily sprinkled with swimmers and sunbathers. A busy swish of traffic rose up from the highway. A parking lot on the beach was filled up with the trucks and vans of a movie or TV shoot. The cast and crew were having lunch at blue tables under white tents. A catering guy was cooking at a grill. He started cutting up what looked like a long sausage; the chopping sounds, lagging an instant behind the flashing knife, reached me with surprising clarity. A group of circling seagulls drifted my way, and I was surrounded by their circling shadows.

I just couldn't do it. Nope. I couldn't make myself make that right turn. Much of my life had been spent in the mindless pursuit of pussy, but I just couldn't follow Maggie Peek home.

The deal was, see, that I didn't like her. I didn't like it when she sang "Happy Birthday" and diverted the attention to herself and away from the woman whose birthday it actually was. I didn't like her making fun of sweet little Apple. I didn't like the fact that I was clearly just another "what" that she wanted and was certain she was going to get.

Ordinarily whether or not I liked a girl had minimal connection to the question of whether or not I wanted to fuck her—but today, for some reason, it was different.

A homeless guy approached me, smiling tentatively.

"Anything you got, man—it'd really help."

I put my hands in my pockets, but came up empty.

"Sorry. I don't have any change."

"I'm just so hungry," he persisted. "Anything you got."

His sour breath gusted over me. I doubted he wanted the money for food, but who was I to deny a man his daily grog, his ration of rum? I pulled out my wallet. I looked through it for a one or a five, but all I had was twenties. I was aware of his avid eyes on all the money.

"Anything you got."

I plucked out one of the twenties and handed it to him. He looked very happy.

"You really are the best."

"Good luck," I said as he walked away. He mumbled something I couldn't understand. He went over to where two of his buddies were sitting in the shade. He showed them the twenty, then, in eerie unison, the heads of all three of them turned towards me.

All at once I became anxious. I was the only non-bum-type person in sight. I remembered the fate of the decadent Sebastian in *Suddenly, Last Summer*, set upon in broad daylight by depraved Spanish street urchins, chased down and torn to bits and cannibalized. As casually as I could, I started walking back the way I had come. I was prepared to break into a panicked and undignified run, but that didn't prove necessary. Soon I had reached a more populated part of the park. A squirrel loped gracefully through the grass. A bald guy in a coat and tie sat on a bench reading a Michael Connelly novel and eating a sandwich and potato chips. A couple dozen little kids trooped by, holding each other's hands and gabbing cheerfully at the top of their lungs, accompanied by two really spectacular-looking young women in tight jeans, how come I never had teachers that looked like that?

I sat down on a green bench. South of me the park ended at the Santa Monica Pier. I could see its Ferris wheel going round and round. Far beyond the pier jetliners were taking off from LAX over Dockweiler Beach and my sea-swallowed wife.

I felt inert inside. I felt like just another stone or tree in the park. I felt as though I could sit here on this green bench till the end of time.

A gangbangery guy wearing a hooded gray sweatshirt with the sleeves cut off and baggy orange shorts that looked like underwear slouched by, holding a leash with a pit bull at the end of it. The pit bull was moving in a delicate, nearly mincing way, as if he were walking along on his tiptoes. He was packing a pair of big balls, and I had a sudden epiphany. That was it. Balls! Basically the cause of all the world's problems.

It wasn't something I heard. It wasn't something I saw. But something made me turn my head in the other direction.

A brown blur was streaking across the park toward me.

"Topper!" I cried in a strangled voice as I stood up, and then he was upon me.

20

"Topper! Stop it!" I yelled, as if finding myself in the middle of some old familiar nightmare. He had sunk his teeth into my pants leg, and was yanking and shaking it and savagely snarling.

"No, Charlie! No!" I heard, and then I saw a girl running across the grass, a leash dangling from her hand. "Let go! No! No, Charlie, I mean it!" she said and then bent down to grab him.

I was afraid that Topper would rip her wrist open. "Look out!" I said. "Be careful!" but I needn't have worried. He let go of my pants and allowed the girl to clip the leash on his collar and pull him away, though he continued to glare and bark at me.

"Hush, Charlie! What's gotten into you?"

She was wearing a long, pale-green skirt covered with tiny pink flowers, a pink T-shirt, and tan sandals. She had a roundish face and shoulder-length, red-blonde hair. She was about five five, in her mid to late thirties, and had a nice figure, though she was carrying maybe six or eight extra pounds. Now she turned to me; her eyes were hidden behind large, dark sunglasses.

"My god, I'm so sorry! I've never seen Charlie behave like that!"

"Oh, I have. And his name's not Charlie, it's Topper."

"Topper?"

The girl looked at Topper, who gave a confirmatory bark.

"Look," I said, "I'm confused. What are you doing with him? Are you a friend of Larry's? Larry Hochheiser?"

"No. I don't know anybody by that name. Maybe you're confusing this dog with some other dog."

"No, that's definitely Topper."

"And you're saying he belongs to this Larry guy?"

"Well, sort of. He did belong to me, but I gave him away to Larry about a month ago."

"Oh. That's about when I found him."

"Found him where?"

"Wandering around on Montana Avenue. Not far from where I work. He didn't have a collar on. I took him all around the neighborhood, but nobody knew who his owner was."

The enormity of what she was saying began to sink in.

"Jesus Christ! You're saying you found him a *month* ago?"

"Yes."

"I must have talked to Larry a dozen times since then, and he always says that Topper's doing great. He tells me these detailed stories about all the fun stuff they're doing together."

"I guess Charlie—Topper—must've run away, and your friend's too afraid to tell you."

"He oughta be afraid, the lying bastard. My name's Dustin, by the way. Dustin Prewitt."

"Penny Ruemmler."

"Well, thanks for looking after Topper, Penny."

"It was my pleasure." Topper had calmed down, and had begun to follow our conversation with interest. Penny looked down at him, crestfallen. She scratched his head, and he licked her hand. She said in a small voice: "I guess you'll be wanting to give him back to Larry now, huh?"

"That won't be possible."

"Why not?"

"Because Larry's going to be dead because I'm going to kill him."

"You know," she said, hopefulness rising in her voice, "I've really fallen in love with Charlie. I mean Topper. I know you don't know me or anything, but I promise you I'd take good care of him. I mean, assuming you don't want him back yourself. You said you gave him away."

"No, I don't want him back. No offense, Topper."

None seemed to be taken as Topper looked up at me, his tail stump wagging.

"I'm good with animals. And I think Topper's taken a real shine to me."

"Yeah, I can see that."

Her sunglasses really were a distraction. They seemed to take up half her face.

"You got eyes under those glasses?"

"Uh-huh," she said, and slipped them off. She did indeed have eyes. Brown, bright, warm, and eager.

"What do you do?" I said. "For a living."

"I work in this little clothing boutique. I don't make a lot, but I make enough. Look, I'm not a Satan worshipper or anything. I don't have some crazy boyfriend that'll be mean to him. I'm the perfect person to take care of Topper!"

"Okay. He's yours."

She squealed, and threw her arms around me. Her warmth and softness pressed up against me, then she pulled back, embarrassed.

"Oh, I'm sorry, I—"

"No, no, it's okay."

We looked at each other. A butterfly fluttered by. Topper barked at it.

"Were you taking him for a walk?"

She nodded. "I probably shouldn't have taken him off his leash, but I'd done it before and it was okay. I was trying to teach him this twirling trick. He loves to learn new things. But as soon as he looked over and saw you, that was it. He made a beehive straight for you."

I smiled a little.

"I think you mean 'beeline.'"

"What did I say?"

"Beehive."

She laughed—a big, unselfconscious, completely charming laugh.

"You've got a great laugh," I said.

"Oh, thanks."

"Topper's mad at me 'cause I gave him away. That's why he came at me."

"So why'd you do that? Give him away?"

"Well, we never really got along very well, for some reason. He was really my wife's dog. And then when she died, I just thought he'd be happier with someone else."

Penny was staring at me.

"Your wife died?"

I nodded.

"When?"

"In late May."

"Jeez. It just happened."

Topper whined and pulled at his leash.

"I think he wants to resume his walk," I said.

Penny nodded. The three of us began to walk. We were silent for a bit, but somehow it didn't seem like an awkward silence. Finally I asked, "So you're off today?"

"No, I'm on my lunch break. I brought Topper to work with me."

"You mean he doesn't bite the customers or pee all over the merchandise?"

"Of course not. Renée, the owner, she likes having him around, 'cause the customers love him."

She was contemplating me with a faintly puzzled half smile.

"You look *so* familiar. Are you an actor?"

"No. But I'm in the business. I'm a screenwriter."

"Oh really! Have you written anything I might have seen?"

"Well, my first movie was called *Strike Four.* Matt Price was in it?"

Penny bit her lower lip, then shook her head.

"No, I don't believe I know that one."

"*Code 7*? A comedy cop movie starring Brendan Fraser and Charlie Sheen?"

Penny's brow furrowed, then she reluctantly shook her head again.

"I don't think so."

"There's this one movie, it was kind of a bomb but I'm still proud of the work I did on it. It starred Sharon Stone as a recovering alcoholic. But I didn't wind up getting a credit, there were some other writers involved and it went to arbitration and I got screwed by the Writers Guild."

"Oh, too bad. So what was it called?"

"*Turn Out the Lights*?"

She thought long and hard about it, then looked at me and sighed.

"No?" I said.

"Sorry."

"Okay, let's see. Have you ever heard of a movie called *Avatar*?" Her face lit up.

"Oh my god! Of course! Yes!"

"Well, I didn't have anything to do with it."

She looked at me a moment, then burst out again into that laugh. She laughed like a person who liked to laugh.

My phone began to ring—I mean to *really* ring, in the old-fashioned way, I'd eighty-sixed "La Bamba."

I took my phone out and looked at it. Wasn't surprised to see it was Ben Benjamin calling.

"Excuse me, Penny, I better take this."

"Sure, go ahead."

"Hello, Ben."

"Dustin!" Ben cried. "What have you done?"

I could hardly hear him above a hubbub of conversations and

laughter and clinking silverware, he was obviously having lunch at one of those crowded acoustically awful Hollywood places.

It was the voice of doom in my ear and I knew it. I had fallen off the mountain, I had broken through the ice. And yet I felt oddly calm.

"I don't know, Ben. Why don't you tell me what you've *heard* that I've done?"

"Maggie Peek says you got drunk at lunch, followed her into the ladies' room, and then—well, you practically tried to rape her."

"Oh, bullshit. If anybody nearly got raped it was *me*. She followed *me* into the *men's* room."

I noticed Penny listening, wide-eyed. The gravelly voice of doom continued.

"She said she used martial-arts techniques to fight you off. Then she ran out of the ladies' room in tears and drove home and called Scott Kelly. Scott's still on the phone with her, trying to calm her down, he says she's hysterical."

"Look, none of this is true. She didn't leave the restaurant in tears. We left together. She was happy, she was laughing, she was signing autographs. You can ask the people at the restaurant."

"Dustin, this is an entertainment agency, not an investigative agency."

I saw Penny check her watch; I could tell she wanted to talk to me.

"Ben, hold on a sec."

"I have to go," said Penny. "I have to get back to work."

"Okay. Well listen, it's been great meeting you," and we shook hands.

"It's been great meeting *you*. And don't worry about Topper, he'll be just fine."

"Maybe I could drop by sometime and see him."

"Oh, I'm sure Topper would love that."

"What's the name of the shop?"

"Renée's. It's on Montana, between Fifteenth and Sixteenth," and then she gave me a concerned look. "So is everything okay?"

"Sure." I shrugged. "It's just Hollywood."

"I guess it's pretty crazy sometimes, huh?"

"Yeah."

"Well—bye."

"Bye."

"Let's go, Topper."

But Topper hung back, looking up at me and whining.

"He doesn't seem to want to go," said Penny.

"Yeah, he wants to bite me some more."

She laughed. "No, he loves you, I can tell. Come on, Topper. Hurry, boy! Let's run to the car! Let's race!"

Penny began to run toward the street with Topper bounding along beside her, as I put the phone back to my ear.

"Okay, Ben. Sorry."

"Who were you talking to?"

"This girl I just met in the park."

"Dustin—the police may be looking for you at this very minute, and you're wandering around in a park trying to pick up girls."

"She's not gonna call the police. She and I both know she made this whole thing up."

"But why would she do such a thing?"

"Revenge. I was supposed to follow her back to her condo to have sex with her, but at the last minute I changed my mind because she's so obnoxious. I guess she felt humiliated."

Penny and Topper reached the sidewalk, and then Penny unlocked the door of a red Honda Civic with a big dent in the side. Topper hopped in the back seat.

"That's a sordid story, Dustin."

"Very sordid. But all true."

Penny went around to the driver's side. She had put her big sunglasses back on. She saw me watching her, and waved. I waved back. She opened the door and got in.

"Unfortunately," said Ben, "the truth is usually irrelevant. Maggie

Peek is now a force of nature in Hollywood, like a hurricane or an earthquake. In regards to you and the agency, I'm afraid there's nothing I can do to save you now."

"I understand, Ben," I said as I watched the red Civic pull away from the curb, become lost in the traffic of Ocean Avenue.

21

When I got home, I called Larry Hochheiser. After we shot the shit for a minute or two, I asked, "So how's Topper?"

"Oh, he's great, man. You know, he did something so cute last night. He grabbed one of my socks and just ran around the house with it. Sometimes he'd throw it up in the air and catch it then he'd run around some more! I nearly laughed my ass off."

"Sounds hilarious!"

"Oh, it was." Larry chuckled. "You should've seen it."

"I really miss that little guy."

"Yeah."

"Hey, you know what? I think maybe I'll drop by later and see him."

"Honestly? I think maybe it's still a little too soon."

"Think it might confuse him?"

"Yeah, I think he's still in this very delicate transitional place. Caught between two worlds, you know?"

"What about next week? Will that still be too soon?"

"Well, we'll just have to—"

"Or next year. Or five years from now. How about it, Larry? Will five years from now still be too soon?"

"What's the deal, man? You're sounding kind of weird."

"I'm *on* to you, you lying sack of shit."

There was a long silence, and then: "What do you mean?"

"I mean I just saw Topper in Santa Monica. He was with this girl who said she'd found him wandering around on the street a fucking *month* ago."

Larry didn't respond, but I could hear him breathing heavily.

"Larry?"

Then I heard coughing and gasping noises.

"Larry, what's going on?"

More coughs and gasps.

"Larry! Larry! What's the matter? You want me to call 911?"

"No—no—I'm glad, man—glad it's over—worst month of my life. And Topper's all right, huh?"

"Yeah, he's fine. What the hell happened?"

"It was just two days after I picked him up. He was in the back yard. The gardener left the gate open. I'd warned him to keep it closed, but—one minute he was there, and then—and then—"

"Just calm down."

"I went running around the streets like a crazy man calling his name, and then I got in my car, I drove around all day, all night, but he'd just vanished, man! I put up lost-dog posters all over the neighborhood offering a big reward, I've been scared to death you'd be driving around and see one of them—"

"You should've just told me the truth."

"I know, but I thought I'd find him and you'd never have to know, my life's been hell, I haven't been eating, I haven't been sleeping, I've lost ten pounds—"

"How come he wasn't wearing his collar?"

"I took it off when I gave him a bath, then I forgot to put it back on. I'm just a dumb fuck, man. A big piece of shit walking around in human form."

"Come on. Let's don't go overboard."

"It's true!"

"Look on the bright side. Topper's okay, and you've lost ten pounds. That's a good thing, right?"

"It's a very good thing," he said, beginning to perk up. "So am I still your lawyer and your pal?"

"Yes. But I'll never give you another dog."

"I don't blame you. So is Topper with you now? Maybe you can have him bark into the phone. I'd really like that."

"The girl's still got him. I'm letting her keep him. They seemed to really be into each other."

"Tell me about this girl."

"What do you want to know?"

"What do you think, asshole? What does she look like? Is she a babe?"

"She's cute, definitely. But not my type."

22

ourth of July found Pete and me drinking mai-tais by my pool. Pete was stretched out in the sun in a bathing suit, his flesh glistening with sweat and suntan lotion. He'd been working hard on his tan, and underneath all the swirls and tufts of black body hair he had become a crisp golden color like a roasted turkey.

I was sitting in the shade, wearing a flowery pair of board shorts and reading a biography of Wilfred Owen. Recently I'd become interested in the English soldier-poets of the Great War; I'd already read books about Rupert Brooke and Siegfried Sassoon. I thought Owen was the most appealing character of the three. Shy, short, and earnest, with an accent that betrayed his lower-middle-class background, he had fallen in love with the tall, haughty, well-to-do Sassoon. Lieutenant Owen was machine-gunned to death as he led his men across the Oise-Sambre canal only a week before the Armistice. He was just twenty-five—same age at death as his hero, Keats.

I sighed and put the book aside and reached for my mai-tai and took a long drink. Owen and Keats had died young but had left behind them many wonderful and permanent poems and here I was at forty-four and what the hell had I done? I knew I was no genius, but I wasn't totally without ability; had I squandered my talent in a classically clichéd fashion? As I'd struggled to come up with a movie I'd worked on that the girl who found Topper had heard of,

I had become acutely aware of how nearly empty the cupboard of my accomplishments actually was.

Well, maybe the Maggie Peek debacle was a blessing in disguise. Perhaps I was a pariah, but I was a very rich pariah, or at least would be as soon as my high-priced probate lawyer convinced a court that Laura really was deceased. There was no reason now that I had to suffer the slings and arrows of outrageous studio executives. I intended to finish the rewrite I was doing on *The Ladies' Man* for Magnus Storndrop, but after that I could do whatever I wanted. Return to my English-major roots. Write novels, or villanelles, or Petrarchan sonnets. No longer was I in thrall to Hollywood. It wouldn't have Dustin Prewitt to kick around anymore.

I chewed on a chunk of pineapple from my drink. I couldn't see Pete's eyes behind his sunglasses, and he'd been uncharacteristically quiet for so long I thought he must have nodded off, but then "Prewitt?" I heard.

"Yeah?"

"You ever wonder what it'd be like to be a woman?"

"Not really. Have you?"

"I was just sitting here thinking about it."

"Come to any conclusions?"

"Yeah. I think I'd hate it."

"How come?"

"I'd hate wearing a dress, wearing a bra. Having big hairy guys like us leering at me wherever I went. Scheming to get their hands on me."

"Yeah, must be terrible."

We thoughtfully sipped our mai-tais as we imagined our Kafkaesque metamorphosis into women; then: "Hey, Prewitt?"

"Yo!"

"'Member 'The Pecker Song'?"

I did, and we sang it . . .

"I'm a little pecker, short and stout,

When I am handled, sperm does spout!"
That's it. "The Pecker Song" only has two lines.

~

Pete was a patriot who took the Fourth of July very seriously. He was determined to see fireworks that night but, overwhelmed by a rising tide of mai-tais, I took a pass. Pete left about six in his Durango to see the show at Marina del Rey.

I don't remember going up the staircase and then into mine and Laura's bedroom; it was as if I had simply materialized there, like a ghost. I looked around, thinking about the last time I'd been in here—after our house had been plundered, and I was helping our housekeeper Rufina get things back in order. (Sluggo and Jodi, incidentally, were still on the run, like Bonnie and Clyde; a surveillance camera had caught them knocking over a convenience store in Redding in the northern part of the state, indicating that although they might be traveling around with millions of dollars' worth of art and jewelry, they were low on cash; police had ID'd Sluggo via fingerprints he had left on the mystic warrior as Mickey Culp, paroled last year from a Colorado prison, with a long rap sheet that included burglary, armed robbery, kidnapping for ransom, indecent exposure, grand theft auto, and attempted murder; the police told me I'd been lucky to have made it through that day alive.)

The floor of the bedroom had been strewn with Laura's beautiful clothes; Jodi must have been trying on and discarding outfits like a capricious princess getting ready for the ball. Laura had loved very little in life as much as she had loved her clothes. To see them there on the floor was shocking and sad, like coming out in the morning and finding that the neighbor's dog has killed your pet peacock, and a breeze is scattering its iridescent feathers all around your lawn. The clothes were carefully rehangered by me and Rufina, who sniffled a little and whose eyes dripped tears, somewhat surprising in light of how harsh Laura had often been with her.

And now, on Independence Day, I opened the door and entered

Laura's enormous walk-in closet. It seemed as silent and airless as a tomb. Her clothes hung in tiered and orderly rows. Maybe I should give them away, I thought. To the Salvation Army, or even to Rufina, for although Rufina herself was squat and homely, she had, as in a fairy tale, seven beautiful daughters. And then there was another strange transition, like a movie dissolve, and I found myself on the balcony outside the master bedroom, walking slowly toward the balustrade. The garden was filled with the mellow light of the end of the day. Beyond the vine-covered wall Magnus Storndrop's French chalet-type mansion was mostly hidden by some trees.

I heard above me a faint buzzing.

A small plane was skywriting a message across the high azure. I looked and looked, but couldn't make heads or tails of it.

I seemed to see a *P*. Although it could have been a *D*. And that was definitely an *X*. But was that a *C* or just another sloppy *D*?

I decided the pilot must be drunk.

23

I drove down Montana, past cute boutiques and chic shops and ficus trees. Reached Fifteenth, then saw Renée's on the other side of the street. It took a bit before I found a parking spot. As I crossed the street, I met in the crosswalk a twelve- or thirteen-year-old girl, very pretty and quite precociously developed, walking along with a chubby friend. The girl was wearing a tight T-shirt, and I read the message on it: "I caught you looking at my tatas." Then I looked up, right into her eyes, as she gave me a nasty, knowing sneer.

I entered Renée's. I was expecting Topper to greet me with barks and bites, but I didn't see him. Penny Ruemmler was standing with her back to me, reaching up with a stick with a hook on the end of it to a handbag hanging high up on the wall. She brought it down, and gave it to a customer. It was a puny little thing; probably twenty or thirty of them could've been fit into Maggie Peek's magnificent Chanel bag.

Now Penny looked around and saw me, and it was pleasant to feel one had occasioned such a nice smile.

"Oh, hi! I'll be with you in a minute."

"Take your time."

As the customer tried to decide whether or not to buy the bag (I don't blame her for agonizing; I heard Penny tell her it cost "six-fifty," and I don't think she meant six dollars and fifty cents), I took a look around. It was a long, narrow space. The merchandise was mostly sweaters, stacked in cubicle-type shelves all along the walls; there were also a few skirts, dresses, pantsuits, and purses. In the middle of the room was a counter where the cash register was. On the counter was a little box filled with pins made out of metal and bits of colored glass; a hand-lettered sign said: "SAVE A DOG'S LIFE! All pins cost $45. The sale of these pins goes directly to the rescue and care of needy dogs taken off the street. Checks should be made out to: Santa Monica Pet Clinic."

I looked through the pins. There were insect pins, flower pins, bird and star and crescent-moon pins. A dragonfly pin caught my eye.

The customer left without the handbag. Penny hung it back up on the wall with her stick, then came my way.

"I was wondering if I'd see you again," she said.

"Had to come see Topper. Where is he?"

"I left him at home today. Sorry. I've got three kittens in the back room. I figured that's enough critters in the store at one time."

"How come you got kittens?"

"One of our customers found them in a dumpster. Everybody knows how I am about animals, so she brought them to me. Need a kitten?"

"No thanks." I heaved a sigh. "Damn. I was really looking forward to seeing that little devil."

"We'll make it another time. Just give me some advance notice."

"Okay."

She was wearing a gauzy black top, and a long khaki skirt with embroidered black flowers and colored beads. She raised one hand to push back a stray wisp of red-blonde hair; several silver bracelets dangled on her wrist.

"I googled you," she said.

"You did?"

"Now I know why you looked so familiar. I saw you on TV . . . when your wife disappeared."

"Oh."

"Any more news about her?"

"No. Her body never turned up. I guess now it never will."

"I'm sorry."

"Thanks."

"So Topper," she said musingly, "was Laura Keene's dog."

"That's right."

"Poor Topper. He must've been used to living this glamorous Hollywood life. And now he's stuck with *me*."

Didn't seem like such a bad fate. I looked around. "You here by yourself?"

"Yeah, Renée's having her hair done."

"How long have you worked here?"

"About five years."

"You like it?"

"It's not what I imagined myself doing at the age of thirty-seven, but—it's okay. I get all my clothes at a discount. And Renée's the best. I can't believe she puts up with me."

"Are you so difficult?"

"No, it's just that these crazy, stupid things keep happening to me."

"Hm. I think we've got a lot in common."

She laughed. I gestured at the box on the counter. "So what's the deal with the pins?"

"Well, Topper's not the first dog I've rescued. There's been lots of them. Usually I find homes for them, but Topper was just so special I couldn't bear to give him up. Anyway, a lot of the dogs are in pretty bad shape. Just before Topper I rescued this adorable little border collie puppy, he came from one of those puppy mills in Mexico, they're terrible places, he was skin and bones, he had hepatitis, he's fine now and I've found him a good home in Culver City, but I've run up a huge bill at the Pet Clinic. They've been great, but they know someday I'll pay off every penny. So selling these pins is one way I kind of chip away at it."

"How much do you owe?"

"You don't wanna know."

"Sure I do."

"*About $8,000*," she said in a voice filled with hushed awe.

I whistled.

"I better buy one then. How's about . . . *this* one?"

I held up the dragonfly pin. She smiled.

"That's my favorite. I love dragonflies."

"Yeah, there's something kind of magical about them."

"One day the biggest dragonfly I ever saw flew in here. It got trapped in the front window. It took Renée and me forever to get it out without hurting it. We had to be really careful, 'cause dragonflies bite, you know."

I didn't know. One more thing in the world to watch out for. I took my billfold out; I always kept a spare check in it.

"Where do you get them? The pins."

"I make them."

"Really? You do a nice job."

She seemed pleased. "You think so?"

"Uh-huh."

I filled the check out and handed it to her.

"Thanks, Dustin. I really appreciate this."

"Glad to help out."

She put the dragonfly in a little pink plastic bag. Another customer came in.

"Guess I better go," I said.

"You're coming back, aren't you? To see Topper?"

"Absolutely."

"Just give me a little warning."

"I will. Bye."

"Bye."

I was about fifty feet down the sidewalk, passing through the shade of a ficus, when I heard behind me: "Dustin! Dustin! Wait!"

I looked around and saw Penny running toward me, her khaki skirt swirling around her knees. She caught up to me and thrust out the check.

"I can't take this!"

"Why not?"

"It's for $8000!"

"So?"

"It's . . . it's too much."

"Penny, listen. I'm lucky enough to have plenty of money, so this is an easy thing for me to do. And it's the least I can do considering you saved Topper's life."

She didn't say anything; she stared at the check.

"You know what? If you give it back, it'll embarrass me. You'll make me feel like I've done something inappropriate. You don't want that to happen, do you?"

Then she surprised the hell out of me by bursting into tears.

"Penny? Penny, what's the matter?"

But she just kept crying. It seemed natural at this point to put my arms around her. It wasn't lost on me that I'd been in this girl's presence for maybe a total of ten minutes and this was the second time she had been in my arms. I awkwardly patted her back, and said, "It's okay."

"I'm sorry. It's just that things have been so lousy for me lately. My car broke down and it's gonna need a new transmission, and my computer crashed and I'm gonna have to buy a new one, and I just found out this girl I know back home has cancer and she's probably gonna die, and . . . now *this*." Then she gave a sort of laugh and said, "I'm crying all over your beautiful shirt."

"I don't mind."

She moved away. Her eyes were red and her cheeks were wet. She sniffled, and took a self-conscious swipe like a little girl with the back of her hand at her nose.

"I must look horrible."

"No."

She looked at the check again.

"Well—I don't know what to say about this, except . . . thank you."

I nodded.

"I need to get back," she said.

"Sure. I'll be talking to you."

"Okay."

I watched her walk back down the sidewalk toward the shop. I told myself: If she looks back at me and waves, that means I'm going to fall in love with her.

When she reached Renée's, she looked back, waved, then disappeared inside.

I jaywalked across the street to my Maserati.

24

Early the next morning, I went in my office to put the finishing touches on my rewrite of *The Ladies' Man*. Pete was a late riser, so the house was nice and quiet. I sipped my coffee and pondered my climax. The young Dustin had given it a mildly cynical twist, which the very-early-middle-aged Dustin, though no less cynical, now took out, bestowing on the ending a sunny sentimentality I was sure Magnus Storndrop would love.

By ten I was done. I had recently bought a new printer that was very fast, and it spewed out the pages of my script with a brisk, optimistic energy.

I walked—briskly, optimistically—around the block to Storndrop's house on Camden Drive. It sat behind a stone wall and a stern iron gate and tall eucalyptus trees. I pressed the buzzer two or three times, but got no response. I saw a metal box in the wall marked DELIVERIES, and opened the door and put in the script. But as I turned to leave, I heard what was unmistakably Storndrop's booming Viking-in-Valhalla laugh coming from somewhere beyond the wall.

"Magnus?" I called. "Magnus! Are you there?"

But now everything was silent, except for a hot, dry breeze moving through the eucalypti. Still, though, as I walked away, I considered the laugh to be a good sign. It's a common practice in Hollywood to slap a new title on an old script and present it as a fresh creation.

With that in mind, I had changed the title of *The Ladies' Man* to *The Girl Who Liked to Laugh.*

~

I didn't call Penny for several days. I played golf with Larry and ping pong with Pete. One night Pete and Larry and I drove out to Anaheim to see the Angels play the Pirates (although interleague play in baseball still strikes me as a profoundly disturbing rupture in the Nature of Things. Perhaps a sign of the End Times). With a vague idea of maybe writing some kind of noirish novel, I began a biography of Bugsy Siegel (who'd had one of his baby-blue eyes shot right out of his head and knocked fifteen feet across the room by a slug from a thirty-thirty as he sat on a sofa at 810 North Linden, just a few blocks away). I hoped every day Magnus Storndrop would call me about my script and every day was disappointed when he didn't. After dinner, Pete and I would drink and watch TV. For a long time, I'd been in the habit of spending each evening with the liberal line-up of shows on MSNBC so I could be shocked, horrified, and depressed by whatever the malignant moron Trump had been up to all day, but that didn't work with Pete around. The house had to be declared a Trump-free zone so we wouldn't kill each other, and we would watch noncontroversial fare like *Savage Pampas* on the Western Channel, *Sex Sent Me to the ER* on TLC, and *The Beach Party at the Threshold of Hell,* starring one of the more obscure Baldwin brothers, on Amazon. Usually the night would end with one of us shaking the other one awake, then we would soddenly trudge up the stairs together and collapse into our respective beds.

What I didn't do was let myself think about Penny. Whenever I found her in my head, like the manager of a tony store on Rodeo Drive into which a homeless person had wandered, I would call security and have her firmly escorted out. I had been buffeted too much by the events of the last few months to want to have strong feelings towards a girl or anything else. I just wished to be left alone in my little corner of Beverly Hills to read, drink, and beat Pete at ping pong. But then one night I had a dire dream.

Penny and I were in a plane taking off from the airport of a large city. We were sitting in the very back row. I looked out the window, and saw the plane that had taken off behind us explode and plummet toward the ground. I was horrified. I looked around and saw that none of the other passengers knew what had just happened. But before I could say anything there was a jolt, and then our plane began losing altitude fast. I understood this was a coordinated act of terrorism, that our plane was probably one of many that were going down at the same time. The plane flew lower and lower over the crowded city as the pilot looked for a place to make a crash landing. The passengers were all screaming. Penny was clutching my hand tightly. I said, "Don't worry, I'll get us out of this," and then I woke up.

I lay there in the dark, disturbed by the dream, and trying to puzzle out what it might mean. I concluded my subconscious was trying to warn me that getting involved with Penny would be a disaster. But the dream had the practical effect of making it impossible for me to stop thinking about Penny. Larry had a client who was throwing a party to celebrate the opening of her trendy new business, and Larry had invited me. I'd said no, since I hate stuff like that, but the next morning I began to reconsider. A little before noon, I called Renée's.

An unfamiliar female voice answered. Renée, presumably. I asked if I could speak to Penny.

"She's with a customer right now. May I ask who's calling?"

"Dustin Prewitt."

There was a change in her voice, and I could tell she knew all about me.

"Oh, hold on. Penny? Dustin Prewitt's on the line!"

I could hear in the background Topper beginning to bark; evidently it took just the sound of my name to set him off.

MAKE BELIEVE · 171

"Topper, be quiet!" I heard Penny say, and then she reached the phone. "Hi, Dustin!"

"Hi. How are you?"

"Fine. Well, I guess you hear Topper. Are you coming by to see him?"

"No, I wasn't calling about him. Actually, I was wondering if you could help me out with something."

"Of course, if I can."

"I'm supposed to go to this party tonight, on Venice Beach. I'm not a party kind of guy, but this is sort of a business obligation. I realize it's last minute and all, but I know if I can talk you into coming with me, the whole thing would be a lot more painless."

Silence. For several seconds. I thought I must have asked her out in such a clumsy way as to insult her.

"Penny?"

"I'm here," she said, and then: "I'd love to come."

25

The sun had just gone down beyond the ocean when I got to Venice Beach. A great glow filled up the western sky. The boardwalk was emptying fast of tourists. The guitar players and T-shirt sellers and fortunetellers and barefoot-walkers-across-broken-glass were all packing up and going home.

The new business, called Codename: Chaos, was located in Gingerbread Court. An Asian guy in a suit stood at the entrance. He found my name on his list, and allowed me to pass. I walked up four brick steps and into a long, narrow, red-brick courtyard. It was lined with little shops selling clothes and ice cream and beachy bric-a-brac.

I walked toward Codename: Chaos. The small space was jammed with dozens of people and dozens more spilled out into the courtyard. I'd offered to pick Penny up but she said she'd just meet me, and I scanned the crowd for her. I could see right away she wasn't here, since a normal person would have stuck out like a sore thumb. It was all tattoos and pierced body parts and crazy-colored hair. Larry had told me many celebrities would attend, and I actually saw one right away: Dennis Rodman, the former Bull and Laker. He rose at least half a foot above everybody else. He was wearing a baseball cap, and had silver rings in his left ear, both nostrils, and lower lip.

"Heeey, Dustin! You're here!"

Some fat little freak had grabbed hold of my arm, and then I realized it was Larry. His curly hair was emblazoned with half a dozen different neony colors.

"My god! What have you done to yourself?"

"Isn't it great? And what's really cool is, all these colors glow under a black light!"

We both had to shout to be heard above a punk song about blow jobs that was blasting out of a sound system.

"Larry, you've really lost it. You've got a certain standing in this town. You can't have hair like that!"

Larry laughed.

"Hey, chill out! It's not permanent. Washes right out with shampoo."

"You sure?"

"Of course. Kooby flew this guy Damien in from New York, he's a famous hair artist, he normally charges hundreds of bucks to do this but he's in there now doing it for free."

"Kooby?"

"She's my client. Kooby D'Allesandro. Codename: Chaos is her creation. It's the world's greatest punk boutique. She's already got stores in New York and Miami. After this? Destination Tokyo! The sky's the limit for that girl."

"So where's all the celebrities?"

"They're everywhere, man. Right in front of your eyes."

"Okay, I see Dennis Rodman. Who else?"

He began pointing them out to me.

"Well, there's Suzy Hotrod, the roller derby queen. And that kind of scary-looking chick to the left of Suzie is Kembra Pfahler, she's a singer and performance artist, she once had her own vagina sewn shut. There's three of the four Cancer Bats, I don't remember what their individual names are. They're kind of a sludge metal group. They are so dope. Oh, and see Franko B? The body modification and blood artist? The girl talking to him? That's Kooby."

Kooby was a waifish creature with spiky green hair. She looked like she ought to be smoking a joint in the bathroom in high school, rather than being on the cusp of running a worldwide punk-boutique empire.

"Come on," said Larry, "I'll introduce you."

"Later. Where can I get a drink?"

"Inside the store. Check out the merchandise. And get Damien to give you a hair job."

"Yeah, I'll be sure to do that."

I maneuvered my way through the crowd and into Codename: Chaos. The music was even louder inside. The air was hot and smelled like punk rockers, and the room shuddered with strobe lights. A video crew was shooting Damien hard at work on somebody's head. People were clustered around and cheering each inspired new splash of color. Damien had white skin and a white mane of hair combed straight back from a widow's peak, giving him the look of an albino werewolf.

I fought my way toward the back of the room where the bar was, past shelves and counters filled with cosmetics, hair products, wigs, faux eyelashes, and cruelty-free non-feather boas. Not one person I encountered even gave me a cursory glance; it was as if my age and appearance had rendered me invisible. The bartender was a short, heavily muscled and tattooed Hispanic guy. He had gold grills on his teeth, inlaid with diamonds and rubies.

"What'll it be, bro?"

I didn't have much of a choice: red or white wine or something called Vampyre vodka. I asked for a vodka tonic. Vampyre vodka, it turned out, was red. Laura would have loved it.

I took a quick gulp, then, as I made my way back toward the entrance, somebody pierced my cloak of invisibility and looked right at me. This was doubtless explained by the fact that she too was relatively normal-looking: an attractive black woman, wearing white corduroy pants and a yellow blouse, her hair in braids.

"Dustin?" she said. "I'm Mandy Jenkins. Remember me?"

Then I did remember. She had acted with Laura some years back in a ridiculous western about a gang of female outlaws.

"Mandy, how are you? You're looking great!"

"You too. So what are you doing here? Doesn't seem like your kind of scene."

"My lawyer invited me. He also represents Pooky."

"Who's Pooky?"

"She's the owner. This is her store."

"You mean Kooby."

"Kooby. Right. So why are you here?"

"Kooby and I are old friends. I knew her in New York."

I grinned and nodded. I hated having to have meaningless hollering-to-be-heard conversations like this. Inviting me to this party was just one more reason that Larry would someday have to be killed.

"Dustin, I'm so sorry about Laura. I couldn't believe it when I heard about it."

"It was pretty unbelievable, all right."

"She's the last person I'd have thought would've done something like that. She seemed like such a strong lady."

"She was strong, in a lot of ways. But in other ways—"

I shrugged. Mandy nodded sympathetically. Somebody lurched into me from behind, spilling some of my drink.

"I'll never forget when I first met her," said Mandy. "I got cast at the last minute, and shooting had already started. And I showed up on set, and I didn't know a soul. It was the first really decent role I'd ever gotten, and I was really nervous. And then Laura saw me. She came over and introduced herself. And then she said, 'Give me your hand.' And so I did. And she held it for a moment, and then she said: 'My god! It never fails! Any time I touch the hand of a black person, it's icy cold!'"

"Hm. And what did *you* say?"

"I said: 'How bizarre!'"

I nodded without surprise—this all sounded exactly like Laura—and took a sip of my crimson drink.

"What is that?" she said. "It looks delicious."

"A Vampyre vodka tonic."

"I think I'll get me one of those. Great seeing you again, Dustin!"

"Great seeing you, Mandy!"

We cheek-kissed, and parted. For the record, the Vampyre vodka tonic was not delicious. It was vile. Something was wrong with either the vodka or the tonic. But it had alcohol in it, so I had little choice except to drink it as I struggled to get back outside.

I saw Penny standing uncertainly on the outskirts of the party, trying to find me. I waved and caught her eye and she laughed with relief and waved back and I made my way over to her.

"You made it!" I said as we gave each other a clumsy half hug.

"Yeah! Looks like quite a party!"

"Can I get you a drink?"

"I'm fine for now. Maybe later."

We stood together and surveyed the orgiastic scene like Dante and Virgil looking over Hell. She plucked at her clothes.

"I don't think I'm dressed right."

She was wearing a rust-colored paisley skirt sprinkled with sequins around the bottom, a matching silk tank top, and strappy high-heeled sandals.

"I think you're dressed exactly right," I said.

She smiled.

"I think you're dressed exactly right too."

I don't know if you've inferred it already, but I'm a bit of a clothes-horse. Laura wasn't the only one who had a big closet. Tonight I was wearing pleated toffee-colored linen pants, a long-sleeved white ineffably soft linen shirt with the sleeves rolled up to an inch and a half below the elbows, a braided-leather belt, and Silvano Lattanzi loafers.

"How's Topper?"

"He's fine. Mrs. Stallings is babysitting him. She lives in the apartment next to mine."

"So what is Mrs. Stallings like?"

"She's kind of this lonely little old lady. She's glad for the company. Hey! Isn't that Dennis Rodman?"

"Yeah. You a basketball fan?"

"Not really. But I'm from Illinois originally, and everyone there loves the Bulls."

Larry's multihued hair came bouncing toward us out of the crowd. He looked curiously at Penny. I noticed they were exactly the same height.

"Hey, man. Who's your friend?"

"Penny, this is Larry Hochheiser, my lawyer. His hair's not usually that color. It washes out, he says. Larry, this is Penny Ruemmler. She's the person who found Topper."

"Oh, wow," said Larry, as he shook Penny's hand. "Dustin said he was bringing a girl tonight, but I didn't know it was gonna be *you*. So I guess you know all about me, huh? I'm the bad guy. The fat little idiot that lost Dustin's dog."

Larry was still moving Penny's hand up and down as if it were a pump handle. He was swaying slightly and his eyes were glassy and he had this silly grin on his face. In the short time since I'd last seen him, he'd somehow managed to get extraordinarily drunk.

"Dustin spoke very highly of you," Penny lied smoothly, finally freeing her hand.

"Really? Damn!"

"Tell Penny about the store," I said.

"*You* tell her. I'd rather just look at her."

He gazed fixedly upon her, his mouth hanging open a little.

"Well," I said, "it's the world's greatest punk boutique. And it's run by a girl with green hair!"

"Cool," said Penny.

"My god you're cute," Larry said. "You look like a Penny. Cute as a penny."

"Thanks."

"Don't let Damien do your hair. It's perfect the way it is."

I'd seen Larry loaded many, many times, but never like this. How did he do it so fast? He must have been shooting it straight into his veins.

"Don't you agree with me, Dustin? Don't you agree she has beautiful hair?"

"I certainly do."

Then he slowly started shaking his harlequin head.

"You know what, Penny? You are so my type. It's just unbelievable."

"Thank you."

"You'd just be wasted on a guy like Dustin. 'Cause a guy like Dustin wouldn't appreciate you like a guy like me. He's had so many women, he can't even keep 'em straight."

Death would be too good for this guy once he sobered up. I grabbed Penny's hand.

"Hey, are you hungry? I think I saw some food up this way."

I plunged with her into the maelstrom. Pulled her along till we got to a table laden with vegetarian fare. I piled high a paper plate with stuff I didn't really want, and Penny did the same. We tried to eat our bean-sprout wraps as we were jostled by punks. Dennis Rodman accidentally stepped on Penny's foot, turned around and apologized nicely. And then disaster. Her paper plate gave way, and dumped her food at our feet on the bricks of the courtyard.

"Oh shit!" she said. "I'm such a klutz!"

Something was going on inside the store. We were carried along by everybody as they surged towards the entrance. And then we saw that a girl had collapsed on the floor and was having some kind of seizure or fit. Maybe it was epileptic, triggered by the strobe lights, or maybe she'd OD'd on something.

"Wanna get outa here?" I asked Penny.

She nodded eagerly. We headed toward the ocean.

"Wait! Wait!"

A guy with a big shiny forehead and wild frizzy hair like Larry of the Three Stooges was running after us.

"You can't leave without your gift bag!"

He thrust a plastic bag heavy with stuff into my hands; it had a green-haired image of Kooby on it.

Near the entrance to Gingerbread Court, the video crew was shooting an interview with the real Kooby. "Success is so cool," we heard her saying. "It's like a drug without taking a drug. I just look around me and I'm like, 'Wow!'"

Then we quickly went down the four brick steps and the sea breeze hit us in the face.

26

"Like, wow!" said Penny as we walked along the boardwalk, and I laughed.

"Sorry. I had no idea it was gonna be like that."

"Oh no, it was great. Not every girl can say she had her foot stepped on by Dennis Rodman!"

"Listen, about my friend, Larry. He's not usually like that. He's really a pretty good guy. But his wife left him and now he seems to be having some kind of nervous breakdown or midlife crisis."

"Poor guy."

We strolled past closed-down businesses on one side and a straight line of palm trees and light poles on the other. We could hear the ocean's faint, sad swish and swash. We couldn't see any stars but we could see a big bright moon. Just a scattering of people were left. A cadaverous man sucking on an oxygen tank as he walked his plodding, aged beagle, who looked as though he could use an oxygen tank too. A pair of down-and-outers sitting on steps and sharing a bottle in a brown paper bag. A very fit-looking girl zooming by on roller blades, perhaps dreaming of being the next Suzy Hotrod. Two fat teenage girls, wearing ridiculously tight and revealing clothing, marching along on quivering thighs, one talking on her phone and the other texting on hers, oblivious to each other and the palm trees and the ocean and the moon.

"You've got an advantage over me," I said.

"What?"

"Well, you've googled me, so presumably you know all about me. But I don't know anything about you. Except you work on Montana and you're from Illinois and you've got a nosy old neighbor named Mrs. Stallings."

"I don't think I mentioned her being nosy."

"Is she?"

She giggled. "Yep. Nobody can sneeze on our street without Mrs. Stallings saying gesundheit."

"What part of Illinois are you from?"

"Anna. It's just this little dink-water town. Very Republican. Very white. I couldn't wait to get out of there. When I got out of high school, I moved to Chicago. I was there till I was thirty. And then I decided it wasn't happening for me in Chicago and I came out here. And that's the thrilling story of Penny Ruemmler!"

"You still got family back in Anna?"

"Last time I checked, my mother was still alive."

"I take it you're not close to her."

"She's only close to people she thinks will buy her a drink or loan her the rent money."

"Brothers? Sisters?"

"I had one sister."

I noted the past tense.

"What was her name?"

"Jacqueline. Jackie. She was four years older than me. She'd take care of me when Mom was off on one of her benders. When she was fourteen, she was playing softball at the park. She put her hand on a metal fence, and then she just dropped dead. A power line had come down and was touching the fence about a hundred feet away, and she got electrocuted."

"Jesus."

"Yeah. Jackie deserved better. She was the best person I ever knew. Really brave. Always determined to never let life get her down. Oh, look! What is that?"

Penny was pointing into the sky. Above the palm trees, a flashing light descended slowly. Then I saw it was a plastic toy, spinning like a helicopter. It drifted down at a slant, till it was snatched out of the air by a scrawny guy with a big brown moustache. He hooked it onto a kind of slingshot and shot it into the air again, towards the ocean. He didn't have to move a step as the breeze carried it right back to his hand.

Several people were gathered around, and they cheered and applauded his expertise. The man was selling the toys. They were called Nightfliers.

"Man," I said, "that's exactly the kind of thing I would've flipped over when I was a kid."

"Not me," said Penny. "I was a real girlie girl. I liked to play make-believe with my dolls."

We passed several tents with a lot of ragged, depressed-looking homeless men and women sitting or lying around. The long night looming ahead of them like some great, dark mountain.

"Poor people," murmured Penny.

"Yeah."

"Things are so terrible in the world. Especially since Trump got elected. How did that ever happen?"

"It was a fluke. There's going to be another election next year. Trump's going to lose, and then things will be fine. Everything will be normal again."

"I hope you're right."

"I am. You'll see."

"So what about your family? Are your parents still alive?"

"No. They died a little over a year ago."

"You mean . . . at the same time?"

"Uh-huh. Car wreck. They were on their way home from play-ing golf. They were enjoying the hell out of their retirement. They were both in really good health. They were probably good-to-go for another twenty or twenty-five years."

"How'd the wreck happen?"

"Some moron was moving a refrigerator, and it fell out of the back of his truck. I guess the only good thing about it was, they were so in love with each other, and that way neither had to bear the loss of the other."

Penny was quiet for a moment, then said, "Sounds like you really miss them."

"I do. They were good people. And for some strange reason, they always seemed to believe in me. No matter how bad I screwed up."

I felt grief beginning to clamp down on my windpipe, so I switched the subject.

"You wanna go someplace? Get a drink? Or something to eat?"

"No thanks. I should probably go soon."

"But why? You just got here."

"I have to get up really early. I have to take a friend to the airport."

"Let 'em take an Uber."

"They don't have the money for an Uber."

"I'll pay for it. How's that?"

"Dustin, you can't just go through life throwing your money around like a crazy man."

"Why not? It's my money."

Penny shook her head. "Thanks anyway."

Then we saw something remarkable: a giant, multicolored mass of flowers, with a pair of skinny legs sticking out the bottom, was walking toward us. And then a voice spoke out of the flowers: "Y'all gotta help me out here. It's the end of the night and I'm stuck with all these damn flowers."

Now we saw the face of a young black man peering out at us through his armload of bouquets.

"Sir, I got your best interests at heart. I see how the young lady here's lookin' at these flowers. I just wanna make sure you don't have to sleep on the couch tonight."

Penny laughed.

"How much?" I said.

"Ten bucks a bunch."

I gave him the ten and took a bouquet of yellow roses.

"You can have all of 'em for twenty."

"No thanks."

"Well, y'all have a nice night. And sir, just remember. Whatever happens tonight, you owe it all to me."

"Okay. I'll remember."

Penny and I watched the animate mass of flowers walk away. I handed her the roses and she stuck her nose in them.

"Thank you. They're beautiful."

We walked on. I saw a rat sniffing around an overflowing trash can. It became still as we went by, its black, dotlike eyes watching us.

We sat down on a bench. We opened the Codename: Chaos gift bag to see what goodies we had got.

A black Codename: Chaos T-shirt. Codename: Chaos cosmetics, nail enamel, hair-color creams, and body jellies. A red cotton belt with DANGER repeated again and again on it. A can of Vampyre black-cherry soda laced heavily with caffeine. A keychain with a heart bearing a message that Penny read aloud.

"Live Every Life Like It's Your Last."

"Reincarnation? Is that what it's talking about?"

"Mm-hm. I think it's kind of a neat thought, don't you? That you have lots and lots of lives."

"Sorry, but I think that's superstitious bullshit."

"So what do you believe?"

"When you die, you're dead. Your body's recycled by nature, and eventually becomes part of other bodies. Worms, birds, cows. Fat guys eating steaks at Tony Roma's. If that's any consolation."

"Oh, yeah. Just makes me feel all warm and cozy inside."

We fell silent. The moon touched the frondy tops of the palms with silver. Penny stared into her lap, fiddling with the keychain. I looked at the curve of her cheek, her coppery hair.

"Penny?"

She looked up at me. I leaned towards her and we kissed. It was a short kiss, maybe two seconds. She looked at me musingly when I moved away. Then she looked up at the sky and said, "Nice moon."

"Thank you."

"You're responsible for the moon?"

I nodded. "There wasn't supposed to be a moon tonight, but I pulled a few strings."

She smiled. I leaned in to kiss her again, but she was having none of it.

"I gotta go."

We got up, and began walking back up the boardwalk, Penny carrying the roses and I the gift bag.

"I know what," I said. "I can follow you home. Make sure you don't get carjacked."

"*I* know what. No."

We heard singing and strumming, and saw an old man walking toward us. He had a tan face and a carefully trimmed white beard, and was wearing blue jeans and a blue baseball cap. He was playing a black and orange guitar and was singing "Mystery Train" in a low, harsh voice. He nodded at us as we passed. We looked over our shoulders at him. There was something nice about the way he was obviously singing just for the fun of it as he walked alone along the edge of the windy sea.

My Maserati and her Honda Civic were parked in the same lot. We watched two punk rockers from the party running along, giggling and trying to goose each other, then they climbed into a black Lamborghini and screeched away.

I pointed at the dent in the side of the Civic.

"How'd that happen?"

"Oh, it was all my fault. I was backing out of a space at a shopping center and somebody hit me. I'm a terrible driver. I never pay attention."

I was hoping we could linger together by her car a bit, but she immediately unlocked the door and got in. She put the roses on the seat beside her, then looked up at me.

"Thanks for inviting me. I had a great time."

"Me too. So when can I see you again?"

"I don't know."

"Why don't you know?"

She didn't say anything.

"Penny?"

"Look, I understand. You just lost your wife, and you're lonely. But I'm not a stop-gap kind of a girl."

"But I really like you."

"I know. And I like *you*. I like you so much it scares me."

She started up the engine.

"Good night," she said.

"Good night."

She turned her headlights on, and began to drive off. At which point I realized I still had the gift bag. I went running after her, yelling, "Penny! Stop! Wait!"

Her brake lights flared and the car stopped. I caught up with her, and held the gift bag up in an alarmed fashion.

"You nearly left me holding the bag!"

She rolled her eyes at my feeble joke, took the bag and put it beside the roses. Now she looked back at me. Suddenly she reached up and grabbed the back of my neck and pulled my head down and kissed me. It lasted about twice as long as the first kiss.

She let me go. We looked at each other. She said, in a voice barely above a whisper: "'Night."

"'Night."

She drove away. Out of the corner of my eye I saw a flashing. I looked and there was the Nightflier, floating down slowly under the perfect moon.

27

Pete and I had got in the routine of working out together every morning, hangovers allowing. I would spend most of my time on the stationary bike because it was easy on my hip, while Pete would run on the treadmill and lift weights. This morning, Pete was curling dumbbells in front of the mirror, admiring his popping biceps, while I pedaled hard, dripping sweat, as I watched the battle of Stalingrad on the American Heroes Channel.

"I don't think it's gonna work out," said Pete.

"Huh?" I said, hardly listening; I was imagining I was a young Russian private riding my bicycle through an artillery barrage with an important message for General Chuikov.

"My job. Being your assistant. I don't think it's gonna work out."

"Why not?"

"'Cause I don't ever do anything for you."

"Not true. Just last week, you took my car in to be serviced."

"Yeah, that was really hard work. Driving through Beverly Hills in a Maserati."

"Being my assistant doesn't have to be horrible or unpleasant. It can be fun and interesting."

"I just feel weird about all the money you're paying me."

"Like I told you. Money's not an issue."

Which was not quite as true as before. The hastily dashed-off check to the Santa Monica Pet Clinic had pretty much dealt a coup de grace to mine and Laura's joint checking account. But that was okay, since I had plenty of credit cards to tide me over till I was rich.

"Hey, Prewitt?" said Pete.

The Germans and Russians were fighting each other hand to hand in the tractor factory.

"Yeah?"

"How would I go about getting hold of Matt Price?"

I quit pedaling and looked at Pete. He'd put down the dumbbells and was toweling sweat off his head and his thick neck.

"Why?"

"I just thought he'd probably like to get together with me."

"Why?"

"Well, he really wasn't anything till he played me in *Strike Four*. In a way, I made him a star."

"I doubt that Matt Price looks at it like that. Anyway, you still haven't told me why you want to see him."

"Well, in the first place, it'd be a blast. Knocking back some brewskis with Matt Price!"

"And in the second place?"

"I have an idea for a movie for him."

I was afraid to ask.

"What?"

"A sequel. To *Strike Four*. I've even got a title for it. *Strike Five*!"

"*Strike Five*'s a ridiculous title. It doesn't make any sense."

"Okay. *Strike Four Two* then."

"So what's it about? What happens?"

"Well, basically it follows my life since I got out of prison."

"But you never were in prison."

"But I was in the book. All the ups and downs of running an electrical-supply company. And man, there's been shit with women you wouldn't fucking believe!"

"I don't doubt it, but—"

"Matt would star and you'd write the script. It'd be a big hit, man! I just know it!"

"And what would your role be in all this?"

"I'd be the producer. And maybe play some small part. Bartender, old baseball buddy, something like that."

"So you're thinking about pursuing a producing and acting career in Hollywood."

"Hey, I gotta start thinking about my future. I can't just be your assistant the rest of my life."

"I don't want to pop your bubble, Pete, but I've got zero interest in writing a sequel to *Strike Four*."

"Why not?"

"It's just a bad idea. Trust me."

Pete looked disappointed.

"Okay. But I still think I'm gonna give ol' Matt a jingle. You got a number for him?"

"No. I haven't seen him since the premiere of the movie."

"Well, I'll just do what I did with you. Call his agent. You know who he's with?"

"CAA, I think. But don't get bummed out if he doesn't call you back. Movie stars like him have people coming at 'em from all sides."

"Don't worry, buddy. I can handle rejection. I know it's the name of the game out here."

I went back to pedaling, and Pete sat down at the Bowflex machine and began doing leg raises. He could see the TV in the mirror. My Stalingrad show had gone to commercials, and a trailer for *Thunder* came on. That was Dick Downward's movie. It had been out for nearly two weeks now and was playing like a monster, both here and abroad. My reluctant Polish princess was on her way to becoming an international star.

Pete and I watched Thomas Thunder, an operative with an agency so secret that even *he* didn't know its name, saving America from hordes of malevolent Muslims. When Helena rose from a

Mesopotamian marsh clad in skimpy, nearly transparent clothing, Pete exclaimed, "Holy shit, man! Look at that!"

I decided not to tell him about her and me. But the interesting thing was this: I didn't feel an intolerable stab of loss and longing at the sight of Helena. I had moved beyond her, because of Penny.

"Looks like a great movie," said Pete. "Wanna go see it?"

"I've already seen it."

"Yeah? What did you think?"

"I think you'd fucking love it."

~

Later, Larry called.

"I'm sorry about last night," he began, but I irately interrupted.

"You damn well oughta be! I can't believe all the shit you were saying!"

"I know, I know, I know," he said miserably.

"I've never seen you get that smashed before."

"But that's the thing, Dustin. I wasn't smashed! All I had was one glass of that red vodka."

"Then what the hell was wrong with you?"

"I just got off the phone with my shrink. He said this new anti-anxiety drug he put me on must've had a bad interaction with the alcohol. He said it was the equivalent of a chemical car wreck taking place in my brain. Kooby's mad at me too. Evidently Suzy Hotrod left the party in a huff because of all these lewd, horrible things I supposedly said to her. I don't remember. It's all a blur. I feel like my life's spinning out of control. Ever since Sarah left me. For that Jerry asshole. Whenever I think about Sarah and Jerry in bed together . . . !" I heard a shaky sigh. "I've been thinking a lot about buying a gun."

"And doing what with it?"

"Who knows?"

"My god. Get a grip."

"Anyway. I liked your girl. Penny. You get laid last night?"

"Not that it's any of your business, you pill-popping lunatic, but no."

"You should thank me, man."

"For what?"

"Penny. If I hadn't've lost Topper, then she never would've found him, and you guys never would've met."

I thought about it. He was right. The gate bell rang. I got off the phone with Larry and hit the intercom.

"Who's there?"

"It is Director Who Likes to Laugh!"

"Magnus!" I said, and buzzed open the gate.

He was walking up the curving drive when I opened the front door. He had my script in one hand and a white paper bag in the other.

"My genius!" he cried.

I went out to meet him and he grabbed me and hugged me and laughed. His coarse whiskers scratched my cheek.

"You read my script?"

"Yeah, you bet," he said as he finally let me go. "It is fucking fantastic."

"Thanks," I said, thrilled.

"I brought you present. From Sweden."

He thrust the white bag at me. I opened it and peered in. Wasn't sure what I was seeing.

"Licorice," Magnus said. "You like licorice?"

"Are you kidding?" I said enthusiastically.

"They make in Sweden best licorice in the whole world. In America, licorice is no good. It is like dog doodie, yeah."

I invited him in. We went in the living room. He laughed at the mystic warrior. He took a licorice stick from my bag and sat down on the down-stuffed chocolate-colored sofa. I sat down in an armchair across from him.

"So you think it's something you might be interested in directing?"

Magnus's little blue eyes squinted intently at me.

"Have you wanted ever to fuck a woman so bad you don't think about nothing else?"

"Sure."

"Sometimes I read a script and it is like woman I have to fuck. I am saying, Dustin, this to you in the form of promise: Magnus Storndrop will direct *Girl Who Likes to Laugh*!"

"Wow. That's great news!"

Zhizn eto zhizn! Life can go from shit to sugar and sugar to shit so fast it takes your breath away. It's always an ominous moment for your script when someone says he has some notes. I fetched us coffee and we began going through the script page by page. I was relieved as I realized his notes were smart and incisive. There were eight sticks of licorice in the bag. Over the course of the next two hours, Magnus devoured seven of them. I pretended to take an occasional nibble of the eighth, breaking off small bits of it and sticking them in my pocket or hiding them under the seat cushion when Magnus wasn't watching.

28

Penny and I had dinner at a restaurant on Pico in Santa Monica. It was dimly lit, like I like, quiet so we could talk, or rather so I could talk and she could listen, because I was made voluble by vodka tonics prepared by a pretty young bartender with long brown braids. Our table was near the bar, a magnificent structure of carved mahogany, with an elegant arch containing mirrored rows of coolly glistening liquor bottles. I ate beef short ribs and she ate wild Columbia River sturgeon as I regaled her with tales of Hollywood, of the bad and the beautiful, and the quick and the dead, and I had her laughing so much that heads were turning though not in irritation because who wouldn't be charmed by Penny Ruemmler's laugh?

Our waiter came by and asked us how we were doing in the drink department. I was tempted to get a third vodka tonic, then decided not to. I wanted to keep my edge, since I intended to have my way with Penny before the night was through. On her part, Penny had hardly touched her glass of Sleepy Hollow Chardonnay.

"I take it you're not much of a drinker," I said.

She shrugged. "I used to drink a lot. I have to be careful with it now."

"Really?"

"I used to do everything a lot."

"Are you talking about drugs?"

"Yeah. I even married my drug dealer."

"What was his name?"

"Rick."

"What was Rick like?"

She thought about it.

"Here's what Rick was like. We had a cat named Elvira. One day I came home from work, and found Rick passed out in front of the TV. And Elvira had had a litter of kittens in his lap!"

She laughed, and took a sip of the Sleepy Hollow.

"Of course, it's not like I was any prize. If Rick's still alive, he's probably telling stories about his crazy exwife Penny."

"How long were you married?"

"Four years. When I left Rick, I left Chicago too. Just jumped in my crummy car with Elvira and headed west. They call it the geographic cure in A.A. Where you think it'll help you kick your addiction if you move somewhere else. But it seems to have actually worked in my case. Knock wood," and she knocked on the table twice. "What about you? Any pre-Laura Keene wives?"

As I indicated earlier, the subject of my first wife is a black hole from which not a single illuminative ray of light will be permitted to escape, so I'll be forced to skip over the rest of this conversation. We finished off our ribs and fish, then shared a piece of warm apple pecan crumble pie. Then I heard "Dustin," as a hand fell on my shoulder.

I looked up. It was Ben Benjamin.

"Ben!"

"Don't get up," said Ben, but I got up anyway and we shook hands.

"Ben, this is Penny. Penny, this is Ben Benjamin. He used to be my agent."

Ben and Penny exchanged pleased-to-meet-you's. He looked crisp and perfect as usual, in a blue and white seersucker suit. I asked him if he'd like to join us.

"No, I won't intrude. I'm here with Miriam," and he gestured toward a table on the other side of the room, where sat a handsome, blue-eyed woman with obviously dyed bright-orange hair. Rumor had it that he had met her right after he had got out of the joint and that she had helped him to go straight. She smiled and waggled her fingers at me, and I waved back.

"So how are things with you, Dustin?" Ben said solemnly in his growly voice.

"Great. Remember that spec script I wrote? *The Ladies' Man*?"

"Of course."

"Well, Magnus Storndrop loves it, and wants to make it his next movie."

"Well, that's wonderful news. Storndrop's a bit unstable, but he's a very talented fellow."

"Unstable?"

"One hears things, about this and that . . . mental hospitals, restraining orders, and so forth and so on . . . but I'm sure it's all been greatly exaggerated," and then his demeanor changed, and he began rubbing the bump on his nose. "I suppose you heard about Brian Nasry."

"No," I said, my blood running cold. "Is he dead?"

"No, but it was a close call. I talked to his father. Brian and the fellow that was working with him, I forgot his name—"

"Grayson Neihardt?"

"He and Neihardt were with a rebel group in Syria in some terrible, bombed-out city. An artillery shell landed right in the middle of them. Several of the rebels were killed, and Neihardt suffered a serious injury to his leg."

"My god! Was Brian hurt?"

"He was knocked unconscious, and he had several shrapnel wounds, nothing life-threatening fortunately. They were trapped in the city for days with no real medical care. Finally the rebels got them back across the border into Turkey."

"Jesus. Where's Brian now?"

"He and Neihardt are in a hospital in Ankara, recovering. But

Neihardt's leg had become infected and they had to amputate it. The poor bastard."

I shook my head. "Ben, I can't believe this."

"But listen to this. Brian's father is with him now. He's begging Brian to come back to America with him, but Brian refuses. He says as soon as he recovers and he gets a replacement for Neihardt, he's going back into Syria and finish his film."

~

Penny and I had come separately to the restaurant; this time when I suggested I follow her home, she didn't say no. She lived in Mar Vista, and as I tailed her Honda Civic as it headed east then south, I tried to get my mind around what Ben had told me.

Brian Nasry a wounded hero in a savage faraway land! He'd been just like me, dismayed by the unending catastrophes we human beings inflict on one another, and for a while it had been enough for him just to watch CNN and MSNBC and shake his head and sigh and be sickened by what he saw. But then something had happened in Brian's brain. He had chosen to step through the looking glass, to enter into the nightmare and document it. *And* (and here I banged the heel of my hand on the steering wheel as the thought came to me with the ecstatic force of a revelation) if Brian could do it . . . *so could I!*

I would begin making plans tomorrow to join Brian in Ankara. I would be Grayson Neihardt's replacement. I mean, how hard could it be to learn to work a video camera? I had always been interested in war, and now I would do the Hemingway thing and find out for myself what it was all about. People in the fancy eateries of Los Angeles would say: "Did you hear about Dustin Prewitt? He went to Syria to make a documentary about the civil war!" Boy, would Brian be surprised when I walked into that hospital.

The left turn signal on Penny's Civic began to throb, and my Maserati followed as she turned off Centinela onto Charnock. It would be tough, I thought, to leave Penny behind, and then I realized with a mixture of disappointment and relief that the idea that I was about to catch a plane to the Middle East was just more of the same old Dustin Prewitt bullshit.

29

Penny lived on the interestingly named, considering her background, Stoner Avenue. It was a densely populated street, and it wasn't easy to find a place to park. Finally I squeezed into a space in front of a small green stucco house. Three young Latino males were standing around in the yard drinking beer. As I got out and shut the door, they eyed me and my silver Maserati in a way that made me nervous.

"How's it goin'?" I said, perhaps a little too loudly and heartily.

"Great, man. Thanks for askin'," said Looks Like a Dangerous Gangster But Is Probably a Perfectly Nice and Hard-Working Young Man Number One.

"I like your fuckin' car," said Looks Like Etc. Number Two.

"Don't worry, man," said the third guy. "We won't let nobody steal it."

"Thanks," I said.

"No problem," said the first guy.

Penny had the lower right unit in a blue cement quadruplex with white trim. She was next door at Mrs. Stallings' retrieving Topper as I came up. My intense yearning to see Topper was the ostensible reason I had come here.

"Hey, Topper!" I said. "It's me!"

He looked around, and I saw his face clearly register unpleasant surprise. Penny introduced me to Mrs. Stallings. She was small and hunched-over, and had a nimbus of white hair which her pink scalp glowed through. She extended a hand that felt to me as dry, fragile, and weightless as a bird's nest.

"Nice to meet you, Mrs. Stallings."

She scrutinized my face. "You know who you look like?"

"No, who?"

"Tyrone Power. And you probably don't have a clue who that is."

"I love Tyrone Power. *The Mask of Zorro. The Razor's Edge. Captain from Castile.*"

Mrs. Stallings looked pleased.

"To me, actors today are just a bunch of mumbling bums, but Tyrone Power was every inch a movie star. I saw him once with Lana Turner, at a nightclub called Ciro's. He smiled at me. I didn't imagine it. He really did," and then she shook her finger in my face, as if daring me to disagree with her. "They said he was the best swordsman in Hollywood! They said that in a real fight, he would have cut Errol Flynn to ribbons!" and then she sighed. "He died so young."

"How did he die?" asked Penny.

"He was making a movie, in Spain, I believe. He was filming a dueling scene, one of those furious sword fights he was so famous for. And he had a massive heart attack and dropped dead on the spot!" and then she peered thoughtfully up at me. "He was probably just about your age, Mr. Prewitt."

We took our leave of Mrs. Stallings, and went into Penny's apartment. A pudgy black and white cat curled up in an armchair lifted its head and blinked at us.

"Hi, Miranda," said Penny, and she petted her. The white blades of a ceiling fan whirled and stirred up the air.

"Sorry it's so hot in here," she said. "The air conditioner's on the fritz. The landlord's been promising to fix it."

"It's not that hot. Don't worry about it."

"I gotta feed Topper. Have a seat. You want something to drink?"

"Okay. Whatcha got?"

"I think I have a bottle of red wine somewhere."

"Sounds good."

She left. I looked around the living room. There was a blue calico couch with a red-ladybug and yellow-daisy pattern. The butter-yellow armchair with the cat in it. A battered wooden trunk serving as a coffee table. A standing lamp with an ivory shade with elephants walking around it, the trunk of each holding on to the tail of the one ahead of it.

I had come here with one idea: to get Penny out of her clothes quickly and efficiently, with no wasted motion, as though I were peeling a banana. In pursuance of that goal, I entered the kitchen.

It was small, with old appliances. An open door gave onto a tiny back yard. Topper was crunching up kibble from a gleaming silver bowl. Penny stood with her back to me on her tiptoes, peering into a cupboard, moving bottles and cans around. She glanced over her shoulder at me as I moved forward.

"I know it's here someplace—"

I put my hands on her waist, plunged my lips into her hair. I felt her shiver as I found her ear and then her neck, but then she laughed and shrugged me off. She returned to the cupboard, then "Here it is," she said.

She turned to me, holding up a bottle of wine.

"All I got's Two Buck Chuck."

"That's fine."

She pulled the cork out of the bottle. It was about half full. She took two drinking glasses from the cupboard.

"Sorry, I don't have any wine glasses."

"That's fine too."

She poured and we clinked glasses and said cheers and sipped.

"Maybe you'd like to go out in the back yard and play with Topper," she said.

"Love to. Just as soon as I finish my wine."

We went back in the living room. I gestured at the elephant lamp. "I like that. Where'd you get it?"

"Garage sale. For ten dollars."

We sat down on the couch. On the coffee-table trunk was a shiny sculpture of a naked guy, reclining, his genitals lolling on an indolent thigh. "Garage sale?" I said.

"No. I did that."

"No kidding."

"Uh-huh. You like it?"

"Yeah. So you sculpt."

She shrugged. "I've taken a few classes. This is the only thing I've done that I thought was halfway decent."

"What's it made out of? Bronze?"

"No, just clay. I fired it and patina'd it with different paints. Making a bronze is expensive."

"Laura was really into art. Buying it, not making it. We had a pretty valuable collection of paintings. But they're gone now. They all got stolen."

"Oh, that's awful. Do you have any idea who did it?"

"I know exactly who did it. I was there when they did it. They tied me up. I thought they were going to kill me."

"When did this happen?"

I found myself telling Penny all about Pete, Jodi, Sluggo, and me. I hadn't talked about it before except with the police and an unsympathetic and insultingly suspicious fat-assed pantsuited insurance lady and Larry Hochheiser. Because of the brief notoriety I had attained after the death of my wife, I knew the media would have jumped all over this, but I was able to keep it from them. In the weeks since, it had been like some black terrible bird that was always perched upon my shoulder but that only I could see.

When I got through, Penny reached out, touched one of my suddenly graying temples. "Jesus. You've been through a tough time."

It felt good the way her brown eyes were looking at me. A skinny orange tabby cat came walking into the room.

"Who's that?" I said.

"That's Ralph. I found him hiding under a car in a Ralphs parking lot." Ralph sniffed at her leg and mewed, and she bent down and scratched his ear. "You were so little and so scared, weren't you, baby?"

"How does Topper get along with the cats?"

"Oh, fine. They just kind of ignore each other. When Topper gets too close, they'll hiss at him, and he'll back off."

"So where's Elvira?"

"She died. About three years ago. Cancer."

"Sorry."

"But I know her spirit's still here. She had a funny little croaky meow, and I hear it sometimes when I'm about to fall asleep. And sometimes when I'm at the sink washing dishes, I can feel a cat rubbing up against my legs and I'll look down and nobody's there and I know it's Elvira."

I nodded solemnly—trying not to look too skeptical. She laughed and leaned toward me, and we kissed for a bit, and I became lost in the moistness and sweetness of the lips of Penny Ruemmler. Time to peel that banana. But my hand hadn't been on one of her breasts for more than three or four seconds when there came a sound in such a low register that I seemed to be less hearing it than feeling its vibrations on my skin. Our heads turned. Topper was standing a foot away. Teeth bared and body trembling.

"Topper! Bad dog!" said Penny, and then she got up. "I'll put him in the back yard." She grabbed his collar and escorted him out. "Sorry, boy. Out you go."

She was back in my arms quickly. Ralph had jumped up in the chair with Miranda, and it looked as if the two of them and Elvira's ghost were about to get an eyeful. But then something changed. Penny's body seemed to tense up. She pushed my hand away from one breast and then the other. I moved back from her and said, "What's the matter?"

She turned her head away. The fair skin of her cheeks and neck bore a rosy flush. Her red-blonde hair was lit by the elephant lamp and was blowing a bit in the breeze from the fan.

"Penny?"

"This is crazy."

"What is?"

"You and me."

"It's not crazy. Why do you say that?"

"We're so different. We're from different worlds. It'll never work out."

"Now *that's* crazy."

"Dinner was wonderful. Thank you. But I think you better go."

"You serious?"

She nodded. I could have argued with her some more, but I suddenly felt exhausted and exasperated. Maybe I *would* go to Syria. I took a baffled gulp of my wine, and got up.

"Fine. Whatever you say."

We walked to the door.

"You don't really want me to go, do you?"

"Yes."

"I'll call you tomorrow."

"Good night, Dustin. Drive safe."

And then I was expelled into outer darkness. I walked slowly down the deserted street. The air was hot and still. The world was becoming unhinged. I couldn't figure Penny out. She definitely didn't strike me as the frigid type. I suspected there was something she wasn't telling me. She was gay. She was being stalked by a deranged exboyfriend. She was a man.

I reached my car. The three beer drinkers were no longer in the yard of the green house, but three empty cans of Bud Light were lined up neatly on my hood. Not wanting to litter, I gathered up the cans and took them inside the car with me.

I'd gone only a few blocks when my phone rang. As I pulled it out of my pocket I smiled a little because I was positive it was a repentant Penny, wanting me to come back.

"Hello?"

"Alex! You motherfucker!"

It was a snarling drunken female voice.

"This isn't Alex. You have the wrong number."

"You're gonna die, you asshole!"

I repocketed my phone. Drove home, and dreamt that night of blood and fire.

30

I woke up late. On my way outside to get the paper, I found Pete in the living room. He was sitting on the sofa, wearing a stained pair of Pitt Panther gym shorts, and having one of his favorite meals: a plate of microwaved corndogs.

"You know, Pete, I think I've told you before I'd kind of rather you not eat in here."

"Oh, right. I forgot. Sorry," he said, continuing to eat. He was staring at the mystic warrior. "I can just look at this thing all day. What a piece of art, huh?"

I sat down on the sofa beside Pete, and looked at the statue.

"So you really like it."

"Yeah."

"It's yours."

Pete gave me a surprised look.

"Get outa here."

"You *should* have it. You like it a lot more than me. Plus, it's got some painful memories tied up with it. Laura bought that on the last day we spent together. I'd just as soon not be reminded of it."

Pete chewed on his corndog and gazed upon the statue.

"I'll treasure it, man. For the rest of my life. And I don't care if it's worth a million bucks someday, I won't ever part with it."

He picked up a yellow squeeze bottle of mustard and squirted a squiggly yellow line on a new corndog.

"Wanna go to the Dodgers game tonight?" I asked. "They're playing the Cardinals."

"Aw, I'd love to, buddy. But I got a hot date."

"Really? Who with?"

"Just this girl I met."

"Come on. Give me some details. Where'd you meet her?"

"'Member the Fourth of July? When I went out to Marina del Rey to see the fireworks? I met her there."

"What's her name?"

"Irene."

"How old is this Irene? Sixteen? Eighteen?"

"Hey, I learned my lesson with Jodi. Irene's no kid. She's probably nearly thirty."

"God. So old. Does she get around without a walker?"

"She gets around just fine. In fact, she walks so fast I have trouble keeping up with her."

"What does she do?"

"Works in an eye doctor's office."

"So you got in her pants yet?"

Pete grinned.

"Oh yeah. I been pounding some serious pussy."

"I thought you seemed like you were in a really good mood lately."

"Nothing like getting laid, buddy. Does wonders for the old self-esteem."

"You haven't been bringing her here, have you? When I'm not around?"

"No. But what are you saying? I can't bring girls here?"

"I'm just a little concerned about getting tied up and robbed again by one of your girls. That's all I'm saying."

"Irene's not like that."

"Good."

I got the paper and went to my office. "Planet To Die Tomorrow, Leading Scientists Say," was the main headline. A smaller headline read: "Experts Call For Mass Evacuations Via Spaceships And Time Machines."

I called Penny at work. Renée picked up the phone. She told me Penny had just stepped out but she would have her call me the moment she returned. I had been doing some desultory research on my noir novel, so while waiting for Penny I got on a website that had the prices of things in the 1930s. A dozen eggs cost eighteen cents in Ohio in 1932. A Packard Club sedan cost $2995 in California in 1933. Applesauce cost—

The phone rang. Penny!

But I got faked out again.

"Dustin!" roared Magnus Storndrop. "I have got fantastic fucking news!"

31

Magnus told me his manager had given *The Girl Who Liked to Laugh* to Martin Joiner, president of a company called Monarch Pictures. Monarch was a big independent that financed its own films and released them through Warner Bros. Joiner had flipped over my script and wanted to meet on it as soon as possible.

The next evening, I was waiting outside my front gate for Magnus to pick me up. We were supposed to meet Joiner for dinner at a restaurant in Beverly Hills at 7:30, and it was already 7:38. I pulled out my phone and was in the process of placing an anxious call to Magnus when a royal-blue Aston Martin DB9 appeared, accelerating down the street as if Bedford Drive were but a drag strip. It screeched to a stop in front of me, then Magnus was yelling, "Hurry up, you fucking Dustin!" and beeping his horn.

Magnus and I had been hitting it off famously. At our script meetings, we would drink cup after cup of black heavily sugared coffee and eat candy and mixed nuts and swap stories about wild women we had known and he would laugh until he turned purple and sometimes he would rant about his faithless French wife, an actress living in Paris, which would also make him turn purple. He said our souls were brothers and we had perhaps known each other in a past life. We discussed other projects. He wanted to do a movie about Emanuel Swedenborg, the Swedish mystic who conversed with angels. I feigned interest in that, then gave him a copy of *Tender Is the Night*.

Now I got in his car and we took off. Palm trees whipped by us dizzyingly on both sides, as if we had entered some kind of space-time tunnel from which we'd emerge on the opposite side of the universe. Magnus was looking at me with his blue jolly eyes.

"You will see, Dustin, a movie with Magnus Storndrop is like going up Amazon River in small leaky boat or racing to South Pole but getting lost in blizzard and you must eat the poor sled dogs. You understand? It is life and death struggle to make a great movie, yeah. And more fun than even fucking!"

"Sounds great, Magnus," I said, tensely watching the road since Magnus was paying no apparent attention to it. "By the way, we're approaching," and then I shouted, "*a stop sign!*"

Magnus laughed, and slammed on the brakes. We skidded to a stop in the middle of the intersection, then sped off again.

As we headed east through Beverly Hills, "Twist and Shout" came on the radio. Magnus reached over and excitedly grabbed my arm.

"Dustin, Dustin! When I was young skinny boy in Sweden I was in band and we always play this song! It is sign of good luck, yeah. Tonight is very lucky for you and me!"

Since moving to L.A., I had often had the unsettling sensation that I was a real person living in a fictitious place, and as I listened to Magnus beginning to sing along with the Beatles in Swedish, I felt that way now.

~

The restaurant occupied a huge, loftlike space on the ground floor of an office building on Wilshire. It was very modern and loud and crowded, with a New York, Soho-ish feel. The front was lined with booths with big windows looking out on the street. Magnus and I followed a beautiful hostess to one of the booths and Martin Joiner.

He was absorbed in his phone, but he jumped up when he saw

us and shook our hands with the strong grip of a short man. He was wearing a lightweight cream-colored suit with a dark-blue shirt and a crazy psychedelic-looking tie with a disembodied eye in the middle of it. The whiskers of his meticulous beard were about a quarter of an inch long and merged with his close-cropped hair so that beard and hair seemed to make a single seamless thing.

"Sorry we're late," I said.

"No problem," said Martin Joiner. "I just got here myself."

I suspected that wasn't true; he probably just didn't want to admit he'd been there for more than a minute or two since a measure of power in Hollywood is who's kept waiting on whom and for how long.

Magnus and I slid into the booth across from him.

"What a fucking tie," said Magnus.

"Oh, you like it?" Joiner looked down at his tie and gave it a saucy flip. "I was just down in BVI with my family, and my daughter bought it for me. Which means I have to wear it at least once! An old American hippie has a shop down there filled with shit like this. He says he eats bushels of psilocybin mushrooms and then just paints what he sees."

"At the risk of sounding unhip," I said, "what's BVI?"

"British Virgin Islands. One of my favorite places. Those people down there really know how to live."

A waiter handed us menus and asked if we wanted drinks. Magnus ordered an Absolut martini, which made it seem okay for me to order a Glenlivet on the rocks. Joiner wanted a Red Bull cocktail.

"I've been your biggest fan for years," said Joiner, obviously not speaking to me. "And I'm just incredibly thrilled to finally be getting into the Magnus Storndrop business."

"So you're gonna make this fucking movie, yeah?"

"If the stars align, I don't see why not. And I'm talking about of course movie stars. Who do you see in the lead?"

"We both think Bradley Cooper would be a terrific Eric," I said. "And for the girl we're thinking—"

"Who cares about the girl? We can have our pick of girls. The actresses in this town will mud-wrestle each other to get a decent part."

A busboy brought bread, butter, and water. Joiner clammed up, as though he might be a spy.

"Brad's a good friend of mine," he went on when the busboy left. "I think he'd respond to this. And I can put the script right into his hands."

Take my word for it. This is how movies happen! I was dealing directly with the big boys, circumventing all of the bullshit. A year from now, *The Girl Who Liked to Laugh* might be in three thousand theaters, might even be "the laff riot of the summer"!

Magnus stuffed some thickly buttered bread into his little red mouth and said, "Fifty."

"Fifty?" said Joiner.

"Budget for fucking movie. Not penny under fifty."

"Well, of course it depends on the cast. And logistically the movie seems pretty simple. But I don't think fifty is wildly out of line."

The waiter came back with our drinks. I grabbed my scotch and lifted it up.

"To the movie," I said ebulliently, and we all clinked glasses.

"To the movie," said Joiner.

"What a fucking tie," said Magnus.

~

I had followed up my scotch with a glass of a nicely dry Australian Riesling, and was enjoying a delicious dinner of sand dabs, shoe-string potatoes, and coleslaw. Joiner was having the grilled halibut, and Magnus was slicing his way through a thick, practically raw steak. Joiner didn't seem like such a bad guy for a movie executive. He had a decent sense of humor and was a Yankees fan. And we had great though not very gentlemanly fun comparing notes when we discovered that as younger men we both had dated a certain wild young D-girl who was presently the plump, self-important president of production at one of the major studios. Magnus laughed heartily as he listened to us, opening his mouth and showing us his chewed-up food.

Maybe it was the martinis that Magnus was quaffing like water. Or maybe it was simply that Magnus was mad, as Ben Benjamin had hinted. At any rate, disaster struck. Magnus said to Joiner: "Take off fucking tie."

Joiner stared at Magnus.

"What?"

Magnus gestured at Joiner's tie with his knife.

"Take fucking tie off."

"Why?"

"I don't like the goddamn thing."

"You're joking, right?"

"No. Not joking."

"Magnus," I said, "come on. Just relax. Eat your steak."

"Dustin, I don't like goddamn tie of Martin."

"What about it bothers you?"

"I was in Siberia making movie, and I was very sad. I want to blow my brains off, yeah. And then shaman says he will make me to feel better and he gives me mushrooms to eat. Just like fucking hippie in BVI! And I fall asleep and go to crazy place of spirits. Beautiful Siberian girl takes me into hut and takes clothes off, and I am about to fuck her but she turns into wolf and tries to kill me. And so I run out of hut and run through fucking snow without no clothes on, yeah. I see tree with big eyeball in the trunk. And I know it is evil eye, yeah, most evil eye in all of world."

Magnus's face had gotten very red, and there was a shine of sweat on his forehead. Now he pointed across the table with his knife at the eye on Joiner's tie. "Eye on tree looks like that eye, yeah."

"Magnus," Joiner said, "I think you've had a little too much to drink—"

Hoarsely screaming some horrible Swedish oath, Magnus lunged across the table at Joiner. He grabbed Joiner's tie with one hand and with the other hand started trying to cut it off with his knife. Joiner, gasping and grunting, unsuccessfully tried to pry loose Magnus's hands, then he grabbed a handful of Magnus's beard and began twisting and pulling on it. Magnus bellowed and water, wine, and martini glasses toppled and broke as I tried to get in between them and push them apart.

"Stop it, guys, stop it!" I said, and then at about the same moment Joiner cried out in pain and clutched his chest, and like a Comanche taking the scalp of a dying cowboy, Magnus held high with a laugh of triumph the two severed ends of Joiner's tie.

"I've been stabbed!" Joiner said in disbelief. "He stabbed me!"

I couldn't believe it either. "Let's see."

Joiner was panting in a panicky way; now he moved his hand to reveal a small dark splotch on his blue shirt.

"See? I'm bleeding!"

He unbuttoned his shirt with trembling fingers and pulled it open. Near his right nipple, a small cut trickled blood.

Magnus gave a derisive snort.

"You call that bleeding? When bear attack me in Siberia, that was fucking bleeding, yeah," and then he stood up.

I thought he was about to pull down his pants and show us his mangled butt.

"Magnus, what are you doing?"

"I am going to take piss."

Then Magnus tossed the tie down on the table and walked away, scratching his beard and laughing to himself.

We had created a bit of a stir, of course. People all around us were gaping in alarm and holding up their cellphones toward us. Now I saw the busboy talking to our waiter, and pointing in our direction.

Joiner was dabbing at his wound with his napkin.

"Martin, are you all right? Do you want me to call 911?"

"Christ, no. The last thing I want to do is make a big scene."

The waiter came over. He was a sensitive-looking young man, almost certainly an actor. His face blanched as he looked at the bloodstained napkin and the shards of broken glass that littered the table and glittered in the remnants of our food.

"What happened?"

"Just a little horseplay that got out of hand," I said. "Everything's fine now."

"That's right," said Joiner, then he took out his wallet and handed the waiter a credit card. "Could you take care of this for me quickly please?"

"Yes sir."

Our waiter hurried off. Joiner began to slide out of the booth.

"I'm going to get out of here before that lunatic gets back."

"What about the movie?"

"What movie?"

Now Joiner stood above me—not very far above me, since he was a short man—still holding the napkin to his chest under the stumps of what was left of his tie. Whatever look was on my face seemed to elicit his pity.

"Look, Dustin. For me this falls into the life's-too-short category. But you've written a nice script, and Storndrop's a hot director. I'm sure you'll be able to get it set up somewhere."

"Thanks for dinner."

He nodded, and walked off.

The busboy came over. He was hardly a boy though. He was probably pushing fifty. He had a sad, pockmarked face. He, too, seemed to feel sorry for me, and gave me a kind smile as he cleaned up the mess. Only one thing was left on the table when he was done. Joiner's tie.

The eye stared up at me.

I turned the tie over, eye-down on the table.

It seemed as if Magnus was taking an inordinate amount of time in the men's room. I looked out the window as I waited at the traffic passing on Wilshire. And then I saw Magnus driving by at the wheel of his Aston Martin.

I just sat there in the booth for another minute or two, my mind more or less blank. Then I took out my phone. I was going to call Pete to come get me. But then I remembered that Pete had said he was going out with Irene tonight.

I decided to walk home. It wasn't far, and a walk would be nice. I could burn off some of the calories from the tasty meal that now seemed to sit in my stomach like a lump of lead.

A hot dry wind was blowing hard down Wilshire between the tall buildings. It blew at my back, and seemed to impel me along. I felt almost as though, if I were to start running down the sidewalk and flap my arms, the wind would pick me right up, and I could fly down the wide, meandering boulevard till I looked beneath me and saw the white statue of Saint Monica, and then the sea.

32

The next morning, Pete and I drove to the Pavilions on Olympic and Beverly. Pete pushed the shopping cart and I strolled alongside. We loaded up on food of the meat-and-potatoes, early-death-inducing variety, since Pete did most of the cooking and that was what he liked.

A tall, leggy redhead in Capri pants was standing in front of a pile of dark-green avocados, picking through and palpating them with her slender, many-ringed fingers.

Pete grinned at her as we passed, but the brief look she gave us couldn't have been less interested.

Pete shook his head. "When we're out shopping together, women completely ignore us. And I think I've just figured out why."

"Why?"

"They think we're a couple of aging fags."

"Could be."

"You think you're born a fag or become a fag?"

"Born. But Pete, you oughta be careful about throwing the word 'fag' around out here. You're not in Pittsburgh anymore. Some people might be offended."

"Yeah, fags might be offended."

"Just say 'gay,' all right?"

"All right. What kinda ketchup you like?"

"It doesn't matter."

"Heinz?"

"Fine."

"What kinda bottle you want? They got all these different kinds of bottles."

"Pete, I really don't care."

My phone rang. I looked at the number. It was Penny.

I'd been leaving her messages for the last two days that she hadn't been returning. Now my smitten heart leapt as I said, "Hello?"

"Hi. It's Penny."

"Hi, Penny. How are you?"

"I'm okay. I'm sorry I took so long to call you back."

"That's okay."

"I hope I'm not interrupting your writing or anything."

"No. Just grocery shopping with Pete."

Pete, I noticed, was listening closely, so I stopped and let him trundle the cart away up the aisle.

"Are you at work?" I said.

"No, I took the day off. I'm about to take Topper on a hike. Do you want to come?"

33

I dashed home and donned my hiking togs then drove to Stoner Avenue to pick up Penny and Topper.

Penny looked cute in her long khaki shorts and chartreuse T-shirt and hiking boots with chartreuse socks and big floppy hat and big sunglasses. I popped the trunk so she could put away her backpack.

"So where are we going?" I said.

"Will Rogers Park. It's one of the only parks around here that still allows dogs, if you can believe it. It's getting harder and harder to find a place to take your dog in L.A."

"That's outrageous. A dog like Topper should be allowed to go wherever he wants to go."

Penny tousled Topper's fur. "I agree."

We drove up the PCH. The day was hot and cloudless and there were a lot of people swimming in the sparkling magic sea. Some kids were flying a blue Dumbo kite and I was happy to be with Penny and even with Topper and I had a Beach Boys album playing. *"Round round, get around, I get around . . ."* Penny looked over at me and smiled and there was something in the smile that made me think she was in love with me and then I turned off the highway onto Chautauqua and then onto Sunset and then it was just a short jog to the northeast to the turnoff for the park.

I paid twelve bucks to a guy in a green uniform in a booth, and drove to a parking lot. Will Rogers, the great humorist and movie star, mostly forgotten now except for a witty remark or two, had a ranch here back in Hollywood's golden age. South of the parking lot was a polo field, where Will used to gallop around with buddies like Clark Gable and Gary Cooper and Mrs. Stallings' favorite, Tyrone Power. We got our backpacks out of the trunk then slathered on sunscreen. A car rolled by, an old man at the wheel and a gigantic dog in the back seat. It had its basketball-sized head stuck out of the window and thunderously woofed at Topper. Topper went berserk, barking and lunging at the end of his leash and rearing up and pawing the air like an out-of-control polo pony. Whatever else you could say about Topper, he was a feisty little fucker who never backed down from anybody or anything.

"Look at all the grass!" said Penny, gazing out on the polo field. "Topper loves to run in the grass!"

She and Topper ran down a gentle slope and onto the field. I sat down on a bench and watched them. They zigged and zagged, Penny laughing and Topper expelling joyful laughlike barks. It was true, I remembered, Topper did love to run in the grass. When he was a puppy, I used to play chase with him in our big yard in Mandeville Canyon, but as the novelty of having a dog had worn off, I had played with him less and less and then not at all. Maybe that was where the rift had started.

I think I've made clear I am not a mystic kind of guy, but I have to admit a funny thing happened. I seemed to be seeing Penny and Topper not from where I sat on the bench but from the point of view of a crow or an eagle, floating high above the trees, higher even than the encircling hills. They were very small against the vivid green grass as they laughed and ran upon it. Penny in her chartreuse shirt and Topper in his auburn coat seemed less like the children of time and chance than indestructible beings, an eternal dog and an eternal girl.

The hiking trail led up through tall eucalyptus trees. We were headed toward Inspiration Point. Steady walking would have gotten us there in twenty minutes or so, but Topper dawdled, barking at skittering gray lizards and pawing at a brown-green mound of horse manure and pissing on a bush and taking a dump.

"Do you go hiking a lot?" I asked Penny.

"Probably once or twice a month. I'd go more, if I had time. I love to hike. How about you?"

"Can't say I'm a big fan of the Great Outdoors. I've spent a lot of time outside in my life, but mostly playing sports."

"I'm terrible at sports. When I was in grade school, one time we were playing softball, and they put me in the outfield. I was happy about that, since balls hardly ever got hit out there, but then one time this girl hit the ball really hard and it came my way. I started running to get it, but then I stepped in a bee hole. Some of the bees flew up and stung me, and I jumped around and hollered, and all my teammates were yelling at me to get the ball but I didn't. The girl just kept running around the bases till she scored a home run."

I laughed. She hit my arm and told me it wasn't funny. Suddenly a guy wearing tight black shorts and a green and black helmet came careening around a curve on a mountain bike. I grabbed Penny and she pulled Topper's leash and the three of us jumped out of the way as the guy flew past us down the hill.

"Slow down!" I shouted at him, and he called back over his shoulder, "Sorry!"

"Hiking's dangerous," I said.

"No it's not," said Penny.

We continued up the broad, pebbly path. Vistas widened out and we began to catch glimpses of the ocean at this turning or that. The eucalypti stopped abruptly and left us shadeless. We began to sweat and thirst. Topper's tongue was hanging out. Penny and I took bottles of water out of our packs and drank and Penny knelt and poured water in a collapsible plastic container for Topper to lap.

A hawk went dreamily drifting over the brushy hills and canyons. We also saw a mockingbird and five crows.

My hip began to hurt and I was limping by the time we reached Inspiration Point. We had a panoramic view of the ocean, hills, and city. A woman built like a fireplug and covered with tattoos was up there peering through binoculars like Patton. One tat depicted a ferocious but beautiful bare-breasted angel with a submachine gun; another said "SHE-MONSTER" in flaming yellow letters. But as formidable as she was, she just went icky and gooey when she saw Topper.

"Oh, that's just the cutest dog! Look at those *ears*!"

He graciously allowed her to pet and fuss over him without attacking her.

The woman left, and we sat down at a picnic table. Though inspiring things could indeed by seen from there, Inspiration Point itself was a rather bleak, ugly spot. The only shade was provided by the picnic table, which Topper immediately plopped down under. Penny had packed lunch: tuna salad sandwiches and Oreo cookies for her and me, salmon chips for Topper. And I pulled from my pack plastic cups, a corkscrew, and a bottle of Panilonco, a cheap Chilean wine that I liked.

The picnic table was weather-beaten and gray with just a few green flecks of paint clinging to it. A brisk wind came off the ocean. We had to put our water bottles on the paper napkins to keep them from blowing away.

I poured the wine and it sparkled in the sunlight and we drank.

"Like it?" I asked.

"Mm," said Penny, nodding.

"Why'd you throw me out of your apartment?"

"I didn't."

"You did."

She was silent. I could hear Topper under the table crunching up his salmon chips.

"Penny?"

"I got scared."

"Of what?"

She shrugged.

"So does the fact you're here with me now mean you're not scared anymore?"

"I'm not sure what it means."

I poured myself some more wine. The sun shined through the cup and threw on the gray table a dancing red dab of light.

We finished lunch and then just stared oceanward as if hypnotized by the sky and water. Seven or eight seagulls were like a flurry of white dots fleeing down the coast.

"The perfect time for a joint," Penny sighed wistfully.

Topper began to bark. A gaunt bearded man was walking up the hill toward us. With him was a lean greyhound. I put a cork in what was left of the wine and we dropped our trash in a barrel and headed back down the trail. We walked by a thicket of small trees. A narrow path descended into it.

"Wonder where that goes," I said.

"Let's find out," said Penny.

It went straight down the hill and met up again with the main trail as it looped around. But just before it ended another path went off to the right. A sun-dappled tunnel through the trees. It seemed like an enchanted path in a fable. Penny said, "Oh, let's go that way!"

I liked it much better than the roadlike trail we'd been on before. One could imagine one was in real wilderness here. No other people within hundreds of miles.

The Daniel Boone feeling was dispelled when we saw a young woman jogging toward us, her blonde hair in a metronomically swinging ponytail, boobs bouncing under a T-shirt that bore the sober message: "Prepare now for an overheating planet."

We came out of the thicket and the trail continued along the side of the steep, brush-covered hill. We could see in the distance below us a patch of green, the polo field. We decided we could follow the trail all the way down.

I was beginning to limp more and more and, my pioneer spirit waning fast, was glad the hike would soon be over. The wine had stimulated my kidneys and I needed to pee. I told Penny to keep going and I would catch up with her. As she and Topper walked on, I stepped a couple of feet off the trail and unzipped. I sent my stream arcing as far as I could down the slope. It made a satisfying, pattering noise in the chaparral.

I saw the five crows again, gliding around the canyon at about eye-level. One of them let loose with three harsh croaks. A quick little black fly flew around my face. I was zipping my shorts back up when something caused me to look a foot or so to my right.

I sucked in my breath.

A snake was there. Lying half hidden in some dried-up vines and decaying plant life. A diamondback rattler, judging by the pattern that ran down the length of its terrifying body.

I spun around and lunged back up toward the trail, and then pain stabbed through my left calf. I let out a yell and fell onto the trail and grabbed my leg and rolled over and scooted away several feet on my butt, looking down the slope, afraid the rattler might be coming after me.

"PENNY!" I shouted. "PENNY! PENNY!"

Penny and Topper came running back down the trail.

"Dustin, what happened? What's wrong?"

"Snake got me! A rattlesnake! In the leg!"

She reached me and knelt beside me.

"My god! You've been bitten by a rattlesnake?"

"Yeah! Can you fucking believe it?"

She looked around wildly.

"Where is it?"

I gestured down the hill.

"Down there somewhere. I nearly stepped right on it!"

"Where'd it bite you?"

"Right around here."

I touched the midpoint of my calf. The intense pain continued. We both peered at my leg.

"I don't see any bite marks," she said.

"Wait a second! There's a little red spot!"

"Oh my god! I see it!"

She started fumbling through her pack.

"I'll call 911."

She found her phone then forced a smile as she punched in the number. "You're gonna be okay. Don't worry."

I nodded, trying to smile too.

"Shit!" said Penny.

"What?"

"It won't work! I can't get a signal!"

"I'll try mine."

But mine wouldn't work either.

"It's these fucking mountains," I said.

"Dustin, you're not looking good. Your face is as white as a sheet!"

I tried to tamp down the panic growing inside me. I said: "Let's start heading down. We've seen lots of people. I'm sure we'll run into someone who can help us."

"Can you walk?"

"I think so."

Penny helped me to my feet. I leaned on her heavily as I hobbled forward a few steps, wincing and gasping. Now she stopped.

"I don't think this is gonna work," she said. "Why don't you stay here while I run for help? I can run really fast! I promise I'll be back in no time."

I didn't argue with her. She helped me to the shade of a small scruffy tree, and I sat down. She pressed Topper's leash into my hand.

"Topper'll keep you company."

She started to move away but I grabbed her wrist. "Look, I just want you to know, I really think I'm in love with you. From the first day, in Santa Monica—"

Her face lit up. "Oh, I love you too!" she said and gave me a quick kiss, then went running away down the trail. I watched her round a curve and disappear.

I was alone. Except for Topper, of course. He stared down the trail where Penny had gone and whimpered a bit, then flopped down in the ragged shade and went to sleep.

The tree was at a part of the trail that jutted out and formed a little point, providing me with a great view. I could see the terracotta roofs of Pacific Palisades, and further down the coast palm trees and Santa Monica, and I could see all the way to the Palos Verdes Peninsula, and out across the ocean to Catalina. In the other direction were the high-rises of Century City, and then downtown, with the San Gabriel Mountains towering beyond.

All at once I saw people. A man and a woman. Across the canyon, walking up the trail through the eucalyptus trees that we had taken.

I stood up and began to shout and wave my arms.

"Hello! Hello! Help! It's an emergency! Call 911! Hello!"

But they never even glanced at me as they slowly trudged upward. They seemed as intent on reaching the top of the hill as mountaineers slogging up the final slope of Everest. The man was holding a walking stick, and I could see now they were bent-over and elderly, and apparently deaf too.

Topper had raised his head and was looking at me with irritation; now he sighed, and went back to sleep.

I was feeling weak and light-headed. A result of the heat and excitement, or of the venom beginning to reach my vital organs? I sank back down. Picked up my water bottle and took a drink. Took off my baseball cap and poured water over my head.

I heard the buzz of a helicopter and then saw it but it was a long way off. I watched it disappearing over the hills.

A dry clicking noise arose behind me out of the brush, its source a complete mystery to a city fellow like me.

I saw the five crows again, arrogantly gliding around like the kings of the canyon. They flapped my way. Seemed to be eying me. They probably knew somehow. Knew a dying, snake-bit creature when they saw it.

I saw movement at the bottom of the canyon. There was a grassy little meadow there, and a deer was grazing. The scene seemed as peaceful as the Garden of Eden.

How could I have been bitten by a poisonous snake? It was one of those one-in-a-million things. I could imagine the (probably very small) headline in the *L.A. Times:* "Dustin Prewitt, Screenwriter, Dies Strange, Lonely Death."

I guessed we were just a doomed couple, Laura and I. She had drowned in the ocean and just a couple of months later here I was dying in the hills. We had both checked into the Hotel California and now we could never leave. I remembered the euphoric feeling I'd had flying into L.A. for the first time and looking at the Hollywood Sign, but my life here really hadn't amounted to much. It had all been a big joke, really. And the funniest part of the joke was that I was sharing my very last moments on this earth with Topper.

"Dustin! Dustin!"

I saw Penny running towards me up the trail. Behind her was the tough-looking woman from Inspiration Point. Topper woke up and began wagging his tail stump. Penny was breathing hard as she reached me, and her T-shirt was blotched with sweat.

"Dustin, this is Angela! She's a registered nurse, can you believe it?"

"Really? That's great!"

"Okay, Dustin," said Angela as she bent over me, "let's see what we got."

She had a calm, seen-it-all manner that inspired confidence.

"A rattlesnake bit me here. On the back of my leg."

228 · TOM EPPERSON

"Where?"

"Right here. See that kind of red thing?"

She scrutinized my leg, frowning.

"Hm."

"What?"

"Looks like a pimple. Or maybe an insect bite."

"Well, the fang marks are there somewhere."

Angela looked at my leg a bit longer, then patted my knee.

"I got good news for you, Dustin. You haven't been bitten by a snake."

Penny and I exchanged a bewildered look.

"But I felt it bite me. Just when I was jumping away from it."

"You probably just have a cramp," said Angela, already bored with me and beginning to play with Topper's floppy ears. "Or maybe you pulled a muscle."

34

Penny and Angela helped me down the trail and back to the Maserati. I wanted to drive, but Penny insisted on getting behind the wheel. While she drove us out of the park, I called Dr. Houghteling. He worked at a sports-medicine clinic in Marina del Rey. I had gone to him for my hip, and had figured I would probably like him when I saw one wall in the examining room was covered with framed and autographed photos of him in a Yankee cap and pinstripe shirt posing with various smiling Yankee luminaries: Joe Torre, Bernie Williams, Derek Jeter, Don Mattingly, Tino Martinez, Roger Clemens. Turned out he had grown up right over the river from Newburgh in Beacon, had played second base at Cornell, and was a fan of my book. He told me to come right over and he'd squeeze me in.

I'm sure the odds were quite low that within a space of less than twenty-four hours I would find myself a passenger in cars driven by two such anarchic drivers as Magnus Storndrop and Penny Ruemmler. Her whimsical and hair-raisingly sudden lane changes tossed around Topper and me as we sped down the PCH. My calf was swelling up and turning purple and I gritted my teeth against the jostling, while Topper got carsick and threw up his salmon chips all over the back seat. Penny didn't want to take the time to stop and clean it up, so we had to lower the windows because of the smell, which made the wind roar in and added to the frantic feeling of the whole thing.

"Penny, would you please slow down? This isn't an emergency situation."

"You're right, I'm sorry. I'm just not used to driving a car like this."

Maybe she did slow down for a minute or two, but I didn't begin to breathe easier until we reached the nearly impenetrable traffic of Santa Monica.

Dr. Houghteling was tan, fit, fiftyish. He seemed glad to see me, as always. He loved to talk baseball with me and get the latest inside dope on Hollywood. He poked and squeezed my calf, and laughed till his eyes got teary as I told him how I thought I'd been bitten by a rattlesnake. He sent me across Lincoln Boulevard to Marina del Rey Hospital where I was MRI'd. Angela's diagnosis was a little off—I had not a pulled muscle but a torn one. I went back to Houghteling's office and he put a compression stocking on my calf and prescribed ice, elevation, and Vicodin. He was still shaking his head and chuckling about the snake as I laboriously left the clinic on crutches.

We got the Vicodin at a pharmacy across the street. The plan was for Penny to drive us to Mar Vista, where she'd drop Topper off with Mrs. Stallings and feed Ralph and Miranda, and then to take me home to Beverly Hills. We headed east on the Marina Freeway through rush-hour traffic. I took a Vicodin, and sat there in silence. I felt enveloped in a sort of hot pink haze of humiliation. Penny asked me what was wrong.

"I'm just embarrassed, is all. I made such a scene."

"Oh, come on. It was totally understandable."

"You should've heard Dr. Houghteling laughing at me."

"I'm sure he wasn't laughing *at* you, he was laughing *with* you."

"No. At."

It was after six by the time we finally rolled through the gate of my house. I was relieved Pete's Durango wasn't parked out front.

Pete could be merciless in situations like this. Penny helped me out of the car and opened the front door for me and I crutched myself inside.

We went in the den. I went behind the bar and grabbed the Gray Goose by the neck. Penny walked over to the French windows that Laura had hurdled through so gracefully not all that long ago, and gazed out on the verdurous garden.

"It's so beautiful," she murmured.

"Thanks. Name your poison."

"Just some water. By the way. Do you think you should be mixing vodka with Vicodin?"

"I think it's an absolutely capital idea."

Penny helped get me and my rattling glass of vodka and ice ensconced on the couch, my left leg up on the coffee table, an ice pack strapped to the calf.

"Well," she said. "I guess I should go."

It was a question. I sipped my drink and pondered it.

"Why?"

"I don't know."

"I don't know why either."

She sat down beside me. I lifted up my arm. She snuggled up against me, laid her head on my shoulder and her hand on my chest.

"It's been quite a day, huh?" she said.

"Mm."

"How are you feeling?"

"Better and better," I said, and drank some vodka.

"I used to love Vicodin. I thought it was like heroin in a pill."

"Want one?"

"No. I'm trying to be a good girl."

"I don't want you to be *too* good," I said, and kissed her hair.

"Dustin? The snake?"

"Yeah?"

"Did you hear it rattling? Is that how you knew it was there?"

"No, I don't think I heard it rattling. I just remember looking over and seeing it."

"Don't they usually rattle before they bite?"

"I don't know. I guess so," and then I said, "What are you suggesting?"

"What do you mean? I'm not suggesting anything."

"I mean, what, you think I just imagined it?"

"No, it's just that—"

"I'd have to be some kind of hysterical neurotic idiot to hallucinate a snake and then think that it bit me!"

"Dustin, calm down. Why are you so mad?"

Here's why. I was remembering what I'd been thinking as I'd stood by the trail and looked to my right: Was that a snake I was seeing, or just an optical illusion, an ephemeral construct of shadow and light and leaf and stick? That thought had been dispelled by the undeniable reality of the pain in my leg as I had jumped away, but now it all was coming rushing back.

"Listen to me," Penny said. "I don't care if there was a snake or not. All I know is, when Angela said she didn't think you'd been bitten, it was one of the happiest moments I've ever felt. And if there's anything neurotic about any of this, it's just that you're not happy right now. You're okay, Dustin! You haven't been poisoned! You're not gonna die! You have your whole life ahead of you, and you're gonna do amazing things!"

I was taken aback; finally I said, "You really think that? That I'm gonna do amazing things?"

"Yes."

"How do you know?"

"I just do."

And then we relaxed into each other's arms again.

"Thanks for taking care of me today."

"You're welcome," she said, then murmured shyly, "Did you mean it?"

"Mean what?"

"What you said. You know. On the trail?"

"Hm. 'What I said on the trail.' Give me a hint."

"Dustin—"

I laughed. "Of course I meant it. I love you, I'm crazy about you."

We kissed, and I tumbled into a radiant vortex of vodka, Vicodin, and kissing, but then Penny pulled away and said, "There's something I have to tell you."

I was right. There was something. Now here it was.

"Okay."

"When I was four, I was in the kitchen with my mother. She was making supper. Spaghetti. And her boyfriend was there, and they got in a fight. They were both probably drunk, I don't remember, but . . . there was a pot of boiling spaghetti sauce on the stove. She took it, and threw it at him."

"The whole pot?"

"No. Just the sauce. He jumped out of the way. I was standing behind him. All I was wearing was my underpants. Some of the sauce landed on me. Around here," and her hand touched the center of her chest, and then circled across her right breast, "and down to here," and her hand slid down over her stomach. "I got burned pretty bad. It left scars."

"How bad are they?"

"They're . . . horrible."

"Let me see."

"No."

"Yes."

Penny looked at me, and nodded, then scrunched her eyes shut, and I helped her take her T-shirt off. I looked, and then I took off her bra, and looked some more. I could certainly see the scars, and they certainly were not horrible. And then I proceeded, thoroughly and systematically, to kiss the scars, not leaving a square quarter-inch of them untouched; then I removed the rest of her clothes, and she helped me remove mine.

"I'm so sweaty and awful," said Penny. "You should let me take a shower."

"Sex first. Shower later."

She laughed. "Okay, Tarzan."

My injured calf made things a bit awkward, but we figured out a way, and then fifteen minutes later we figured it out again.

"My god," Penny gasped as we finished.

"Yeah," I agreed.

We went upstairs and took a shower together, then, Adam-and-Eve naked, with me lurching along on crutches, we ambled about the house. I asked her how it had been to grow up with the scars. She said it had made her pathetically grateful for the attention of any boy. She said that in high school for a while she had found herself oddly popular with members of the football team, and then she found out there was a competition among the players to see who could sleep with the grossest girl and she had been voted the grossest girl at Anna High.

"The bastards," I growled. "If I could, I'd go back in time and kick their butts."

And then we went outside. We walked around in our walled garden. The grass was crisp and cool to our bare feet, then we lay down on our backs in the middle of the yard and looked up at the sky. There were about as many stars up there as you're ever likely to see in Beverly Hills. Just think, said Penny. Our souls had had all of space and time to wander through, but somehow they had come together, hers and mine, right now, beneath these stars.

Just think.

KITTY

35

About a week and a half after the hike, Penny and I drove down to Laguna Beach. It was a Sunday. My leg had slowly been getting better, turning an array of interesting, putrescent colors as it did so, and I had graduated from crude crutches to a genteel cane. The plan was for Penny to check out some of Laguna's many art galleries and arts and crafts shops while I limped along beside her like a dutiful boyfriend till the pain became too great and we had to retire to the nearest bar for a drink. Halfway down there, though, I noticed Penny had become pale and silent and was massaging her temple with her fingertips. I asked her what was the matter.

"I'm getting a migraine."

"You get migraines?"

"Yeah. They're pretty brutal."

"Can you take something for them?"

"I've got some medication at home. Not that it always helps that much."

We decided to call our outing off, and returned to Mar Vista. Penny took her medicine, tremulously took off her clothes, and crept into bed with her cats. I offered to stay, but she said there wasn't any point, she just needed to sleep for a few hours, and she'd call me when she woke up. I kissed her on the forehead, then went in the living room. Topper was on the couch, gnawing noisily on a foul-smelling stick made out of bull's testicles.

"Take care of Penny, Topper."

He ignored me, and I left. I went back to Beverly Hills, stopping off at Barney's on Wilshire to buy some shirts. The bill came to six hundred or so bucks. My credit card was rejected; I had maxed it out. I produced another one that did the trick, but still, it was disturbing: this was the second credit card in the last ten days to go belly-up.

When I pulled through my front gate, I saw a yellow Subaru Impreza parked behind Pete's Durango. Irene's, I assumed. When Dustin's away, Pete will play. I took my bag of shirts inside. As I walked past the living room, I caught a fleeting glimpse of a naked girl with short blonde hair and a tattoo of a sunflower on her left buttock dashing away, holding her clothes in her arms. Then Pete's head and hirsute shoulders rose up above the back of the couch. He looked around at me, wiping off his mouth and moustache with the back of his hand.

"Prewitt, what the fuck? What are you doing back already?"

"Sorry," I said and kept walking. "Penny got a headache. Don't let me interrupt you."

I mulled over what I'd just seen as I headed for my office. After my experience with the snake I didn't know if I could always believe my eyes, but I was ninety-nine percent sure the girl was Ben Benjamin's assistant, Chelsea.

I sat down behind my desk, determined to be productive. First, I dialed Magnus Storndrop's number. I got his voicemail.

"Hey, Magnus, it's Dustin again. Just checking in. I've come up with some more casting ideas, in case Bradley Cooper doesn't work out. Well, take care. Bye."

This was the third message I'd left for Magnus since our calamitous dinner, and I'd yet to hear back from him. It was, I feared, the beginning of the Big Silence. That's how dreams usually end in Hollywood. Not with a no, but with nothing.

I had a tall stack of books on my desk, research for my 1930s noir project (for which I had come up with the hopefully catchy title of *Diary of a Dead Man*). Most recently I had read *The Maltese Falcon* and *Farewell, My Lovely*. I was surprised by how good a writer Chandler was. Also surprised by how bad a writer was Hammett. I picked up another book, but after a page or two, set it aside with a sigh. Who wants to work on Sunday? I turned to my computer, and opened up *Wolfenstein*, a video game I was fond of. It was World War II, and I was an agent for the Office of Special Actions, blowing away Nazis by the dozen.

"Hey, buddy."

Pete slouched into the room, wearing only a pair of shorts and holding a can of Coke.

"Hey. Was that Irene?"

"Yeah."

"She gone?"

"Yeah."

He dropped into the chair on the other side of the desk.

"She didn't have to go."

"I know. But she wanted to. She felt embarrassed you saw her naked."

"She looked hot."

"She is. Damn hot."

"You know who she kinda looked like?"

"Who?"

"Chelsea."

"Who?"

"Chelsea? My agent's assistant? You talked to her a couple of times on the phone."

Pete's face turned red, and he took a gulp of his Coke.

"Oh yeah. Right."

"In fact, I'm nearly positive it *was* Chelsea."

Pete gave me a sheepish smile.

"Busted!"

"Man, you and Chelsea," I said, shaking my head.

"I would've told you from the beginning, but she didn't want you to know."

"How long's this been going on?"

"Well, the fucking part, since the Fourth of July. Before that, we'd just been talking on the phone. We just kind of hit it off on the phone, you know?"

"You in love?"

"Hell, no. Well, kind of." He pulled pensively at his chest hairs; I noticed he'd sprouted quite a few gray ones. "I've never met anybody like Chelsea before. She's so smart. So funny. So pretty."

"Why do you think she didn't want me to know?"

"I don't know."

"Has she introduced you to any of her friends?"

"Nope."

"Why do you think that is?"

"What are you getting at, Prewitt? You think she's embarrassed by me and it's all about the sex for her?"

Well, yes, I thought. Exactly.

"Pete, all I'm saying is, I know Chelsea, and I know Chelsea's type. She's very ambitious. Ultimately, she's gonna be with guys she thinks can help her climb up the Hollywood ladder."

"Hey, maybe I know Chelsea too. Maybe I know her better than you do."

"I hope you're right." I switched gears. "I've got a little problem."

"What?"

"I'm nearly out of money. It's just a cash-flow, red-tape kind of thing. Because Laura's body was never found, the county hasn't issued a death certificate. I have a lawyer working on it, and he says it should be resolved soon. When it is, Laura's estate will pass to me. But till then, I'm stuck. And I can't pay you anymore to be my assistant."

"Aw, hey, buddy, don't worry about it."

"But I feel bad."

Pete jumped up and headed for the door.

"Let's go!"

"Let's go where?"

But Pete just gave the follow-me signal and kept going. I grabbed my cane. We went upstairs to his room. He opened his closet and pulled a gym bag off a high shelf. Then he carried the bag over to his bed.

"What's the big mystery?" I said.

He just smiled, unzipped the bag, and opened it. I saw dirty T-shirts, an old pair of tennis shoes. Then he lifted off the clothes and there was money. A wrinkled, amorphous mass of fives, tens, twenties, fifties, and hundreds filling the bag up to nearly the brim.

"Shit, Pete. How much you got there?"

"About 19,000 bucks. It's my rainy-day money. I been squirreling it away for years. Hiding it from my wife and my creditors and the IRS. Take some."

"Oh, no thanks, I don't need it."

"Sure you do. You need some walking-around money. Here," and he plunged both hands into the bag then thrust a massive wad of cash at me. "And don't try giving it back or I'll shove it up your ass."

I took the money and gazed down bemusedly at it, as a few stray bills fluttered to the floor.

"You're lucky Jodi never knew about this."

Pete nodded somberly.

"She probably would've cut my head off."

"And kicked it around like a soccer ball."

~

Penny called me later, said she was feeling better but the migraine had worn her out and she thought she would just stay in tonight and rest. It was the first night Penny and I had spent apart since the day of the hike, and I didn't like it. I went to bed early but woke up a little after midnight from a ghastly dream about Laura. It was like the short story "The Monkey's Paw," where a deceased loved one is wished back from the grave but it's a mutilated corpse that comes knocking at the door. I dreamed Laura came walking up out of the waves, her hair stringy and dripping, her skin bloated and white in the eerie light of the moon, then she set her plodding course for Bedford Drive and me.

I was awake for hours after escaping the dream. I was haunted by the absence of Penny and the way time passed and you couldn't stop it and how you never knew what was around the corner. Sure, everything might seem to be okay, just hunky-dory, fine and dandy, and peachy-keen. But each of us at any time might be incubating the terrible tumor that will kill us, or be moving inexorably toward that intersection where the drunk will run the red light and knock us ass over appetite into eternity.

I tried to work the next day but was too groggy to get much done. I went in the kitchen for more coffee. On the marble top of the island, a half-eaten plate of spaghetti and meatballs was growing cold. This was odd. Ordinarily Pete would leave barely a speck of nutritive matter behind on any plate he'd been eating from or even near.

"Pete?" I called. "Pete?"

I walked around the house looking for Pete. Stuck my head out the front door and saw his Durango was still there. I started to get worried. Had he just disappeared like Laura? Then I went back in the kitchen and looked out the window and saw him by the swimming pool.

I walked outside. Pete was standing with his hands on his hips and the sweat running off him right out in the scorching early-August sun. He was gazing fixedly into the empty pool.

"Pete, what's up?"

"Chelsea called. She's dumping me."

"What did she say?"

"You know. The usual bullshit. She really fucking likes me but she thinks our fucking relationship has run its fucking course. It's your fault, Prewitt. You made it happen. You cursed me."

"Look, Pete. I just had a strong feeling she was going to end it because I knew about it. So it just ended today instead of next week or next month. Which allows you to move on. It's probably better this way."

"It's not better for my dick. My dick doesn't think like that."

"Your dick'll survive."

We stood side by side staring into the blue blankness of the pool. Then some kind of little bright bug came veering past us and crash-landed in the water. Its tiny strugglings sent out concentric rings.

I heard Pete sigh.

"How come pussy's got so much power over you?"

I shook my head.

"I don't know, Pete. It just does."

36

Penny and I had one last idyllic day before the tsunami hit. We'd been planning a day trip to Catalina; I wanted to cheer Pete up, so we invited him along. We drove down to San Pedro early in the morning, trooped aboard the *Catalina Express* with dozens of other tourists. The boat slowly motored out of the Port of Los Angeles. Enormous, science-fictionish-looking cranes lifted cargo containers off gargantuan ships. When the boat got out of the port, it roared ahead, sending out white wings of spray over the blue-gray sea. We went outside. Pete's Steelers cap promptly flew off his head and sailed off the end of the boat. I laughed at Pete as he cursed at his cap. It bobbed in our wake, dwindled in the distance. A pelican that looked more like a pterodactyl than a bird glided over and took a look at us then swerved away. Penny was hoping to see whales or dolphins; as she scanned the horizon, her red-blonde hair blew prettily in the wind. But we were lightly dressed and the wind was chilly and it wasn't long before we were all back inside. There was a bar selling drinks and snacks. Pete and I got Bloody Marys in plastic cups, Penny potato chips and Oreo cookies. We settled down in our seats, drank and ate.

"This is the best bloody Mary I've ever had," said Pete, pulling a pickled green bean out of the cup and munching on it. I agreed. After about an hour, Catalina appeared out of the mists, like a dream-island some powerful magician was making materialize just for us.

The boat entered a harbor and docked at Avalon. We filed off with the other tourists, then went walking down a pathway that curved along the shore. Rugged hills rose up steeply all around. White boats floated on the blue water. Sunbathers crowded narrow strips of sand. Three stunning teenage girls in bikinis pranced together toward the water. Pete openly ogled them, while Penny's presence made me eye them casually, just another part of the scenery: fat family eating red wedges of watermelon, three stunning, practically naked teenage girls, weather-beaten old couple with skin like leather.

Nearly everything about the town was small: its population, its houses, its motorized vehicles, most of which were golf carts. Strict restrictions had been placed on so-called "development," so that the island hadn't suffered the mainland's dystopic fate. It had a lot of interesting history. The Chicago Cubs used to have spring training there. Movie-star sailors like John Wayne and Errol Flynn once glamorously plied its waters. Marilyn Monroe lived there for a year and a half with her Merchant Marine husband when she was still just Norma Jean. Natalie Wood drowned on the other side of the island.

We went in Luau Larry's, where we breakfasted and Bloody Mary'd and studied glossy tourist brochures, planning our day. I was the only one who'd been here before, with my parents and Laura, not long after we'd gotten married. I remembered we'd spent a pleasant time together (and now I was the only survivor of the foursome!) playing miniature golf, so we decided to start there.

A bent-over old man named Bob gave us clubs and colored balls. The course meandered over a lovely acre of trees, its shade pierced with shafts of crystalline sunlight. Wherever you looked there seemed to be a cat, licking itself, or watching you with cool, incurious eyes, or walking delicately away. I got off to a poor start, bogeying the first hole. Penny made a lucky putt and parred it, while Pete double-bogeyed it. By the sixth hole, Pete was gone. He gave his purple ball a kick and announced that miniature golf was a goddamn stupid kids' game. There was a hamburger stand next to the golf course, and he said he was going to have a beer and wait for us there, and stalked off through the trees, frightening one of the cats. But the thing was, I wasn't doing much better than Pete.

You need to understand that I'm a scratch golfer. Even in my forties, with a bum hip, I still consistently hit the ball three hundred yards and seldom miss a fairway, and my short game is excellent. I believe if I had set my mind to it, I could have played on the pro tour. In fact, since I would soon be rich and wouldn't have to worry about making a living, I'd been toying with the idea of giving up writing altogether and devoting myself to golf. In six years, I'd be eligible for the Champions Tour, and that old dead dream of playing sports professionally could be resurrected.

So you can see that it was maddening that Penny was beating me in miniature golf. I couldn't seem to get used to the fast greens— you'd barely tap the ball and it would roll forever; plus I made some tactical errors, going for the tough shots when I should have played it safe, while Penny was sinking in a nearly supernatural way putt after putt, and not being very gracious about it either, jumping up and down and screaming and chortling and pumping her fists in the air. In the end, it wasn't even close; Penny beat me by three strokes. But at least I took my defeat in a mature fashion, throwing down the scorecard and stomping on it. Penny immediately snatched it up, gleefully pointed out the imprint of my shoe, and said she was keeping it forever as a souvenir.

Bob observed all this with a lopsided grin from behind the counter of his office. He said as we returned our clubs that for some reason the women usually beat the men. A gray tabby cat was stretched out on the counter. Penny petted it and asked Bob if all these cats belonged to him. Bob said they did. They were all cats he'd rescued and now their home was the golf course. Bob said he was a retired airline pilot and his wife had passed away and he loved cats and he loved working here but he was worried because the owner of the golf course had told him he was thinking about tearing it down and building condos and then what would happen to Bob and all his cats?

We walked over to the burger joint. Pete wasn't there. I felt a throb of worry, but when I called his cell, he answered immediately. He said he'd gotten bored waiting and had rented a golf cart and was now tooling around the town and would catch up with us later.

Penny and I strolled back down to the waterfront, went in some shops. I bought a blue and white Catalina coffee mug. She bought a turquoise cotton skirt, which I insisted on paying for (Pete's gym-bag cash was coming in handy). Then Penny took my arm and we walked along the breezy shore to the Casino.

It was an exception to the Catalina smallness rule, a magnificent round building ten stories high, out on a rocky point at the north end of the bay. During the thirties, up to fifteen hundred couples would toss each other around to joyous swing music in its vast circular ballroom. I thought it might be a nice setting for an episode in my noir novel that I would probably never write but when we reached it we were disappointed to find all the entrances either locked or blocked off by construction workers. Outside the main entrance were murals of undersea scenes, one of which showed a bare-breasted, utterly bewitching mermaid, long, sinuous, more girl than fish, with a tuft of pubic hair.

"Anybody need a taxi?!"

We looked around. Pete was there in his golf cart, grinning at us from under a spanking-new Catalina cap. I was still hobbling around with a cane, so was glad for the ride. We glided down Casino Way back toward the town. I liked how the air was so fresh and cool after the noxious heat of L.A., and liked that Penny was sitting on my lap, and liked that I was in love with her, because I was used to love being angsty and crazy, but with Penny there was something calm about it and it made me feel stronger and not weaker.

We left the golf cart at the rental place, went out on the pier, and boarded the *Nautilus*. It was a kind of faux submarine for fish watching. We had the illusion of being not five feet down but deep under the sea as we looked out windows and glided by undulating beds of brown-green kelp. You could press a button that sent fish food shooting out into the water, and our windows were swarmed with hundreds of fish with eerie violet eyes. Then we returned to land, and we were hungry again, and had Mexican food and margaritas at Coyote Joe's, and by then it was time to end our trip and catch the *Express.*

The boat sprouted its white wings again and took us toward San Pedro. Perhaps afraid of losing his new cap, Pete had gone inside, but Penny and I stayed on deck. I stood behind her with my arms around her. "Look," she cried, "dolphins!" and I saw them too, leaping into the ecstatic late-afternoon sunlight. Then she said something else, but I couldn't quite hear it above the roar of the engine and the rush of the wind.

"What?"

"I said, you take me to the moon!"

"What do you mean?"

"Everything about you . . . the way you talk, the way you move . . . the way you got so mad when I beat you at miniature golf . . . the way you make love to me . . . the way you make me laugh . . . it just knocks me out . . . you take me to the moon!"

"You take me to the moon too."

We kissed for a bit, then went inside. Pete's arms were crossed, his eyes were closed, and fitful snoring issued from his open mouth. We sat down near him. Penny said I ought to write a book or a movie about the old man and the cats at the miniature golf course. The cats could band together to save the golf course from greedy developers. I could call it *The Cats of Catalina.* I told her that was a great title. I began to think about it. A tough island cat could say to a newcomer cat from the mainland: "Us cats run this island, see? They don't call it Dogalina, do they?"

All the liquor I had drunk combined with the thrum of the

engine and the gentle rising and falling of the boat to make me start nodding off. Penny put her arm around me and I laid my head down on her shoulder. And then somehow the cats of Catalina got mixed up with the boat's sound and motion. Dozens, hundreds, thousands of cats were on the move. It was dusk, and the dusk was deepening, till all I could see was the violet eyes of the marching cats . . .

~

I dropped Pete off in Beverly Hills, then Penny and I went to Mar Vista. There was a message from Annabeth, her friend from Chicago who had cancer, on her answering machine. Annabeth said she was having a bad time of it with her chemotherapy, and didn't feel like she could handle things anymore, and wanted to know if Penny could come and help her. When the message was over, Penny looked at me, and I asked her if she had to go, and she said a few years back she'd bottomed out and didn't think she would've made it if not for Annabeth. Then she called Renée to see if she could get time off, then went online to book a flight.

37

S he would be gone for two weeks. She said that Mrs. Stallings would take care of Ralph and Miranda, but Topper was just too much of a handful for her and would I mind taking him because after all he was used to me and my house. I could hardly say no.

I drove Penny to the airport, Topper in the back seat. We didn't say much.

It was a real bummer, her leaving.

Ever since 9/11 I had hated coming to airports—not because I was afraid of terrorists but because I hated the hysteria and paranoia of those who would protect us from terrorists. LAX was crowded and frenzied. I maneuvered through the traffic and pulled over and parked. Topper licked Penny's face as she told him good-bye, then we got out and I helped her with her luggage. We spoke fast and hurriedly hugged and kissed, then I walked back toward my car. A sweating, red-faced policeman yelled at me to get a move-on. I told him I was getting a move-on and he should keep his shirt on, which made his face turn even redder. So lest I be arrested or maybe even tasered I clamped my mouth shut, and Topper and I left the airport as quickly as we could.

He sat up in the seat and looked around alertly as we drove into Beverly Hills. He began to whimper as we turned up Bedford, started to bark as we went through the front gate. I couldn't tell whether he was sad or happy to be back. Probably he was just confused.

I got his food and doggie paraphernalia out of the trunk and carried it all inside. Topper trotted along behind me, then bounded up the stairs and disappeared. I just let him go. I couldn't spend all my time following him in case he might be up to no good. I put his food and water dishes in their old spot in the kitchen, then went outside.

I walked around like a country squire inspecting his estate. This really was a great place. The world was going to go to hell, with or without me, so maybe the best thing to do was just stay home. Cultivate my garden, as Voltaire said. I could hole up here with Penny and never leave, except to play golf.

I heard somebody sneeze on the other side of the adobe wall. Magnus, perhaps. But I wasn't about to call out to him. I'd chased him enough. I still had a little bit of pride left.

I noticed a butterfly fanning its wings in the trumpet vines. Sorry, can't tell you what kind, I'm an idiot in insect matters. But I can say its wings were gorgeous, black and trimmed with gold. Then I saw a few inches away the grayish tatters of a cocoon and realized the butterfly had just emerged. I stood there and watched, an accidental witness to the dramatic goings-on in this one tiny corner of the universe. The butterfly seemed so alone and vulnerable. I didn't know how long a butterfly lived, but I doubted it was more than days or weeks—but butterflies had lived for millions of years. I was struck by the scariness of existence and the durability of life.

I encountered more insects near the swimming pool. Under one of the curving arms of a tall cactus, a small nest of yellow jackets was tucked away. The enemies of my boyhood. Today was a Cesar day, and my first thought was to have him exterminate them. But then ah, let them live, I thought. They weren't bothering anybody.

38

Penny and I talked each night. She didn't have a lot to say about Annabeth and her treatments; I sensed that things were tough. She just wanted to hear all about me and Topper. I was glad to report that Topper wasn't doing bad at all. He seemed less overtly hostile to me that he used to be. And, taking to heart her dictum, "A bored dog is a bad dog," and its corollary, "A tired dog is a happy dog," I was doing my best to keep him busy, with lots of walks and tedious games of fetch in the yard. It helped that Pete liked dogs. In fact, the only time he seemed happy was when he was playing with Topper. A bored Pete was a bad Pete. A tired Pete was a happy Pete.

~

Larry Hochheiser invited Pete and me to his house in Brentwood to watch his new state-of-the-art TV which, he said, was "as big as a pool table." I hadn't seen Larry since the night of the Codename: Chaos party, and I was shocked when he opened the door.

"Good lord. What happened to you?"

Larry laughed, and ran his hand over his gleaming pate.

"I shaved my hair off! Come on in! What are you guys drinking?"

"Got any tequila?" said Pete.

"Sure, whatever you want. Dustin?"

"Yeah, tequila. But why'd you shave your head?"

"Remember Damien? The hair artist from New York? He said all those colors he put in my hair would wash right out, right?"

"Wrong?" I ventured.

"I don't know whether he was just incompetent or was some kind of psychopath consciously trying to destroy my hair—Pete, you're gonna love this tequila, it's the smoothest I've ever tasted! Anyway, Renata, my hair stylist, almost got physically sick when she saw my hair. She said the best thing to do was just shave it all off and start from scratch."

"What's that thing in your ear?" I said.

"A diamond earring, what's it look like?"

"You're wearing earrings? What's come over you?"

"If you shut up, I'll tell you. I'm not through with my story yet. Salud!"

"Salud!" said Pete and I, then we all clicked our shot glasses together and tossed back our el Jimador.

"The day after I get my head shaved, I have a dental appointment. And Maricar's cleaning my teeth. I got some killer paté here, guys, dig in."

"Who's Maricar?" said Pete.

"She's the dental assistant. A cute little Filipino girl. And Maricar says," and Larry adopted a high-pitched voice, "'Oh, Larry, I love your head, it is *so* sexy! All you need is a diamond in your ear!'"

"I like the falsetto," I said. "You should think about keeping it."

"You gotta understand, Maricar's been cleaning my teeth for two or three years, and she's always been friendly, but kind of impersonal. And now suddenly her whole attitude toward me is, like, *transformed*! All because of my shaved head. So, cut to the chase—we're dating now."

"'Dating' means 'fucking'?" I asked.

"Absolutely."

I gave him a high-five, and he laughed giddily as he got one from Pete too.

"Way to go, buddy!" said Pete.

"Thanks," he said, pouring himself more tequila. "I can't believe how lucky I am. Maricar's really beautiful. She's kind of on the short side, but I'm kind of on the short side too—but she's got this body that won't fucking quit, man. And big brown eyes and fat red lips. And she comes from a culture where the man is *numero uno*. She'll do anything to please me."

"Wow, this is quite a turnaround," I said. "Just a few weeks ago you were despondent. You were talking about getting a gun, remember? I was afraid you were about to go on a murder-suicide spree."

"What can I say? Maricar's just good for me. Did you notice I've lost weight? That's because she has me eating better and doing Pilates. The Pilates instructor said my core is weak. I didn't even know I had a core." He dragged a corn chip through a bowl of guacamole and popped it in his mouth. "There's one thing about her that bugs me though."

"What?" I said.

"She thinks I drink too much. She wants me to start going to AA."

Pete and I were both indignant.

"That's ridiculous," I said. "Sure, you like to have a drink or two, like me, but—"

"A fucking A," Pete sneered. "A bunch of fags holding hands and saying God'll help them."

We ordered in Chinese food, and sat ourselves down in front of Larry's wonderful new TV. We watched a baseball game for a while, then a show about vampire bats in Mexico on the Discovery Channel, then settled in with *Bikini Spring Break* on Amazon.

"Incredible, isn't it?" said Larry. "It's almost like 3D."

"Yeah," said Pete. "It's like you can just reach out and touch those tits." And then Pete casually dropped, as they say, a bombshell. "Matt Price called me."

I looked at him.

"Matt Price?"

"Yeah."

"When did this happen?"

"Just a couple of hours ago. Not long before we left."

"Why didn't you tell me about it?"

"Well, I was going to, but you were taking a shower. So I decided to wait. Make it kind of like a surprise."

He skewered a scallop in black bean sauce with a chopstick and stuck it in his mouth.

"Why would Matt Price call you?" said Larry.

"Well, he was calling me *back*. I'd called and left a message with his agent."

"So how'd it go?" I said.

"Great. We talked for about ten minutes. Matt's a great fucking guy. He said Lumpy Ogonowski's one of his favorite roles and he'd love to get together with me and talk to the real Lumpy. Oh, and he said to tell you hey."

Larry and I looked at each other. The diamond in his ear twinkled. I can't say I was in love with the new look, but what Maricar thought was all that mattered.

"So when are you getting together with him?" I asked.

"Tomorrow. Lunch. One o'clock."

"God, Pete, that's terrific," said Larry. "You know, Matt Price is probably the biggest movie star on the planet right now."

Pete nodded, and kept eating.

"Where are you having lunch?" I said.

"Barney's Beanery."

"The one in West Hollywood?"

"Yeah."

"Barney's Beanery," said Larry, smiling and rubbing his hand over the top of his head, which seemed to be his favorite new all-purpose gesture. "Man, I haven't been there in years."

Tequila has always given me nightmares, and did so that night. There was some kind of emergency or natural disaster, and I was carrying Penny piggyback to safety, but she kept dementedly biting my neck and shoulders. And then I awoke soon after sunrise with a churning in my guts, and jumped out of bed and scuttled toward the bathroom, holding my lower stomach. I made it to the toilet, barely beating a Krakatoic explosion of anus-scorching, lavalike stool. As I sat there gasping and rocking back and forth, I had no doubt what the cause was. Larry had bought a big cellophane bag of hot, spicy pecans from Trader Joe's. Knowing it was a bad idea, but unable to stop, I'd single-handedly eaten nearly the entire bag. I tottered back to my bed and fell facedown upon it. Next thing I knew I was having a dream that Sluggo had punched his fist through a window, was breaking into the house. I woke up. The closet door was open, and I could hear somebody rustling around inside. If Sluggo came walking out of the closet, I thought, I would die of a heart attack. Instantly. Like Tyrone Power.

"Who's in there?" I yelled.

"Pete, who do you think?"

"Oh. Pete."

Pete came out, holding a peach-colored silk shirt up in front of him.

"Can I wear this?"

"Sure."

"Great," he said, looking at himself and the shirt in a mirror.

"You wearing that to lunch? With Matt?"

"Yeah."

"Nervous?"

"Nah. What for? Matt's just a human like you and me, right? Puts his pants on one leg at a time?"

Later, while I was taking Topper for a walk, I pondered Pete. His nonchalant attitude about this whole thing didn't strike me as very Pete-like. Plus Barney's Beanery was great if you wanted to eat potato skins and drink some beer with your pals, but it seemed an unlikely place to meet a movie star for lunch. The more I thought about it, the surer I became that Pete, in a pitiful attempt to feel important, had made up his phone call from Matt Price.

He'd left by the time Topper and I got back. He was certain to return grinning and smelling of beer and telling me what a great time he'd had with Matt, but I wouldn't let him get away with it. I'd ask for details. He'd tell me a story that wouldn't hold up. For his own good, I'd swing the truth like a baseball bat and hit him smack between the eyes. I'd tell him he needed to grow up and live in the real world, not one of make-believe.

And when he and my peach-colored shirt came through the door of the den at around 3:30, it was exactly like I'd thought it would be.

"How'd it go?"

"Fucking amazing, dude! What a great guy!"

He flopped down in a chair and belched and sighed.

"So was Matt on time? Usually stars make you wait."

"Oh yeah. Him and me both got there right around one."

"What did you guys talk about?"

"Oh, all kinds of shit."

"Like what exactly?"

"Well . . . you know why he wanted to meet me at Barney's Beanery?"

"No, why?"

"He said he'd come out from Oklahoma to be an actor, but all he'd got was a couple of crummy parts in slasher movies. He says he's practically starving, sleeping on people's couches, then one day he gets a call from his agent and he tells him he's got the role of Lumpy. Well, ol' Matt said he let out a holler and called up all his buddies and they got together at Barney's to celebrate. He said that was the happiest day of his life till the day his baby got born."

"That's a nice story."

"Yeah."

It was the kind of nice story he could easily have gotten by googling Matt. I needed to probe deeper.

"So what was he wearing?"

"What was he wearing?" Pete repeated; he seemed a little surprised by the question.

"Yeah. You know, I'm kind of into clothes. I like to know what other people are wearing."

Pete shrugged. "I'll show you." He got up and pulled his phone out of his pocket. He showed me a picture of him and Matt Price standing together in front of a pool table. Matt was wearing a gray T-shirt, olive-green cargo pants, and a baseball cap on backwards. He and Pete were both holding pool sticks and were both laughing.

I stared at the image and thought: I'll be damned.

"So what are you guys laughing about?" I said.

Pete shook his head and chuckled. "Shit if I know. The dude just kept me laughing all day!"

The "dude" thing was new for Pete; I assumed he'd picked it up from Matt.

"He's got some sense of humor," continued Pete. "Better than anybody I ever been around."

I was a little hurt.

"But . . . don't I have a pretty good sense of humor?"

"Yeah, pretty good. But not like Matt's though. Hey, you want a beer, dude?"

39

Kitty called. She said she'd finally come to terms with the fact that Laura was gone and was never coming back. She and Buzzy wanted to fly out and have a memorial service for her, and she wondered if this weekend would work for me. I said I thought it would work very well. You see, it seemed better to do it when Penny wasn't around. I couldn't very well have asked her to attend, could I? Or even let Laura's family know she existed. I would have hated to have had to hide her away.

Kitty and I both agreed we didn't want another media circus. The service should be small, just family and close friends. Also, since Laura had been an atheist ever since she'd had an atheist boyfriend in college, there wouldn't be any religious element. We would all just share fond thoughts and happy reminiscences of the departed.

Her mother Peggy wasn't well enough to travel, so only two relatives, Kitty and Buzzy, would be there. Three, if you count me. As for "close friends," well, hm—it was hard for me to think of any. I suppose that *I* had been her best friend, God help her. She didn't really have any girlfriends that she hung out with. Any childhood or college chums had long since vanished into the murk of the past. One might think some of her professional colleagues would like to attend, but I suspected her of having slept with most of her male costars, so fuck them, and she usually regarded her female costars as malignant bitches who were out to get her. Obviously we didn't want this to be like Gatsby's funeral; I needed to come up with at least a few people who could pass as friends. I called Jay Norberg, her manager, but his assistant said he was in Oregon at a Buddhist retreat, where he and several other managers and agents had hilariously taken a vow of silence for a week. Next I tried Puppy Morone, Laura's agent. First she said no, she was going to be out of town, then she called back an hour later and said she'd rearranged her schedule and she'd love to come. Then I came up with the perfect people, Phoebe and Coco, who'd been Laura's favorite hair person and makeup person respectively. They both seemed to have genuinely loved and admired Laura, and were thrilled to be asked, and I felt could be counted on to supply much of the requisite tears and laughter. I also invited Detectives Dempster and Gunston, who'd been checking in with me periodically all summer to see how I was doing and to give me updates on the wild rumors about Laura they'd been having to chase down (Laura had been kidnapped by a Columbian drug cartel which was seeking a billion dollar ransom from the Keene family; Laura had entered a convent in Nova Scotia; Laura had been spotted walking barefoot on the beach near a little fishing village in Mexico). I rounded out the guest list with Larry, Pete, and Ben Benjamin.

When I called Ben's office, Chelsea answered.

"Hi, Chelsea. It's Dustin."

"Dustin, how are you? It's so great to hear your voice!"

We chatted about this and that for a minute or two. No mention, naturally, of Pete. One would never have known she knew I knew she had a sunflower tattooed on her butt.

Ben sounded glad to hear from me, and when I invited him to the service, he said it would be his honor to attend. He asked how my project with Storndrop was going. I said it seemed to have fizzled out. He didn't seem surprised.

"You've got to take the long view," he rasped. "Life's up and down, yin and yang, Macy's and Gimbels—there's no Gimbels now, but you get my point. Anyway, I was just about to call you. I have some good news."

"About what?"

"Rob Crisafulli, young producer, very well-respected, has a deal at Paramount. I sent him some of your work just before the Maggie Peek, um . . . lunch. I spoke to him yesterday. He'd read your scripts. He raved about them, Dustin. He said it was the best material he'd read in years."

"Really?"

"He wants to set up a meeting, he's got a couple of projects he'd like to present to you. Chelsea can give you the contact information."

"Okay, great. And I know you don't represent me anymore, but if anything comes of this, I'll make sure you get the commission."

"Dustin, please," he said, sounding pained. "This isn't about commissions. This is about you getting back on your feet."

"I get it, Ben. Thanks."

40

The memorial service was set for nine a.m. Saturday morning on Dockweiler Beach, where Laura had disappeared. Kitty and Buzzy flew in from New York via private jet on Friday night. I met them at eight the next morning in the lobby of the Four Seasons. Kitty was wearing a long flowing gauzy white skirt and a white Mexican-peasant blouse and a wide straw hat and flat sandals and big sunglasses. The corner of her mouth grazed the corner of mine as we hugged and kissed, then I hugged Buzzy and he also kissed me.

Kitty lowered her sunglasses and looked me over. "We match!" She was referring to my white linen shirt and pants.

"Kitty," said Buzzy, "Dustin's not wearing a tie. Why should I have to wear a tie if he's not wearing one?"

"Gee," I said, "maybe I *should* wear one. I'm not really sure what the dress code for a memorial service on the beach is."

"I don't think you boys need a tie," said Kitty. "Buzzy, just take it off, if you want to. Put it in your pocket."

"I *will*," said Buzzy, very pleased, a smile lifting his apple cheeks. "I *will* put it in my pocket."

We headed toward the beach in my Maserati, Buzzy in the front seat and Kitty in the back.

"What's this?" asked Kitty, leaning over the seat and holding out one of the empty Bud Light cans I'd acquired on Stoner Avenue.

"Why, it appears to be a beer can, Kitty," said Buzzy.

"That was a rhetorical question, Buzzy. What I meant was, what's it doing here?"

"Well, I don't know, Kitty. Maybe you should ask Dustin."

"I *was* asking Dustin. I mean, the floorboard back here is literally littered with empty beer cans."

"They don't belong to me," I said. "I totally forgot they were back there."

But Kitty, obviously entertaining an image of me driving around town drinking beer and tossing the empties over my shoulder into the back seat, just sighed and said, "Oh, Dustin."

Traffic was light, and we got down to Dockweiler Beach twenty minutes early. I pulled off on the side of Vista del Mar. Many cars were already parked there. I'd thought that this early on a Saturday morning we'd pretty much have the beach to ourselves, but as we got out I saw I'd miscalculated; there weren't any swimmers or sunbathers yet, but the bike path was thronged with bikers, skaters, walkers, joggers, even two big-armed young men in wheelchairs. It was misty out in the ocean but cloudless overhead and the day was already getting hot, with only feeble puffs of breeze. We went down a paved path to the beach, then walked across the sand to a clump of palm trees and terra-cotta-roofed restrooms. Kitty went into the ladies' room. Buzzy took out his phone and made a call. I put one foot up on a low wall and gazed out on Santa Monica Bay, thinking about Penny. I'd been missing her like crazy. She was due back in five days.

I saw a moustached man, a big bouquet of red roses in his arms, walking down the path toward the beach; it was one of the homicide detectives, Steve Gunston or John Dempster. I waved to him and he waved back and as I headed to meet him I could now see it was definitely Dempster.

"Something came up and Steve couldn't make it," he said, then he handed me the roses—"but these are from both of us."

"Thanks, John. Laura loved roses."

He put his hands on his hips and regarded the ocean.

"Great day, huh?"

"Yeah."

"You know, I come out here a lot."

"You do?"

"Middle of the night sometimes. I just look out at the ocean and wonder about her. I guess you gotta be feeling like the loneliest person in the world to do something like what she did. It drives me nuts we never found her. I feel like we've let you down."

I pictured this tough cop in his cheap suit and hard leather shoes wandering around the beach and anguishing over my lost wife—and I felt a little guilty over my own lack of anguish.

"Hey, no way have you let me down. You guys have been great."

Dempster looked past me and his eyes widened a little, and I turned and saw Kitty and Buzzy coming toward us.

"Oh, that's the sister," Dempster said. "For just a split second—"

Over the next quarter of an hour, the rest of the guests arrived. Ben Benjamin, with his silver hair and broken nose and dove-gray suit with the white carnation in the buttonhole, looked like the distinguished and dangerous Mafia figure I think he'd always aspired to be.

"Dustin," he said, "have you made an appointment to see Rob Crisafulli yet?"

"Tuesday. Three o'clock."

"Wonderful." He glanced around, as if concerned the feds might be trying to listen in, and lowered his growl a little. "I've got some inside information for you. He's got a go picture with Jimmy Ning, a very talented young Chinese director. It's a big romantic thriller set in France in World War II, and they're looking for someone to do a rewrite. I think that may be what he wants to talk to you about."

"Wow. World War II. That sounds great."

"I know you can be very charming, Dustin, when you want to be."

"Don't worry, Ben. I'll charm the fillings right out of his fucking teeth."

Phoebe and Coco came traipsing across the beach, holding their black high heels in their hands. Phoebe was tall, with platinum-blonde swirly hair. Coco was short and plump, her mahogany hair teased and banged. They both were wearing black dresses that showed lots of cleavage and were in full makeup. They rushed upon me and squeezed and kissed me and giggled with delight when I told them how great they looked.

"Phoebe did my hair!" said Coco.

"And Coco did my makeup!" said Phoebe.

They left some lipstick on my face, which Kitty, with a slight, ironic smile, rubbed off with a tissue. Then I became aware of Pete standing off to the side, grinningly waiting to be introduced. He looked good, in tan slacks and one of my Barney's shirts.

"Kitty, this is Pete Holacek. We played baseball together. Pete, this is Kitty Keene, my sister-in-law."

"Hey Dustin," said Pete as they shook hands, "how come you never told me you had such a beautiful sister-in-law?"

I got the ironic smile from Kitty again.

"Thank you, Pete. You know, I'm a big baseball fan."

"Oh yeah?" said Pete, practically panting, his tongue all but hanging out.

"Who is *that*?" Kitty said.

A fat little bald guy in a red and white striped shirt and black shorts was walking towards us.

"My lawyer," I said, and went to meet him.

"Am I dressed okay?" Larry asked anxiously. "I notice I'm the only one wearing shorts."

"Well, let's see. You do look kind of like a referee for some weird foreign sport."

"Shit. You made it sound like this was gonna be this relaxed, beachy thing."

"Don't worry about it. But maybe you should've worn a cap. Your head's gonna get sunburned."

Larry smiled and proudly patted the top of his head. "Maricar's way ahead of you, man. She put on sun block!"

It was nine now and all were here except for Puppy Morone. I led my little band of mourners toward the ocean. We crossed the bike path and got gawked at as people wondered who we were and what we were up to and then we stopped about a hundred feet from the water, near a straggly line of eight or nine seagulls sitting on the sand. I had made a few notes for what I intended to be a short and simple, but powerful and eloquent speech; I pulled them out of my pocket and glanced over them.

"Thank you all for coming," I began, unexpectedly feeling a touch of stage fright. "We are here on this beautiful morning to remember Laura and to mourn her and to celebrate her remarkable life."

"Amen!" said Buzzy with a sad smile, pushing his glasses back up his nose.

"Can I say something?" asked Coco.

"Coco, please," said Phoebe. "Let Dustin talk. Don't you see he's got a little speech all written up?"

"Oh, I'm sorry, honey, you go ahead!"

Two short Asian guys and a tall ponytailed white guy walked slowly past with a metal detector that was beeping steadily like a heart monitor, but then that sound was drowned out by the gathering rumble of a green vehicle with huge back tires; it was dragging behind it some kind of wide agricultural-looking implement to smooth out the sand.

"As clearly as I can see the faces of each of you today," I proclaimed loudly, "I can remember the first time I saw Laura—"

A jetliner lifting off from LAX blasted me into silence. Kitty gave me an encouraging smile. She was now in custody of the detectives' roses, and she began to move among the mourners and give each a rose. As the jet soared away above the sea, I continued.

"There is an irony here—"

Suddenly I saw a skinny guy with an orange mohawk filming me with his phone.

"Excuse me," I said. "Would you mind not doing that? This is a private service."

"Private service, public beach, dude," the guy said, and kept filming.

Pete walked toward him with his hand out. "Give me the phone, asshole."

The guy looked startled. "Huh?"

"Give me the goddamn phone!"

Pete lunged at the guy, and he dodged away, then Pete went after him again and the guy took off. Their feet kicked up sand as Pete chased him around the beach. Finally he ran across the bike path, nearly colliding with a gaggle of swerving bikers. Pete stopped, and began to walk back toward us.

"Hey Pete," yelled Larry, clapping his hands, "way to go!"

"Well done, Pete!" said Buzzy.

Meanwhile, the skinny guy was shooting himself and his mohawk as he screamed at me.

"Eat my shit, dude!"

Pete rejoined us, breathing heavily. Detective Dempster slapped him on the back. Pete stood with his arms crossed on his chest, basking in his hero status.

"There is an irony here," I repeated, my speech beginning to sound absurdly solemn to me, like the Gettysburg Address. "Most of you probably know I used to play baseball, both in college and professionally—"

A bright-yellow Beamer came tearing down Vista del Mar. It veered off the road and stopped with a sharp screech.

"I was a pitcher, and—"

Two females, one older and one younger, jumped out of the car, and began hurrying down the path to the beach. The younger was carrying a green parasol.

"And many years after I'd pitched my last game, when I met Laura for the first time, I was also a pitcher."

I began losing my audience, as they turned and took a look at the women.

"Dustin," said Kitty, "who are they?"

"The one in front's Puppy Morone, Laura's agent. I don't know who the other one is."

"Go ahead, Dustin," said Ben, who detested Puppy. "Don't let them distract you."

"Yeah, honey, we're all ears," said Coco.

"You were just saying how you met Laura at a baseball game," said Phoebe.

"Oh no, it wasn't at a baseball game—"

"Okay," said Phoebe, "I'm confused."

"Hi, Dustin!" called Puppy, as she and the mystery girl scurried towards us over the sand. "Sorry we're late!"

I don't think "Puppy" was her real first name, but if it was a nickname, it was singularly unsuitable. "Alligator" or "Wolverine" would have been better. She was famously ferocious, and also one of the homeliest women in Hollywood, with a pug nose and jug ears and a tiny, nearly dwarfish body. But she always dressed herself in the best clothes; today she was in an azure satin blouse and matching pants and was atwinkle and aglitter with exquisite jewelry.

The girl with the parasol was one of those creatures of such flaw-less beauty as to barely seem human; one had trouble imagining that she ate and drank like regular people or ever went to the bathroom. She had long, light-brown, silky hair, dreamy, pale-as-a-princess-hidden-away-in-a-lofty-tower skin, and high cheekbones and green eyes. She was wearing a sundress with green polka dots.

"Dustin," said Puppy as I did the hug-and-kiss thing with her, "I brought a guest, I hope it's all right, this is McKay!"

"Hello," the girl said with a shy smile.

"That's your first name?" I said. "McKay?"

"It's not like a first or a last name. It's just my name. I'm just McKay."

Everyone gazed at McKay with fascination, as she peered out at us with a fawnlike uncertainty from her parasol's delicate shade.

"Are you one of Puppy's clients?" Larry asked.

"Yes."

"McKay is hot and happening. She's on the cusp of stardom," said Puppy.

"How delightful!" said Buzzy.

"I'm ninety-nine percent sure they're going to cast her in *California Dreamin'*, that's the Mamas and the Papas biopic, she'd play Michelle Phillips, ha ha, well of course it wouldn't be Mama Cass! Every girl in town wants this part but McKay owns it, baby, it's hers!"

"Hey," said Pete, "congratulations!"

"Well," said McKay, "I haven't got the role yet."

"You will!" said Dempster.

"McKay," said Puppy, "who's your favorite actress?"

"Laura Keene. I've loved her ever since I was a little girl. That's why I asked Puppy if I could come today."

I hoped when she'd auditioned for *California Dreamin'* she'd delivered her lines with a little more conviction. I wondered why Puppy had taken the trouble of dragging her out here.

"Puppy, Dustin was in the middle of some prepared remarks," intoned Ben gravely.

"Oh, I'm sorry, Dustin, I'll shut my big mouth."

"Sorry, Mr. Keene," said McKay.

A respectful silence settled down upon the mourners. I looked at my notes. I wanted only to get to the end of this infernal thing, but I'd barely begun it. The world would little note, nor long remember. I decided to just skip past the pitch meeting where Laura and I had met, move on to the honeymoon.

"The snow was deep in St. Moritz—and as Laura and I stood on the balcony of our hotel, I was reminded of the lines of the great Irish poet, William Butler Yeats—"

"Uh-oh. We got company," Larry said.

Up on Vista del Mar, a news crew was piling out of a Channel 7 van. Cameraman, soundman, leggy brunette in a tight skirt.

"Oh Dustin," Kitty wailed, "what are they *doing* here? This is exactly what we didn't want!"

"I told everybody not to tell anybody," I said, pointedly looking at Puppy.

"You don't think *I* told them, do you?" said Puppy. "Come on! Give me a break!"

McKay carefully stared off into the distance, giving her parasol little twirls back and forth.

"It's not relevant how they found out," Ben said practically. "Now they're here, we have to deal with them."

They came at us in a brisk trot across the sand. I recognized the brunette as Lisa Larrabee, one of Channel 7's star reporters.

"Let's moon 'em," said Pete.

"You know what they are?" said Dempster. "Pond scum. That's all. Best thing to do is just ignore 'em."

"Or we could do this someplace else," said Larry. "Maybe go to Dustin's house?"

"Look, we're here," I said. "Let's just"—I nearly said *get it over with*—"continue."

"Dustin," said Buzzy, smiling wistfully, "would you mind if I asked McKay a question first?"

Kitty rolled her eyes. "Buzzy, please—"

"I don't mind," I said, beginning to consider the possibility that if we wandered far enough afield everyone would forget that I'd ever begun a speech. "Go ahead, Buzzy."

"You're a singer as well as an actress?"

"Well, I'm mainly an actress. But I sing okay."

"McKay's being modest," said Wolverine. "She's phenomenal!"

I noticed that the boom mike was floating in our direction, the cameraman had begun to film us, and Lisa Larrabee had taken off her shoes and her toenails were painted shrimp pink.

"Do you know 'Catch a Falling Star'?" Buzzy asked McKay.

"No sir, I don't. Sorry."

"That was Laura's favorite song, when she was a little girl. Remember, Kitty?"

"Not really, Buzzy. But it's a moot issue. She said she doesn't know it."

"Maybe McKay could sing another song for us," said Buzzy. "In memory of Laura."

McKay's translucent cheeks colored a little and she shook her head but Larry and Pete and Dempster and Coco and Phoebe and several members of the growing crowd that had been attracted to us by the arrival of the camera crew all chimed in. Modest McKay seemed at the point of being talked into it. I caught smiles flashing between Puppy and Lisa Larrabee.

But the god of the sea, Poseidon, foiled Puppy's plot. The three metal-detector guys went running past us toward the water, the tall guy's ponytail flopping against his neck. Somebody yelled, "What's going on?" and somebody yelled back, "There's something dead down there!" McKay was forgotten as the spectators began to break away from us, to surge towards the ocean.

"Let's go take a look!" said Buzzy.

"No, Buzzy, wait!" said Kitty, but Buzzy ignored her, Buzzy too was running through the sand. The rest of us joined him. I wasn't using my cane any longer but my calf was still sore and I limpingly ran and remembered the terrible dream I'd had of Laura returning from the sea. Detective Dempster was running beside me in a weird repeat of that morning in May, and the sand sucked at our shoes, and the indolent seagulls scattered up into the air, and Kitty as she ran had one hand on her hat to keep it from blowing off, and then we saw it—bulky, dark, bloated, and half-shrouded in gold-green tangles of kelp—rocking a bit in the sudsy wake of a receding wave.

"Sea lion," said Dempster. "There's been a lot of 'em dying this year. Because of the poison algae."

"Oh, Dustin," said Kitty, "I thought it might be—"

Then she sagged against me, and would have fallen had I not caught her.

41

I took Kitty and Buzzy back to the hotel. Kitty said she'd hardly slept the night before and hadn't eaten and the heat and stress had gotten to her and she would be fine after a few hours sleep. We made plans to have dinner together, then they would fly back to New York on Sunday morning. I was glad my time with them was being minimized; not that I didn't enjoy their company, but Kitty possessed a combination of attractiveness and vulnerability that was unsettling to be close to.

When I got home, I found Pete in the workout room lifting weights.

"Hey, wanna go see a movie?" I said.

"Can't," he grunted.

"Why not?"

"I'm going over to Matt's house. He's having some buddies over. He's gonna barbecue a whole pig."

"Oh. Okay."

"Hey, maybe your sister-in-law would like to come. I could call Matt to see if it's okay."

"She's worn out. She's going to rest all afternoon."

"Too bad. But hey, gimme a rain check on the movie, dude."

I went downstairs and turned on a baseball game. But it began raining, and the tarps came out, and there were close-ups of rain-stippled puddles, and soaked fans sitting stoically in the emptying stands.

If there was an afterlife, I thought, maybe this was what it was like: chewing tobacco in a dugout, frowning out at the rain, wondering when it would end—a rain-delay lasting for eternity.

~

I woke up on the couch, the phone ringing—it was Penny. She wanted to know how the memorial service for Laura had gone. I told her it went well, but I could only talk a minute or two because it was already after six and I needed to get ready for my dinner with the Keenes.

We were supposed to meet in Kitty's suite for a drink, then go on to dinner at a new restaurant in West Hollywood that was alleged to be totally jumping. I rode the elevator up to the fifteenth floor, pressed Kitty's doorbell. It took a minute or two for the door to open.

"Sorry," said Kitty, "I just got out of the shower."

Her hair was damp and her feet were bare and she gave me a fragrant, humid hug.

"Feeling better?"

"Oh yes. I slept and slept and dreamed and dreamed. Have a seat."

I walked across the mauve carpet, sat down on a gold sofa with embroidered, tasseled pillows.

"Where's Buzzy?"

"He's not here," said Kitty, stating the obvious as she walked off. "Be right back, okay?"

It was a nice room. A room for rich people. French doors gave onto a wraparound balcony and I could see through them the Hollywood Hills, burnished by the sinking sun.

Kitty returned, holding a small, gift-wrapped box.

"What's that?" I said.

She handed it to me. "Open it and find out."

"It's cold."

"It's been in the fridge."

"Been in the fridge. How mysterious."

I tore off the wrapping paper. It was a six-pack of Bud Light.

"Wow," I said.

"Your favorite."

"Thanks, Kitty."

She had sat down beside me on the sofa, tucking her feet up under her. She was wearing an apricot-colored blouse and white cotton pants. She was smiling at me.

"Want one?" I said.

"If you're having one."

I popped the tops on two cans and we said salud and drank.

"Nothing like a good beer every now and then," I said. "But you know, those cans in the car really weren't mine."

"Oh, give it up, Dustin. You think I'm judging you? I'm the last person in the world to judge anybody about anything."

"Why, are you such a sinner?"

"I'm a terrible sinner. Didn't you know that about me?"

I smiled uncomfortably, took a gulp of my beer. I was getting unmistakable erotic vibes—her voice a flirty purr, her eyes flickering over my face, her body cozily close, and leaning closer . . .

"You want to call Buzzy?" I said. "Let him know I'm here?"

"Buzzy won't be joining us."

"Why not?"

"He found out Queen Latifah's singing tonight at the Hollywood Bowl. He sends his apologies. I know, it's rude, but you can't be mad at him. Buzzy's Buzzy. It would be like being mad at a small child or a pet."

"He's going by himself?"

"Oh, no. Coco and Phoebe are going with him."

"You're kidding."

"He was quite taken with both of them."

Her perfume was drifting over me like a narcotic mist. I looked at my watch.

"We should probably leave soon. I made reservations for 7:30."

"Dustin, would you mind awfully if we just had dinner in the room? It's been go, go, go, rush, rush, rush, for weeks with me. It'd be such a luxury just to spend a quiet, simple evening with a friend."

Okay. There wasn't any doubt any longer. This was a setup. Tonight I was expected to join hands with my sister-in-law and take a running leap into the hay. And, knowing Kitty, I wouldn't have been a bit surprised if ultimately she had marriage on her mind. Granted, being bedded and wedded by a beautiful billionairess was hardly a fate worse than death, but I was in love with Penny Ruemmler, so I wasn't tempted in the least. Not mentally tempted, anyway.

"Room service is fine with me," I said. "Wanna take a look at the menu?"

"What's the hurry? Let's relax a little. Enjoy our beers."

I nodded. We sipped.

"I'm sorry about this morning," I said. "I guess it was kind of a fiasco."

"You have nothing to be sorry about, and I don't think it was a fiasco. We met to remember Laura, and Laura was remembered. I think there was a lot of love on that beach." Kitty pensively ran one finger around the rim of her can of beer. "I don't know where people go when they die, or even if there's anything left of them to go anywhere. But for the first time, I feel like Laura really is *gone*. That's a sad thing, and it's also a good thing. Because I feel now like I can move on with my life. Do you know what I mean, Dustin?"

"I think so."

She reached out, laid her hand over the back of mine; and, swear to God, an instant before she said them I knew what her next two words were going to be.

"Remember Nantucket?"

"Of course. Of course I remember."

She looked at my lips.

"You know what?" I said. "I should call the restaurant. Let them know we're not coming."

She smiled a little and patted my hand. "You do that."

As I made the call, I watched Kitty walk across the room, pass through the French doors and onto the balcony. She stood at the railing, sipping her Bud Light and waiting for me. A breeze rippled her apricot top and beyond her the hills were golden and when I walked out she looked around and brushed the windy hair out of her eyes.

"How's the writing going? Anything exciting happening?"

"Well, I don't want to jinx it, but I've got a big meeting on Tuesday. At Paramount."

"Great. What's it about?"

"I might be doing a rewrite on a World War II movie that's about to go into production."

"Dustin, that *is* exciting! Well, break a leg!"

We looked out together on the vast city, flaring up into a final brightness as night approached.

"What do you think of this place?" said Kitty.

"Fitzgerald wrote a novel called *The Beautiful and Damned*. That's what I think of this place."

"Would you like to live somewhere else?"

"Probably not. It's kind of gotten in my blood."

"Can I make a confession?"

I nodded.

"Ever since we first met, I've been a little bit in love with you. But I never let it go any further than that. Because of Laura."

"Kitty, I—"

"Don't say anything," she said, setting her beer down and moving up against me. I could smell her hair and feel the plumpish warmth of her breasts against my chest. "There's nothing to stop us now, darling," she whispered, sliding her arms around me and beginning to kiss my neck, at which point—and don't think it didn't take some will power—I began to gently disengage myself.

"Kitty—this is a bad idea."

"But why? What's the matter?"

"I've met someone. There's someone else."

Kitty was backing away, all flushed and flustered.

"Who?"

"Just—a girl. My dog ran away, and she found him. That's how we met."

"When did this happen? After Laura—?"

"Yeah. Look, maybe I should've told you and Buzzy about her, but I guess I thought it would make me look bad—finding someone else, so soon—"

"You're right. It makes you look bad."

"But you and me? That would've been okay?"

"We've known each other for *years*. I'm not some little chippie you picked up while you were out walking your dog."

"I wasn't walking my dog—"

"What does she do? Is she another one of your little actress bimbos? Oh yes, Laura told me all about them."

"Penny's not like that at all. She works in a dress shop."

"Oh, 'Penny,' what a sweet name. And she works in a dress shop! A poor little shop girl! And you're the handsome Hollywood prince that's going to take her away from all that!"

"Kitty, come on. Don't be mad."

"So what's Poor Little Shop Girl up to tonight? Are you going to go see her after you've discharged your wearisome family obligations with me?"

"She's not here. She left town for a couple of weeks."

"Oh really. I'm puzzled about something."

"What?"

"I know you're not the faithful type. And it's clear you're attracted to me, at least a little. So what's the problem? Why not jump in the sack with compliant Kitty? What Penny doesn't know won't hurt her, will it?"

"I know I wasn't a very good husband to Laura—but I'm trying to be a better person now."

"Oh yes. You must keep yourself pure for your precious little Penny. Not soil yourself with rich corrupt old Kitty—"

"Kitty, stop it!" I said, grabbing her shoulders.

"Let go of me!" she said, trying to wriggle away. "I hate it when you touch me!"

If this had been a scene in the noir novel I was contemplating writing, Kitty would have lost her balance and toppled over the railing and plunged fifteen stories to her death and there would have been some cockeyed witness who said I pushed her and I would have been charged with murder and then Penny would have come to visit me while I was awaiting execution in San Quentin. But all that really happened was, Kitty disconcertingly burst into tears, and I did my clumsy best to comfort her.

"Kitty, honestly—I think the world of you, and I think you're tremendously attractive, but—the timing between us has just always been off."

"Shut up. Get me some tissues."

I went inside and found some tissues then hurried back out. Kitty dabbed at her eyes and blew her nose, then grabbed her beer and took a drink, then regarded the can with a tight, bitter smile.

"You know who Kitty Keene is? The champion idiot of the world."

"No, I hold that title. We should still have dinner."

"Okay," she said sadly, and then, as we went in: "I'm ready for a real drink. How about you?"

42

On Tuesday afternoon, I drove east into Hollywood for my meeting with Rob Crisafulli. I felt good. A well-received rewrite on a big studio movie would make me hot again. Melrose unrolled like a welcoming carpet before my silver Maserati. I passed Bogie's Liquor and Lucy's El Adobe Café, then went through the storied gates of Paramount Pictures.

I parked the car and then, guided by a map provided to me by the guard at the gate, struck out across the lot. I sauntered by sound stages and office buildings. A pretty young thing smiled at me, and I smiled back. Crisafulli's office was in the Gloria Swanson Building, which was tucked away in the northwest corner of the lot. It was a long four-story tan stucco structure. I climbed stairs to the second floor and arrived for my meeting at three o'clock sharp.

I had to wait, of course; they always make you wait at least ten minutes (and don't bother being purposely late; the ten-minute clock doesn't start running until you get there). A girl with an unsightly nose ring brought me a bottle of water. I took out my phone and perused my emails. There was a breaking news alert from *Deadline Hollywood*. The headline reached up and grabbed me by the throat: "Storndrop To Direct 'Tender Is The Night.'"

I skimmed the article for the salient points: Movie to be financed by Fox . . . Ryan Gosling and Jennifer Lawrence in talks to play Dick and Nicole Diver . . . Reginald Perry hired to write the script . . .

"*Reginald fucking Perry*?" I said out loud. My heart was thudding. The girl with the nose ring was staring at me from behind her computer. Reginald Perry, a dismal limey hack with yellow teeth who had once drunkenly insulted me at a post-screening party.

A frizzy-haired girl named Dorian came out and, in apparent contravention of the ten-minute rule, escorted me down a hallway—but when she led me into an empty conference room and told me Rob had gotten hung up on a call and was running a few minutes late, I saw the rule remained in force. Dorian said she too had read my stuff and was in agreement with Rob that it was wonderful, then she gave me a big smile and left.

I took some deep breaths and tried to calm down. In difficult situations, one needed to rely on the corny lessons of sports. So what if your last pitch got pounded into the stands? The pitch you were about to throw was the only one that mattered. Forget about Magnus. This was a huge important meeting. Be relaxed. Be charming. Be Dustin Prewitt.

I walked over to a window, which had venetian blinds pulled halfway up. The window overlooked Gower. I took a swig of my water and watched the traffic. Across the street was a day-care center. Little kids were running, playing, laughing, shrieking—

"Hi, Dustin," I heard behind me, "sorry to keep you waiting"

I turned from the window, and the smile on the face of the young man walking toward me froze, and then twisted into a grimace of disbelief.

"It's *you*!" he said. "The asshole at Geoffrey's!"

And then recognition clicked in for me too. He was the guy with the older woman who I'd thought was a gigolo and whose water glass I'd tipped over into his lap.

I stood there, speechless, immobile.

"You remember that woman I was with?" said Rob Crisafulli. "That was my mother. It was her sixtieth birthday. I'd flown her out from Florida to spend it with me. She has asthma and a heart condition. Your girlfriend's smoke was blowing all over her. You scared her so bad that after lunch, I had to take her to a doctor."

"I, I didn't mean to harm or offend your mother," I said feebly. "That girl—I was upset—we'd just broken up—"

Crisafulli seemed to be trembling a little as he struggled to control himself. He said, slowly and softly: "Get out of here. Before I throw you out."

I trudged numbly down the stairs and exited. Perhaps because this was the Gloria Swanson Building, an image of the corpse of William Holden floating facedown in the swimming pool in *Sunset Boulevard* flashed through my mind. I didn't even think about heading to my car; instead, I just walked aimlessly. There were smears of cloud high in the sky and it was hot and unusually humid and sweat began to soak through my shirt. I found myself on a phony big-city street, walking between tall brick buildings. I felt weightless, as unreal as the street, as if Dustin Prewitt were just a configuration of colored smoke that one good puff of wind would disperse and carry away.

Ahead of me, I saw a girl standing alone, her back to me. She was wearing a purple tank top, and tight ragged blue jeans faded nearly to white, and her shoulders were brushed by honey-colored hair. I knew before she turned around it was Helena.

She smiled, with no apparent surprise, as though my appearance had been expected.

"Hello, Dustin."

"Hello, Helena."

We quick-kissed on both cheeks.

"What are you doing here?" I asked.

"Oh, you know. I had one of those silly meetings. And you?"

"The same."

"How did your silly meeting go?"

"I think I might have set a record."

"A record? For what?"

"Shortest meeting in Hollywood history. How was yours?"

"It maybe was the longest in history. At least, that's how it felt."

We began to stroll together down the street, past the blank facades of the empty buildings. I considered telling her about the remarkable coincidence of running into her right after I'd encountered the Armani guy from Geoffrey's, but I sensed she wouldn't have found it odd or even interesting. Just McFate at his most ham-handed. Or had I got it all wrong? Dazed by disappointment, had I tripped going down the stairs and broken my neck, and these were just the final wistful visions of an oxygen-depleted brain?

"I've been seeing you everywhere," I said. "On magazine covers, billboards, TV."

"Just what the world needs. Endless replications of my stupid face. My freckles multiplying uncontrollably. Like a virus."

"You don't sound happy about becoming a star."

She gave me a crooked smile. "Yes, it's a tragedy, but I'll survive. And how is Hollywood for you?"

"Hollywood is a nightmare from which I am trying to awake."

"Ah. James Joyce."

"*Portrait of the Artist as a Middle-Aged Fart.*"

"You're not a fart."

"Thank you."

Helena looked at me thoughtfully. "I've missed you, Dustin."

"And I've missed *you.*"

"I saw you on TV. At the memorial thing for your wife."

"Ghastly, wasn't it?"

"Was it?"

"Yes."

"I'm sorry."

"It's okay. My life's actually taken a turn for the better."

"In what way?"

"I've met someone. A girl."

"I hope someone not like me. I hope someone better than me."

"She's not better. But she's different."

She stopped, and pulled cigarettes and a lighter out of her purse. "Yes, I'm still smoking. And don't nag me about it."

"Okay."

"Are you writing?" she said, lighting up.

"Not exactly. But I'm making notes. For a book."

"A book!" she said, blowing out enthusiastic smoke. "You mean a novel?"

I nodded.

"Will you do one thing?"

"What?"

"Make the ending happy. Joyous. Confetti being thrown in the air."

"I wouldn't have figured you for a happy-endings kind of a girl."

"Why not? This is a sad country, Dustin. The saddest in the world. Let's have our happy endings. Even if they're just make-believe!"

～

That night Pete and I were watching TV in the den. The gate bell rang. I looked at the clock. It was after 10:30.

"Jesus," I said. "Who could it be at this time of night?"

"Beats me," said Pete.

"Guess one of us needs to get up and find out."

"Uh-huh."

Pete was staring at the TV, a can of beer in one hand and a huge banana-nut muffin in the other.

I sighed, and got up. Went to the intercom and pressed the button.

"Who's there?"

"Dustin, darling!" said a voice from the intercom. "Open the gate!"

"Who is this?" I said.

But I knew who it was.

DUSTIN

43

A yellow cab eased down the driveway, then the door opened and Laura leapt out and flung herself into my arms. Being the big girl she was, she knocked me back a bit and we stumbled and Laura laughed and kissed me.

"Laura, I—I can't believe it's really you," I managed to say, and Laura said, "Yes, Dustin, it's me, it's me, I'm back, I'm back, I'm alive, alive!"

She was dressed in a strangely un-Lauralike way—blue jeans, a lettuce-green T-shirt, and simple brown sandals—but she looked better than she'd looked in years, her hair lustrous, her eyes sparkly, her skin smooth and tanned.

"But, but what happened," I stammered, "where have you been, everyone thought—"

"Oh Dustin, it's a long story but it's really a very short story, I was lost and then I was saved and—"

"Hey, lady, I gotta go!" the cab driver said.

Laura went back to the cab, pulling a wad of cash out of her pocket. The driver, who looked like a seedy eastern-European criminal, seemed pleased by his tip. Topper came running out the door as the cab pulled away. When he saw Laura, he practically skidded to a stop.

"Topper, my baby, did you miss Mommy?" Laura cried as she

swooped down on him, but Topper crouched down, growling, then turned around and scampered away.

"What's wrong with him?" said Laura.

"I think he's just kind of in a state of shock. Like me."

"Poor Dustin. I suppose I should have called ahead but I wanted it to be a surprise."

She grabbed my arm and we went inside.

"Oh it's so good to be *home*! I feel just like Dorothy in *The Wizard of Oz*!"

We went in the living room and she saw the mystic warrior. "I'd forgotten all about this! I bought it on our last day together, remember? 'Cause I thought it looked like *you*. And it does. But not half as handsome."

"Laura, you've been gone three months. Everyone thought you were dead! And then you just come driving up in a cab! You've got to tell me what happened!"

"Well," she began, and then Pete walked in. Laura looked startled. "Who's that?"

"That's Pete, he's an old friend. He's out here visiting from Pittsburgh. Pete, this is . . . Laura. My wife."

Pete stared at her. "Holy shit."

Laura eyed his beer and his muffin and his mussed-up hair and his hairy legs with obvious displeasure.

"Would anybody like a drink?" I said.

"Not me," said Laura. "I don't drink anymore."

"Really?"

"Don't look so shocked. God helped me to quit. But I'd love a Diet Coke."

I looked at Pete. "Would you mind getting Laura a Diet Coke?"

"No, buddy, course not."

"And get me a scotch on the rocks."

His heavy brow knit with puzzlement, Pete nodded, and left.

"What's this about God?" I said.

"Oh Dustin," she said rapturously, "I could talk for hours about God!" and now she flumped down on the sofa. "But tell me who this Pete guy is."

I sat down beside her, and she snuggled up to me. "We played baseball together. Remember Lumpy in *Strike Four*? Basically Pete's Lumpy."

"How long's he been here?"

"Since not long after you, uh . . . left."

"What is he, a permanent house guest?"

"He's really helped me out a lot, Laura. This has been a tough time for me."

"Oh, I'm sure it has, baby. What I did to you was *so* bad. But I'm gonna make it up to you, I promise. Okay?"

I was about to do it, right at that moment—about to tell Laura I was happy she was alive but things had changed between us because I had walked in Palisades Park and met a girl named Penny.

I took a deep breath and said: "Laura?"

"Who was the cunt in the polka dots?"

"Huh?"

"At my memorial service. I saw her on TV."

"She was just some actress. One of Puppy's clients. You know Puppy. She'll do anything to get her clients publicity."

"When's the last time she ever did anything for *me*? You know the first thing I'm going to do tomorrow? Fire Puppy! That way she'll have more time to devote to Little Miss Polka Dot!"

Pete padded in barefoot with our drinks.

"Thank you, Pete," said Laura as she took her Diet Coke from him, and then she shrieked, "Oh my god! Where is it?"

"Where's what?" I said.

"My Jackson Pollack!"

She was pointing toward a spot on the wall where the invaluable rectangle of splattery paint used to hang.

Pete and I exchanged a look.

"Something happened to it," I said.

"What do you mean something happened to it?"

"It was stolen. A lot of other stuff was stolen too."

"Oh, Dustin, no! But who did it? How did they get in?"

I looked at Pete again; he was rubbing his stomach, as though he had heartburn, and his face was turning red.

"What do you keep looking at *him* for?"

"Laura, look, I can tell you all about this later. But first you've gotta tell me where the hell you've been!"

~

In the weeks leading up to her attempted suicide, she had feared she was losing her mind. Wherever she was in the house, she felt invisible eyes glaring at her. Sometimes when she entered a room, she felt like she was walking through cobwebs, they would cling to her face and stick to her arms and she could feel them on her fingers as she tried clawing them away and yet nothing was there. One day she opened her lingerie drawer and it was empty save for a single one of my socks. When she came out of the shower twenty minutes later and looked in the drawer again, there was no sign of the sock, but her lingerie had been restored. And then suddenly the sock seemed to come dropping out of nowhere and landed softly at her feet.

"Why didn't you tell me about any of this?" I said. We were sitting in the kitchen at the island, where I was downing another scotch and she was ravenously tearing apart with her fingers a roasted chicken.

"What for? So you could smirk at me and roll your eyes and tell me I oughta go see a shrink?"

Things had gone from strange to stranger on the day of the art show. Laura had come home furious at what she saw as her public humiliation because I wouldn't dance with her. She tried to swim off some of her anger in the pool, but after she climbed out, she glanced back, and saw a dead woman floating facedown in the water. She had short, wavy, bleached-blonde hair and was wearing an old-fashioned-looking bathing suit. And then the woman began to grow transparent till she blended in completely with the blue water of the pool.

Laura took a bottle of vodka up to our bedroom and locked herself in, and drank and paced and wept for hours, and listened to a voice that never stopped. It said there was only one way out of this mess, and that was to make herself like the woman in the pool. Eventually she got in her car and started driving. She ran out of vodka, and stopped at a liquor store in Playa del Rey. The door was locked, but she could see a man inside behind the counter. She began to bang on the door, and he yelled at her *what do you want?* and all at once it wasn't about the liquor anymore, she was scared to death and she yelled back *I want you to help me! I want you to help me!* But he just scowled and threatened to call the cops, and she drove to the beach.

She wrote her suicide note to me and shed her clothes and ran with a sudden sense of exultation and liberation, like one escaping a terrible prison, across the sand through the rain and wind and plunged into the violent sea. She fought through the breaking waves and swam up and down the ink-black swells and felt strong enough to swim to China. It was her intention to continue to the point of complete exhaustion, whereupon she would sink gently and peacefully to the bottom of the sea. But then something changed. Fear crept in, or the will to live. She stopped, she treaded water, she gasped and spluttered, she tried to get her bearings. She saw the lights of the shore. She turned around. And now the ocean was an obliterating black horror that she flailed across, and the cold soaked into her bones, and she could feel her muscles failing, and then there were lights, not the lights of the shore but practically right on top of her, they were about to run her down, and she waved her arms and screamed. A life buoy with a rope attached plopped down beside her, but her benumbed fingers couldn't hang on, then someone was in the water with her, and then she was naked on the deck and then darkness possessed her.

She woke up in the cabin, wrapped in blankets. The boat was

owned by Rudy Botana, who had jumped in the sea and saved her, and his younger brother Narciso. There were three other fishermen on board. They gave her hot coffee and hot soup and asked her her name and what she was doing swimming naked in the ocean in the middle of the night in a storm but she replied not a word. Her mind and heart were wrapped in silence. They were returning home with their catch, and not knowing what else to do they took her with them. And that was how she found herself in Baja California, south of Ensenada, in the paradisal little town of Santo Tomás.

Now dressed in rough fishing clothes, she was taken by Rudy and Narciso to their house. It was modest, clean, and pleasant. The brothers lived there with their mother, Amelia. Laura was installed in the spare bedroom. She lay on the bed and listened to Spanish songs on the radio and still she didn't speak. Antonio, one of the fisherman, had been sure their mysterious passenger was the American movie star, Laura Keene, but nobody had believed him. But now Rudy and Narciso saw the reports about Laura on TV. They went in her bedroom, and told her America was going loco because it thought she was dead. They said they were going to call the police and inform them of her whereabouts. Laura no longer wanted to die, but the thought of going back was unbearable. She wanted only to be in this simple room with the sunlight on the wooden floor and the radio playing its sad love songs, and for the first time she spoke, begging them not to call the police and asking if she could stay. And so she stayed for nearly three months.

It was a week before she came out of the room, two weeks before she smiled or laughed, three weeks before she found God. Narciso was a runner, and he persuaded her to get up early and, before it got too hot, to run with him up and down the hills around Santo Tomás. She saw eagles in the sky and whales out in the ocean and on the third day of running, she came upon a white doe with soft blue human-looking eyes. But when she pointed it out to Narciso he didn't see a thing. She was afraid she might be losing her mind again, but the elderly mother told her she had seen the same doe when she was a little girl, and an old half-Indian priest had told her it was a manifestation of the Virgin Mary.

Amelia took her to Sunday mass. God exploded like a star inside her. She saw how full of sin she was. She resolved to change her life.

And so the summer passed in Santo Tomás. She ran and read and listened to the radio and watched TV and didn't drink and walked by the ocean and thought and prayed. It soon became common knowledge to the people of the town that a missing American movie star was in their midst, but out of respect to the Botanas, and because they began to feel protective of her, they kept her secret.

"I know how your mind works, Dustin," said Laura, gnawing on a tawny wing. "I know you think I was fucking Rudy. But I wasn't. Or Narciso either. Not that they didn't want to. But I was married to you, and that's all there was to it."

I seriously suspected there was much more to it, but I decided to move on.

"It all sounds so idyllic. Why did you come back?"

"Because of *you*, darling. Saturday night I was watching TV, and suddenly there you were. On the beach, at my memorial service. You were dressed all in white, and you were so handsome, but your face was so sad, and I realized how much I'd hurt you, and it was just selfish of me to stay away.

"I wanted to come back quietly, without any publicity. I didn't have my passport or driver's license or credit cards or anything, so I couldn't just catch a plane or drive across the border, so I had Rudy and Narciso bring me back on their boat. They dropped me off at San Pedro and gave me some money for a cab. And here I am!"

"And it was that easy? You weren't stopped by the Coast Guard or Immigration?"

"No. Seems like Rudy and Narciso knew how to avoid them."

"Why couldn't you have just let me know you were okay? If you'd wanted to stay in Mexico for a while, that would have been fine."

"Oh darling, I thought about calling you a thousand times but . . . something inside me kept telling me I needed a complete and total break with the past. That was the only way I could heal. Do you forgive me?"

I nodded. She napkined chicken grease off her mouth and fingers, then leaned toward me and kissed me. "I'm gonna make myself look nice for you. And then I'm gonna show you how much I've missed you. Okay?"

I nodded again. She left. I sipped my scotch, and contemplated the skeletal remains of the chicken.

The story she'd just told me—how both her body and soul had been saved by noble Mexican fishermen—seemed wildly improbable. How could I know if any of it was true? Maybe, for example, they hadn't been fishermen, but drug smugglers. I thought it over. The modest *casa* in Santo Tomás became a giant garish mansion filled with mirrors, red rugs, and pornographic statuary. The little radio playing romantic ballads turned into a state-of-the-art sound system blasting out decadent pounding technopop or nasty snarling hip hop. The party went on day and night. Piles of coke glittered on chrome and glass coffee tables. Laura gazed into the feral eyes of Narciso. In the bathrooms, snitches were being dismembered by chainsaws.

Or maybe she'd never been in Mexico, had never swum into the sea. She could have been anywhere, with anybody, doing anything. Maybe it *had* all been just a publicity stunt to revive her career.

And yet her narrative of what had led up to her disappearance, with her hallucinations of ghosts in swimming pools and supernatural socks, had had the ring of truth. I believed she had been in a precarious mental state, and perhaps still was. It had been the right thing to not tell her about Penny tonight. I must be careful with her lest she relapse and do something crazy.

I went in the den for some more scotch. Pete had already gone up to bed. He'd left empty beer bottles and crumbs of muffin on the coffee table. He'd have to quit being such a slob now with Laura around. Laura was a neat freak, and he was on thin ice with her already.

I went in my office. I sat down at my desk. I took a long drink of my scotch.

A faint whimper came from the doorway.

Topper was standing there, looking in at me.

"I know, boy. I know."

He turned around and plodded off.

I reached for the phone. I was going to call Penny. I put in the area code, and then I paused. It was after midnight here, after two in Chicago. Why wake her up with some nerve-jangling phone call in the middle of the night? As if this were some emergency. Which it wasn't. Laura was alive. That was a good thing. It wouldn't have any effect on Penny and me. Not in the long run, anyway.

I put down the phone, picked up the scotch. Overhead, the floorboards creaked, as Laura moved about. I finished up the scotch and went upstairs. Laura, looking very nice indeed, was waiting for me in our bed. I took off my clothes and got into bed too. Immediately Laura was all over me, but, pleading exhaustion and too much booze, I asked if we could just hold each other. Laura seemed okay with that, and within a few minutes was snoring on my shoulder. But I lay awake for a long, long time.

44

I woke up. It was morning. I lay in bed, pondering a bizarre dream I'd had: A taxi had driven up to the front door and my dead wife had jumped out. Then I saw Laura's blue jeans draped over the back of a chair, and the depression of her head in the pillow next to me, and I got up and got dressed and went downstairs.

I found her on the phone in the kitchen.

"Absolutely! There's no doubt about it!" Laura was saying, then she smiled at me and kissed the air. She was sitting at the island with a mug of coffee; of the dozens of cups and mugs we had, she had picked the one I had bought in Catalina. "Well, I haven't decided that yet. I'm gonna be rethinking everything."

"Who are you talking to?" I said.

"Kitty."

My blood ran a little cold as I went to the cupboard and got a mug. I thought about Kitty kissing my neck, about me telling Kitty all about Penny.

"Dustin?" said Laura. "Kitty wants to say hello."

"Okay." I poured myself coffee then took the phone. "Hi, Kitty."

"Isn't it just amazing?!" Kitty exclaimed. "Isn't it just the biggest miracle ever?!"

"It sure is! It's unbelievable!"

"It's funny, I never wanted to have that memorial service because

I thought she might come back—but it's *because* of the memorial service that she *came* back!"

"Kind of ironic, huh?"

And then Kitty's tone changed. "*So.* Isn't life interesting?"

"Yes, it certainly is."

"A penny for your thoughts."

I glanced at Laura. She was unpeeling a banana. She saw me looking at her and smiled.

"What do you mean?"

"Obviously you haven't told her about the poor little shop girl."

"No."

"When are you going to?"

"It won't be long now."

"You know what I predict? I predict you never tell her."

"Why do you say that?"

"Because I know you, Dustin. You like the good things in life too much. Poor Mother may not even make it to Christmas. And then Laura will be one of the richest women in America. You're not going to walk away from that. For what? For 'love'? You haven't got it in you."

Laura chewed on her banana, watching me, and I got the unsettling feeling she was somehow hearing both ends of the conversation.

"Well, you never know," I said vaguely.

"I do hope you get all this worked out. Honestly. You're a vain, shallow, foolish man. But you're not a cruel man. You're not unkind. And I guess that's why I still give a damn about you."

"Well, thanks, Kitty. I'll give you back to Laura now."

I went to the refrigerator to get some milk for my coffee. "Do me a favor," I heard Laura say into the phone. "Call Mother and Buzzy and tell them what's happened. Tell them I'll call them in a little while. I love you too. Bye-bye," and then she said to me: "I'm starving. How about I make us some breakfast? Bacon and eggs? With the bacon really crisp, like you like it?"

"Okay. You know, you haven't made breakfast in years."

"It's the new me."

"You seen Pete? Is he up?"

"He's up. He's outside. With Topper. Who hates me."

"Oh, he doesn't hate you."

"He acts like it. He's mad at me 'cause he thinks I abandoned him. I'm afraid he'll never forgive me."

"I'll go out and have a talk with him," I said, and started for the door.

"Could you have a talk with Pete too?"

"About what?"

"Look, I'm glad he's been such a good friend to you. But maybe you could ask him to start looking for another place to stay. 'Cause I want you all to myself!"

I found Pete and Topper playing with Topper's teddy bear near the big cactus by the swimming pool.

"Hey, buddy," said Pete. "So how's it going?"

"Shit, man, I don't know. This has kind of knocked me for a loop."

"So I guess Penny's history now, huh?"

"What, are you kidding me? Of course not. I love Penny."

"You told your wife about her yet?"

"No. Not yet. I'm looking for the right moment. She tried to off herself three months ago. I have to be careful not to push her over the edge again."

Pete stuck his lower lip out, and nodded judiciously.

"Makes sense. But tell me something."

"What?"

"If you do decide to dump Penny, you think I'd have a shot at her?"

"Goddamn it, I'm not gonna dump her! And you stay away from her!"

"Okay, Prewitt, okay. Just chill."

Pete flung the teddy bear across the yard, and Topper raced after it.

"Pete? Don't take this wrong, but—Laura wants you to leave. It's nothing personal. She just wants more privacy."

Pete nodded, not seeming surprised at all. "Okay."

"I feel bad about this."

"Hey, man, don't sweat it. If I was Laura, I wouldn't wanna have some asshole like me hanging around either."

"You know, I'll bet Larry would love to have you. He's got plenty of room, and you guys have really hit it off. You want me to call him for you?"

"Sure. I won't be needing a place to stay for long anyway."

"Why not?"

"I'm going to Thailand."

"Thailand? What for?"

"Matt's making a movie there. He says it's like a modern-day version of *The Magnificent Seven*. There's this poor little fishing village in Thailand, and there's this gang of pirates that's always robbing the village and raping their women and shit, so they hire these American mercenaries to get rid of the pirates. Matt's gonna play the Steve McQueen role."

"Sounds great. But how come you're going?"

"Matt's got this buddy that's been his stand-in in all his movies, but the dude just wrecked his motorcycle and broke his leg. So Matt wants *me* to be his stand-in. And he says he'll make sure the director gives me some little part so I can get my SAG card."

"Wow! Congratulations. How long you gonna be gone?"

"Five months." He and Topper had been tug-of-warring with the teddy bear, but now Topper let go and lunged at a yellow jacket on patrol from the nest in the cactus. His jaws snapped shut but missed the yellow jacket and it zoomed away. "I can't wait, dude. I hear Bangkok's got the best pussy in the world!"

I took a bemused sip of my coffee as I walked back to the house. Seemed like nothing could stop Pete Holocek in his climb to the top of the Hollywood mountain. I should write something about him. *All About Pete. What Makes Petey Run? A Star Is Born (and His Name Is Pete!).*

Uproarious laughter was coming out of the kitchen. I wondered what could be so funny about making breakfast. But when I went through the door, I found my wife on the phone again.

"Who you talking to?"

"Puppy."

It didn't sound as though Puppy was in the middle of getting fired. I walked through the kitchen and to my office fighting a rising tide of panic. If Puppy Morone knew Laura was back, then in ten minutes the whole town would know, and then the whole world ten minutes after that. And I still hadn't called Penny!

I got her voicemail.

"This isn't an emergency!" I began rather breathlessly. "But please call me right away. Call me on my cellphone. Bye."

I sat there at my desk. I stared up at the framed photograph on the wall of eleven-year-old me posing with Don Mattingly. If only I'd had a better fastball, my whole life would have been different. But then again, who knew? Kerry Wood of the Cubs could throw 102 miles per hour and struck out twenty batters when he was twenty, but then his career was derailed by one injury after another.

I became aware that I was breathing through my mouth and that my chest felt like it was wrapped up in a very tight piece of plastic sheeting. But I was not about to be the comical fool who cried wolf again. I was not having a heart attack. It was just stress.

I got up and went in the den. I could faintly hear Laura still talking and laughing in the kitchen. It had been years since I'd had a drink this early in the day, but it felt like the right thing to do. I made it vodka, so nobody could smell it on me.

45

By noon, they'd arrived. They were clustered outside the walls like besieging barbarians. The media, I mean. Laura and I sat on the sofa in the den in front of the TV, Laura wielding the remote, flipping channels. She was breaking news in big red capital letters on CNN, MSNBC, Fox News, and all the local stations. Puppy had arrived about an hour earlier, along with Laura's publicist, Kim Loori. They were fielding dozens of calls and texts. They were in ecstasy. Kim had a cellphone in each hand, like a gunslinger with two guns, and was a sight to see.

We heard the clatter of a helicopter, then Laura switched to Channel 7 just as our back yard hove into view. Now the clattering was coming out of the TV as well. The camera zoomed in on the swimming pool as Pete hauled himself out. He was wearing a black Speedo and the water streamed off his hairy body, and then he turned his moustache heavenward and gazed into the camera. The Channel 7 reporter identified him as Laura Keene's husband, Dustin Prewitt.

My cell rang. It was Penny.

Laura was looking at me inquiringly. "You need to get that?"

I shrugged. "Nah."

I turned off the phone.

Puppy came rushing over, her jewelry flashing.

"Lifetime wants to do a movie! Right now! Starring you as you! You'll have total creative control, anything you want!"

"But they don't even know what happened to her yet," I said.

"They don't care about that. They just wanna make a deal."

"Dustin would have to write the script, of course," said Laura.

"Dustin would have to write the script of course *not*," I said.

Laura looked puzzled. "But why not, honey?"

"Laura, do you really want to play yourself in some cheesy cable movie?"

"Dustin's right," said Laura to Puppy. "Let's hold out for a feature."

"Got it," Puppy said and rushed away.

"That's not really what I meant," I began, but Laura, continuing her channel flipping, said, "Who's the bald guy?"

"Don't you recognize him? That's Larry."

He was driving up to the gate in his Escalade. Reporters surged toward him, yelling questions, surrounding the car, seeming on the verge of grabbing it, rocking it, turning it over, and setting it on fire. Larry reached out and pressed the gatebell and I heard it ring. It felt weird, watching my life unfolding live on TV, as though there'd been an ontological fracture and I no longer quite existed on my own.

Laura greeted Larry with hugs and kisses. She couldn't get over how great he looked, and indeed, he had transformed further since I'd last seen him, somehow acquiring a glowing tan. Right on the heels of Larry, Detectives Dempster and Gunston arrived. Dempster's face as he looked on my wife was filled with such wonderment and bliss it occurred to me that during his heartrending search for lost, tragic, beautiful Laura he must have fallen in love with her. In a just universe, when she got to know him a little better, Laura would reciprocate, and his and hers and mine and Penny's problems would all be solved.

The detectives took Laura into another room, so she could tell them her tale of being rescued by possibly fictitious Mexican fisherman, and I took Larry into the den to get him a Diet Coke and me more vodka.

"Looks like you've been catching some rays," I said.

Larry laughed, and ran his hand over his bronzed noggin.

"It's not real, man. It's a cream you rub on. I got it at Chocolate Sun in Santa Monica. And there's no dangerous chemicals. It's totally organic."

"Looks good."

"Thanks. Maricar loves it. I'm tan all over. No tan lines. Even my dick has a tan."

I tried my best not to imagine that. I rattled my ice cubes to make the vodka colder, and took a drink.

"So what does Penny think about all this?"

"I don't know. I haven't talked to her."

"Shit. Why not?"

"We've just been missing connections. She probably knows about it by now though. She's probably seen it on TV."

"You gonna dump her?"

"*No.* Course not. You and Pete. Jeez."

"If I were you, man? I'd try calling her again right this fucking second. She must be going bananas."

My god, I thought, he's right. I need to call her this fucking second. I asked Larry to please beat it. Penny picked up on the first ring.

"Dustin?"

"Penny—listen—"

"I'm really happy she's okay."

"I know. Me too."

"It's incredible!"

"Yeah."

"What happened to her? Where's she been?"

"She tried to drown herself, but she was rescued by Mexican fisherman. She's been in Mexico with them."

"Wow."

304 · TOM EPPERSON

I could hear through the phone Wolf Blitzer of CNN: "A Hollywood movie star makes the ultimate comeback! She returns from the dead!" And then Penny said, "Why didn't you call me?"

"I did, didn't you get my message?"

"No, I mean last night. They're saying on TV she came home last night."

"I didn't have a chance. I mean, she was right there—"

"All night?"

"More or less, yeah."

"You haven't told her yet. About me."

"No. Not yet."

"Do you plan to?"

"Of course. Look, she hasn't even been home twenty-four hours yet. I need to break it to her gently. I don't want her to go nuts again."

"I'm coming home tomorrow morning."

"I know."

"My plane lands at 11:05."

"I know I said I'd pick you up, but—it might not be possible. How about I just send a car for you?"

"Don't bother. I'll Uber."

"Come on, don't be mad. Try to understand—"

"Oh my god! There's Topper!"

"Where?"

"He's in the back yard. Playing with Pete."

I walked over to the French windows. His teddy bear clamped between his jaws, Topper zigzagged across the lawn as Pete gave chase. I watched Pete cavorting for the cameras of the hovering helicopters in his little black bathing suit, his body gleaming with sweat. He'd been working out hard recently, and I noticed how well-toned his muscles had become.

"Pete's getting out of fucking control," I said.

"Dustin?" said Penny in a small voice. "What's going to happen with Topper?"

I'd known this question was coming.

"Penny, you've got to understand. Topper was always really Laura's dog, not mine."

"Are you saying I've lost him?"

"Maybe for now you have, but—"

I heard a catch in her breath, and a little sniffle.

"Oh great, are you crying? Over Topper? He's really a horrible little dog—"

"What else have I lost?"

"What?"

"You heard me."

"You haven't lost anything, baby, I love you!"

"Do you?"

"Of course I do. You just have to be patient—"

Laura walked in.

"Anyway," I continued. "It was great talking to you."

"Oh. *She's* there."

"That's right. I'll talk to you soon."

Silence, except for Mr. Blitzer.

"Okay," I said. "Bye-bye."

I hung up. Laura was looking at me.

"Who was that?"

"Ben Benjamin. He said to give you his love."

"Oh, fuck *him*." I'd told her a highly expurgated version of the events leading up to Ben and his agency dropping me. "Now that he smells a buck, he's gonna try and crawl back in your good graces."

"Ben's not like that."

"He's Jewish. He can't help it."

"Jesus, Laura. What's the good of finding God if you're still gonna be a bigot?"

"You're right. I'm sorry. That just popped out. Forgive me?"

I nodded. Took a grim sip of vodka, and stared out at Pete and Topper. Laura slipped her arm around my waist.

"I love being here with you. I love this house. You don't really appreciate what you have until you go away and then come back. You see everything different. Even Topper. I see him different. Is that vodka? It's a little early in the day for you. Do me a favor? Clean up a little bit? Shave? 'Cause I'm having a press conference at three, and I want my handsome honey-bunny standing right there beside me!"

46

There's an old saying in England: long runs the fox, but eventually the fox gets caught. I felt caught there in our courtyard, standing with a stiff smile on the front steps alongside Laura behind a bristling bank of microphones, facing a feverish mob of media. Beyond the walls I could hear honks and shouts. Beverly Hills cops were out there, trying to keep order on the carnival-like street. Choppers throbbed ominously overhead, and several crows swept by with raucous squawks, upset, it appeared, over the intrusion into their airspace.

Phoebe and Coco had hurried over (Phoebe had gotten a speeding ticket, which she unsuccessfully tried to get Dempster to fix) and had frenziedly worked on Laura, with the paradoxical charge from her to make it look as if she hadn't been worked on at all. She was after a simple Nature Girl kind of look, and I don't think I'd ever seen her more beautiful than she was that afternoon. She was wearing blue jeans and a black T-shirt, and her hair fell on her shoulders in glossy cascading curves, and her eyes were as clear and blue as the skies over the mystic mountains of Mexico. She had done plenty of publicity in her time and was good at it and the media listened raptly to her now-familiar (to you) story of despair, rescue, and redemption. I saw a few reporters crying. A hulking cameraman with a grizzled beard sheepishly rubbed his runny nose. There was applause when she finished. Kim Loori ducked in for a moment and said we would take a few questions.

"Laura, to what do you attribute your survival?" solemnly asked a Latina babe in a leather miniskirt, and as Laura gave her answer (Guess what it was! I'll give you a hint! It's the kind of animal that Topper is spelled backwards!), I was feeling a little bit like I was about to pass out. It had been another day of hideous heat, and I hadn't eaten at all but had drunk *mucho*, and I could feel the plastic sheeting beginning to tighten around my chest again. All at once I became aware that everyone was looking at me, and I realized that the moon-faced, bow-tied little entertainment reporter for Channel 11 had just asked me a question.

"I'm sorry," I mumbled, feeling as though my mouth had been shot full of Novocaine. "Could you repeat that?"

"You bet. Dustin, could you tell us what your very first thoughts were when you realized that, against all the odds, Laura had come back to you?"

"That's a very difficult—it's not easy to—to put into—" and then somebody shouted: *"She's not real! She's a fake!"*

Laura, as in a dream, was no longer standing at my side wearing a T-shirt and blue jeans but was out in front of me in a black cocktail dress and high heels, her face contorted with rage as she pushed through the crowd.

"I'M Laura Keene!" she screamed. *"She's trying to take over my iDENtity!"*

But then I saw that Laura *was* still beside me, which meant the wrathful figure in black stumbling toward us was probably Brenda Caskey, the Laura Keene impersonator. Suddenly Caskey reached in her handbag and pulled out a gun. Shrieks and cries arose from the startled media and people began diving out of the way and then out of nowhere Dempster appeared. He grabbed the arm with the gun in it and it terrifyingly fired into the air and then he wrested it away from her and took her roughly down to the cobblestones. He had his knee in her back and was twisting her arms up behind her as cops came running from the street. Caskey was thrashing around and screaming bloody murder, and then our handlers, Puppy and Kim, hustled Laura and me back into the house and I saw no more.

~

Laura and I sat in the kitchen at the island eating pizza and watching the six o'clock news. Our press conference had become a national sensation. For the umpteenth time they were showing me inanely stammering and then the yelling and the wildly swinging camera and the beautiful broad in black with a gun. That the gun turned out to be a fake, a harmless prop pistol, obviously didn't diminish in the least Dempster's bravery.

I could have been chewing on Topper's kibble for all the pleasure I was taking in the pizza. Each time I saw myself I felt more disgusted. I had always wanted to be a hero. Not just a sports hero, because I'd had my moments of glory at the Hill School and Dartmouth, but a *real* one. I'd have fantasies with the detail of short stories about saving a pretty girl from a gang of ruffians, or plunging into the smoke of a burning building in search of kids and kittens, or dashing across a battlefield to rescue a wounded buddy as machine-gun bullets kicked up dirt all around me (He, gasping: *Prewitt . . . I knew you'd come . . .* Me, with a jaunty grin: *I had no choice. You still owe me twenty bucks!*).

And today when a real-life lunatic with a gun had come charging at my wife, I'd done what exactly? Thrown myself in front of Laura to take the bullet? Leapt off the steps like Tyrone Power and tackled her? No, I'd just stood there gaping at her like the big doofus that I was.

"What the fuck are they doing?" said Laura.

A live helicopter shot showed Pete and Larry carrying the statue of the warrior out the front door and toward Pete's Durango.

"They're stealing my fucking sculpture!" she said, and jumped up.

"Laura," I said, "wait!" but she was already gone.

She was outside by the time I caught up with her, hollering at

Pete and Larry, who had the statue half in and half out of the SUV. "Are you guys crazy?! What are you doing!?"

They looked confused.

"I was just taking my statue over to Larry's," said Pete.

"*Your* statue?"

"Yeah. Dustin gave it to me."

"Yeah, I did give it to him," I said. "Pete really fell in love with it."

Laura gave an uncomfortable laugh.

"I'm sorry, Pete. Looks like there's been a misunderstanding. It was something *I* bought. It really wasn't Dustin's to give."

"He thought you were dead," Larry pointed out.

"Exactly. But I'm not. And I happen to love it too. So, if you guys don't mind

"No problem," said Pete. Grunting and gasping, he and Larry wrestled the statue out of the Durango and began to lug it back into the house.

"Sorry, Pete," I said.

"Hey, don't sweat it, buddy."

I glanced up at the TV chopper hovering overhead; we'd been giving viewers their money's worth today. Laura and I went back in the kitchen.

"Why can't we just give it to him?" I said.

"Dustin, how would you like it if I started giving away your stuff to my girlfriends without your permission? Besides. I just realized something."

"What?"

"It was probably an inside job and he was in on it."

"What are you talking about?"

"Those creatures that robbed us. Pete was probably in cahoots with them."

"Come on. That's crazy."

"Is it? How come he conveniently wasn't there when they took all our beautiful paintings? And then he just happened to show up right after they left? I'll bet they split it a-third-a-third-a-third."

"Laura, you're really off-base. Pete's a good guy."

"Maybe. But I think just to be on the safe side, Pete shouldn't come around here anymore. Unless you want to take a chance on being tied up and robbed again. What a day! I'm just wiped out. I'm going to take a long bubble bath. You're welcome to join me."

"Thanks. But I think I'll finish my pizza."

Laura went upstairs. I went in my office and called Penny. I got her voicemail.

"Hey, Penny. Sorry I had to get off the phone so fast. Have a good flight tomorrow. I'll see you soon. I can't wait to see you. I love you."

There is a gap in my memory and next thing I see is me standing out in the back yard by the cactus near the swimming pool. It's nearly dark. I'm very drunk. I am gazing up into the cactus. A spider is building a web there. I see it silhouetted against the faint glow of the sky. I am blown away, as though I'm on an acid trip. It's such an intricate thing that it is doing and yet it knows exactly what to do. And then I lie down and curl up on my side on the grass and go to sleep.

47

Okay. I have to confess. I was having second thoughts about Penny.

Sure, I was in love with her, but what did that mean? A few months ago I'd been in love with Helena. I was always falling in love. I'd never been a womanizer in the sense of ever having had multiple girlfriends. It had always been one girl at a time (excluding my wife). Penny happened to be the girl of the moment. She seemed unique and special and all that, but that was precisely what being in love was all about. The adored object is so wrapped in illusion that it's almost impossible to make out what she or he is really like. The love affair with Penny may have peaked already and I didn't even know it. Maybe Catalina had been the high point. I needed to think very carefully about ending a marriage of nine years over a girl that might not even be around in a couple of months. As for Laura . . .

I was skeptical that much of a conversion had actually taken place, in Mexico or wherever the hell she'd been. The new Laura seemed about like the old one, except for the sobriety, but who knew how long that would last? But Kitty had nailed it. It would be tough to give up my easy life with Laura. Say I left her for Penny. I had no money. All my credit cards were maxed out. I owed money to Pete. Eventually I ought to be able to pry some money loose from Laura in a divorce settlement, but she wouldn't make that easy. She'd drag it out as long as she could. And what was I supposed to do in the meantime?

Live crammed in with Penny, Ralph, Miranda, and the stray dog *du jour* in Penny's little apartment? Go out and get a job? Doing what exactly? I'd never had a real job in my life. The closest I'd come was working for my dad during the summers in high school and college at his department store, but I'd been the archetypal worthless boss's son, goofing off, chasing girls. So I would live on Stoner Avenue, looking for a (gulp) "day" job while I tried to revive my moribund screenwriting career and, if I could overcome my customary sloth, began writing my noir novel, and Penny would go off to work every day and support both of us on her pathetic paycheck, and sooner rather than later we'd start to resent each other and to fight and then it would all be over and I'd move out and . . . and then what? Go slinking back to Laura? Beg her to take me back?

And yet the moment I'd decide *be smart and stick with Laura*, I'd find myself dizzyingly whipped in the opposite direction. Penny *was* unique and special and nobody had ever loved me like she did and I'd regret it the rest of my life if I messed it up with her. Thursday morning it was as if I were perceiving in some extrasensory way her plane taking off from Chicago. I could see her face looking out the window as the plane soared upward into a cumulus cloud, I could see in her eyes that she was thinking about me, and wondering what she was returning home to, and all morning, as I drank coffee and read the paper, as I exercised with Laura (she wanted to go for a run through Beverly Hills, but paparazzi were spotted skulking about, so she ran on the treadmill and I biked beside her), as I pretended to work in my office, drinking vodka and playing Wolfenstein, some part of my brain was receiving images of Penny floating over the cornfields of Nebraska, the mountains of Colorado, the deserts of California, and then when I seemed to hear the landing gear grindingly deploying I went outside and looked up as if I might actually see her, and Topper looked up too.

A big powwow was held at our house at one o'clock. Present were Puppy Morone, accompanied by three young savagely ambitious

314 · TOM EPPERSON

acolytes from her agency; Jay Norberg, Laura's manager, raring and ready to go after a week of silence at his Buddhist retreat; and Kim the publicist. Their mission? Seize the moment. Make Laura a star again.

I'd been dithering about whether to try to get away to see Penny today. As soon, though, as Laura sat down with her people in the living room around a platter of fruit and cheeses, I called Penny, found her home, and told her I'd be there in half an hour. Then I walked into the living room, wincing and holding my jaw.

"Dustin," said Laura, "what's the matter?"

I said a tooth had been bothering me for days and the pain had suddenly become unbearable and I'd called my dentist's office and they told me he could see me now if I came immediately.

Jay Norberg told me chanting *om mani padme hum* would help with the pain. Laura gave me a sympathetic kiss good-bye. I felt a twinge of guilt as I left. She had always been so easy to fool.

48

Penny opened the door. She was wearing the turquoise skirt she'd bought on Catalina. She came into my arms and smelled like Penny and we hugged and kissed. Then she laid her head on my shoulder, and sighed. "Seems like I've been gone forever."

"Seems like that to me too." I caressed her hair. "How was your flight?"

"You know. Okay. No screaming babies."

Now we walked into the room. The ceiling fan was going. Miranda was snoozing in the yellow armchair.

"I think I'll have a glass of wine," she said. "Wanna join me?"

"Sure."

She went in the kitchen. I sat down on the ladybugs and daisies of the blue couch. The last time we'd made love had been right here. It had been great. I intended to do it again before I left.

Penny came back with glasses of cold, pale-gold wine. I took a drink, and diminished my glass's contents by a third. I was already quite drunk, though it probably wasn't apparent to Penny. I'd never been a slurrer or a stumbler. I'd always held my liquor well.

I looked her over. There was something a little different about her.

"Have you lost some weight?"

"Yeah. Annabeth was sick all the time 'cause of the chemo, and that made me not have any appetite either."

"How's she doing?"

"The worst is over for now. But she'll probably end up dying anyway. She's not even forty yet."

"That sucks."

Skinny little Ralph came in, and jumped up on her lap.

"I guess your kitties missed you."

"And I missed my kitties." Ralph set up a noisy purring as Penny stroked him. "But Miranda's mad at me. She always ignores me for a day or two when I come back from a trip. To punish me." She took a drink of her wine and looked at me. "How's Topper?"

"He's been missing you too."

"I was hoping you might bring him along."

"That wouldn't have worked."

"Where'd you say you were going?"

"Dentist."

"Dentist," she repeated, as though it were a word she wasn't sure she knew. Then she picked up Ralph and put him down beside her and got up.

"Where you going?"

"I'll be right back."

She went in the bedroom. A moment later she returned with a gift-wrapped package, flat and about three feet tall and two feet wide.

"Aw, come on," I said as she handed it to me. "What is this?"

She shrugged. I tore the wrapping paper off. It was a framed poster of the mural of the mermaid we saw at the Casino on Catalina.

"Oh man! This is incredible!"

Penny smiled. "You really like it?"

"Oh yeah."

"I saw how you were looking at her. Kind of like you were entranced by her."

"Where'd you get this?"

"I went on the Internet. The Casino has this little museum and gift shop that sells them."

"I feel bad. I don't have anything for you."

"*You're* here. That's all I care about."

"I love it," I said. "Thanks," and I kissed her.

"You want some more wine?"

My glass was almost empty already.

"Okay."

She went in the kitchen. Ralph departed the couch, and jumped up on the chair and joined Miranda. I tugged at my shirt collar. Even with the fan, it was very hot. I'd offered to buy Penny a new air conditioner but she wouldn't let me. Of course now I'd be hard pressed to buy her a pack of gum. I needed to get Laura to replenish the coffers of our joint checking account.

Penny came back with the wine. It was good, whatever it was. Cold and fruity, perfect for the heat. I couldn't seem to drink it fast enough.

I looked at the sculpture of the naked guy on the coffee-table trunk.

"So did you have a model for that?"

"Uh-huh."

"What was his name?"

"Fernando."

"Is that what Fernando did for a living? Pose in art classes?"

"I think so."

"How much can you make doing that?"

"Thirty an hour? Maybe thirty-five?"

"That's not bad. For just taking off your clothes and sitting around."

"It's a lot more than I make."

"Can you read a book while you're doing it?"

"No. You have to just sit there or stand there. Whatever your pose is."

"Have you ever seen a male model get a boner?"

"A boner?"

"Yeah. There's probably a lot of good-looking women in these classes. I think that'd be embarrassing."

"No, I've never seen that." She gave me a puzzled smile. "Why all the questions?"

"Oh, you know, I'm a writer. We're always asking questions."

She looked at me over her wine.

"When are you going to tell your wife about me?"

"As soon as I can. I told you. It's a delicate situation."

"And what are you going to tell her exactly?"

"The truth, of course."

"And what's the truth?"

"I love you. You know that."

She gave me a long, searching look.

"What?" I said.

"There's something wrong. I feel it. You're acting different to me."

"Penny, this is Thursday, right? My wife, who I think's been dead for three months, rings the fucking doorbell on Tuesday. No wonder if I'm acting a little different. I've got a lot on my mind."

She was quiet. She kept looking at me.

"You know," I said, "has it occurred to you that you're acting a little selfish?"

I could tell that it had not. "How?"

"All you're thinking about is you. You're not thinking about me, you're not thinking about Laura. I mean, my god, what if she tried to kill herself again?"

"I saw that press conference thing yesterday. She seemed fine."

"She's an actress. She's good at hiding things. Who knows how she really feels? Plus, she was pretty shaken up after that nut with the gun came at her."

I put my glass of wine down by Fernando and reached for her.

"I've been missing you like you wouldn't believe. So let's just enjoy being together, okay? Let's not ruin it."

I tried to kiss her, but she pulled away.

"Stop it, Dustin."

"What's the matter?"

"You can't just pop over here for a quickie with me then go back to your wife. I've been the other woman before. It made me feel cheap and crummy. I'm not gonna do it again."

"Nobody's asking you to."

"Have you slept with her? Since she's been back?"

"As a matter of fact, no."

"How do I know you're telling the truth?"

"'Cause I *am*, all right? And I don't appreciate being accused of being a liar!"

I grabbed my wine and indignantly got up and walked to the middle of the room. I stood there with my back to Penny. I swallowed some wine.

"Dustin?"

My gaze fell on the cats. They were curled up together on the chair nose to tail in such a way as to form a nearly perfect circle. They looked like a yin-yang symbol.

"Dustin, would you turn around? You're acting like a kid."

I turned around. We looked at each other.

"You're drunk," she said.

"Yeah, maybe a little, so what? Maybe you'd be drunk too if you'd been through what I have the last couple of days."

"Oh, stop feeling sorry for yourself. I hate it when you're like this. You're so much better than this."

"What are you saying? You think I'm just some kind of sniveling weakling?"

"No . . . but I think *you* think that."

"Oh really. Why don't you expand on that?"

Penny seemed hesitant. "Well, I—I think you've lost confidence. You haven't worked in a long time—"

"Yeah, well, there's a reason for that. If you wanna work in

Hollywood, you gotta be willing to kiss an infinite amount of ass. And I won't do that."

"And I think the death of your parents really hit you hard. 'Cause you were so close to them and—"

"Look, don't try to fucking psychoanalyze me. I hate that. I think it's bullshit!"

"You think everything's bullshit!"

"That's RIGHT!" I said, seeming to see myself from the outside as I whirled and threw my glass against the wall. It exploded, drenching the wall with wine, and glittering fragments of glass bounced on the floor like hail.

My heart was pounding and my breath was coming fast as I surveyed what I'd done. The cats, startled out of their nap, crouched on the chair, their luminous green eyes looking around wildly. I moved toward them, putting my hand out to pet them. "I'm sorry, guys, I—" But they bailed, Miranda diving under the chair, Ralph running into the bedroom.

"You're scaring them, you bastard!" Penny said, coming up off the couch. She knelt by the chair, peered under it at Miranda. "Miranda, baby, it's okay."

"Penny, I'm sorry."

"Get out of here. You fucking asshole."

"Look, let's talk."

She jumped up and faced me. "You can't come in here drunk and yell at me and break things and scare my cats! I don't let anybody treat me like that!"

Such anger was blazing out of her brown eyes that I was afraid she might pick something up, Fernando maybe, and clobber me with it.

"Please, I'm sorry. Can't we just start over again?"

"No! Get out!"

I protested weakly as she pushed me toward the door. In a flash I found myself on the outside. Penny disappeared as the door slammed shut and then I heard the click of a lock.

I knocked on the door and rattled the doorknob. "Penny? Come on, let me in!"

I stepped back on the little porch. Put my hands on my hips, and stared at Penny's apartment as though waiting for some brilliant idea to strike me.

Out of the corner of my eye, I thought I detected a presence in the window of Mrs. Stallings' apartment, but when I looked that way no one was there, though the curtain seemed to be swaying a little.

Short of breaking the door down, there was nothing else to do, so I turned and started to walk away.

Behind me, I heard the lock unclicking and the door opening. With a rush of relief I turned around. "Penny?" I said.

Penny was holding the framed poster of the mermaid. "And take this with you!" she shouted as she threw it at me.

I made a pretty deft catch for a drunken man, and then Penny again was gone.

49

Laura's meeting was still going strong when I got back. I snuck past it without being seen and went straight upstairs and fell down upon the bed and immediately went to sleep, passed out, whatever. I woke up later to find Laura sitting on the bed and looking down at me.

"You okay, honey?"

"Dentist said terrible cavity," I mumbled. "Worst he'd ever seen. Gave me some Vicodin. Really knocked me out."

"Can I get you anything?"

"Glass of water."

She brought me the water and I drank about half of it then rolled over and went back to sleep. When I woke next it was dark outside but a light was on in the room. Laura was moving around, getting ready for bed. When I woke up again, the room was dark. Laura was sleeping beside me. I got up and went in the bathroom and peed interminably. I felt wretched. I wasn't sleepy anymore. I went downstairs to the den and turned on the TV.

As I channel-flipped, I heard claws clicking, then Topper walked in.

"Hey, boy. Can't sleep either?"

He stopped and stared at me, then jumped up on the other end of the sofa and settled down with a sigh.

An old black and white movie caught my attention. A conservative young man was in love with a wacky girl. They were walking through the city when they saw a bus taking on passengers. The girl suggested they get on the bus. The young man protested that they didn't know where it was going. The girl said that was the whole point, they should do it for the adventure of it.

But the experience turned out to be dismal. The bus driver was a crabby old guy. The passengers were all weary and depressed. The route of the bus took them past warehouses and shabby storefronts. The girl told the driver he ought to take his bus down to the beach and drive along the ocean because everything was so much prettier there. The driver said that was crazy, he couldn't do that, he'd been driving this route for twenty years, the route was the route! The passengers overheard the girl and the driver and began to join in the discussion. A man was on his way to a job he hated. Two down-and-out musicians were looking for work. A woman was going home to cook dinner for a husband who didn't like the way she cooked. All of them were living difficult, circumscribed lives, and they came in on the side of the girl: Why couldn't they just do what they wanted to for once? Why did they have to travel through this lousy part of town when they could drive down to the beach?

Dissolve to the beach. It was night. A big moon hung over the ocean. The bus was cruising along the beach just a few feet from the water.

Inside the bus, the musicians had taken their violins out and were playing a soothing, lovely tune. The girl, her guy, the bus driver, and all the passengers were listening to the music and gazing out the window at the moonlit sky and sea. They all seemed peaceful and happy. Soon they would have to return to the "real" world, but for now they were exempt from time and tide, they'd made a daring escape into a silvery black and white realm of dreams.

This was an obscure film from eighty or ninety years ago and I was pretty up on old Hollywood but I didn't recognize any of the actors and yet I thought this was one of the most beautiful scenes

I'd ever seen. I felt the need to get up, to breathe fresh air, to look at the sky.

Dawn was barely beginning to glimmer in the east. A crescent moon was rising over the trees. An extraordinarily bright star was shining above and to the right of the moon. A planet, probably.

I heard a car out front, and then the paper flew over the gate and thumped down on the driveway. A bird was waking up. I seemed to feel a sliver of sanity inserting itself into my heart.

TOPPER

50

Laura and I lunched at the Grill. We were here because it had sentimental value for us, or at least for her. We had dinner here a few days after we met, then went to her house and had sex for the first time. Since we still hadn't had sex since she came back, I had no doubt what was expected of me post lunch.

No jeans for Laura today. I guessed that phase had passed. She was wearing a pumpkin-colored sheath dress with matching pumps. The dress was very short, and her golden legs looked awesome. All eyeballs moved to her as we came in. This was her first time out of the house since her resurrection, so her appearance was big news. Crazed paparazzi had pursued us as we'd traveled here in Laura's white Mercedes.

Laura ordered an iced tea, I a glass of iced Evian. She cocked her head a little and looked at me.

"Not having a drink?"

"No. Thought I'd follow your lead. Go on the wagon for a while."

"Oh Dustin, that's great!"

"Just don't start talking to me about God though."

She reached across the table, gave my hand a cheerful squeeze. "We're gonna have so much fun together, being sober. You'll see!"

I smiled as slightly as it was possible for a human being to smile. She looked around, saw people she knew, laughed and waved and kissed the air. "Wow! It's so great to be back."

"In this toxic town?"

"One thing I learned in Mexico, Dustin. Life is what you make of it. And I'm going to make my life terrific from now on!"

The waiter brought us our tea and water and a shrimp cocktail, which we split. For her main course, Laura ordered the blackened ahi tuna salad. Something to do with my hangover made me crave fat and salt, so I got the pepper bacon cheeseburger and French fries.

Austin du Plooy, a movie producer, stopped at our table on her way out. She had silver-blonde hair and heavy eyeliner and a silver handbag and silver shoes. She was reputed to be a very aggressive skirt-chaser. Ignoring me, du Plooy complained to Laura that Puppy hadn't returned her calls, which was unfortunate, since she felt that she'd been born to bring the Laura Keene story to the big screen, and didn't she think Gael García Bernal would be perfect to play Rudy Botana?! Laura said she'd have Puppy call her back, but she needed to realize that her husband—the silent moron sitting across from her eating the shrimp—was a brilliant writer and was part of the package. "No problem!" du Plooy chirped, then leaned down and kissed Laura on the lips and left.

"Laura, please—don't try and sell me like a used car. I can't stand it."

"But Dustin, you *are* a brilliant writer and I just want the whole world to know it."

"I get it. Thanks. But just leave me out of this."

"Why are you so grouchy?"

"I'm not."

"Does your tooth hurt?"

"No. It's fine. I'd look out for du Plooy. She wants in your pants."

"Nobody gets in my pants but *you*."

"Do you want this last shrimp?"

"No. You take it. I was talking about casting with Puppy. Don't you think Colin Farrell would make a great you?"

"Not really."

She looked irritated. "It's like you're not even interested in all the amazing things that are happening for me. I mean, did you know the USA Network is offering me a series to produce and star in?"

"Really? What is it?"

"It's called *The Dead Detective*. I'd play a private investigator that gets murdered. And she comes back as a ghost and helps people solve crimes and find missing loved ones and all that. And at the same time she's trying to find out who her murderer was."

"Sounds great. Congratulations. Cheers."

Laura laughed happily, and we clicked glasses. Our food came. I tore into my cheeseburger. It was like insulin to a diabetic.

"Topper bit Blair," Laura announced.

"Who's Blair?"

"Puppy's assistant."

"Why'd he bite her?"

"No reason at all. Blair was just trying to pet him. Luckily he didn't break the skin, but still . . . He's just been acting so crazy ever since I came back."

"Maybe we should give him away," I suggested hopefully.

"But would that be right? To pass along our problem to someone else?"

"I'll bet we could find a good home for him. Some people are really good with problem dogs."

The waiter came by and asked us how our food was. Mouth full, I gave him a thumb's-up, but Laura said her tuna was overcooked. He said he'd be back in a jiff, and whisked the offending food away.

"Want some of my cheeseburger?" I said.

"Ugh. No. I found something odd in the closet this morning."

"What?"

"Crutches. And a cane."

"Oh. I tore a muscle in my calf a few weeks ago."

"Oh, poor Dustin."

"Yeah."

"I've noticed you limping a little bit. But I thought it was because of your hip."

"Nope. Hip's on the right side. This is on my left."

"How'd it happen?"

"I kind of slipped while I was hiking."

"Hiking? That doesn't sound like you."

"Well, you know . . . thought I'd try something different."

"I love to hike. We can start going together."

"Mm."

She took one of my French fries, dabbed it in some ketchup. "I hope you haven't made any plans for next week."

"Why not?"

"'Cause we're going back east to see my family."

"We are?"

"Well, they're dying to see me, just like you were. And poor Mother . . . who knows how much longer she'll last."

I suddenly lost my appetite because I suddenly knew what I had to say. I wiped my mouth with my napkin as I tried to work up to it.

"And Puppy wants me to take some meetings in New York. There's big interest in me on Broadway. How'd you like to see me in a musical?!"

"Laura . . . you were right about the hiking."

"What do you mean?"

"It's not something I'd normally do."

She looked at me curiously.

"I did it," I said, "because I went with somebody else. A girl. We've been having a . . . a relationship. We—"

Laura leaned across the table, put her fingers on my lips. "Honey . . . honey . . . you don't have to say another word."

Now she made a bridge of her hands and propped her chin on it, and gazed fondly across the table at me. "It's sweet you think you have to confess this to me, but it's really not necessary. You thought I was dead. There wasn't any reason you shouldn't've been with somebody else. The old me might've been jealous, but not the new me. *The new me understands.*"

"But I don't think you do. You're not getting the full picture."

"So what's the full picture?"

"I'm in love with this girl. I want to spend the rest of my life with her. I want to marry her. I want to everything with her."

Laura didn't say a word. Her blue eyes became icy as she stared at me.

"Laura?"

"What's her name?" she said softly.

"Does it really matter?"

"What's her *name*?"

"Penny."

"How'd you meet her?"

"Not long after you disappeared, Topper ran away. He was missing for about a month. And then one day I was walking in this park, and there he was. With this girl. Penny. She'd found him and rescued him. She's really into animals."

"So that's why Topper hates me. He loves Penny now."

"Topper doesn't hate you."

"You're saying you want a divorce, right? That's the big picture? Divorce me and marry her?"

She was still possessed of an ominous calm. I would've preferred yelling and screaming.

"Laura, I—I think you've forgotten how things were with us. Our marriage was on the rocks. We've been cheating on each other for years, making each other miserable—"

Then her breathing began coming quick and shallow and her eyes became bright with tears. "But I've, I've become a new person! And you can too! We can be new people! We can start over again!"

I shook my head. "We *should* start over again. But not with each other."

As if those icy eyes were melting, tears spilled over her lower eyelids and ran down her cheeks.

"This can't be happening."

"Laura," I said, feeling awful, "I'm sorry—"

Our waiter inopportunely returned at this moment with Laura's new ahi tuna salad. "Here we go, Miss Keene!" he said as he set it down in front of her.

Laura looked down at it as though she'd just been served a broiled rat. Suddenly she stood up and grabbed the dish and lifted it over her head, her face fixed in a terrible grimace; it was like Lon Chaney in *The Phantom of the Opera* after he's been unmasked. I raised up my right forearm to try to block the dish, but she shifted her body a little and smashed it on the floor by my chair. Then she lunged across the table and grabbed my glass of ice water and flung it in my face and then she and her pumpkin-colored dress and shoes stormed out magnificently.

I was too stunned to do anything except sit there as water dripped off me. The Grill was never a very loud place but suddenly it might have been empty it was so quiet, as every last mover, shaker, waiter, and busboy stared at me. Finally I wiped my face and shirt with my napkin. I decided not to go after Laura. I had a feeling it would end badly for me if I did. I had no trouble imagining her running me down in her Mercedes as I tried to stop her. That would be a great Hollywood ending. Right up there with Peg Entwistle jumping off the Hollywood Sign. I asked the waiter for a check, then took my phone out and called Pete.

51

"Way to go, dude," Pete said when I told him all about it.
"So you think I'm doing the right thing?"
"Abso-damn-lutely. You're finally growing some *cojones*. Now if you could just get me my fucking statue back."

We drove through Beverly Hills in Pete's Durango, then he dropped me off in front of my house. I was prepared to find my clothes in a burning pile in the courtyard or my Maserati with slashed tires and smashed windows, but everything seemed normal on Bedford Drive. The house was quiet. Laura's Mercedes was parked in the garage. I wondered what she was doing. I felt bad for her, but I had to take care of myself now. I got in my car and drove out through the gate.

I wanted to tell Penny the good news in person. I'd go to Renée's first. If she wasn't there, I'd go to her apartment. I felt exhilarated as I headed to Santa Monica. I felt like a rocket that was about to launch itself into the sky. I imagined Penny's face as I asked her to marry me. She'd think she hadn't heard me right. She'd ask me to repeat myself. She'd probably start to cry, she'd throw herself in my arms, she'd kiss me all over my face. Customers would be watching us with big smiles. I'd just walk into her workplace like Richard Gere did with Deborah Winger at the end of *An Officer and a Gentleman* and carry her right out of there.

My heart began thumping with anticipatory joy as I drove down

Montana, found a place to park. I waited for the light, then walked across the street. A small, ugly bulldog was plodding along at the end of a leash held by a plump, red-haired woman. The dog was wearing a shirt that said BITCH MAGNET. I laughed out loud at the shirt, and the woman smiled at me.

I went in Renée's. Renée was with a customer. At first I thought Penny wasn't there, but then I saw her toward the back, standing in front of a shelf and straightening up a pile of sweaters. Renée saw me, glanced at Penny, then, more as a warning to her, I thought, than an actual greeting, loudly said, "Hi, Dustin!"

"Hi, Renée," I said, as Penny looked around at me. No smile from her as she watched me approach.

"Hi," I said.

"Hi."

Her face was very pale. It always was easy to look in Penny's eyes and see exactly what was going on with her, and now I saw hurt and sadness, but that was okay, because I was about to change all that.

"You look tired," I said.

"I didn't sleep much."

"Me neither. Look. I screwed up bad yesterday and I'm really sorry. But I didn't come here to apologize."

I expected her to ask me why *did* I come, but she was silent so I went on.

"I just came from lunch with Laura. I told her everything about us. It's over with her. I'm getting a divorce."

"How'd she take it?"

"She was—upset."

"Poor thing."

She went back to her sweaters as though I'd told her something completely inconsequential, it's supposed to rain tomorrow or I saw a dog with a funny shirt.

"Penny, please—stop it—look at me."

She looked at me.

"I love you. I want to marry you."

Now I saw a change in her eyes all right. Anger appeared.

"I'm not your fucking yo-yo."

"What?"

"I can't take this. I can't be up one day and down the next."

"You're always gonna be up with me. Believe me."

"Why should I? Why should I believe anything you say anymore?!"

She turned away from me again and began to fumble blindly with the sweaters. I was shocked.

"Penny, I—"

"Dustin, just leave me alone, I have to work!" and then suddenly she winced a little and put her hand on her stomach.

"Penny, what's the matter?"

She was going from pale to white. "I think I'm gonna be sick," she said and then scurried away, disappearing through the door that led into the back.

I looked at Renée and her customer, a willowy aging blonde. They were doing their best to pretend they hadn't been doing their best to listen in.

I wandered over to the counter and the "SAVE A DOG'S LIFE!" sign. I looked through the box filled with Penny's pins, the butterflies and flowers and moons and stars. I tried to remember what I'd done with my dragonfly pin.

The customer left and Renée came over. She was late-fortyish, petite, with straight black hair falling in bangs to her eyebrows. I'd always had the feeling that she liked me and was on my side.

"What's up with Penny?" she asked.

"She said she was feeling sick. She's been in the bathroom for a while. You think maybe you could go check on her?"

"Sure."

Renée left and then came back and said, "She's gone."

"What do you mean she's gone?"

"She wasn't in the bathroom. Then I went out in the alley and her car was gone. She took off."

"Jesus. Where do you think she went?"

"I have no idea."

"Shit."

I stood there, with not the slightest notion of what to do next. Renée regarded me sympathetically.

"This is so Penny," she said. "When she's scared, she runs away."

"What should I do?"

"Well, I don't think chasing her will do any good. Maybe just give her some space?"

I went back to my car. It was pointed west, so I continued that way. After a while I found myself on Ocean Avenue. There was the white pious statue of Saint Monica. I pulled my Maserati over and got out. I think that I was looking for a happy ending here, that I was halfway hoping this is where Penny had come when she had fled the store and in a neatly symmetrical way we would find each other again in Palisades Park. But there was no Penny. Only homeless dudes and squirrels and birds and tourists. I walked down to the Santa Monica Pier. An old bronze artillery piece pointed out at the ocean, as if still waiting on the Japs. I went out on the pier. A breeze was blowing. The water was a dingy green. A small plane droned by, trailing a banner that said: DR. TATTOFF TATTOO REMOVAL 1-888-TATT-OFF. A guy was juggling, and a crowd had gathered. A little girl was moving along with mincing steps, making sure she stepped on every plank of the pier.

I walked past a man leaning on the railing, watching the waves come in. He was wearing a baseball cap and had a brown bushy beard and for one jolting second I thought it was Sluggo, but then I got a better look at his face and saw it wasn't him. There had been no further sightings of Sluggo and Jodi since they'd robbed the convenience store in Redding. None of our paintings and jewelry had turned up. The two of them had simply vanished. I often found myself thinking about him. Dreaming about him too. He was the stuff that nightmares were made of. I felt as though he and I were permanently bonded in some terrible way. Sometimes I had the eerie feeling that he didn't exist independently of me, that I'd summoned him up out of some dark and chaotic part of myself. But even if Sluggo was a creation of my mind, that didn't mean he wasn't real.

I sat down on a bench. A seagull floated virtually motionless in front of me, facing into the breeze, seeming to balance on it as on a tightrope. I was suddenly seized by the fear that I would never see Penny again. I felt a dull ache in my chest, and the plastic sheeting beginning to tighten. Calm down, I told myself. This is just a panic attack. Take some deep breaths. Look at the ocean. See how peaceful it is. It doesn't know a thing about Dustin Prewitt and it doesn't care. Look at the seagull. Breathe slow. Breathe deep.

52

I drove from the beach back to Beverly Hills. I found Laura sitting in the den, leafing through one of her glossy magazines, drinking a Diet Coke. "I guess I'm gonna have to have the locks changed," she said languidly, without looking up. "I can't have you just wandering in and out."

"Laura, this is as much my house as it is yours."

"Like hell it is. I paid for it."

"But it's in both our names."

Now she tossed the magazine aside and glared up at me. "Listen to me carefully. I want you out of here. Today. *Now.*"

"You know, this is difficult for both of us, but it doesn't have to be bitter and horrible. We can work everything out like calm, rational people."

"Fuck yourself. Don't give me one of your fucking speeches. You talk to me like I'm ten years old and you're some kind of wise father figure. Well, fuck that. No more speeches. That's all over."

I sighed, walked over to the French windows. There was a little shimmer of déjà vu as I saw Cesar outside, trimming the trumpet vines. Topper was dozing on the patio.

"I'm surprised you even want to stay here," I said.

"Why?"

"Well, you think it's haunted. You think we've got dead women in the swimming pool."

"I don't think that anymore. I was sick. But I'm okay now."

"I'll move out for now. But that doesn't mean I'm conceding anything. About the house, I mean."

"You never did love me, did you? It was always all about my money."

"No. That's not true."

"Just go, all right? You said you were going, so go!"

"Are you gonna be okay?"

"I'm not gonna try and kill myself over you again, if that's what you mean. I'm not that stupid."

"Can I take Topper with me?"

"No."

"Why not? You clearly don't want him anymore."

"I'm gonna give him to you so you can give him to your little bitch?" She laughed drearily. "I don't think so."

"So you're gonna keep a dog you don't even like anymore just to spite me."

"Maybe I won't keep him."

"Then what'll you do?"

"I'm thinking about having him put to sleep."

"*What*?"

"It's like I said at lunch. He's become vicious. Dangerous. And it wouldn't be fair to pass along my problem to someone else."

I turned back to the window. I could see Topper's chest rising and falling as he snoozed on his side in the shade. Laura read my mind.

"If you take him," she said, "I'll call the police and tell them you're stealing my dog. And then when I get him back, I'll call the vet and have him put down."

I stared at her, hardly believing what I was hearing.

"This is a new low, Laura. Even for you."

She shrugged, picked her magazine back up, and opened its shiny pages. I went upstairs, packed up some stuff. I found the dragonfly pin in a drawer in the guest room. Then I drove over to Larry's.

~

That night, we watched a baseball game and, in honor of Pete's upcoming trip, ordered in Thai food. The season was entering the homestretch and there were some great races going on and the Dodgers were having a terrific year, but right now I didn't care about baseball. I'd left two or three hopefully not-too-desperate messages for Penny, and all I wanted was for my phone to ring and it be her.

I nibbled on some crunchy noodles but I wasn't really hungry. I envied Larry and Pete their booze but sobriety was the hair shirt I'd put on to punish myself for my misdeeds.

"What's Maricar up to tonight?" asked Pete.

"She's having one of those girls'-night-out kind of things. Where they sit around and drink margaritas and laugh hysterically and talk about their boyfriends' dicks."

"So things are still going good?" I said.

"Oh yeah, she's great. But you know, I've been thinking: Why limit myself to one girl? Why not play the field a little? Have some fun? Sow my wild oats?"

"Larry, if I were you," I said, "I'd just keep my wild oats in my pants, and stick with Maricar. You don't want to screw up a good thing."

Larry nodded thoughtfully. "Yeah. Or I might wind up like *you*."

"Right. So was your divorce attorney any good?"

"Nah, he sucked. Sarah's attorney kicked his ass. Schulman. He's a beast. A monster. *That's* who you should get."

"Great. Give me his number."

"He's not cheap, but he's worth every penny. You didn't have a prenup, did you?"

"No."

"There's no reason you shouldn't walk away from this with a bundle. I'll bet Schulman could even get you alimony."

Pete snorted. "Alimony!? Why don't you just start wearing a fucking bra and panties, dude?"

That stung. I felt my face getting hot.

"Would you quit saying 'dude'? You never said that till you met Matt Price. And now you've become part of his little entourage. All these guys have that . . . little flunkies that kiss their ass and laugh at their jokes and do what they're told."

Pete's face turned red, and I thought for a moment he was about to punch me. Then he threw his chopsticks down in his plate, and got up and left the room.

Larry was fixing me with a stern stare, his diamond earring catching the light as he shook his head a little.

"What?" I said.

"What's the matter with you, man? The poor guy finally catches a break, and you piss all over him."

I found Pete in the back yard, standing under a pine tree, sipping a can of beer.

"Pete? I'm sorry. Really."

"No, you're probably right. That's probably what I am with Matt. His flunky."

"I'm sure that's not the case."

"Maybe that's what I've been with *you*. Your assistant? Isn't that kinda like a flunky?"

"You're my *friend*, Pete. Period. I didn't mean what I said. It's just that all this Laura and Penny stuff has been driving me fucking crazy. I feel like I'm on the verge of just totally losing it."

Pete gave me a long look.

"You know what?" he said.

"What?"

"I'm not going."

"To Thailand?"

"Nope. I'm gonna stay here with you. You need me."

"Pete, I appreciate that. But there's no way I'm letting you not go to Thailand. It's too big an opportunity for you. I'll be fine. Don't worry."

"You sure?"

"Absolutely."

A wind went through the pine tree. The stars glittered through the needles.

"'Cause I owe you a lot," said Pete. "I don't know where I'd be now without you."

"Well, same here."

"But let's don't get all slobbery about it."

"No," I agreed, and we went back in.

53

I slept on the couch in the living room that night, if sleep is the right word. I had a series of dreams so awful I don't even want to tell you about them. I would wake up thrashing and moaning, and would try not to go back to sleep, but would helplessly sink as in quicksand into a new bad dream, or sometimes the old bad dream would pick up right where it had left off.

"You look horrible, man!" Larry cheerfully observed at the kitchen table when Saturday morning finally came. "What's that phrase? 'Like death warmed over'?"

"Yeah, that's how I feel."

I was having only coffee and orange juice for breakfast. Larry was eating a big bowl of the weirdly named Ezekiel 4:9, a supposedly super-healthy cereal that Maricar had gotten him. Pete shuffled in yawning and scratching, and put a Jimmy Dean Bacon Breakfast Bowl in the microwave.

Larry looked at his watch. "Shit, I gotta get moving. I gotta meet Maricar at ten. We're starting a Kata class."

"A what-the-fuck class?" said Pete.

"Kata. It's kind of like karate, only quicker and more deadly. You want to come with us? Check it out?"

"Nah, I got a lotta shit I gotta do. To get ready for my trip."

Larry didn't ask me if I wanted to come. I guess I seemed too far gone for Kata. Pretty soon I was alone in the house. I shaved and showered and tried to figure out what to do next. Penny wasn't calling me back. I'd been trying to follow Renée's advice and give her some space, but by noon that had all gone out the window and I was on the way to Santa Monica.

Penny usually worked on Saturdays, but today just Renée was there.

"Where is she?" I said. "Renée, you gotta tell me!"

She seemed a little taken aback—I guess I'd come charging in like a nut, waving my arms and shouting.

"Dustin, I don't know where she is."

"Have you talked to her? Is she all right?"

"She's fine. You don't have to worry."

"I think you know where she is. Is she home?"

"Even if I did know I couldn't tell you."

I was out the door, Mar Vista-bound. I barreled down Bundy till it became Centinela, turned onto Charnoff, steered down Stoner. As I approached Penny's blue quadraplex, I looked for her red Civic, but didn't see it anywhere.

I found a parking spot across the street. I rang the doorbell and knocked without much hope. The place didn't seem to be giving off any obvious Penny vibes. Miranda was sitting in the window.

"Where is she, Miranda?"

But Miranda just gave me a calm, blank look.

I went back to my car. Since I had no idea where else to go, I'd wait here awhile. She'd have to come back sometime.

I wasn't in the shade, and the car got hot fast. I turned the engine on so I could run the AC. The sun was bouncing off the back window of the car in front of me, and I closed my eyes against the glare.

Marty Robbins was singing on my Golden Oldies station: *"Out in the west Texas town of El Paso . . ."* I must have heard the song a hundred times before, but now it seemed to take on a strange significance. It was just it and I in the febrile dark behind my eyelids. A young cowboy was narrating the story of his own death. He was on the run from the law, but he couldn't stop himself from returning to El Paso and the Mexican girl he'd fallen in love with. But there were men waiting for him with guns. I was shot in the chest. And then, as I died in the arms of my beloved Felina, I heard a tapping at the window. I opened my eyes and saw, startlingly close, the pink face and white hair of Mrs. Jennings.

I buzzed the window down. "Are you looking for Penny?" she asked.

"Yes! Do you know where she is?"

"I don't know for certain—but she gave me this."

She handed me a flier. It advertised a big pet adoption event that was taking place today at Westchester Park. That was on Lincoln Boulevard, near the airport, not too far from here.

When I looked back up, Mrs. Jennings' tiny, hunched figure was moving very slowly away across the street.

"Thanks, Mrs. Jennings!"

She turned her head slightly and raised one hand in farewell.

And then I was off again. I sped down Centinela to Jefferson, and thence to Lincoln. I reached the park. Next to a baseball field were dozens of white tents. The parking lot was filled up. I followed some signs to La Tijera and the parking garage of the Otis Art Institute.

I walked back down Lincoln. When I got among the tents, I realized it wasn't going to be easy to find Penny, even assuming she was here. So many tents, so many people, so many dogs. Not only were there the dogs that were up for adoption, but people had brought their own dogs. The air was filled with yaps and yips, growls and howls, whimpers and whines. I passed by the tents for the Riverside Dachshund Rescue, Beagles & Buddies, A Dog's Life Rescue, Chow Dog Rescue, the Canine Adoption and Rescue League, Pugs 'N Pals. I paused at a tent filled with pit bulls. Most were in crates, but two had been brought out to meet prospective owners. Without warning, one lunged at the other and there was a frightening fight till they were separated by their handlers and banished back to their crates, by which time the prospective owners were nowhere to be seen.

I walked and I wandered, seeking a glimpse of red-blonde hair. When I went by Beagles & Buddies for the second time I felt I was going in circles and might never find her unless I got more systematic about it, going up one row and down the next, and that was when I saw her, not twenty feet away.

She was standing by the tent of the blandly named Neighborhood Animal Group. She was wearing a pink skirt and a green top and the same oversized sunglasses she had on the day we had met. She was showing a homely black and white dog to a slumpy, soft-bellied man and his pretty young daughter. She was smiling and then I saw the sunglasses turning toward me and the smile faltered.

"Michelle?" she said. "Could you give me a hand with Grover for a minute?"

Michelle, a profoundly obese young woman, arose with an effort from a metal folding chair. Penny turned dog, dad, and daughter over to her, and then we were face to face, I smiling nervously and she not smiling at all.

"How'd you find me?"

"Mrs. Stallings. She gave me the flier you gave her."

"I wish she'd mind her own business for a change."

"You can't blame her for liking me, can you?" I said, still with the same stupid little grin.

"Dustin, I'm really busy now."

"Yeah, I can see."

I looked at the dogs under the tent. There were about a dozen of them, an eclectic bunch, all kinds and colors. Each had a rakish red bandana that said "Adopt me" tied around his or her neck.

"Where'd they all come from?" I said.

Penny looked them over speculatively. "Different places. They all have their own stories."

"I've been so worried about you. Why'd you disappear?"

"Because—I can't deal with this."

"Deal with what? I've left Laura, I'm getting a divorce, I've moved in with Larry, and I love you! There's nothing in the way, there's nothing in between us. So why are you freaking out?"

"Because you were all set to leave me—I could see it in your eyes."

"Okay, I was confused, but I'm not confused anymore. Don't you believe in giving a guy a second chance? And would you mind taking off those glasses?"

She took them off. Her eyes were red. It looked like she'd been crying.

"Look," she sighed, "it's as much me as it is you. You don't really know me."

"Then *tell* me. Tell me what it is I ought to know about you."

"I'm *afraid*, all right?"

"Of what?"

"Of—going back to the way I used to be—I was so lost—"

"That won't happen. I won't let you be lost."

"I don't think I can be in a relationship. It hurts too much."

"It doesn't have to hurt."

"Hey, Penny?" It was Michelle, still with the father and daughter, and now two more people had come up. "They'd like to meet Casey?"

"Oh, Casey's a sweetheart!" Penny said to the people with a smile, and then turned back to me, the smile fading, Dustin the smile-killer. "I gotta go."

"Can we talk later?"

She shrugged. "How's Topper?"

"He's—fine."

She nodded. I was hoping to hug or something but it didn't seem to be in the cards. "Bye," she said, putting her sunglasses back on.

"Bye."

I watched her walk to a crate and take out Casey, a wiggling little tail-thrashing mutt, and then I left. I walked numbly among the tents, through the milling crowds of people and dogs. It felt like

Penny was slipping away from me and I couldn't stop it. I wondered if there was something she wasn't telling me. Maybe some old boyfriend had slithered back into the picture. Fernando, maybe, the sculpture model. Charming, no-good Fernando.

I heard a voice booming over a P.A. system, then saw people gathered in front of a small stage where a man was standing with a little brown dog with pointy ears. "Jasmine just came in from Mexico, she was stuck on a roof in the blazing hot sun!"

I left the clamor of the dogs behind, and entered the strikingly hushed world of the cats. The adults sat stoically in their cages, paws tucked beneath them, trying to endure with some measure of dignity the importunate stares of strangers, while the kittens wrestled around and batted at pieces of string or slept exhaustedly in each other's arms. Then I walked by a tent with twenty or so gentle rabbits hopping about cautiously, then under the last tent, squawking, whistling, and saying hello, were two parrots, one white, one turquoise, saffron, and green.

I turned around, with the vague notion of heading back to my car and then, after that . . . *what?* I came upon an open space ringed with people sitting in folding chairs with more people standing behind them. I lingered, wondering what they were all waiting for. Then a woman came out with a microphone and announced the beginning of the Pet Parade, for rescued animals and their owners, and then I heard the opening notes of Dire Straits' "Walk of Life" and the parade began. It was people with their dogs mostly, though there were two or three cats, including one perched like a parrot on the shoulder of a ZZ Top-looking guy with a cowboy hat, sunglasses, and a big beard, and one guy had an adorable half-grown goat on a leash. There was a beautiful golden retriever with a beautiful golden-haired little girl, and a stalwart-looking German shepherd with a buff young man with a buzz cut, but most of the people weren't handsome or pretty and most of the animals weren't beautiful and strong. There was a three-legged dog, hopping along happily. A one-eyed dog, with a piratical black eye patch. A skeletally thin woman who appeared to be ill, wearing a baseball cap with a blue star on it with an identical blue star tattooed on her arm, walking with an old limping chocolate Lab. A fat black guy, wearing a gray T-shirt that said Air Force Institute of Technology, rolling along in a motorized wheelchair, with a tattered-looking Toto dog trotting by his side. And yet I thought I had never seen such proud, joyous faces as on these men, women, dogs, and kids, and as they paraded round and round within the circle of chairs with the exuberant music playing the spectators began to applaud, they rose from their chairs and clapped and cheered and a savage sob ripped through me. It had been pretty loud, judging by the curious looks I was getting. I turned and began to walk away rapidly. I could see people looking at the weeping man with the twisted face but I couldn't seem to stop and then it hit me! I knew exactly what I had to do! I began to run. I ran until the tents were behind me and my timing for the red light was perfect and I ran across the street and up Lincoln Boulevard. A gigantic plane was thundering down in front of me for a landing at LAX and the sun was hot and high and I was gasping and the sweat was pouring off me and a part of me was aware of the plastic sheeting getting tighter and tighter on my chest but the rest of me ignored it and I reached the Art Institute.

I jumped in my Maserati, and tore out of the parking garage. Up Tijera, back down Lincoln, on my way to Beverly Hills.

54

Laura hadn't bothered to bring in my *L.A. Times*. It was still lying where it had landed on the cobblestones of the driveway. I got out of the car, and looked at the house. Pleasant white stucco. Pretty green trim. A nice house, but now it seemed like some dark castle I had come to for some kind of ultimate confrontation.

I went inside. The mystic warrior gleamed in the empty living room.

"Laura?" I called. "You here? Topper? Hello?"

I went in the den, then into Laura's office. No Topper or Laura. Then I entered the kitchen. Nobody in there either, but something on the marble island caught my attention.

A cake. With a wedge cut out of it. White frosting, with a message written in pink. Upside-down, from my vantage point. I walked close, until I could read: WELCOME HOME, NEIGHBOR!

By the cake were two small plates, a half-eaten slice of cake on one and on the other just a few crumbs and smears of frosting. There were two rumpled napkins, and two shot glasses. A little liquid remained in one. I sniffed it, took a taste. Vodka.

The door that led to the back yard was open. I walked over to it and looked out. Near the swimming pool, by the big cactus, in the shade, on the grass, a naked Magnus Storndrop lay on top of my naked wife.

I walked toward them. Scattered around them were their clothes. A bottle of Pravda vodka sat on the grass, tilting a little, looking in danger of toppling over. I gazed with fascination at Storndrop's bobbing, bear-scarred butt. He grunted in rhythm to his thrusts as Laura emitted small, sharp cries. I got to within a few feet and still they didn't know I was there. Laura's hands clawed at his already clawed-up back and clutched deliriously at his red tangled hair. Then she opened her eyes and saw me.

"Magnus! Magnus, stop!"

But Magnus in rut was not to be stopped easily. She beat on his back, then tried to push him off.

"Magnus, stop it, stop it!"

I joined in. "Stop that, Magnus! Magnus! Stop that!"

Magnus glanced over his shoulder, then gave a dazed, interrogative grunt and rolled off her. He snatched up a pair of blue shorts and wiggled into them, but not before I caught a chilling glimpse of his erect penis: a thick, purplish, brutal-looking thing.

Meanwhile, Laura was scrambling into her own clothes, eager to conceal from me the nakedness I'd seen only about a jillion times.

"Dustin, what are you doing here? I should call the police!"

"I live here, remember? This is my house too. Hi, Magnus."

"Fucking Dustin, goddamn, ha ha ha, how are you, my Jesus, yeah!" he babbled uneasily, his small cunning eyes watching me closely; maybe he was concerned that like a good American I was about to pull a gun out and fill him full of holes.

"How's *Tender Is the Night* going?" I asked.

He put on a red plaid shirt and began buttoning it.

"That goddamn Reggie Perry," he said, shaking his head. "I want you but fucking producers make me take him, yeah. Maybe you do rewrite, Dustin, what do you fucking say?"

I didn't say anything. He grabbed the bottle of vodka and took a long, hard pull at it; it overflowed his mouth, spilled into his beard. He laughed, and held the bottle out to me.

I shook my head.

He looked at Laura. "Maybe I go now, yeah?"

"You don't have to go," I said. "This won't take long."

"What do you want, Dustin?" Laura sighed, straightening her clothes out, smoothing down her hair.

"I just wanted you to know I've hired a high-powered divorce attorney. Schulman. Maybe you've heard of him."

"No."

"I told Schulman what I wanted and he said he could get it for me, no problem."

"And what do you want?"

"Money. Lots of it. And the house."

"You're not getting the house."

"Okay. I'm willing to sell the house, and we can split the money."

"I'm going to hire a lawyer that will step on your lawyer like a fucking ant."

"Listen. It looks like this is gonna be a long, ugly process. But I'm willing to make a deal. We can settle this whole thing today."

"Oh really," said Laura skeptically.

"I'll give up everything. My half of the house. Any claim I might have on any of your money. I'm willing to walk away from this without a dime. But I want two things."

Laura looked intrigued. "What?"

"The statue in the living room. The warrior guy."

Laura looked at Magnus and laughed. Magnus stroked his beard and chuckled.

"What else?" she said.

"Topper."

She looked surprised. "Topper?"

I felt a tingle of panic. What if she'd already taken him on a one-way trip to the vet? "Where is he?"

"He's around somewhere," she said, looking around. "Oh, there he is. Digging up the rosemary bush that Cesar planted yesterday."

MAKE BELIEVE · 353

I saw him now in a far corner of the garden, paws flashing as he dug diligently in the hot sun.

"So you want the sculpture for your awful friend and Topper for your little whore," Laura sneered. "How noble."

"Deal or no deal?"

"We'll have to put it all in writing, of course."

"Of course."

"All right, Dustin. You're an idiot to the end. You can go now."

"I'll take Topper with me. I'll come back later for the statue and the rest of my stuff."

"Just call first, all right?"

"See you around, Magnus. Look out for bears."

"Ha ha ha! See you, my friend! You are man of the world! God-damn Dustin!"

I went to collect Topper. It could be a problem to get him on a leash but he didn't give me any trouble today. He liked to ride in cars, and jumped eagerly up into the front seat.

"Say good-bye, Topper. You're never gonna see this place again!"

We went out through the gate and down Bedford.

"You know where we're going, boy? We're going to see Penny! Yeah, that's right! Penny!"

Topper jumped up on the window and scrabbled against it with his paws. He loved to ride with the window down. I lowered both our windows and I got the music going, and we drove out of Beverly Hills, then turned south on the 405. I felt exuberant. Some of my imaginings hadn't matched up very well with reality as it unfolded, but how could Penny's face do anything other than light up with astonished joy when she saw me walking up to her tent with Topper? It would be like at the end of *The Searchers* when Natalie Wood, after years of being held captive by the Indians, is brought back to her family by John Wayne. We exited the freeway at Jefferson, and now Penny was just minutes away. There wasn't much traffic and I could drive pretty fast, and the Go-Go's "We Got the Beat" was playing, and I mumbled and hummed along with those bouncy gals from the long-lost eighties. The warm air of summer's end was gushing in through the windows. Topper, tongue dangling, was gazing into the wind. We zoomed past a Home Depot, and then—

It was sort of like I'd been shot in the chest. I cried out. At first I was more flummoxed than frightened. I had felt pain in my chest before, but nothing like this. I put my hand on my shirt, felt around. Maybe I had somehow torn a muscle or—

The pain came again and I cried out again.

This was no torn muscle. I was coming up on Lincoln. Left lay Penny. I turned right. The hospital in Marina del Rey across from Dr. Houghteling's office was only about a mile away.

I looked over at Topper. His head was still hanging out the window. He was oblivious to what was happening to me. Not that he would have cared. Now I most definitely was afraid, indeed had moved well past fear into the icy realm of terror. The pain wasn't sharp now but was a constant throbbing ache, and I couldn't seem to catch my breath.

I had to talk to Penny. I got my phone out and called her. *"Please, please, please pick up!"* I whispered, but I got her voicemail.

"Penny, it's me! I'm in the car! Something's wrong! I'm in a lot of pain! In my chest! I'm going to that hospital in Marina del Rey, the one where I had the MRI! Could you meet me there? Topper's with me! I love you so much! I'm sorry I hurt you, I—"

It was like another bullet hit me, and I groaned loudly and dropped the phone. I didn't try to pick it back up. I was focused on reaching the hospital. An intersection was clotted with traffic. I was stuck at a red light. My breaths were coming short and shallow. I felt dizzy. A flurry of spots appeared in front of my eyes, faded away, came back. I thought I might pass out. I considered pulling over and calling 911 and waiting to be rescued, but then the light changed and traffic began to creep forward. I was nearly there. If I could just hold on for another minute or two.

And then I seemed to have some kind of hallucination. I was looking at a little kid in a red bathing suit, holding a helium-filled balloon. The kid was me, and I watched me let the balloon go, watched me watch it float away.

I saw I was at the hospital. A sign pointed the way to the emergency room. I pulled into the parking lot. I got out of the car. I could feel the heat coming up off the concrete. Too hot to leave Topper, so I reached back in and grabbed his leash. "Come on, boy," I gasped.

We walked toward the door. My legs felt wobbly as if my knees were double-jointed and were bending both ways. We went through the door, and an elderly black security guard came toward us. He had white, lamb-like hair.

"Sir, you can't bring that dog in here—"

But another pain hit my chest. I thought I was going to the floor but the security guard grabbed my arm. He yelled for help. A nurse came running. She asked me what the problem was and I said my chest. And then an Asian man dressed in green appeared with a wheelchair. I was rolled into a room with a row of beds, each with its own set of plastic curtains. I was helped from the wheelchair to one of the beds, and then someone was asking me where it hurt in a lilting, melodic voice. I saw a young, dark, beautiful woman. Her nametag said Dr. Nanda. She helped me to lie back on the bed. The light above me was overwhelmingly bright, and I could hardly see her face against it, but I could hear her soft, lilting voice, saying be calm, breathe deeply, we'll take care of you. I felt a blood-pressure cuff going around my arm, and I was dimly aware of Dr. Nanda unbuttoning my shirt—

Guess what! I got fooled again! There was a yellow jacket inside my shirt! It was crawling around amid my chest hairs, and it had been stinging my chest! The dadgum thing must have been blown in through the window of my car, or maybe it was one of the yellow jackets that lived in the cactus by the swimming pool. Anyway, Dr.

Nanda laughed when she saw it, laughed at *me* like Dr. Houghteling had laughed at me, but I didn't mind because I too was laughing.

She plucked it off my chest with tweezers. I didn't feel any hostility to the little critter; actually I felt oddly grateful, and I had her put it in an empty medicine bottle so I could let it go outside. She said I was probably dizzy because the excitement had made me hyperventilate, but she wanted to keep me for a bit to make sure I wasn't having an allergic reaction, and also she wanted to do an EKG on me just in case. She did so, and the results were normal. She gave me some salve to put on my stings and released me.

When I walked out into the lobby, the first thing I saw was Penny. She was standing by the front entrance, talking agitatedly to the security guard, who was holding Topper's leash. And then she looked over and saw me.

"Dustin, are you all right?!"

"I'm fine. It was a false alarm."

And then, oh yes, she rushed into my arms! I was holding my lovely beloved in my arms, and she was kissing me all over my face, and Topper was jumping up on both of us and barking—

I'm Dustin Prewitt, and I get what I want.

About the Author

Tom Epperson, a native of Arkansas, headed west with his boyhood friend Billy Bob Thornton to pursue a career in show business. Epperson's cowritten the scripts for *One False Move*, *A Family Thing*, *The Gift*, *A Gun, a Car, a Blonde*, and *Jayne Mansfield's Car*. His L.A. noir *The Kind One* was nominated for both the Edgar Award and the Barry Award for Best First Novel. Two more books followed, *Sailor* and *Roberto to the Dark Tower Came*. He lives in Los Angeles with his wife, Stefani, three pampered cats, and a frisky dog.

www.tomepperson.com

Made in the USA
Coppell, TX
15 November 2024

40323020R00215